The Firebird in Russian folklore is a fiery, illuminated bird; magical, iconic, coveted. Its feathers continue to glow when removed, and a single feather, it is said, can light up a room. Some who claim to have seen the Firebird say it even has glowing eyes. The Firebird is often the object of a quest. In one famous tale, the Firebird needs to be captured to prevent it from stealing the king's golden apples, a fruit bestowing youth and strength on those who partake of the fruit. But in other stories, the Firebird has another mission: it is always flying over the earth providing hope to any who may need it. In modern times and in the West, the Firebird has become part of world culture. In Igor Stravinsky's ballet *The Firebird*, it is a creature half-woman and half-bird, and the ballerina's role is considered by many to be the most demanding in the history of ballet.

The Overlook Press in the U.S. and Gerald Duckworth in the UK, in adopting the Firebird as the logo for its expanding Ardis publishing program, consider that this magical, glowing creature—in legend come to Russia from a faraway land—will play a role in bringing Russia and its literature closer to readers everywhere.

Without a Dowry and Other Plays

Alexander Ostrovsky

Translated from the Russian
and with an Introduction by

Norman Henley

ARDIS PUBLISHERS
NEW YORK, NY

This edition first published in paperback in the United States and the United Kingdom in 2014 by
Ardis Publishers, an imprint of Peter Mayer Publishers, Inc.

NEW YORK:
The Overlook Press
141 Wooster Street
New York, NY 10012
www.overlookpress.com
For bulk and special sales, please contact sales@overlookny.com,
or write us at the above address.

LONDON:
Gerald Duckworth & Co. Ltd.
30 Calvin Street
London E1 6NW
info@duckworth-publishers.co.uk
www.ducknet.co.uk
For bulk and special sales, please contact sales@duckworth-publishers.co.uk,
or write us at the above address.

Library of Congress Cataloging-in-Publication Data

Ostrovsky, Aleksandr Nikolaevich, 1823–1886
[Selections. English. 1995]
Without a dowry & other plays / Alexander Ostrovsky; translated
with an introduction by Norman Henley.
p. cm.
Includes bibliographical references.
Contents: A profitable position – Ardent heart –Without a dowry
– Talents and admirers.
ISBN 0-88233-933-8
1. Ostrovsky, Aleksandr Nikolaevich, 1823–1886–Translations into
English. I. Henley, Norman. II. Title.
PG3337.08A24 1995 95–23736
891.72'3–dc20 CIP

Printed in the United States of America
ISBN US: 978-1-4683-0858-7
ISBN UK: 978-0-7156-4738-7

2 4 6 8 10 9 7 5 3 1
Go to **www.ardisbooks.com** to read or download the latest Ardis catalog.

For Chris and Frannie

CONTENTS

PREFACE

Despite Ostrovsky's high stature in Russian letters he has fared relatively poorly in English translation. Much of the translation was done before World War Two, and for that we are largely indebted to George Rapall Noyes (1873-1952), an eminent American Slavicist and strong champion of Ostrovsky. Since World War Two there have been scattered translations of Ostrovsky, but some of his worthy plays have not yet been translated into English.

Some appreciations are in order. To my ex-wife Nancy and Robert M. Slusser, former colleague at Johns Hopkins, for their encouragement when it was most needed. To Dorothy Magner and my son Christopher, whose suggestions and corrections improved the translation. And to the Johns Hopkins University for a special grant, which helped me to finish the basic project.

N.H.

INTRODUCTION

Alexander Nikolaevich Ostrovsky (1823-86), son of a judicial official, was raised in Moscow. He studied law at Moscow University, but did not finish his degree, and took a job as a legal clerk, in which capacity he learned much of value for some of his plays. During his university and law-court years he became passionately devoted to the theater and dreamed of working for it.

In 1847 Ostrovsky's first complete play, a one-acter entitled *Picture of Family Happiness,* was published but immediately forbidden theatrical presentation by the censor. Ostrovsky's first full-length play, *It's All in the Family,* was published in 1850, and it also was banned from the stage. While this play earned Ostrovsky instant fame, it also brought attention from the authorities, who were disturbed both because the play portrayed merchant immorality as a typical phenomenon and because the main culprit escaped unpunished. Ostrovsky was placed under police surveillance and soon felt compelled to leave his government position. In effect this sentenced Ostrovsky to a life of constant struggle and near poverty, particularly noticeable in his letters, where he frequently begs his friends for a loan to carry him through a pressing financial crisis. It should be noted here that in that period Russian playwrights had almost no rights, and though Ostrovsky's plays were being performed continuously, he received very little income from the performances, deriving his basic income from their publication.

Henceforth Ostrovsky generally wrote a play or two every year until his death, compiling a total of forty-seven original plays. In addition, he collaborated on seven plays and translated several others. Always concerned with the lot of the Russian theater and its actors, Ostrovsky served as president of the Society of Russian Dramatic Writers and Operatic Composers from its founding in 1870 to his death some sixteen years later.

On the personal side Ostrovsky had many friends, especially in the theatrical and literary worlds. Unlike many of his contemporaries he shunned feuds and controversy. Though some of his plays stirred up heated debate, notably that engaged in by the Westerners and Slavophiles over some of his early plays, Ostrovsky himself shied away from such controversy.

Brief as this sketch is, it is probably not unfair in suggesting that Ostrovsky's personal life was unglamorous. He was an unpretentious literary hero, who wrote as steadily and honestly as he could under difficult censorship conditions and without compromising his integrity. His writing is that of the self-effacing artist, and in contrast to a playwright like Strindberg, it is almost impossible to see anything of Ostrovsky the outer man in his plays. Ostrovsky was a keen and sensitive observer of Russian reality, and this became the raw material for his plays. Although the well-known literary historian D. S. Mirsky made some bad and misleading observations about Ostrovsky, he was perceptive in describing Ostrovsky as "the least subjective of Russian writers."

INTRODUCTION

During his "early" period, from 1847 to 1860, Ostrovsky wrote fifteen plays, notable among them being *It's All in the Family, Poverty's No Vice, A Profitable Position,* and *The Thunderstorm.* Although *The Thunderstorm* is performed less often than a number of Ostrovsky's other plays, it has often been considered his masterpiece. Paradoxically, the success of this play in western drama anthologies may have hurt Ostrovsky in the West by giving him the reputation of writing plays too "Russian" to be understood readily by non-Russian audiences. However, it should be stated that *The Thunderstorm* is hardly a leading candidate for Ostrovsky's most typical play and that, in any case, many of his plays do have universal interest.

The early plays impressed everybody with their brilliant characterization and language. But they also provoked controversy on sociological and political grounds. On the basis of these plays Nikolai A. Dobrolyubov (1836-61) wrote two famous essays, "The Kingdom of Darkness" (1859) and "A Ray of Light in the Kingdom of Darkness" (1860). The former essay considered the plays primarily as social documentation, dwelling on the morally unworthy characters (often enough the uncouth self-willed characters known as "samodurs"), whose power, derived from money or the authority of elders, was used arbitrarily to exploit the weaker members of society. In the latter essay, inspired by *The Thunderstorm,* Dobrolyubov saw a glimmer of hope, interpreting the heroine Katerina as a basically Russian type whose way of thinking in itself constituted a kind of protest against the inhuman world around her.

At this point I feel that I should take the time to object strongly to the opinion sometimes expressed or implied in western criticism that Ostrovsky's powers declined after *The Thunderstorm.* Ostrovsky's artistic powers developed steadily throughout his career, and it is only with his very last play *Not of This World* that one can say that Ostrovsky "lost his touch." In any case, it is a matter of record that for some time Soviet theaters performed Ostrovsky's later plays much more than his early plays.

The next period, from about 1860 to 1868, may somewhat awkwardly be labelled "historical." While Ostrovsky wrote some plays based on contemporary life during this period, his main concern was the writing of versified historical chronicles intended for reading rather than the stage. Actually Ostrovsky was trying to make an escape from the theater, for his bitter experiences with the censor, the lack of proper recognition, and his impecunious state had left him disillusioned and discouraged. In a letter written in 1866 to his close friend, the actor Burdin, Ostrovsky declared, "I'm letting you know that I'm giving up the theatrical realm completely... I receive almost no profits from the theater although all the theaters in Russia live by my repertory... Believe me that I shall have much more respect, which I have earned and deserve, if I separate from the theater. Having given the theater twenty-five original plays I haven't had any success in being distinguished from some bad translator." Fortunately for us Burdin and others insisted that Ostrovsky not leave the theater, though one can easily imagine that Ostrovsky's love of the theater made it easy for him to change his position. Although his historical plays are of justified interest to some, as a whole they are the least valuable of Ostrovsky's plays and are seldom performed.

The third period, from 1868 to 1878, may be considered Ostrovsky's satirical period. While there had been satire in some of his previous plays, it is now more dominant, being especially brilliant in *To Every Sage His Share of Folly* and *Wolves and Sheep*. Other important plays of this period are *An Ardent Heart; Easy Come, Easy Go; The Forest; Feasting Can't Last Forever; Not Even a Copper, Then Lo a Goldpiece; The Snowmaiden; Late Love; Truth Is Fine, but Good Luck's Better*. *The Snowmaiden* (1873) deserves special mention as a highly esteemed though seldom performed fairy-tale play in verse. Rimsky-Korsakoff wrote an opera based on it, and Tchaikovsky wrote incidental music for it around 1900.

B.V. Alpers calls the plays of Ostrovsky's fourth and final period (1878-1885) "sad comedies." Largely devoted to the slavish plight of women (Ostrovsky was definitely a philogynist), these plays are characterized by fine psychological delineation as well as a sad poetic atmosphere of unfulfilled love and deceived hopes. Notable plays of this period are *A Last Sacrifice; Without a Dowry; Talents and Admirers; Without Guilt Guilty*.

It is sometimes difficult to do justice to Ostrovsky in translation or, for that matter, even by reading him in the original. Ostrovsky was highly stage conscious, and, with the exception of the historical plays, he always wrote his plays with performance in mind, sometimes with specific actors in mind for certain roles. He was especially language conscious, listening carefully to any speech within hearing, and while working on a play he read all the lines aloud to himself, striving above all for natural speech.

If critics agree that Ostrovsky is unsurpassed in his use of colloquial language, they also agree that he is a master of characterization. His characters are convincingly real, interesting and varied. However, though there is an astonishing diversity in his vast gallery (E. Kholodov calculates a total of 728 speaking characters in Ostrovsky's 47 original plays), some types recur rather frequently, such as the parasitic idler (especially the unscrupulous male seeking wealth through marriage), the powerful self-righteous bully, the helpless woman, the capitalistic entrepreneur as exploiter of individuals, and the rebellious crusader. The frequent classification of Ostrovsky's characters into the exploiters and the exploited ("wolves and sheep") needs special mention, for personal conflict of a quite direct nature, one-sided as the contest often is, is at the heart of Ostrovsky's plays. It is probably this rather traditional feature which most obviously distinguishes the plays of Ostrovsky from those of Chekhov, whose dramatic characters are portrayed not so much as victims of other individuals as of themselves or their frustrating and unfriendly environment. It is indeed unfortunate that some Westerners have typed Ostrovsky as a playwright of the merchant class. In actuality only a small number of Ostrovsky's plays deals to any great extent with merchants, and in those the merchant's significance is as a human being, not as a businessman. Offhand I can remember only one instance (in *The Forest*) when one of Ostrovsky's merchants makes a business transaction on stage.

Ostrovsky is a brilliant psychologist. However, since the deservedly influential D. S. Mirsky didn't understand this properly, it should be pointed out that Ostrovsky is primarily a *social* psychologist rather than what might loosely be called an "individual" psychologist. He introduces ready-made characters with significant traits or ambitions which are manifested as the characters interact with other characters. Ostrovsky does not ordinarily delve into the consciousness of individual characters to reveal their psychoses, to try to show how they "got that way," an approach better suited to a novel, where time is not so limited. As psychologist, Ostrovsky is more subtle in his later plays.

Ostrovsky's plots tend to subordinate themselves to the portrayal of character and the social situation. However, this generalization is much more applicable to the earlier plays, as one will see if he compares the plot of *A Profitable Position* with that of *Talents and Admirers*. Ostrovsky was sometimes guilty of resorting to abrupt endings of a *deus ex machina* nature. Yet we should refrain from judging him too hastily since some of his seemingly abrupt and "happy" endings may be ironic, suggesting to the sensitive viewer or reader that in the kind of social milieu portrayed in the play it is only the very lucky who escape unscathed. Such is the case in *Truth Is Fine, but Good Luck's Better,* where the virtuous hero-knight is reminded at the end that his deliverance from an unjust imprisonment was due not to his virtue but sheer good luck. Such endings can be frightening, and one can see how easily some of Ostrovsky's so-called comedies could have turned into what we may loosely call tragedies. Incidentally, it is certainly worth considering the view of one critic who felt that Ostrovsky sugarcoated his endings as a compensatory consolation to the viewer/reader for the dark realities just portrayed which might unrelieved be morally discouraging.

Relatively objective, Ostrovsky nevertheless does have his tendentious side and is frequently a propagandist for social justice. This is most obvious when some of his rebellious and morally good characters engage in excited moralistic preaching, usually near the end of the play. However, what probably influences us more is Ostrovsky's satirical portrayal of the oppressive and insensitive characters. And yet Ostrovsky rarely insists too much. His satire is sharp but seldom bitter. He was not a misanthrope or pessimist. Painfully aware of the grim realities in his society he also had an optimistic faith in the power of education, considering the stage to be an educational forum.

Why was Ostrovsky so popular during the Soviet period? Was it because with some reason he could be considered anticapitalistic? Because he believed in education? Because he exalted work? Certainly such factors would have him congenial to the officialdom, but they were hardly the reasons why normal Soviet citizens would have wanted to take in an Ostrovsky play on a cold winter's night. They must have gone simply because of Ostrovsky's dramatic art, because they found his plays entertaining and worthwhile.

I. A. Goncharov best summed up Ostrovsky's significance for Russian drama when he wrote to Ostrovsky in 1882, "You have made a gift of an entire library of artistic works; you have created for the stage your own special world. You alone have finished the building for which Fonvizin, Griboedov, and Gogol set the cornerstone. But only after you can we Russians say with pride, 'We have our own Russian, national theater. By rights it should be called *The Theater of Ostrovsky.'*"

WITHOUT A DOWRY

&

Other Plays

A PROFITABLE POSITION

A Comedy in Five Acts
(1857)

CAST OF CHARACTERS*

ARISTÁRKH VLADÍMIRYCH VYSHNÉVSKY, a decrepit old man with symptoms of the gout.

ANNA PÁVLOVNA VYSHNÉVSKY (MME. VYSHNEVSKY), his wife, a young woman.

VASÍLY NIKOLÁICH ZHÁDOV, a young man. Vyshnevsky's nephew.

AKÍM AKÍMYCH YÚSOV, an old official serving under Vyshnevsky.

ONÍSIM PANFÍLYCH BELOGÚBOV, a young official under Yusov.

FELISÁTA GERÁSIMOVNA KUKÚSHKIN (MME. KUKUSHKIN), widow of a collegiate assessor (a rank in the civil service giving the right to hereditary nobility).

JULIE and PAULINE, her daughters.

ANTÓN (ANTÓSHA, ANTÓSHKA), a servant in Vyshnevsky's home.

STÉSHA, a maidservant in Mme. Kukushkin's home.

MÝKIN, a teacher. A friend of Zhadov.

DOSÚZHEV.

GRIGÓRY and VASÍLY, waiters.

FIRST and SECOND OFFICIALS.

A BOY SERVANT.

GUESTS and WAITERS in another room (in Act Three).

---

*Meanings which might be suggested to Ostrovsky's contemporaries by some of the family names: Vyshnevsky—high; Zhadov—avid, eager; Yusov—legal chicaner; Belogubov—white-lipped; Kukushkin—cuckoo; Mykin—living in need; Dosuzhev—clever.

ACT ONE

A large and richly furnished reception room in Vyshnevsky's home. On the left is a door to Vyshnevsky's study, on the right a door to Mme. Vyshnevsky's rooms. Each side wall has a mirror with a small table below. An entrance door faces the audience. Vyshnevsky, without his wig, is wearing a cotton frock coat. Mme. Vyshnevsky is in morning attire. They are coming from her rooms.

VYSHNEVSKY. What ingratitude! What spite! *(He sits down.)* We've been married five years now, and in all those five years I haven't been able to do a thing to gain your favor. I just don't understand. Is there perhaps something that doesn't satisfy you?

MME. VYSHNEVSKY. Not at all.

VYSHNEVSKY. I should think not. Wasn't it for you I bought and decorated this house so splendidly? Wasn't it for you I built the summer house last year? is there anything you don't have enough of? I suppose there isn't even a merchant's wife who has as many diamonds as you have.

MME. VYSHNEVSKY. Thank you. All the same, I didn't ask for anything.

VYSHNEVSKY. You didn't ask, but I had to find some way to make up to you the difference in our years. I thought I'd find in you a woman who could appreciate the sacrifices I was making for you. I'm not a magician, you know; I can't build marble palaces with a flick of the hand. For the silk, the gold, the sable, and the velvet you wrap yourself up in from head to foot it takes money; it has to be gotten. And it isn't always easy to come by.

MME. VYSHNEVSKY. I don't need anything. I've already told you that more than once.

VYSHNEVSKY. But I have a need, and that is to win your heart at last. Your coldness is driving me crazy. I'm a man of passion; out of love for a woman I could do anything! This year I bought you an estate outside Moscow. Do you realize that the money I bought it with… how should I tell you?… Well, in a word, I risked more than was prudent. I could be held accountable.

MME. VYSHNEVSKY. For heaven's sake, don't make me part of your dealings if they're not completely honest. Don't justify them out of love for me. Please. That's something I can't bear. Still, I don't believe you. Before you knew me you lived and acted the very same way. I don't want to burden my conscience with your conduct.

VYSHNEVSKY. Conduct! Conduct! Out of my love for you I'm even ready to commit a crime. I'm ready to procure your love at the cost of my honor. *(He gets up and approaches her.)*

MME. VYSHNEVSKY. Aristarkh Vladimirych, I can't pretend.

VYSHNEVSKY *(taking her by the hand)*. Pretend! Pretend!

MME.VYSHNEVSKY *(turning away)*. Never.

VYSHNEVSKY. But really I love you!…*(Trembling, he falls onto his knees.)* I love you!

MME.VYSHNEVSKY. Aristarkh Vladimirych, don't degrade yourself! It's time for you to get dressed. *(She rings.)*

Vyshnevsky gets up. Anton enters from the study.

Aristarkh Vladimirych needs to be dressed.

ANTON. As you wish, it's ready, sir. *(He goes off into the study.)*

Vyshnevsky follows him.

VYSHNEVSKY *(in the doorway)*. Snake! Snake! *(He goes out.)*

MME.VYSHNEVSKY *(sitting and thinking awhile. The boy servant enters, gives her a letter, and leaves)*. Who could this be from? *(She unseals and reads it.)* That's really nice! A love letter. And who sent it! A man well on in years, with a beautiful wife. How disgusting! How insulting! What's a woman to do in such a case? And the vulgar things he writes! Stupid tender things! Should I send it back? No, it would be better to show it to a few friends for a good laugh together… Ugh, how repulsive! *(She leaves.)*

Anton comes out from the study, stopping at the door. Yusov enters.

YUSOV *(with a briefcase)*. Announce me, Antosha.

Anton goes out. Yusov tidies himself up before the mirror.

ANTON *(in the doorway)*. Come in, please.

Yusov goes in.

BELOGUBOV *(enters, takes a comb from his pocket, and combs his hair)*. Tell me, sir, is Akim Akimych here?

ANTON. He just went into the study.

BELOGUBOV. And the master himself, how is he today? Is he in a good mood, sir?

ANTON. I don't know. *(He leaves.)*

Belogubov stands by the table near the mirror.

YUSOV *(coming out and noticeably putting on airs)*. Oh, so you're here.

BELOGUBOV. I'm here, sir.

YUSOV *(looking through a document)*. Belogubov.

BELOGUBOV. What would you like, sir?

YUSOV. Here, my friend, take this home and make a clean copy. Those are his orders.

BELOGUBOV. It was me he ordered to make a copy, sir?

YUSOV *(sitting down)*. You. He said you have a good handwriting.

BELOGUBOV. It's a great pleasure for me to hear that, sir.

YUSOV. So listen, friend, don't hurry it. The main thing is to be neat. You see, where we're sending it'...

BELOGUBOV. Akim Akimych, I understand, sir. I'll use beautiful penmanship, sir; I'll stay up with it all night.

YUSOV *(sighing)*. Oh, oh! Oh, oh!

BELOGUBOV. Akim Akimych, if only somebody could pay some attention to me.

YUSOV *(sternly)*. Are you trying to make some kind of joke?

BELOGUBOV. How could I do that, sir?

YUSOV. Could pay attention... That's easy to say! What more could an official want? What more could he desire?

BELOGUBOV. Yes, sir!

YUSOV. We've paid attention to you; you're a man, you breathe. Are you saying we haven't paid attention.

BELOGUBOV. It's as you say, sir.

YUSOV. You worm!

BELOGUBOV. Akim Akimych, I think I'm making an effort, sir.

YUSOV. You are? *(He looks at him.)* I do think well of you.

BELOGUBOV. I even skimp on food, Akim Akimych, so I can be neatly dressed. Because, sir, when official is neatly dressed, his superiors always take notice. Please, take a look at my waist... *(He turns about.)*

YUSOV. Stand still. *(He examines Belogubov and takes snuff.)* Your waist is fine... But there's something else, Belogubov; you should watch out more for your writing.

BELOGUBOV. It's the spelling that gets me, Akim Akimych; that's what's bad, sir... Believe me, it bothers me myself.

YUSOV. What does that matter, the spelling! It doesn't all come at once; it takes getting used to. The first thing is to write a rough draft, and then you get somebody to correct it; you make a copy from that. Do you hear what I'm saying?

BELOGUBOV. But when I ask somebody to correct it, sir, then Zhadov always laughs at me.

YUSOV. Who?

BELOGUBOV. Zhadov, sir.

21

YUSOV *(sternly).* But he himself, what is he? What kind of a bird is he? He can afford to laugh!

BELOGUBOV. That's the thing, sir. He has to let people know he's been educated.

YUSOV. Ugh! That's him all right.

BELOGUBOV. I just can't make him out, Akim Akimych, what kind of a person he is.

YUSOV. He's nobody!...

Silence.

I was just in there *(indicating the study),* and he told me *(quietly),"* I don't know what to do about my nephew!" You can figure it out from that.

BELOGUBOV. Zhadov really has a high opinion of himself, sir.

YUSOV. He flies high, but where will he land! He couldn't have it any better, living here with all his keep provided. So what do you think, has he felt any gratitude? Has anybody seen any respect from him? Nothing of the kind! Rudeness, freethinking... After all, even if he's a relative, still his uncle's a big man... how can he put up with that sort of thing? So here's what his uncle told that dear boy, "You just go and live with that mind of yours on ten rubles a month, and perhaps you'll wise up."

BELOGUBOV. That's just what acting stupid can lead to, Akim Akimych. You'd really think ... Good God!... what luck! He ought to be thanking God every moment. Isn't that right, what I'm saying, Akim Akimych, shouldn't he be thanking God, sir?

YUSOV. Of course!

BELOGUBOV. The man's running away from his own happiness. What else does he need, sir! He has a rank in the service, related to a man like that, his keep provided; if he wanted, he could have a good position with a big income. You know Aristarkh Vladimirych wouldn't refuse him.

YUSOV. Not a chance!

BELOGUBOV. This is how I look at it, Akim Akimych. Any other man with feelings in his place would be cleaning boots for Aristarkh Vladimirych, but Zhadov has to cause him pain.

YUSOV. It's all from pride and making judgments.

BELOGUBOV. What judgments! What do we have to judge? Now take me, Akim Akimych, never have I...

YUSOV. Of course not!

BELOGUBOV. I never have, sir... because no good can come of it, only unpleasantness.

YUSOV. But how can he keep from talking! He has to show people he's been at the university.

BELOGUBOV. But what's the use of learning if there's no fear in a man… if there's no trembling before his superiors?

YUSOV. No what?

BELOGUBOV. Trembling, sir.

YUSOV. Indeed yes.

BELOGUBOV. Akim Akimych, I wish they'd make me a department head, sir.

YUSOV. You know what's good for you.

BELOGUBOV. The reason I'm saying that, sir, is that I have a fiancée now. A wonderfully educated young lady, sir. Only without a position it's impossible, sir. Who would give her?

YUSOV. So why not show what you're made of?

BELOGUBOV. My first duty, sir… only right now… I need somebody to take the place of a relative for me, sir.

YUSOV. I'll put in a word about a position. We'll think about it.

BELOGUBOV. That position would set me up for life, sir. Though I'd just sign things, because I can't go higher than that, sir. I don't have the ability.

Zhadov enters.

ZHADOV. Tell me, is Uncle busy?

YUSOV. Busy.

ZHADOV. Too bad! I need very much to see him.

YUSOV. It can wait. He has business more important than yours.

ZHADOV. How can you know what my business is!

YUSOV *(looking at him and laughing)*. What your business is! It has to be some kind of nonsense.

ZHADOV. It's better not to talk with you, Akim Akimych. You always provoke me to harsh words. *(He goes away and sits down at the front of the stage.)*

YUSOV *(to Belogubov)*. What do you think of him?

BELOGUBOV *(loudly)*. It's not worth talking about! At your age it can only upset you. Good-bye, sir. *(He leaves.)*

YUSOV *(to himself)*. Ha, ha, ha! Thank God I've lived to see the day. Little boys have begun to act big.

ZHADOV *(looking around)*. What are you grumbling about over there?

YUSOV *(continuing)*. To follow orders, that we don't like, but to make judgments—there's something for us. So how can we possibly stay in the office! They should make us all ministers of state! But what can you do? They made a mistake, please excuse it, they didn't know of your talents. But we'll make you ministers yet, without fail… just wait a bit… tomorrow even.

ZHADOV *(to himself)*. I'm sick of this!

YUSOV. Oh Lord! Lord! No shame, no conscience. Still young and green, but already high and mighty. See what I am! Don't touch me!

Anton enters

ANTON *(to Yusov)*. The master would like to see you.

Yusov goes off into the study.

ZHADOV. Tell Anna Pavlovna I should like to see her.

ANTON. Very good, sir. *(He goes off.)*

ZHADOV *(alone)*. Why did that old fogy grumble so much! What did I ever do to him! I can't stand university people, he says. Is that my fault? Just try serving under such a boss. Still, what can he do to me if I behave well? But if there's a vacancy they'll probably pass me by. Just like them.

Mme. Vyshnevsky enters.

MME. VYSHNEVSKY. Hello, Vasily Nikolaich.

ZHADOV. Oh, Aunty, hello! *(He kisses her hand.)* I have some news for you.

MME. VYSHNEVSKY. Sit down.

They sit down.

What's your news?

ZHADOV. I want to get married.

MME. VYSHNEVSKY. Isn't it early for that?

ZHADOV. I'm in love, Aunty, in love! And what a girl! Perfection!

MME. VYSHNEVSKY. Is she rich?

ZHADOV. No, Aunty. She doesn't have a thing.

MME. VYSHNEVSKY. Then what are you going to live on?

ZHADOV. But what is my head for, and my hands? Am I really supposed to live all my life at somebody else's expense? Of course, some people would be glad, only too happy for the chance, but I can't. Not to mention that I'd have to kowtow to Uncle and go against my convictions. And who is going to work? What were we taught for? Uncle advises me first of all to make my pile, no matter how, buy myself a home, get some horses, and then get a wife. How can I agree with him? I've fallen in love with a girl as only men at my age do. Am I really supposed to renounce my happiness just because she has no money?

MME. VYSHNEVSKY. It's not only from poverty that people suffer. People suffer from wealth too.

ZHADOV. Do you remember our talks with Uncle? Whatever I'd say against bribes or questionable acts in general, he'd always come back with the same answer,

"You go out and live a bit, and you won't talk like that." Well, now I want to live a bit, and not alone but with a young wife.

MME. VYSHNEVSKY *(sighing)*. Yes, you have to envy women who are loved by men like you.

ZHADOV *(kissing her hand)*. And how I'll work, Aunty! I'm sure my wife won't expect more from me. And if we'll have to suffer need awhile, then surely Pauline, out of love for me, won't show the slightest dissatisfaction. But in any case, no matter how bitter life might be, I'm not going to give up even a millionth part of those convictions which I owe to my education.

MME. VYSHNEVSKY. You we can be sure of, but your wife... she's a young woman! It will be hard for her to put up with any deprivation. Our girls are brought up very badly. You young men think we're angels, but believe me, Vasily Nikolaich, we're worse than the men. We're more mercenary, more prejudiced. What can you do! One has to admit we have much less feeling for honor and exact justice. Another bad thing in us is a lack of delicacy. A woman can reproach somebody in a way few grown men would permit themselves. You can hear the most cutting remarks between women who are close friends. Sometimes a woman's foolish reproach hurts worse than a direct insult.

ZHADOV. That's true. But I myself will educate her. She's still only a child; I can still make anything out of her. Only I have to tear her away from her family right away before they spoil her with their vulgar upbringing. For after they've made her a young lady in their fashion it'll be too late.

MME. VYSHNEVSKY. I can't raise doubts, and I don't want to disillusion you. It would be mean of me to dampen your spirit at the start. So give your heart free rein before it begins to get hardened. Don't be afraid of poverty. God will bless you. Believe me, nobody could wish you as much happiness as I.

ZHADOV. I've always been sure of that, Aunty.

MME. VYSHNEVSKY. One thing that worries me is your impatience. You're always making enemies.

ZHADOV. Yes, everybody tells me I'm impatient, that I lose a lot by it. But is impatience really a fault? Is it really better to look with indifference at the Yusovs and the Belogubovs, at all the disgusting things that go around one all the time? From indifference to vice is a short distance. The man who's not disgusted by vice will bit by bit be dragged into it himself.

MME. VYSHNEVSKY. It's not that I'm calling impatience a fault, simply that I know from experience how out of place it can be in real life. I've known cases... you'll see some day.

ZHADOV. What do you think, will Uncle turn me down or not? I want to ask him for a raise. Right now that would come in very handy.

MME. VYSHNEVSKY. I don't know. Ask him.

Vyshnevsky enters in a frock coat and wig, Yusov behind him.

VYSHNEVSKY *(to Zhadov).* Oh, hello. *(He sits down.)* Sit down. Sit down, Akim Akimych. You're idling about all the time; you hardly ever go to the office.

ZHADOV. There's nothing to do there. They don't give me any work.

YUSOV. We have loads of work!

ZHADOV. You mean that copying? No thanks, your obedient servant! You have officials a lot better at that than I am.

VYSHNEVSKY. My boy, you're still at it! Still preaching your sermons. *(To his wife.)* Can you imagine, at the office he preaches morality to the clerks, and they, of course, don't understand any of it, sitting there with their eyes and mouths wide open. It's really funny!

ZHADOV. How can I stay quiet when I see disgusting things at every step! I still haven't lost my faith in people. I think my words will have some effect on them.

VYSHNEVSKY. They already have; you've become the laughing stock of the whole office. You've reached your goal already; you've managed it so that when you come in they all look around with a smile and whisper to each other, and when you leave, they all laugh.

YUSOV. That's right, sir.

ZHADOV. All the same, what's so funny in what I say?

VYSHNEVSKY. Everything, my friend. Starting with your unnecessary indecent enthusiasm and ending with your childish impractical conclusions. Believe me, any clerk knows life better than you. He knows from his own experience that it's better to have a full stomach than to be a hungry philosopher. It's no wonder your words seem stupid to him.

ZHADOV. But as I see it the only thing they know is that there's more profit for a bribetaker than an honest man.

YUSOV. Hm, hm…

VYSHNEVSKY. That's stupid, my friend! Both insolent and stupid.

ZHADOV. But Uncle! What was their purpose in teaching us, why did they fill us with those ideas we can't mention without your accusing us of stupidity or insolence?

VYSHNEVSKY. I don't know who taught you there or what. It does seem to me better to teach people to do their work and respect their elders than to babble nonsense.

YUSOV. Yes, sir, that would be much better.

ZHADOV. Have it your way, I'll keep quiet. But I can't part with my convictions; they're my sole consolation in life.

VYSHNEVSKY. Yes, in an attic eating a crust of black bread. A wonderful consolation! Out of hunger you'll take to praising your own virtue, and you'll curse your colleagues and superiors because they knew how to organize their lives, because they're living in plenty, with a family, happy. Marvelous! That's where envy will help.

ZHADOV. Good God!

MME. VYSHNEVSKY. That was cruel.

VYSHNEVSKY. Please, don't think you've said something new. This sort of thing always was and always will be. The man who hasn't known how or hasn't managed to make a fortune for himself will always envy the man with a fortune; that's human nature. It's easy also to justify envy. Those who envy usually say, "I don't want wealth; I may be poor, but I'm noble."

YUSOV. Honeyed lips!

VYSHNEVSKY. Noble poverty is good only in the theater. But just try it out in life. That, my friend, is not so easy or pleasant as we'd like to think. You've gotten used to thinking only of yourself, but suppose you get married, what then? That's something to think about!

ZHADOV. Yes, Uncle I am going to get married, and that's what I wanted to talk with you about.

VYSHNEVSKY. And no doubt it's for love, to some poor girl, most likely some fool with just as much understanding of life as you. She's probably educated, and, accompanied by a piano out of tune, she sings, "With my darling it's heaven, even in a hut."[1]

ZHADOV. Yes, she's a poor girl.

VYSHNEVSKY. Marvelous.

YUSOV. For the propagation of beggars, sir.

ZHADOV. Akim Akimych, don't insult me. I haven't given you any cause for that. Uncle, marriage is a big thing, and I think that in such a matter a man should follow his own inclinations.

VYSHNEVSKY. Go right ahead; nobody's stopping you. But have you thought about things? You love your fiancée, of course?

ZHADOV. Naturally I love her.

VYSHNEVSKY. So what are you preparing for her, what joys in life? Poverty, all kinds of deprivation. In my opinion, a man who loves a woman tries to strew her path, so to speak, with all kinds of delights.

YUSOV. That's right, sir.

VYSHNEVSKY. Instead of the hats and styles women feel they must have, you'll be giving your wife sermons on virtue. Out of love for you she'll listen, of course, but all the same she won't be getting her hats and coats.

MME. VYSHNEVSKY. At his age love isn't bought yet.

ZHADOV. What Aunty says is true.

VYSHNEVSKY. I agree there's no need for you to buy love, but every man is obliged to reward love, to pay for it; otherwise, the most unselfish love will grow cold. You'll start getting reproaches, complaints against fate. I don't know how you'll be able to stand it when all the time your wife expresses regret that from inexperience she joined her lot with a beggar. In a word, it's your *obligation* to provide for the happiness of the woman you love. And without wealth or at least some abundance there is no happiness for a woman. Maybe, as usual, you'll start contradicting me, so I'll prove it to you. Look around you. What smart girl will think twice before marrying an old or ugly man if only he has money? What mother will hesitate a second before marrying her daughter off to such a man even if the girl's against it? Because she considers her daughter's tears stupid and childish, and she thanks God for sending such good luck to her Mashenka or Annushka. Every mother knows in advance that her daughter will thank her afterwards. And if only for his peace of mind, which also is worth something, a husband has to provide completely for his wife; then even… even if the wife isn't completely happy, she doesn't have the right to… she doesn't dare complain. *(With heat.)* If a woman is snatched away from poverty and smothered with concern for her needs and luxury then who can believe she's unhappy? Ask my wife if I'm speaking the truth.

MME. VYSHNEVSKY. Your words are so clever and convincing they don't need my agreement. *(She leaves.)*

ZHADOV. Not all women are like that.

VYSHNEVSKY. Almost all. Of course there are exceptions, but it's not likely such an exception will fall your way. For that to happen a man has to live a bit, do some hunting around rather than, like you, fall in love with the first girl he meets. Listen, I'll speak to you as a relative, because I'm sorry for you. What are you really thinking about your affairs? How are you and your wife going to live without means?

ZHADOV. I'll live by working. My hope is that for me a peaceful conscience will take the place of earthly blessings.

VYSHNEVSKY. Your work won't be enough to support a family. You won't land a good job, because with your stupid ways you won't know how to get on the good side of any of your superiors; instead you'll turn them against you. And your peaceful conscience won't save you from hunger either. Take note, my friend, luxury is noticeably spreading in society, but your Spartan virtues don't get along well with luxury. Your mother entrusted you to my care, and I'm obliged to do all I can for you. For the last time this is my advice to you. Tone down your character a bit, give up those foolish ideas, give them up, they're ridiculous. Work at your job the way all decent people do, that is, look at life and work in a practical way. Then I can help you with advice, with money, with influence. You're no longer a child; you're getting ready to be married.

ZHADOV. Never!

VYSHNEVSKY. How loud you said that… "Never!"… But it's stupid all the same! I think you'll come to your senses; I've seen a lot of cases like yours. Only watch out you're not too late. Right now you have the opportunity and the patronage, but you might not have it later. You'll ruin your career, your colleagues will pass you by, it will be hard for you to start again from scratch. I'm speaking to you as official to official.

ZHADOV. Never, never.

VYSHNEVSKY. All right then, live as you want, without backing. Don't put your hopes on me any more. I'm sick and tired of talking with you.

ZHADOV. Oh God! My backing will come from public opinion.

VYSHNEVSKY. That'll be the day! My friend, we don't have any public opinion, and there can't be any, not in your sense. Here's public opinion for you: don't get caught and you're not a thief. Society doesn't care what income you live on so long as you live in decent style and act respectably. But if you go without boots and lecture everybody on morality then don't blame people if you're not received in respectable homes or if you're called light-minded or even harmful. I served in some of the chief provincial towns, and people there know each other better than in Moscow or St. Petersburg. They know what each man has and what he lives on, so it's easier for public opinion to be formed. But no, people are people everywhere. Even there, in my very presence, they laughed at an official who lived on nothing but his salary; he had a large family, and the towns-people said he sewed his own coats. Even there the whole town respected the number-one bribetaker because he did a lot of entertaining and had evening parties twice a week.

ZHADOV. Is that really true?

VYSHNEVSKY. Live awhile, and you'll find out. Let's go, Akim Akimych. *(He gets up.)*

ZHADOV. Uncle!

VYSHNEVSKY. What is it?

ZHADOV. I have a small salary; I don't have enough to get by on. There's an opening now; let me fill it. I'm going to get married...

VYSHNEVSKY. Hm... For that position what I need is not a married man but one who's capable. In all conscience I can't give you a higher salary. In the first place, you don't deserve it, and in the second place, you're my relative; they'll consider it nepotism.

ZHADOV. As you wish. I'll live on what means I have.

VYSHNEVSKY. My friend, you're at it again! I'll tell you once and for all; I don't like the way you talk. Your words are cutting and disrespectful, and I don't see any need for you to get so worked up. Don't think I consider your opinions insulting—that would be too great an honor for you—I just consider them stupid. So then, aside from official dealings you can consider our relations finished.

ZHADOV. In that case I'd better transfer to another office.

VYSHNEVSKY. Please do. *(He leaves.)*

YUSOV *(looking right at Zdadov).* Ha, ha, ha, ha…

ZHADOV. What are you laughing at?

YUSOV. Ha, ha, ha… How can one help laughing? Who is it you're arguing with? Ha, ha, ha! Has there ever been anything like it?

ZHADOV. What's so funny about it?

YUSOV. Really now, is your uncle more stupid than you? Is he more stupid? Does he understand less about life than you? It's all enough to make the hens laugh. You could make me die laughing. Have mercy, spare me, I have a family.

ZHADOV. Akim Akimych, you don't understand this matter.

YUSOV. But there's nothing to understand. You could bring in even a thousand men, and they'd all die laughing at you. Here you should be listening to such a man with your mouth wide open, not missing a single word, engraving what he says in your memory, but you have to argue! It's really a comedy, honest to God it's a comedy, ha, ha, ha… And your uncle gave you a good going over, hee, hee, hee, but it still wasn't enough. Now if I were in his place… *(He makes a strong grimace and goes off into the study.)*

ZHADOV *(alone, thoughtful).* Go on, keep talking! I don't believe you, I don't believe that an educated man can't provide for himself and his family through honest work. I don't want to believe society is that corrupt! That's the way old people have of trying to disillusion young people, by showing them everything in a bad light. Old people envy us because we look at life with a light heart and lots of hope. I understand you, Uncle. Now you've gotten everything, a big name and money, you don't have to envy anybody. The only ones of us you envy are those with a clear conscience and a calm soul. You won't buy that for any money. You can say what you want, but all the same I'm going to get married, and I'm going to live a happy life. *(He leaves.)*

Vyshnevsky and Yusov come out from the study.

VYSHNEVSKY. Who's he going to marry?

YUSOV. The Kukushkin girl. She's the daughter of a collegiate assessor's widow.[2]

VYSHNEVSKY. Do you know the woman?

YUSOV. Yes, sir, I knew her husband. Belogubov wants to marry the other daughter.

VYSHNEVSKY. Well, Belogubov's another matter. Anyway, you go see the woman. Make her see she shouldn't ruin her daughter by letting her marry this idiot. *(He nods and leaves.)*

YUSOV *(alone).* What times we've come to! The things that go on in the world these days, you can't believe your own eyes! How can one live in the world! Little boys have started to talk! And just who is talking? Just who is arguing? A nobody, that's who! Just blow on him and phoo! *(He blows.)* There's nobody there. And just who is he arguing with! A genius. Aristarkh Vladimirych is a genius… a genius, a Napoleon. He has a limitless mind, he's quick, bold in his

affairs. Just one deficiency, he's not at all strong in the law, he came from another department. If, with his mind, Aristarkh Vladimirych knew the laws and
all the ins and outs like his predecessor, well, that's all… that's all… no more
needs to be said. You could follow him like a railroad. You could hitch onto
him and be on your way. Promotion, decorations, all kinds of land, houses, set-
tlements with virgin land… It takes your breath away! *(He leaves.)*

ACT TWO

*A room in Mme. Kukushkin's home. An ordinary living room, the kind
found in homes of modest means. A door in the middle and one to the left. Julie
and Pauline are standing before the mirror. Stesha is holding cleaning utensils.*

STESHA. There, my young ladies are all set. Those suitors can come right now, the
display is first rate. We can put on a great show. We wouldn't even be ashamed
to show them off to some general!

PAULINE. So then, Julie, let's get to our posts. We'll sit down the way bright young
ladies sit. Mummy will come any time for the inspection. She wants to sell the
goods at their best.

STESHA *(wiping the dust)*. You can look as hard as you want, but everything's in its
place and neat as a pin.

JULIE. An inspector like her'll find something.

They sit down.

STESHA *(stooping in the middle of the room)*. That's the way of it, young ladies, because
of her you don't have any life at all. She drills you and drills you like soldiers in
training. She keeps you at attention all the time; all that's missing is she doesn't
order you to lift your feet. And she takes it out on me too. She's been after me
all the time about that cleanliness of hers. *(She wipes dust.)*

JULIE. Do you like your suitor, your Vasily Nikolaich?

PAULINE. Oh, he's a real darling! And do you like your Belogubov?

JULIE. No, he's nothing but trash!

PAULINE. Then why don't you tell Mama?

JULIE. That's worse, God forbid! I'd jump for joy to marry him, just to get out of
this house.

PAULINE. You're right there. If Vasily Nikolaich hadn't come along, I think I'd be only
too glad to throw myself at the first man I'd meet. He wouldn't have to be anything, just so he'd rescue me from my misery, take me from this house. *(She laughs.)*

STESHA *(bending under the divan)*. It's the suffering of the martyrs. It's true, what
you're saying, miss.

PAULINE. There are some girls, Julie, who cry when they get married. How can they leave home! They mourn for every little nook. But you and I'd go to the end of the world right now if only some dragon would carry us off. *(She laughs.)*

STESHA. If I don't wipe here I'll get it from her. But who's going to see anything here, who'd want to! *(She wipes under the mirror.)*

JULIE. You're the lucky one, Pauline; everything's funny to you, but I'm starting to think seriously about marriage. It's easy enough to get married—we know how to pull that off, but one has to think how married life'll be.

PAULINE. But what's there to think about? It surely can't be any worse than at home.

JULIE. Can't be any worse! That's not enough. It has to be better. If a woman's going to get married then she should end up a true proper lady.

PAULINE. That would be very nice, nothing better, but how? You're the smart one here, tell me how.

JULIE. You have to tell from what a man says what he's putting his hopes on. If he doesn't have something now, whether he has prospects. Just from what he says you can tell right off what kind of man he is. What does your Zhadov tell you when you're alone with him?

PAULINE. Well, Julie, for the life of me I don't understand a thing he says. He squeezes my hand hard and starts to talk… he wants to teach me something.

JULIE What?

PAULINE. I really don't know, Julie. Something very deep. Wait, maybe I can remember something, only don't laugh; the words are so funny. Hold on, now I remember! *(Mimicking.)* "What is the destination of women in society?" He talked about some kind of civic virtue. I don't know what that is. They didn't teach us that, did they?

JULIE. No, they didn't teach us that.

PAULINE. He probably read it in those books they wouldn't give us. You remember… in the boarding school? But then, to tell the truth, we didn't read any books.

JULIE. That's something to be sorry about! Even without books it's boring enough! Now if we could only go for a ride or to the theater, that would be another matter.

PAULINE. Yes, sis, yes.

JULIE. We'll have to face up to it, Pauline, there's not much hope for your man. Mine's not like that.

PAULINE. What's yours like?

JULIE. My Belogubov may be on the repulsive side, but he gives more hope. He says to me, "You'll come to love me, miss. Now is not the time for me to get married, miss, but when they make me a department head, then I'll get married." I asked him what a department head was. He says, "It's first-rate, miss." So it must be something good. He says, "I may be uneducated, but I have lots of business with merchants, miss, and that means I'll be bringing you silks and different materials from the market, and so far as provisions go, we'll have everything, miss." What about that? It's very good, Pauline, let him bring the stuff. You don't even have to think about it, you've got to marry a man like that.

PAULINE. My man mustn't know any merchants, he didn't say anything about it. Does that mean he won't bring me anything?

JULIE. No, your man must have something too. After all, he's an official, and all officials have things given them, whatever they want. Some married men get different kinds of material. For a bachelor it could be cloth, tricot. If a man has horses he gets oats or hay. Otherwise, money. Last time Belogubov was wearing a vest, you remember, the one with gay colors. A merchant gave him that; he told me so himself.

PAULINE. I'll just have to ask Zhadov if he knows any merchants.

Mme. Kukushkin enters.

MME KUKUSHKIN. I can't help bragging! I have it clean here, I have things in order, everything under control! *(She sits down.)* But what's that? *(She indicates to Stesha something under the divan.)*

STESHA. Really, ma'am, I'm worn out, I broke my back for you.

MME KUKUSHKIN. How dare you talk like that, you nasty woman! That's what you're paid for. I get cleanliness, I get order, and I get absolute obedience. In return for the money you're my slave.

The maid sweeps up and leaves.

Julie!

Julie stands up.

I want to talk to you.

JULIE. What do you want, Mama?

MME KUKUSHKIN. You know, young lady, I don't have anything or any prospects of getting anything.

JULIE. I know, Mama.

MME KUKUSHKIN. It's time you knew, young lady! I don't get income from anywhere, only my pension. I have to make ends meet as best I can. I deny myself everything. I bustle about like a thief at the fair, but for all that I'm not an old woman yet, I could find myself a match. Do you understand that?

JULIE. I understand, ma'am.

MME KUKUSHKIN. I make stylish dresses and all sorts of knick-knacks for you, but for myself I take my old things and cut and dye them. Now you probably think I'm dressing you up for your own pleasure, just so you can look smart. But you're mistaken. I'm doing all this to get you married, to get you off my hands. With my means I couldn't keep you in anything but cotton house dresses. If you don't want or don't know how to land yourself a bridegroom, so be it. But I don't intend to cut down and limit myself for you to no good purpose.

PAULINE. Mama, this is an old story. Tell us what it's all about.

MME KUKUSHKIN. You be quiet! Nobody's talking to you. To make up for your stupidity God gave you good luck, so be quiet. If this Zhadov weren't such a fool, you'd end up an old maid, you're so emptyheaded. What man in his right mind would take you? Who'd want to? You don't have a thing to brag about, not a brain in your head. You can't say you charmed the man, he came running himself, he's putting his own neck in the noose, nobody dragged him here. But Julie's a bright girl, and that's why she's sure to win happiness. Tell me, does your Belogubov show any promise or not?

JULIE. I don't know, Mama.

MME KUKUSHKIN. Then who does? You know very well, young lady, I don't receive just any young men. Only a suitor or one who might be. If a man looks something like that, come right in, please, open house. But when he starts getting evasive it's the gate for him. We don't need that type. I'm protecting my reputation, yes, and yours too.

JULIE. But Mama, what do you want me to do?

MME KUKUSHKIN. Do as you're told. Just remember one thing, you can't stay single. If you do, you'll have to live in the kitchen.

JULIE. I've done all you told me, Mama.

MME KUKUSHKIN. What have you done? Tell me, I'm all ears.

JULIE. When he came that second time, you remember, you almost had to drag him in, I made eyes at him.

MME KUKUSHKIN. And what did he do?

JULIE. In a strange way he stuck his lips together, and then he licked them. I think he was too stupid to understand. Nowadays any schoolboy would do better.

MME KUKUSHKIN. Maybe you know something I don't, but what I do see is that he shows his bosses respect. He knows how to be pleasant and make up to them. That means he'll go far. I understood that right away.

JULIE. The third time he came, you remember, it was a Friday. I read some love poems to him. I don't think he understood any of that either. The fourth time I wrote him a little note.

MME KUKUSHKIN. What did he do then?

JULIE. He came over to me, and he says, "My heart has never turned away from you. It always was, is, and ever will be."

Pauline laughs.

MME KUKUSHKIN *(threatening her with her finger).* Then what?

JULIE. He says, "As soon as I get the position of department head then I'll ask your mama for your hand, and I'll have tears in my eyes."

MME KUKUSHKIN. Will he get it soon?

JULIE. He says it'll be soon.

MME KUKUSHKIN. Come here, Julie, kiss me. *(Julie kisses her.)* Getting married, my dear, is a big thing in a girl's life. Some day you'll understand that. I'm a mother, you know, and I'm a strict mother. If a suitor is serious, you can do what you want; I won't say a thing, dear, I'll keep quiet. But if it's going to be hanky panky with a man just in from the street, no! I won't allow that. Go, Julie, take your place.

Julie sits down.

So when you get married, children, here's my advice to you. Don't indulge your husbands, but keep pecking away at them to bring in money. Otherwise, they get lazy, and later on they're sorry themselves. There's a lot I ought to tell you girls, but I can't say all of it now. If something comes up, run straight to me. You'll always find a welcome with me; I'll never turn you away. I know all the ins and outs, and I can give you all kinds of advice, even on medical things.

PAULINE. Mama, somebody's at the door.

JULIE *(looking out the window).* It's Belogubov and some old man.

MME KUKUSHKIN. Sit in your places. Julie, lower your cape a bit on your right shoulder.

Yusov and Belogubov enter.

BELOGUBOV. Hello, Felisata Gerasimovna. *(To the young ladies.)* Hello, ladies. *(Indicating Yusov.)* Ma'am, he wanted... this is my superior and my benefactor, Akim Akimych Yusov. You know it's better, Felisata Gerasimovna, when it's with your superior, ma'am.

MME KUKUSHKIN. Welcome, welcome! Please sit down.

Yusov and Belogubov sit down.

Let me introduce you to my two daughters, Julie and Pauline. They're absolute children, don't understand a thing; they should still be playing with their dolls instead of getting married. It's a great pity to part with them, but what can you do? Goods like that can't be kept at home.

YUSOV. Yes, ma'am, that's the law of our fates, ma'am. It's the very sphere of life itself, ma'am! Whatever has been foreordained for ages and ages, that is something, ma'am, which man cannot...

MME KUKUSHKIN. I'll tell you the honest truth, Akim Akimych. I've brought them up strictly, away from everything. I can't give a big dowry for them, but when it comes to morality their husbands will be grateful. I love my children, Akim Akimych, but I'm strict, terribly strict. *(Sternly.)* Pauline, go get the tea ready.

PAULINE *(gets up)*. Right away, Mama. *(She goes out.)*

YUSOV. I'm strict myself, ma'am. *(Sternly.)* Belogubov!

BELOGUBOV. What would you like, sir?

YUSOV. Isn't that right, that I'm strict?

BELOGUBOV. You're strict, sir. *(To Julie.)* I have a new vest, miss, take a look.

JULIE. It's very nice. Did the same merchant give it to you?

BELOGUBOV. No, this was another one, miss. This one has a better mill.

JULIE. Let's go into the living room. I'll show you my fancywork.

They leave.

MME KUKUSHKIN. How they love each other, it's so touching to watch them. The young man lacks just one thing; he says he doesn't have a good position. He says he can't guarantee his wife complete tranquillity. If, he says, they would make me a department head, then, he says, I could support a wife. It's such a shame, Akim Akimych! He's such a wonderful young man, so much in love...

YUSOV *(taking some snuff)*. It comes bit by bit, Felisata Gerasimovna, bit by bit.

MME KUKUSHKIN. Still you ought to know if he's going to get this position soon. It might even depend on you. I'll submit a request on his behalf. *(She bows to him.)* You really can't ignore my request, for I'm a mother, a tender mother fussing about for the happiness of her children, her baby birds.

YUSOV *(assuming a serious expression)*. It'll be soon, soon. I've already submitted a report about him to our chief. And that chief is completely in my hands; whatever I say goes. We'll make him a department head. If I want, he'll be a department head, and if I don't, he won't...Heh, heh, he will be, he will. I have that chief right there. *(He shows his hand.)*

MME KUKUSHKIN. I'll have to own up to you I don't even like bachelors. What do they accomplish? All they do is weigh down the earth.

YUSOV *(solemnly)*. They're a burden on the earth, a burden... and empty chatter too.

MME KUKUSHKIN. Yes, sir. And it's even dangerous to admit a bachelor into a home, especially where there are daughters or a young wife. Who knows what he has on his mind? The way I look at it, you have to get a young man married off as soon as you can; later on he himself will want to thank you. Otherwise they're stupid; they don't know what's good for them.

YUSOV. Yes, ma'am. It's because they get distracted. You see, life… is the sea of life… it swallows a man up.

MME KUKUSHKIN. A bachelor can't set up a proper household; he pays no attention to the house; he goes to the tavern.

YUSOV. But some of us go there too, ma'am… it's a repose from our labors…

MME KUKUSHKIN. But there's a big difference, Akim Akimych. You go when you're invited, when somebody wants to treat you, to show their respect. But you don't really go at your own expense.

YUSOV. I should say not. No, ma'am, in that case I don't go.

MME KUKUSHKIN. Take a case like this. A man submitting an official request invites your bachelor to a tavern, treats him to a dinner, and that's the end of it. A lot of money spent but no good from it. But your married man, Akim Akimych, will tell the man making that request, "What good are your dinners to me? I'm better off having dinner with my wife, family style, quietly, in my own little nook. Just give me some pure cash." And he'll bring home the money. From that you have two advantages: he comes home sober, and he has money… How many years have you been married?

YUSOV. It's been forty-three years, ma'am.

MME KUKUSHKIN. You don't say! But your face looks so young!

YUSOV. It's the regularity of my life… Yesterday I had my blood drawn with cupping glasses.

MME KUKUSHKIN. A healthy man is always healthy, especially a man at rest in his soul, a man who's well off.

YUSOV. Let me make a report to you about the game of nature taking its course… with a man… from poverty to riches. They took me, ma'am… this was a long time ago… into the office, I had on a shabby miserable coat, and I'd just learned to read and write… I can see them now sitting there, all older men, looking important, as if they were angry. Those days they didn't shave much,[3] and it made them look even more important. I was so frightened I couldn't say a word. For a couple of years I ran errands, did all kinds of things: went for vodka, for meat pies, and for kvass if somebody had a hangover. And I didn't sit at a table or on a chair but by the window on a pile of papers; I didn't write out of an inkwell but out of an old hairgrease jar. But I made something of myself. Of course it's not all our doing… it's from above… it seems it just had to be that I would become somebody and hold an important position. Sometimes my wife and I wonder: why did God favor us so with His gifts? For everything there's a fate… and one has to do good deeds… help the poor. Yes, ma'am, at the present time I have three little homes, far away, to be sure, but that doesn't stop me, for I have a team of four horses. Their being far away makes it even better; there's more land and less noise made about it, less talk, less malicious gossip.

MME KUKUSHKIN. Yes, of course. I suppose you have a little flower garden near your homes?

YUSOV. Yes, I do, ma'am. In the summer heat it's all good for cooling off and resting the limbs. But I don't have any pride, ma'am. Pride blinds people... Even if it's a peasant... I treat him like my own brother... after all, he's my neighbor... But at work that's out... The ones I especially don't care for are those emptyheaded ones, the educated fellows they have now. With them I'm strict and demanding. They have such a high opinion of themselves. I just don't go along with their crazy notions, as if scholars could grab stars from the sky. I've seen their kind; they're no better than us sinners, and they're not so attentive to their work. I have a rule: I make things as hard for them as I can for the good of the service... because they do harm. Somehow or other, Felisata Gerasimovna, my heart goes out more to the simple folk. Things are so strict now a man can suffer a setback; for failing grades he can be expelled from a district school or from the lower classes of a preparatory school. How can you not help a man like that? He's been killed by fate, deprived of everything, treated badly all around. But in our office those are the very ones who catch on faster and are more compliant; they have a more open mind. Out of Christian duty you make something out of him, and he'll be grateful for the rest of his life; he'll ask you to stand at his wedding, be godfather to his children. You get your reward in the future life... Now take Belogubov. It's true he can't read or write, but I love him, Felisata Gerasimovna, like a son; he has feeling. But I must confess to you, your other suitor... you know, he's under me too... So I'm in a position to judge...

MME KUKUSHKIN. What is it?

YUSOV (makes a serious face). He's not reliable.

MME KUKUSHKIN. But why not? He's not a drunkard or a spendthrift or lazy, is he?

YUSOV. No, ma'am. But... (He takes some snuff.) He's not reliable.

MME KUKUSHKIN. In what way? Explain it to me, my dear Akim Akimych. After all, I'm the mother.

YUSOV. It's this way. He has a certain man for a relative... Aristarkh Vladimirych Vyshnevsky.

MME KUKUSHKIN. I know.

YUSOV. He's a big man, no question, a big man.

MME KUKUSHKIN. I know.

YUSOV. But Zhadov's disrespectful to him.

MME KUKUSHKIN. I know, I know.

YUSOV. He's rude to his superiors... high and mighty above all limits... and the thoughts he has... he's corrupting the youth... above all, his freethinking. His superiors have to take a stern view.

MME KUKUSHKIN. I know.

YUSOV. If you know, then you can judge for yourself. What times we've come to, Felisata Gerasimovna, no real life at all! And whose fault is it? It's that trash, those little boys. They're being graduated by the hundreds; they'll take us all over.

MME KUKUSHKIN. But when he gets married, Akim Akimych, he'll change. If I didn't know all that, I couldn't go through with it; I'm not a mother to rush into things with eyes closed. I have a rule. As soon as a young man starts coming here I send somebody to find out every last thing about him, or I find out from people myself. The way I see it, all those stupid things come from his being a bachelor. But once he's married we women will go to work on him. He'll make it up with his uncle, and he'll be good at work.

YUSOV. If he changes, his superiors will change towards him… *(He becomes silent for awhile.)* We don't have the officials we used to have, Felisata Gerasimovna! Officials are degenerating. They don't have any spirit. What a life it used to be, Felisata Gerasimovna, heaven itself! A man could live that kind of life forever. We were swimming, simply swimming, Felisata Gerasimovna. In those days officials were eagles… eagles, but nowadays youth is emptyheaded, there's something missing.

Zhadov enters.

MME KUKUSHKIN. Welcome, Vasily Nikolaich, welcome. Pauline has missed you terribly. She kept looking for you, running up to one window, then the other. Such love, such love!… Really, I've never seen the like. You're a lucky man, Vasily Nikolaich. Tell me, why is it you're loved like that?

ZHADOV. Excuse me, Felisata Gerasimovna, I'm a bit late. Oh, Akim Akimych. *(He bows.)* What brings you here?

MME KUKUSHKIN. Akim Akimych is kind enough to take good care of his officials… I just don't know how to thank him. He took it on himself to come and get acquainted.

ZHADOV *(to Yusov)*. Thank you. Still, there was no need to trouble yourself.

YUSOV. I came more for Belogubov, Felisata Gerasimovna. He doesn't have any relatives, so I'm trying to act like a father for him.

MME KUKUSHKIN. Don't say another word, Akim Akimych. You're a family man yourself, and I could see right away how you make every effort to encourage young men in the direction of family life. I myself share that feeling, Akim Akimych. *(To Zhadov.)* You can't imagine, Vasily Nikolaich, how much I suffer when I see two hearts in love sharing obstacles. When you read a novel, you see how circumstances keep the lovers from seeing each other, or the parents are opposed, or class considerations interfere, how it makes you suffer. I cry, I just cry! And sometimes parents can be so cruel, parents who don't want to respect their children's feelings. In cases like that some children even die from love. But when you see that everything is leading up to a happy ending, that all the obstacles are disappearing, *(in rapture)* that love is triumphant, and that the young people are joined in legal wedlock, how all that sweetens up your soul. A kind of sweet bliss goes through all your limbs.

Pauline enters.

PAULINE. Won't you come in? The tea's all ready. *(Seeing Zhadov.)* Vasily Nikolaich! Aren't you ashamed to make me suffer so? I waited and waited for you.

ZHADOV *(kisses her hand)*. I'm sorry.

MME KUKUSHKIN. Come here, my child, kiss me.

PAULINE *(to Zhadov)*. Let's go in.

MME KUKUSHKIN. Let's go in, Akim Akimych.

They leave. Belogubov and Julie enter with cups in hand.

JULIE. As I see it, you've been deceiving me all the time.

BELOGUBOV. How could I dare deceive you, miss? Wherever did you get that idea?

They sit down.

JULIE. You can't believe men in anything, anything at all.

BELOGUBOV. What makes you so critical of men?

JULIE. How am I critical when it's the absolute truth?

BELOGUBOV. That's not possible, miss. It's just a matter of talk. It's the usual thing for men to pay compliments, but the young ladies don't believe them. They say men deceive them.

JULIE. You know everything. You yourself have probably paid a lot of compliments in your life.

BELOGUBOV. I didn't have anyone to pay them to, and then again I don't know how to, miss. You know that I've just started coming to the house, miss, and before that I didn't have any acquaintances.

JULIE. And you didn't deceive anyone?

BELOGUBOV. In what regard?

JULIE. Don't talk to me. I don't believe a single word you say. *(She turns away.)*

BELOGUBOV. But what's the point of this, miss? One could take offense.

JULIE. I should think you'd understand.

BELOGUBOV. I don't understand, miss.

JULIE. You don't want to! *(She covers her eyes with her handkerchief.)*

BELOGUBOV. I can assure you any way you want, miss, that I have always... the way it was when I fell in love, miss, that's the way it is now... I've already told you...

JULIE. You're in love, but you keep putting things off.

BELOGUBOV. Yes, miss… Now I understand, miss. But you know, miss, it isn't the kind of business that… you just can't do it right off, miss.

JULIE. Then how come Zhadov can?

BELOGUBOV. That's quite another matter, miss. He has a rich uncle, miss, and he himself is an educated man, he could get a job anywhere. He could even become a teacher; he'll always have his bread, miss. But what can I do, miss? Until I'm given the position as department head there's nothing I can do, miss. And you yourself wouldn't want to eat soup and porridge, miss. Only men can do that, but you're a young lady, miss, that's not for you. But once I get that position then there'll be a real turnabout.

JULIE. And when will that turnabout be?

BELOGUBOV. It'll be soon, miss. They promised. As soon as I get the position, then at that very moment… only first I'll sew myself a new office uniform… I've already spoken to your mama, miss. Don't you get angry, Julia Ivanovna, because it doesn't depend on me. Your hand, please.

Julie, not looking at him, stretches out her hand. He kisses it.

As for me I can hardly wait.

Zhadov and Pauline enter.

JULIE. Let's go. We'll leave them alone.

They go out. Zhadov and Pauline sit down.

PAULINE. Do you know what I'm going to tell you?

ZHADOV. No, I don't.

PAULINE. Only please, don't you tell Mama.

ZHADOV. I won't tell, don't worry.

PAULINE *(thinking a bit)*. I'd tell you, but I'm afraid you won't love me any more.

ZHADOV. Won't love you any more? Could that really happen?

PAULINE. Are you telling me the truth?

ZHADOV *(taking her by the hand)*. I'm not going to stop loving you, believe me.

PAULINE. See that you don't. I'll tell you out of my simplicity. *(Quietly.)* In our house everything is deception, everything, everything, absolutely everything. Please, don't you believe anything you're told. We don't have a thing. Mama says she loves us, but she doesn't love us at all; she just wants to get rid of us the sooner the better. She makes up to the suitors to their face but runs them down behind their back. She makes us pretend.

ZHADOV. Does this disgust you? Does it?

PAULINE. Only I'm not pretending, I really do love you.

ZHADOV. You'll drive me mad! *(He kisses her hand.)*

PAULINE. And another thing, we're not educated at all. Julie knows something, but I'm an absolute idiot.

ZHADOV. What do you mean, idiot?

PAULINE. Just that, the same as any idiot. I don't know a thing; I haven't read anything... Sometimes when you talk I don't understand a word of it.

ZHADOV. You're an angel! *(He kisses her hand.)*

PAULINE. I may be kinder than Julie, but I'm a lot dumber.

ZHADOV. And that's just why I love you, because they haven't managed to teach you anything, haven't managed to spoil your heart. What we have to do is get you out of here as soon as we can. You and I'll begin a new life. I'll take up your education with loving care. What delights are in store for me!

PAULINE. Ah, the sooner the better!

ZHADOV. Then why put it off? I've made up my mind already. *(He looks at her passionately.)*

Silence.

PAULINE. Do you know any merchants?

ZHADOV. What kind of a question is that? Why do you want to know?

PAULINE. No special reason. I just want to know.

ZHADOV. But I still don't understand. There must be a reason.

PAULINE. Well, here's why. Belogubov says he knows some merchants, and they give him vests, and that when he gets married they're going to give him dress materials for his wife.

ZHADOV. So that's it! Well, no, they won't be giving things to us. You and I are going to work. Isn't that so, Pauline?

PAULINE *(with a distracted air).* Yes, sir.

ZHADOV. No, Pauline, you don't yet know the high bliss of living by your own work. You'll be taken care of in everything, God will provide, you'll see. Everything we acquire will be ours; we won't be obliged to anyone. Do you understand that? There are two delights in this: the delight of work and the delight of managing one's own possessions freely and with a calm conscience, not being accountable to anyone. And that's better than any gift. It's really better, Pauline, isn't it?

PAULINE. Yes, sir, it's better.

Silence.

Would you like me to ask you a riddle?

ZHADOV. Go ahead.

PAULINE. What comes down but doesn't have feet?

ZHADOV. What kind of a riddle is that? The rain.

PAULINE. How you do know everything! That's disgusting. I couldn't guess it at all when Julie asked me.

ZHADOV. What a child you are! Always stay such a child.

PAULINE. And can people count stars in the sky?

ZHADOV. They can.

PAULINE. No, they can't. I don't believe you.

ZHADOV. But there's no need to count them; they've already been counted.

PAULINE. You're making fun of me. *(She turns away.)*

ZHADOV *(tenderly)*. Me make fun of you, Pauline! I want to dedicate my whole life to you. Take a good look at me, could I make fun of you?

PAULINE *(she looks at him)*. No, no...

ZHADOV. You say you're an idiot; I'm the idiot. Make fun of me. A lot of people do make fun of me. With no means or money I'm going to marry you with nothing but hopes for the future. Why get married, they ask me. Why? Because I love you, because I have faith in people. I admit I'm going ahead without giving it much thought. But when can I think about it? I love you so much I just don't have time to think.

Mme Kukushkin and Yusov enter.

PAULINE *(with some feeling)*. I love you too.

Zhadov kisses her hand.

MME KUKUSHKIN *(to Yusov)*. Just look at them, cooing like doves. Don't disturb them. It's so touching to see them!

Belogubov and Julie enter.

ZHADOV *(turning around he takes Pauline by the hand and leads her to Mme. Kukushkin)*. Felisata Gerasimovna, give away this treasure to me.

MME KUKUSHKIN. I'll have to confess, it's painful for me to part with her. She's my favorite daughter... she would have been a consolation in my old age... but God go with her, take her... her happiness means more to me. *(She covers her face with her handkerchief.)*

Zhadov and Pauline kiss her hands. Belogubov gives her a chair. She sits down.

YUSOV. You're a real mother, Felisata Gerasimovna.

MME KUKUSHKIN. Yes, that's something I can boast of. *(With heat.)* No, bringing up daughters is a thankless task! You raise them, you cherish them, and then you give them away to a stranger... you're left alone like an orphan... it's awful! *(She covers her eyes with her handkerchief.)*

PAULINE and JULIE *(together)*. Mama, we won't desert you.

ACT THREE

Between the second and third acts about a year has passed. A tavern. In the background is a rear curtain, in the middle a gramophone. On the right is an open door through which another room is visible. On the left is a clothes tree. At the front of the stage are tables and divans.

Vasily is standing by the gramophone reading a newspaper. Grigory is standing by the door looking into the other room. Zhadov and Mykin enter. Grigory shows them in, wipes off the table, and places napkins.

MYKIN. Well now, old friend, how are things?

ZHADOV. Bad, brother. *(To Grigory.)* Give us some tea.

Grigory leaves.

And how are you?

MYKIN. All right. I manage, I get in some teaching.

They sit down.

ZHADOV. Do you make much?

MYKIN. Two hundred rubles.

ZHADOV. Is that enough for you?

MYKIN. I keep within my means. As you see, I don't have too many amusements.

ZHADOV. Yes, a bachelor can do that.

MYKIN. You shouldn't have gotten married! Men like us shouldn't marry. How can we, poor as we are! Just having a full stomach and being protected from the elements, and that should be it. You know the saying: a single person isn't poor, because even if he is poor, he's by himself.

ZHADOV. The deed's been done.

MYKIN. Look at yourself and what you used to be. Have the steep hills worn down the gray horse? No, men like us shouldn't get married. We are workers. *(Grigory serves the tea. Mykin pours.)* If we have to work, then work; we can do our living later if it ever comes to that.

ZHADOV. But what could I do! I was so much in love with her.

MYKIN. What does that matter, that you were in love! Don't you think other people can be in love? I too, friend, was in love, but I didn't get married. And you shouldn't have gotten married either.

ZHADOV. But why not?

MYKIN. Very simple. A bachelor thinks about his work, a married man about his wife. A married man is unreliable.

ZHADOV. That's nothing but nonsense.

MYKIN. No, it's not nonsense. I don't know what I wouldn't have done for the girl I was in love with. But I decided it was better to make a sacrifice. It's better, my friend, to overcome that very natural feeling than surround yourself with temptations.

ZHADOV. I suppose it wasn't easy for you, was it?

MYKIN. What can I say! Denying yourself in general isn't easy, but denying yourself the woman you love when the only obstacle is poverty... Do you love your wife very much?

ZHADOV. I'm crazy about her.

MYKIN. A bad business! Is she smart?

ZHADOV. I really don't know. All I know is, she's unusually nice. If some little thing upsets her, she cries so nicely and so sincerely that just looking at her you cry yourself.

MYKIN. Tell me frankly how you're living. You know, I haven't seen you for a year and a half.

ZHADOV. All right. My story won't be long. As you know, I married for love. I took an uneducated girl, brought up in the prejudices of society, like practically all our girls. I dreamed of educating her in the convictions you and I have, and now I've been married a year...

MYKIN. And has the plan worked out?

ZHADOV. Nothing's come of it, of course. I don't have the time to educate her, and I don't even know how to go about it. So she's left with her own ideas, and in arguments, of course, I'm the one to give in. You can see it's not a good situation, and there's no way to correct it. She doesn't even listen to me; she just doesn't consider me an intelligent man. According to their idea an intelligent man absolutely has to be rich.

MYKIN. So that's how far it's gone! And how's your financial situation?

ZHADOV. I work day and night.

MYKIN. And you still don't have enough?

ZHADOV. We survive.

MYKIN. And what about your wife?

ZHADOV. She sulks some, and sometimes she cries. What can you do!

MYKIN. I'm sorry for you. No, my friend, people like us shouldn't get married. Once I was without work for a whole year; all I ate was black bread. What would I have done with a wife?

Dosuzhev enters.

DOSUZHEV *(sitting down at another table).* Garçon, you there, show some life!

VASILY. What would you like?

DOSUZHEV. Some ashberry brandy. And a side dish appropriate for a man of my position.

VASILY. Yes, sir. *(He goes toward the door.)*

DOSUZHEV. And some French mustard! Did you hear? I can shut down this tavern. Grigory, start that hurdy-hurdy going.

GRIGORY. Right away, sir. *(He winds up the gramophone.)*

MYKIN. That man has just got to be a bachelor.

DOSUZHEV. What are you looking at me for? I'm waiting here for my fish, the carp.

ZHADOV. What do you mean, carp?

DOSUZHEV. He'll come with a red beard; I'll eat him up.

Vasily brings vodka.

Vasily, keep an eye out for him. When he comes, let me know.

The gramophone plays.

Gentlemen, have you ever seen how drunk Germans cry? *(He acts out a crying German.)*

Zhadov and Mykin laugh. The gramophone stops playing.

MYKIN *(to Zhadov).* Well, good-bye. I'll drop in on you sometime.

ZHADOV. Good-bye.

Mykin leaves.

VASILY *(to Dosuzhev).* He's come, sir.

DOSUZHEV. Call him here.

VASILY. He won't come, sir. He sat down in the rear room.

DOSUZHEV *(to Zhadov).* He's embarrassed. Good-bye. If you're going to stay awhile, I'll come talk with you. I like the look of your face. *(He leaves.)*

ZHADOV *(to Vasily).* Give me something to read.

VASILY *(gives him a book).* There's a piece in there you might like to read. People like it, sir.

Zhadov reads. Yusov, Belogubov, and two officials enter.

BELOGUBOV. Akim Akimych, we had dinner there. Let me treat you to some wine here, and we'll have some music, sir.

YUSOV. Treat me, treat me.

BELOGUBOV. What would you like? Some champagne, sir?

YUSOV. Let's have that.

BELOGUBOV. The Rhine brand, sir? Gentlemen, be seated.

Everyone sits down but Belogubov.

Vasily! Bring some Rhine champagne, bottled abroad.

Vasily leaves.

Oh brother, hello there! Wouldn't you like to join us? *(He comes up to Zhadov.)*

ZHADOV. No, thank you. I don't drink.

BELOGUBOV But really, come now, brother! Do it for me!… One little glass… we're relatives now!

Vasily brings the wine. Belogubov goes back to his own table.

Pour it.

Vasily pours.

YUSOV. So, friend, to your health! *(He takes a glass and stands up.)*

THE TWO OFFICIALS. To your health, sir. *(They take glasses and stand up.)*

YUSOV *(pointing to Belogubov's head)*. In this brow, in this mind I have always seen something worthwhile.

They clink glasses.

Let's kiss.

They kiss each other.

BELOGUBOV. No, you must let me kiss your hand, sir.

YUSOV *(hides his hands)*. That's not necessary, not necessary. *(He sits down.)*

BELOGUBOV. It was through you, sir, that I became somebody.

THE TWO OFFICIALS. Sir, allow us. *(They clink glasses with Belogubov, drink, and sit down.)*

BELOGUBOV *(pours out a glass and hands it on a tray to Zhadov).* Brother, do us a favor.

ZHADOV. I told you I don't drink.

BELOGUBOV. You mustn't be like that, brother; you'll hurt our feelings.

ZHADOV. I'm getting tired of this.

BELOGUBOV. If you don't like champagne, is there something you would like? Whatever you want, brother, it's my pleasure.

ZHADOV. I don't want a thing. Leave me alone! *(He reads.)*

BELOGUBOV. Very well, as you wish. I don't know why you want to hurt our feelings, brother. I meant it all for the best...*(He goes back to his table.)*

YUSOV *(quietly).* Let him be.

BELOGUBOV *(sits down).* Gentlemen, another glass each! *(He pours.)* Wouldn't you like a fancy cake? Vasily, bring a large fancy cake.

Vasily leaves.

YUSOV. You're really letting loose! You were smart and caught somebody. Am I right?

BELOGUBOV *(pointing to his pocket).* Right! And who is it I owe it to? All to you.

YUSOV. You caught him pretty good, eh?

BELOGUBOV *(takes out a packet of paper money).* There it is, sir.

YUSOV. I know you. You wouldn't be making a false move.

BELOGUBOV *(puts the money away).* No, really. Who am I in debt to? Would I really have understood things without you? Who made me somebody, who made me begin to live, if not you? I was brought up under your wing! Anyone else wouldn't have learned all that in ten years, all those fine touches and moves you taught me in four. I made you my example in everything, for what could I have done with my mind! Anyone else's own father wouldn't do for his son what you did for me. *(He wipes his eyes.)*

YUSOV. You have a noble soul. You can feel. But there are some who can't.

Vasily brings the fancy cake.

BELOGUBOV. What would I have been? An idiot, sir! But now I'm a member of society, everyone respects me. I go through the market section, and all the merchants bow to me; they invite me to their homes, want me to sit in the place of honor. My wife loves me. Why else would she want to love a fool like me? Vasily! Don't you have any expensive candy?

VASILY. We can get it, sir.

BELOGUBOV *(to Yusov).* It's for my wife, sir. *(To Vasily.)* Look, wrap a lot of it up in paper. You can charge what you want, I won't mind.

Vasily starts to go.

Wait! And put in all kinds of fancy cake.

YUSOV. She has enough; you'll spoil her.

BELOGUBOV. That's impossible, sir. *(To Vasily.)* Put in some of everything, do you hear?

VASILY. Yes, sir. *(He leaves.)*

BELOGUBOV. I love her, I love my wife very much, sir. If I give her a treat, then she'll love me more, Akim Akimych. What am I compared to her, sir? She's educated, sir… I just bought a dress for her, sir… that is, I didn't buy it, I just took it. I'll settle with him later.

YUSOV. It doesn't matter. Why pay money? Maybe some sort of business deal will turn up, and then you and he are quits. A mountain doesn't get together with a mountain, but a man can get together with a man.

Vasily brings the candy wrapped in paper.

BELOGUBOV. Put it in my hat. Another glass each, sir. *(He pours.)* Vasily! Another bottle.

YUSOV. We've had enough.

BELOGUBOV. No, allow me, sir. Here you're not in charge, I am.

Vasily leaves.

FIRST OFFICIAL. Let me tell you something that happened! One of our good- for-nothing clerks really pulled a fast one! He made a false copy of a decision *(what an idea!)*, forged the signatures, and then took it to a plaintiff. It was an interesting case, there was money in it. Only the sly dog didn't let go of that copy; he just showed it. Anyway, he made a lot of money out of it. Later the plaintiff showed up in court, but the case didn't turn out at all the way he expected.

BELOGUBOV. How disgusting! For that he ought to be fired.

YUSOV. Fired is right. Don't stain the reputation of officials. If you take some-thing, do it for something real, not a swindle. Take so the man making a request won't be hurt and you'll be satisfied. Live within the law; live so the wolves have their fill and the sheep stay safe. Why chase after something big! The hen pecks at the grain but is filled. What kind of a man is that! One of these days they'll pack him off to the army.[4]

BELOGUBOV *(pours a glass)*. That's for you, Akim Akimych!… You won't refuse me what I ask? I'll bow down at your feet.

YUSOV. What is it?

BELOGUBOV. You remember the last time, sir, how you danced while the gramophone played "Over the Pavement"?[5]

YUSOV. What will you think of next!

BELOGUBOV. Make me happy, Akim Akimych! I'll remember it all my life.

YUSOV. All right, all right. Just for you! Tell them to play "Over the Pavement."

BELOGUBOV. Hey, Vasily! Play "Over the Pavement." And stand by the door. Make sure nobody comes in.

VASILY. Yes, sir. *(He winds up the gramophone.)*

YUSOV *(indicating Zhadov)*. I don't like that one over there. No telling what he'll think.

BELOGUBOV *(sitting down next to Zhadov)*. Brother, be one of the family. Akim Akimych is embarrassed because of you.

ZHADOV. Why is he embarrassed?

BELOGUBOV. He wants to dance. After work, brother, a man has to have some kind of diversion. He can't work all the time; he has to amuse himself. So what! It's innocent pleasure; we're not hurting anybody.

ZHADOV. Dance all you want. I'm not in your way.

BELOGUBOV *(to Yusov)*. It's all right, Akim Akimych, he's one of the family.

VASILY. Do you want me to start?

YUSOV. Start.

The gramophone plays "Over the Pavement." Yusov dances. At the end all but Zhadov applaud.

BELOGUBOV. No, now you can't get out of it, sir! We have to drink champagne! Vasily, a bottle of champagne! Does it come to much for everything?

VASILY *(calculates on the abacus)*. It comes to fifteen rubles, sir.

BELOGUBOV. Here. *(He gives him money.)* Half a ruble for the tip.

VASILY. Thank you very much, sir. *(He leaves.)*

YUSOV *(loudly)*. I suppose you young whippersnappers are laughing at the old man!

FIRST OFFICIAL. How could we do that, Akim Akimych? We don't know how to thank you.

SECOND OFFICIAL. That's right, sir.

YUSOV. I have the right to dance. I've done everything required in life. My soul is calm, my past doesn't weigh on me, I've provided for my family, and now I can dance. Now I rejoice in God's world! If I see a little bird I rejoice in it, if I see a little flower I rejoice in that too: in everything I see a wondrous wisdom.

Vasily brings a bottle, uncorks it, and pours while Yusov continues to speak.

When I remember my own poverty I don't forget my brother in need. I don't condemn others like some of our young learned whippersnappers! What man can we condemn? Who knows, we ourselves might be in the same boat! Only today you may have laughed at a drunkard, but tomorrow you might be a drunkard yourself. You condemn a thief today, but tomorrow you might be a thief.

How can we know our final end, who is destined for what? We know one thing, we'll all be in the other world. Just now you were laughing *(looking at Zhadov)* because I was dancing, but tomorrow you might be dancing worse. Maybe *(nodding in Zhadov's direction)* you'll even go begging for charity, and you'll hold out your hand. That's what pride can lead to! Pride, pride! I danced from the fullness of my soul. I have joy in my heart, I'm calm in my soul! I'm not afraid of anybody! I'd dance right on the public square in front of everybody. And the people passing by'd say, "That man is dancing, he must have a pure soul!" And each and every one of them would go about his business.

BELOGUBOV *(raising his glass)*. Gentlemen! To the health of Akim Akimych! Hurrah!

THE TWO OFFICIALS. Hurrah!

BELOGUBOV. Akim Akimych, you would make us happy if you dropped in on us sometime. My wife and I are still young, you could give us advice, some lessons in morality, how to live in wedlock and meet our obligations. A man of stone would feel things listening to you.

YUSOV. I'll drop in sometime. *(He takes the newspaper.)*

BELOGUBOV *(pours a glass and takes it over to Zhadov)*. You see, brother, I can't stay away from you.

ZHADOV. Why don't you let me read? An interesting article turned up, and you keep pestering me.

BELOGUBOV *(sitting down next to Zhadov)*. Brother, it's wrong of you to hold a grudge against me. Let's put all this hostility aside, brother. Eat something. Drink something. You'll feel better. On my side there's nothing important, sir. Let's live like relatives.

ZHADOV. It's impossible for us to live like relatives.

BELOGUBOV. But why, sir?

ZHADOV. We're not equals.

BELOGUBOV. Yes, of course, every man to his own fate. Right now I'm living well, and you're living in poverty. So what, I'm not proud of that. After all, that's what fate does to some people. I'm supporting a whole family now and Mama too. I know you're in need, brother. Maybe you need money, don't be offended, I'll give you as much as I can. I won't even consider it a debt. What are accounts between relatives!

ZHADOV. Where'd you get the idea of offering me money!

BELOGUBOV. Brother, I'm well off now. It's my duty to try and help you. I can see your poverty, brother.

ZHADOV. What kind of a brother am I to you! Leave me alone.

BELOGUBOV. If that's how you want it! I meant well. I won't hold it against you, brother. Only I feel sorry looking at you and your wife. *(He goes off to Yusov.)*

YUSOV *(throwing the newspaper aside).* The things they write these days! Not a thing that's morally uplifting! *(He pours for Belogubov.)* Drink it up, and let's go.

BELOGUBOV *(drinks up).* Let's go.

Vasily and Grigory hand them their coats.

VASILY *(hands Belogubov two packages).* Here you are, sir.

BELOGUBOV *(sweetly).* They're for my wife, sir. I love her, sir.

They leave. Dosuzhev enters.

DOSUZHEV. "'Tis not a flock of ravens that flew together there!"[6]

ZHADOV. Right you are.

DOSUZHEV. Let's go to Marya's Grove[7] and have a good time.

ZHADOV. I can't.

DOSUZHEV. Why not? You have a family? You have to take care of children?

ZHADOV. I don't have to take care of any children. My wife is waiting for me at home.

DOSUZHEV. Has it been long since you saw each other?

ZHADOV. What do you mean, long? This morning.

DOSUZHEV. Well, that's not so long. I was thinking you hadn't seen each other for three days or so.

Zhadov looks at him.

Why do you look at me like that! I know what you're thinking about me. You think I'm like those dandies who just left, but you're wrong. They're asses in lions' skins! The skin alone is frightening. All the same, they frighten the common run of folk.

ZHADOV. I have to admit, I can't figure you out.

DOSUZHEV. It's like this. In the first place, I like to have a good time. And in the second place, I'm an awfully good lawyer. You were a student, I can see that, and I was a student too. I took a job with a small salary. I can't take bribes, that just isn't my nature, but a man has to have something to live on. Then I had an inspiration. I took up law and went in for writing up touching legal requests for merchants. So if you don't want to go with me then let's have a drink. Vasily, some vodka!

Vasily goes off.

ZHADOV. I don't drink.

DOSUZHEV. What country were you born it? That's a lot of nonsense! It's all right to do it with me. So, sir, I went in for writing those touching requests. You have no idea what these people are like! I'll tell you.

Vasily enters.

Pour two glasses. This is for the whole bottle. *(He gives some money.)*
ZHADOV. And from me for the tip. *(He gives some money.)*

Vasily goes off.

DOSUZHEV. Let's drink!
ZHADOV. All right, just for you. Only I really don't drink.

They clink glasses and drink. Dosuzhev pours some more.

DOSUZHEV. If you write a request for some beardy old merchant and charge a little, then he'll ride all over you. He'll get familiar and tell you, "Here, you pen-pusher you, here's a tip for you." I've come to have unlimited spite towards them. Let's drink! As the saying goes, "If you drink you'll die and if you don't drink you'll die, so you might as well drink and die."

They drink.

So I started writing them to suit their taste. For example, you have to write a bill for one of them, and all it takes is ten strokes of the pen. But for him you write four pages. I begin this way: "Being encumbered with a multitudinous family numbering a quantity of members…" And you put in all the ornaments. You write it so he cries and his whole family cries to the point of hysterics. You have a good laugh at his expense, take a pile of money from him, and there he is respecting you and bowing to you from the waist. You can wrap him round your little finger. And all their fat mothers-in-law and grandmothers will try to hunt up a rich bride for you. That's the kind of man they like. Let's drink!

ZHADOV. I've had enough!
DOSUZHEV. To my health!
ZHADOV. Well, if it's to your health.

They drink.

DOSUZHEV. You need a lot of will power not to take bribes from them. They laugh at an honest official, and they're only too ready to humiliate him because they find him inconvenient. So you have to be hard as flint! But really now, what's the point in being a hero! Just worm a fur coat out of him and be done with it. The trouble is, I can't do that. So I just take money from them for their ignorance, and I drink it up. Oh, why did you have to get married! Let's drink. What's your name?
ZHADOV. Vasily.
DOSUZHEV. That's my name too. Let's drink, Vasya.

They drink.

I can see you're a good man.

ZHADOV. What kind of a man am I! I'm still a child, with no idea of life at all. What you've told me is all new to me. It's so hard on me! I just don't know how I can bear it! Corruption all around, and I have so little strength! What did they educate us for?

DOSUZHEV. Drink, it'll make things easier.

ZHADOV. No, no! *(He lowers his head onto his arms.)*

DOSUZHEV. So you won't go with me?

ZHADOV. I won't go. Why did you make me drink like this? What have you done to me!

DOSUZHEV. Good-bye then. From now on we'll be friends. You're a bit high, my friend! *(He shakes Zhadov's hand.)* Vasily, my coat! *(He puts on his coat.)* Don't judge me too harshly. I'm a lost man. Try to be better than me, if you can. *(He goes to the door and returns.)* Yes! Here's some more advice for you. Maybe you'll take after me and start drinking. Don't drink wine, drink vodka. People like you and me can't afford wine, but vodka, my friend, is the best thing. You'll forget your troubles, and it's cheap! Adieu! *(He leaves.)*

ZHADOV. No! Drinking's no good! It doesn't make things easier but even worse! *(He becomes thoughtful. Vasily, following an order from the other room, starts up the gramophone. It plays the folk song "O Splinter." Zhadov sings.)* "O splinter, splinter of mine, splinter from birchwood!…"[8]

VASILY. Sir, please! That's not good, sir! It's not proper, sir!

Zhadov puts on his coat mechanically and leaves.

ACT FOUR

A very poor room. A window on the right, a table near the window. A mirror on the left wall.

PAULINE. *(alone, looking out the window).* It's so dull, I'm bored to death! *(She sings.)* "Mother mine, so dear to me, sun so warm and mild! Mother mine, caress your own tiny baby child."[9] *(She laughs.)* What a song to come into my head! *(Again she becomes thoughtful.)* I could get lost just from boredom. Should I tell my fortune from cards? Why not, there's nothing to stop me. That's possible, possible. Whatever else, that's left to us. *(She gets the cards from out of the table.)* I feel so much like talking with somebody. If only somebody would come, I'd be happy, I'd cheer up right away. But the way it is, I'm all by myself, always by myself… And there's no getting around it, I do like to talk. When we were at Mama's morning would come, and we'd chatter away, chatter away, and not notice how the time passed. But now there's not a soul to talk to. Should I run over to sister's? It's too late for that. What a fool I was not to think of that before. *(She sings.)* "Mother mine, so dear to me…" Oh, I forgot I was going to tell my fortune… What should I ask about? I'll ask if I'm going to get a new hat. *(She lays out the cards.)* I'm going to get it, I'm going to get it… I'll get it, I'll get it. *(She claps her hands, becomes thoughtful, and then sings.)* "Mother mine, so dear to me, sun so warm and mild! Mother mine, caress your own tiny baby child."

Julie enters.

Hello, hello!

They kiss each other.

How glad I am to see you. Take off your hat.

JULIE. No, I just came for a minute.

PAULINE. Oh sis, how nice you look!

JULIE. Yes. Now I buy nothing but the best and latest from abroad.

PAULINE. You're lucky, Julie.

JULIE. Yes, I can say that for myself, I'm lucky. But with you, Polly, things are just awful. You're not in style at all. Nowadays everyone is supposed to live in luxury.

PAULINE. But what can I do? It's not my fault, is it?

JULIE. And yesterday we were in the park.[10] What fun, it was wonderful! Some merchant treated us to supper, champagne, different kinds of fruit.

PAULINE. And I stay home alone all the time, dying from boredom.

JULIE. Yes, Pauline, I'm a completely new woman. You just can't imagine how money and the good life ennoble a person. I don't bother any more with housework, that's vulgar. All I bother with now is my looks. But you! You! This is awful! Tell me, please, just what is your husband doing?

PAULINE. He doesn't even let me visit you. He tells me to stay home and work.

JULIE. How stupid! He makes himself out to be a smart man, but he doesn't know the latest style. He ought to know that man is made for society.

PAULINE. What was that?

JULIE. Man is made for society. Who doesn't know that? Nowadays absolutely everybody knows that.

PAULINE. Good, I'll tell him that.

JULIE. Should you try arguing with him?

PAULINE. I've tried that, but it doesn't do any good. He always comes out right, and I'm wrong.

JULIE. But he loves you, doesn't he?

PAULINE. He loves me very much.

JULIE. And you love him?

PAULINE. I love him too.

JULIE. So, it's your own fault, dear. You won't get anything from men with affection. You give him affection, and he'll just sit there not doing a thing, not thinking about you or himself.

PAULINE. He works hard.

JULIE. But what good comes from that work? My husband doesn't work much, and you should see how we live. I must say, Onisim Panfilych is a perfect man for the house, a real head of the household. What we don't have! And in such a short time! Where does he get it from! But your man? Really and truly, it's a disgrace the way you're living.

PAULINE. What he always says is, "Stay home and work. Don't envy the others. We'll live well too."

JULIE. But when will that be? You'll get old waiting, a lot of pleasure you'll get from it then! Everyone's patience can be exhausted.

PAULINE. But what can I do?

JULIE. He's a tyrant, that's all. Why waste words on him! Tell him you don't love him, and that's it. Or here's what's even better. You tell him you're fed up with this kind of life, that you don't want to live with him, that you're moving to Mama's, that he shouldn't have any more to do with you. And I'll let Mama know about it.

PAULINE. Good, good! I'll pull it off with style.

JULIE. Do you think you can?

PAULINE. Of course! I can play a scene as well as any actress. After all, we were trained for that at home from childhood. But now I'm home alone all the time, and working's no fun. I talk to myself all the time; it's amazing how well I've caught onto it. Still, I'm going to feel a little sorry for him.

JULIE. Don't you show him any pity! I brought you a hat, Polly. *(She takes it out of the box.)*

PAULINE. Oh, how charming! Thanks, sis, you're a darling! *(She kisses her.)*

JULIE. Your old one has gotten ugly.

PAULINE. It's disgusting! I hate to go out onto the street. But now I can tease my husband. Look, my dear, I'll say, somebody bought this for me, and you guess who.

JULIE. There's no way out of it, Polly, and Mama and I'll back you up as much as we can. Only please, don't listen to your husband. Make it very clear to him you're not about to love him just for the fun of it. You get this into your stupid little head, why should we love our husbands for nothing? A fine thing! Tell him, "Make sure I'll shine in society, and then I can start loving you." Because of some crazy whim he doesn't want you to be happy, and you keep quiet. All he has to do is ask his uncle, and they'll give him a position just as profitable as the one my husband has.

PAULINE. I'll start working on him right away.

JULIE. Just imagine now. You're so pretty, dressed in style, and you're sitting in a theater… near a light… all the men have their opera glasses on you, staring at you.

PAULINE. Don't talk about it, sis, I'll start to cry.

JULIE. Here's some money for you *(she gets it out of her purse)*; some time you might need something, and with this you can manage without your husband. We have the means, so we've decided to help others.

PAULINE. Thanks, sis! Only maybe he'll get mad.

JULIE. A lot that matters! Why pay any attention to him! It's coming from relatives, not strangers. Why, just because of him, should you go hungry! Good-bye, Pauline.

PAULINE. Good-bye, sis. *(She sees her off. Julie leaves.)* How clever our Julie is! But I'm an idiot, an idiot! *(Seeing the box.)* A new hat! A new hat! *(She claps her hands.)* I'll be happy now for a whole week, if only my husband doesn't get upset. *(She sings.)* "Mother mine, so dear to me…" *(Etc.)*

Mme Kukushkin enters.

MME KUKUSHKIN. You always have songs on your mind.

PAULINE. Hello, Mama! I sing from boredom.

MME KUKUSHKIN. I didn't even want to visit you at all.

PAULINE. Why not, Mama?

MME KUKUSHKIN. It disgusts me, young lady, it disgusts me to visit you. But since I just happened to be going by, I dropped in. It's so wretched here, such poverty… ugh… I can't look at it. I've got cleanliness, I've got order, but what do you have here! It's a peasant hut! It's revolting.

PAULINE. But is that my fault?

MME KUKUSHKIN. What scoundrels in the world! And yet I really don't blame him, I never did have any hopes for him. But you, miss, why do you keep quiet? I kept telling you over and over again, don't indulge your husband. Work on him all the time, day and night. Tell him, "Give me some money and keep on giving it to me; get it where you want just as long as you give it to me." Tell him you need this and that. Tell him Mama is a fine lady and we have to receive her in proper fashion. He'll say, "I don't have it." And you'll say, "What does that have to do with it? Give it to me if you have to steal it." Why did he make you his wife? He knew how to get married, so he should know to support you the proper way. You keep hammering that into him from morn till night, and maybe he'll come to his senses. In your place I wouldn't talk about anything else.

PAULINE. But what can I do, Mama? I'm just not made of stern stuff.

MME KUKUSHKIN. No, what you'd better say is you're made of a lot of stupid stuff, you spoil him. And do you realize that it's your spoiling that ruins a man? All the time you have tenderness on your mind, and you'd just love to hang around his neck. You were only too glad to get married, you couldn't wait. You have no shame at all! Never a thought about life. Whoever could you have taken after! In our family all the women are completely cold to their husbands. They think more about clothes, how to be properly dressed, how to shine in public. You can show affection to your husband, only he has to know what he's getting that affection for. Now take Julie. When her husband brings her something from the market that's when she throws herself around his neck, she's glued to him, you couldn't pull her off. That's why he brings her gifts almost every day. But if he doesn't bring her any she pouts and stops speaking to him for two days. You hang around their necks, they love that, that's all they want. You should be ashamed of yourself!

PAULINE. I have a feeling I'm being stupid. But when he shows me affection I feel as glad about it as he does.

MME KUKUSHKIN. Just wait, you and I'll gang up on him, and maybe he'll give in. The main thing is, don't spoil him and don't listen to his stupid talk. He makes his point, you make yours; argue till you faint, but don't give in. If we give in to them they'll make us carry water. It's that pride of his, it's his pride we have to beat. Do you know what he has on his mind?

PAULINE. How should I know?

MME KUKUSHKIN. It's some sort of idiotic philosophy, I heard about it in a home not too long ago, it's all the rage now. They've taken it into their head that they're smarter than everybody and that the people who take bribes are fools. How unforgivably stupid of them! What they say is, we don't want to take bribes, we want to live on just our salary. But what kind of a life is that! Who could we marry our daughters to? Next thing you know, the human race would die out. Bribes! What kind of a word is that, bribes? They thought it up themselves, to harm good people. It's not bribes but gratitude! And rejecting gratitude is a sin, you offend a man. Now if a man's a bachelor, there's no need to judge him, he can play the saintly fool as much as he wants. He doesn't even have to take his salary. But once he marries he should know how to live with his wife and not deceive the parents. Why do they tear parents' hearts so? Some nitwit suddenly marries a well-brought-up young lady who's understood life from childhood, whose parents didn't begrudge her a thing and gave her principles completely opposed to his, did everything to keep her away from stupid talk like his, and just like that he shuts her up in some stable! What do they want? To turn well-brought-up young ladies into laundry women? It's turning the whole world upside down. If they want to get married, then marry one of those lost women who don't give a hang whether they're a lady or a cook, who out of love will be only too glad to wash skirts and wear themselves out going to the market through the mud. And there are women like that, women without sense.

PAULINE. That's probably what he'd like to make of me.

MME KUKUSHKIN. What does a woman need?... A woman who's well bred, who sees and understands everything about her like the fingers on her hand? That's what they don't understand. What a woman needs is good clothes, servants, and, the main thing, tranquillity, to be isolated from everything because of her noble qualities, so she doesn't have to get involved in petty household cares. Here's how my Julie works it: she's not taken up with anything except herself. She sleeps late; in the morning her husband has to arrange for breakfast and the whole business. The maid gives him some tea, and off he goes to the office. At last she gets up; tea, coffee, it's all ready for her. She eats, dresses to perfection, and sits down with a book by the window to wait for her husband. Evenings she puts on her best dress and goes to the theater or visiting. That's what I call living! That's what's proper! How a lady ought to behave! What could be more exalted than that, more delicate, more tender?... That's what I approve of.

PAULINE. That's heaven! If I could only live that for just a week.

MME KUKUSHKIN. Well, with the husband you have, you've got a long wait coming!

PAULINE. You're really letting him have it, Mama! But to tell the truth, I am envious. Whenever Julie comes she's always wearing a new dress, and I'm always in the same old one. Here he comes now. *(She goes toward the door.)*

Zhadov enters carrying a briefcase. They kiss.

ZHADOV. Hello, Felisata Gerasimovna. *(He sits down.)* Oh, how tired I am!

Pauline sits down next to her mother.

It's work all the time, I don't know what it means to rest. In the morning the office, in the afternoon I give lessons, and at night I work. I bring home extracts to draw up, that pays pretty well. But you, Pauline, are always without work, always idle. I never catch you doing anything.

MME KUKUSHKIN. That's how I raised them, they weren't trained for work.

ZHADOV. That's what's so bad. It's hard getting used to work if you haven't been trained from childhood. But it's necessary.

MME KUKUSHKIN. There's no need for her to get used to it. I didn't prepare my girls to be housemaids but to marry noble men.

ZHADOV. Our opinions differ, Felisata Gerasimovna. I want Pauline to obey me.

MME KUKUSHKIN. What you mean is that you want to make her into a working girl. But you really should have looked for a match to suit you. Excuse me for saying it, but we people don't have those feelings about life. With us nobility is inborn.

ZHADOV. What nobility? That's just so much talk! Something we can do well enough without.

59

MME KUKUSHKIN. Listening to you is sickening. Here's what I have to tell you. If I had known that she, poor creature, would be leading such a beggar's life, then nothing in the world would have made me give her to you.

ZHADOV. Please, I beg you, don't go knocking it into her head that she's an unhappy woman. She might actually believe she's unhappy.

MME KUKUSHKIN. And is she happy? It should be clear enough, she's miserable. I don't know what anyone else in her place might have done.

Pauline cries.

ZHADOV. Pauline, stop being foolish, think of me!

PAULINE. You always find me foolish. Looks like you don't like it when people tell you the truth.

ZHADOV. What do you mean, the truth?

PAULINE. The truth, that's all. Mama's not about to tell lies.

ZHADOV. You and I'll discuss this later.

PAULINE. There's nothing to discuss. *(She turns away.)*

MME KUKUSHKIN. That's right.

ZHADOV *(sighs)*. Troubles!

Mme Kukushkin and Pauline pay no attention to him while they talk together in a whisper. Zhadov gets some papers out of his briefcase, lays them on the table, and, during the course of the following conversation, looks around at them.

MME KUKUSHKIN *(loudly)*. Just imagine, Pauline, I was over at Belogubov's, he bought his wife a velvet dress.

PAULINE *(in tears)*. Velvet! What color?

MME KUKUSHKIN. Cherry.

PAULINE *(cries)*. Oh Lord! When I think how well it suits her.

MME KUKUSHKIN. It's really amazing! Can you imagine what a playful rogue that Belogubov is! He made me laugh, he truly made me laugh. Look here, Mama, he says, I have a complaint to make against my wife. I bought her a velvet dress, and she kissed me so hard she even bit me, and it hurt a lot. Now that's what I call living! That's what I call love! Not what you find with some people.

ZHADOV. This is unbearable! *(He gets up.)*

MME KUKUSHKIN *(gets up)*. Allow me to ask you, dear sir, what is she suffering for? Answer me that.

ZHADOV. She's already left your care and come under mine, so leave it to me to arrange her life. Believe me, it will be better.

MME KUKUSHKIN. But I'm her mother, dear sir.

ZHADOV. And I'm her husband.

MME KUKUSHKIN. We can see what kind of a husband you are! The love of a husband can never be compared with that of parents.

ZHADOV. What kind of parents!

MME KUKUSHKIN. It doesn't matter what kind, you'd still be no match for them. I'll tell you, dear sir, what kind of parents we were! My husband and I put money together coin by coin so we could bring up our daughters and send them to boarding school. And why do you think we did this? So they'd have good manners, wouldn't see poverty around them, wouldn't have to look at common objects. So the child wouldn't be weighed down but from childhood would be trained for the good life, for nobility in word and deed.

ZHADOV. Thank you. For almost a year now I've been trying to knock your training out of her, but I just can't. I think I'd give half my life if she could only forget it.

MME KUKUSHKIN. But you surely don't think I raised her for a life like this, do you? I'd rather have my hand cut off than see my daughter in such a condition—in poverty, suffering, misery.

ZHADOV. Please, we've had enough of your pity.

MME KUKUSHKIN. Do you think they lived this way with me? I have things in order, I have it clean. I didn't have great means, but they lived like countesses and were perfectly innocent; they didn't know where the entrance to the kitchen was; they didn't know what went into cabbage soup. All they troubled themselves about as proper young ladies was conversation about feelings and matters of a noble nature.

ZHADOV (indicating his wife). Yes, and such low depravity as your family has is something I've never seen.

MME KUKUSHKIN. How can people like you have any appreciation of a noble upbringing! It's my own fault, I was in too much of a hurry! If she had married a man with tender feelings and some breeding, he wouldn't have known how to thank me for the training I gave her. And she would have been happy, because decent men don't force their wives to work, that's what they have servants for. But what a wife is for...

ZHADOV (quickly). What is she for?

MME KUKUSHKIN. What is she for? Who doesn't know that? As everyone knows, she's for being dressed up as well as possible, for being admired, for being taken out into society. She should get all kinds of pleasures, have her every whim carried out like a law, be adored.

ZHADOV. Shame on you! You're a woman of years, you've lived to old age, raised daughters and trained them, and you don't know why a wife is given to a man. Aren't you ashamed of yourself! A wife is not a plaything but a husband's helpmate. You're a bad mother!

MME KUKUSHKIN. Yes, I know you'd just love to make your wife into a cook. You're a man without feelings!

ZHADOV. Stop spouting nonsense!

PAULINE. Mama, leave him alone.

MME KUKUSHKIN. No, I won't leave him alone. What made you think I'd leave him alone?

ZHADOV. Stop it. I'm not going to listen to you any more, and I won't allow my wife to. All you have left in your old age is a head full of empty air.

MME KUKUSHKIN. What kind of talk is that, what kind of talk, eh?

ZHADOV. Between you and me there can't be any other kind of talk. Please, leave us alone. I love Pauline, and it's my responsibility to take care of her. Your talk is harmful for Pauline and immoral too.

MME KUKUSHKIN. Don't you get too worked up, dear sir!

ZHADOV. You don't understand one single thing.

MME KUKUSHKIN (spitefully). I don't understand? No, I understand very well. I've seen some of those cases where women perish from poverty. Poverty can lead to anything. Those women struggle and struggle, and then they go astray. You can't even blame them.

ZHADOV. What! How can you say such things in front of your daughter! Spare us your presence... right now, right now.

MME KUKUSHKIN. When there's cold and hunger in a home and the husband's a lazybones, then, whether you like it or not, you've got to look for means...

ZHADOV. Leave us, I'm asking you nicely. You'll exhaust my patience.

MME KUKUSHKIN. Don't worry, I'm going, and I'll never set foot in your house again. (To Pauline.) What a husband you have! It's awful! Terrible!

PAULINE. Good-bye, Mama. (She cries.)

MME KUKUSHKIN. Cry, cry, unhappy victim, mourn your fate! Cry to the grave itself! You'd even do better to die, poor creature, than break my heart so. It would be easier for me. (To Zhadov.) Enjoy your triumph! You've done your work: you tricked her, made her believe you were in love with her, seduced her with words, and then ruined her. That's what your whole aim was, I understand you now. (She leaves.)

Pauline sees her off.

ZHADOV. I'm going to have to talk more strictly with Pauline. If I don't, they'll mix her up completely.

Pauline returns, sits down by the window, and sulks. Zhadov lays out his papers and sits down by the table.

I suppose Felisata Gerasimovna won't be visiting us any more, which makes me very glad. I wish you wouldn't visit her any more, Pauline, or the Belogubovs either.

PAULINE. You're not ordering me to give up all my relatives for you, are you?

ZHADOV. It's not for me but yourself. They have such savage ideas! I'm teaching you good, and they're corrupting you.

PAULINE. It's too late to teach me, I've been taught already.

ZHADOV. It would be horrible for me if I thought what you said is true. No, I hope at long last you'll understand me. I have a lot of work now, but when things lighten up, you and I can occupy ourselves together. In the morning you'll work, and in the evening we'll read. You have a lot to read; after all, you haven't read anything.

PAULINE. So, now I'm supposed to stay home with you! A lot of fun that'll be! Man is created for society.

ZHADOV. What?

PAULINE. Man is created for society.

ZHADOV. Where did you pick that up?

PAULINE. You really take me for a fool. Who doesn't know that? Everybody does. Do you think you took me in off the street?

ZHADOV. But for society one has to prepare oneself, educate oneself.

PAULINE. None of that's needed, that's all nonsense. All you need is to dress in style.

ZHADOV. Well, that's precisely what we can't do, so there's no point in talking about it. You'd do better to busy yourself with something, and I'll get to work. *(He takes his pen.)*

PAULINE. Busy myself with something! Where did you get that idea? You've been giving orders long enough... ordering me about and treating me like a fool.

ZHADOV *(turning around)*. What is this, Pauline?

PAULINE. What it is is that I want to live the way people live and not like beggars. I'm fed up. Living with you has ruined my youth.

ZHADOV. That's something new! I haven't heard that before.

PAULINE. You haven't heard it, then listen. Do you think that because I've kept quiet almost a year I'm going to keep quiet forever? No, pardon me! But why talk about it! I want to live the way Julie's living, the way all noble ladies live. That's it!

ZHADOV. So that's what it is! Only let me ask you this. Where are we going to get what it takes to live like that?

PAULINE. What does that have to do with me! The man who loves finds a way to get what it takes.

ZHADOV. But think of me. As it is I'm working like an ox.

PAULINE. Whether you work or don't work is no concern of mine. I didn't marry you for a life of affliction and tyranny.

ZHADOV. You people have worn me all out today. For God's sake, don't say another word!

PAULINE. You have a long wait before I stop talking! Thanks to you the whole world's laughing at me. How much shame I've had to endure! Sis is taking pity on me already. Today she came and said to me, "You're putting us to shame, our whole family, just look what you're going around in!" Doesn't that make you feel ashamed? And yet you tried to make me believe that you love me. With her own money she bought a hat and brought it here for me.

ZHADOV *(gets up)*. A hat?

PAULINE. Yes, it's over there. Look at it. What do you think, isn't it pretty?

ZHADOV *(sternly)*. Take it back right away.

PAULINE. Back?

ZHADOV. Yes, right away, right away, take it back! And don't you dare take anything from them.

PAULINE. Well, that's something that's not going to happen, you can be sure of that.

ZHADOV. Then I'll throw it out the window.

PAULINE. Oh! So that's what you've come to? Very well, my friend, I'll take it back.

ZHADOV. Take it back then.

PAULINE *(in tears)*. I'll take it back, I'll take it back. *(She puts on her hat and cloak, takes her umbrella.)* Good-bye, sir.

ZHADOV. Good-bye.

PAULINE. It's good-bye for good. You won't be seeing me any more.

ZHADOV. What kind of nonsense is that?

PAULINE. I'm going to Mama's, and I'm going to stay there. Don't you come to us either.

ZHADOV. That's stupid, Pauline!

PAULINE. No, I've been thinking it over a long time! *(She traces on the floor with her umbrella.)* What kind of a life do I have here? Nothing but suffering, no joy at all!

ZHADOV. Aren't you ashamed to talk like that? Have you really had no joy with me?

PAULINE. What joy? If you were rich, that would be something else, but as it is, I have to endure poverty. What kind of joy is that! The other day you came home drunk, you'll probably be beating me next.

ZHADOV. Oh good heavens! Why do you say things like that? One time I came home a bit high… Where's there a man who doesn't get drunk sometimes?

PAULINE. We know what that poverty can lead to, Mama told me. You'll take up drinking, and I'll be ruined along with you.

ZHADOV. This is all nonsense that's gotten into your head!

PAULINE. But what is there for me to look forward to? I've already told my fortune at cards, and I asked a fortune teller too. It all comes out I'm going to be terribly unhappy.

ZHADOV *(grabs himself by the head)*. She tells her fortune with cards! She goes to fortune tellers!

PAULINE. I suppose you think cards are nonsense! No, pardon me, never in my life will I believe that! Cards never lie; they always tell the truth. You can even tell right off what a person's thinking from cards. You don't believe in anything, with you everything is just nonsense; that's why you don't have any happiness.

ZHADOV *(tenderly)*. Pauline. *(He goes toward her.)*

PAULINE *(moving away)*. Do me a favor, leave me alone.

ZHADOV. No, you don't love me.

PAULINE. And why should I love you? Why should one love for nothing?

ZHADOV *(heatedly)*. For nothing? For nothing? For your love I pay you with love. After all, you're my wife! Or have you forgotten? It is your duty to share with me both grief and joy... even if I were the lowest of beggars.

PAULINE *(sits down on a chair, throws back her head, and bursts out laughing)*. Ha, ha, ha, ha!

ZHADOV. This is really disgusting! It's immoral!

PAULINE *(gets up quickly)*. What I don't understand is why you want to live with an immoral woman. Good-bye, sir.

ZHADOV. Go on, good-bye. If you can desert your husband without a care, then good-bye. *(He sits down at the table and supports his head with his hands.)*

PAULINE. But what's so surprising! Fish look for deeper water, people for something better.

ZHADOV. All right, good-bye, good-bye.

PAULINE *(before the mirror)*. A hat's a hat, but it's different when it's mine. *(She sings.)* "Mother mine, so dear to me, sun so warm and mild..." You walk down the street, and someone's sure to look at you and say, "Oh, how pretty!" Good-bye, sir. *(She makes a curtsy and leaves.)*

ZHADOV *(alone)*. What a character I have! What's it good for? I can't even get along with my wife! What can I do now? God! I'll go mad. Without her there's no reason for me to go on living. How this happened I just don't understand. How could I let her get away from me! What will she do at her mother's! There she'll go to the dogs completely. Marya! Marya!

Marya off stage: "What is it?"

Run after the mistress and tell her I have to talk with her a bit. And hurry, hurry!... Really, Marya, how slow you are! Run, run fast!

Marya off stage: "Right away!"

But suppose she doesn't want to come back? And she'd be acting very well, quite within her rights. How is she at fault if I can't support her properly? She's pretty, only eighteen, she wants to live, wants some pleasure. And I keep her shut up in one room, I'm not home all day. A nice kind of love! So now I can live alone! Great! Wonderful!... An orphan again, what better! In the morning to the office, after the office no reason to go home, so I'll stay in the tavern till evening when I'll go home to solitude and a cold bed... I'll burst into tears! And so on day after day. Very good! *(He cries.)* Well, so what! You didn't know how to live with your wife, so live alone. No, I'll have to decide on something. Either I must part with her or... live... live... the way people live. That's something I'll have to think about. *(He becomes thoughtful.)* Part? Do I have the strength to part with her? How long have I lived with her? Oh, how it hurts, how it hurts! No, really it would be better... why try to fight windmills!" What am I saying! What thoughts are coming into my head!

Pauline enters.

PAULINE *(sits down without taking off her coat).* What do you want?

ZHADOV *(runs up to her).* You've come, you've come! You've come back!... Aren't you ashamed! You got me so upset, so upset. Pauline, I can't pull my thoughts together, I've lost all control of myself. *(He kisses her hands.)* Pauline, my friend!

PAULINE. Don't you go playing your tender tricks on me.

ZHADOV. You were joking, Pauline, weren't you? You won't leave me, will you?

PAULINE. What's so interesting living with you? It's just misery!

ZHADOV. You're killing me, Pauline! If you don't love, then at least take pity on me. You know how much I love you.

PAULINE. Yes, it's clear enough. The way some people love.

ZHADOV. How could I love any more? How? Tell me, I'll do anything you say.

PAULINE. Then go right now to your uncle and make it up with him. Ask him for the same kind of position that Belogubov has, and while you're at it, ask for some money, we'll pay it back when we get rich.

ZHADOV. Not for anything in the world, not for anything in the world! Don't say that to me.

PAULINE. Then why did you bring me back? You want to make fun of me? I've had enough of that, now I've gotten smarter. Good-bye. *(She stands up.)*

ZHADOV. Wait! Wait, Pauline! Let me talk with you a bit.

PAULINE *(before the mirror).* What's there to talk about? We've already talked it all over.

ZHADOV *(pleading).* No, no, Pauline, not all yet. There's a lot, there's still a lot I have to tell you. There's a lot you don't know. If I could only tell right away what's in my soul, tell you what I've thought and dreamed about, how happy I'd be! Let's talk a bit, Pauline, let's talk a bit. Only listen, in God's name, I'm asking this one favor.

PAULINE. Talk.

ZHADOV *(heatedly).* Listen, listen! *(He takes her by the hand.)* Always, Pauline, in every era there have been people, and even now there are, people who go against anti-quated social customs and conditions. This is not because of their caprice, not because they will it. No, it's because the principles they have come to know are better, more honorable than the principles which rule society. And these people haven't just thought up the principles by themselves. They've heard them from preachers and professors, read about them in the best literary works, ours and foreign ones. They've been raised on them and want to put them into effect. That this is not easy, I grant you. Social vices are strong, the ignorant majority is powerful. The fight is hard and often fatal, but all the more glory to those who are chosen; on them will be bestowed the blessing of posterity; without them falsehood, evil, and coercion would grow until people are cut off from the sun's light…

PAULINE *(looks at him with amazement)*. You've gone crazy, plumb crazy! And you want me to listen to you; with you I'd lose what few brains I have.

ZHADOV. But listen to me, Pauline!

PAULINE. No, I'd be better off listening to smart people.

ZHADOV. And who are these smart people you'll listen to?

PAULINE. Who? Sis, Belogubov.

ZHADOV. And you compare me with Belogubov?

PAULINE. Oh come now! What makes you so important? Everybody knows Belogubov's better than you. His superiors respect him, he loves his wife, is a wonderful man for the house, has his own horses… And what about you? All you do is brag…*(Imitating him.)* "I'm smart, I'm noble, they're all fools, they're all bribetakers!"

ZHADOV. What a tone you've taken! What manners! How disgusting!

PAULINE. Now you're abusing me again! Good-bye! *(She starts to go.)*

ZHADOV *(holds her back)*. Hold on, wait a bit.

PAULINE. Let me go.

ZHADOV. No, wait, wait! Polly, my friend, wait a bit. *(He grabs her dress.)*

PAULINE *(she laughs)*. Why are you holding me! What a character you are! I want to go, so don't stop me.

ZHADOV. But what can I do with you? What can I do with my dear Pauline?

PAULINE. Go to Uncle and make it up with him.

ZHADOV. Wait, wait, let me think a bit.

PAULINE. Think a bit.

ZHADOV. You know I love you, for you I'm ready to do anything in the world… But what you're proposing to me!… It's horrible!… No, I must think some. Yes, yes, yes, yes… I must think some… I must think some… So, if I don't go to Uncle, you'll leave me?

PAULINE. I'll leave.

ZHADOV. You'll leave for good?

PAULINE. For good. I don't have to tell you ten times, I'm sick of it. Good-bye!

ZHADOV. Wait, wait! *(He sits down at the table, supports his head with his hands, and becomes thoughtful.)*

PAULINE. How long am I supposed to wait!

ZHADOV *(almost in tears)*. You know what, Pauline? It's really nice, isn't it, when a pretty wife is well dressed?

PAULINE *(with feeling)*. It's very nice!

ZHADOV. That's it, yes, yes... *(He shouts.)* Yes, yes! *(He stamps his feet.)* And it's nice to go riding with her in a good carriage?

PAULINE. Oh, how nice!

ZHADOV. After all, a man has to love his young pretty wife, has to cherish her... *(He shouts.)* Yes, yes, yes! A man has to dress her up... *(Calming down)* Very well then, all right... all right... It's easy enough to do! *(In despair.)* Good-bye, dreams of my youth! Good-bye, great lessons! Good-bye, my honorable future! I'll still reach old age, I'll still have gray hair, I'll still have children...

PAULINE. What's wrong with you, what's wrong?

ZHADOV. No, no! We'll raise our children on strict principles. Let them be outside their time. There's no need for children to look at their father for an example.

PAULINE. Stop it!

ZHADOV. Let me cry a bit, since it's the last time I'll be crying in my life. *(He sobs.)*

PAULINE. What's happened to you?

ZHADOV. Nothing... nothing... it'll be easy... easy... everything is easy in this world. The only requirement is that I not be reminded of anything! And that's a simple matter! This is what I'll do...I'll keep away, hide out from my old friends... I won't go to those places where they talk about honor, the sacredness of duty... I'll work all week long, and on Fridays and Saturdays I'll get together with all the Belogubovs and get drunk on stolen money, like some highway robber... yes, yes... And I'll get used to all that.

PAULINE. *(almost crying)*. You're saying something bad.

ZHADOV. And I'll sing songs... Do you know this song? *(He sings.)*

> Just take, no need for rhyme or reason.
> Just take whatever's there to get.
> Men's hands are always in good season.
> They want to get and get and get.[12]

Isn't that a pretty song?

PAULINE. I'll never understand what's happened to you.

ZHADOV. Let's go to Uncle and ask him for a profitable position!

He puts his hat on carelessly and takes his wife by the hand. They leave.

ACT FIVE

Room of the first act. Anton gives a letter on a tray to Mme Vyshnevsky and leaves.

MME VYSHNEVSKY *(reads)*. "Dear Madame, Anna Pavlovna. Pardon me if you do not like my letter; your behavior towards me justifies mine towards you. I have heard that you are making fun of me and showing strangers my letters, written in love and passion. You cannot know of my position in society and to what degree such conduct on your part compromises me. I'm not a child. What right do you have to act this way with me? My attempt to seek your favor was completely justified by your conduct, which, as you yourself must admit, was not above reproach. And though society permits me as a man to enjoy certain liberties, I still don't want to look ridiculous. But you have made me a conversation piece in the whole town. You know my relations with Lyubimov; I already told you that among the papers left after his death I found several of your letters. I offered to give them to you. All you had to do was overcome your pride and agree with social opinion that I am one of the handsomest of men and enjoy unusual success with the ladies. It was your pleasure to treat me with scorn. In such a case you must excuse me, but I have decided to hand those letters over to your husband." There's nobility for you! Ugh! How disgusting! Oh well, it doesn't matter, it all had to end sometime. I'm not one of those women who, with calculated depravity, try to cover up an act of passion. What nice men we have! A man forty years old, with a beautiful wife, starts making advances to me, saying and doing stupid things. What's his justification? Passion? What passion? He must have lost the ability to fall in love at the age of eighteen. No, it's very simple. He heard some gossip about me, and he considers me an accessible woman. And so, not standing on ceremony, he starts writing me passionate letters, full of the cheapest kind of tender sentiments, obviously thought out very deliberately. He'll make the rounds in ten living rooms, and then he'll come to comfort me. He says he's above cold heartless society with its proprieties and laws, that he scorns social opinion, that in his eyes passion justifies all. He swears he's in love, speaks cliches, and when he wants to give his face a passionate expression he puts on strange and sour smiles. He doesn't even go to the trouble of pretending he's in love. Why bother? It'll all work out all right just so long as the formalities are observed. If you make fun of a man like that or show him the contempt he deserves, he thinks he has the right to avenge himself. For him ridicule is more horrible than the worst of vices. He can brag about an affair with a woman, that does him honor, but show his letters and that's a calamity, it compromises him. He himself feels that his letters are ridiculous and stupid. What does he take those women for, the ones he writes such letters? His like has no conscience! And now, in a burst of noble indignation, he is acting meanly toward me, no doubt considering himself in the right. And he's not the only one, they're all like that… Well, so much the better, at least I'll have things out with my husband. I even want to have things out. He'll see that if I'm guilty towards him, then he's even more guilty towards me. He destroyed my whole life. With his self-ishness he dried up my heart, deprived me of family happiness, made me cry over my lost youth. I spent my youth with him in trivialities, without feeling, at a time when my soul was craving for life, for love. In the empty and petty circle of his acquaintances which he led me into, all my best spiritual qualities were strangled, all my noble aspirations were frozen. And besides that my conscience bothers me for an act I was not in a position to avoid.

Yusov enters, noticeably upset.

YUSOV *(bowing)*. He hasn't come yet, ma'am?

MME VYSHNEVSKY. Not yet. Sit down.

Yusov sits down.

Has something upset you?

YUSOV. There aren't any words for it, ma'am… my mouth can't speak.

MME VYSHNEVSKY. But what is it?

YUSOV *(shakes his head)*. Man all the same… is a ship at sea… suddenly a ship-wreck, and nobody there to save him!…

MME VYSHNEVSKY. I don't understand you.

YUSOV. I'm talking about frailty… what is enduring in this life? What will we take with us when we enter that life?… Certain dealings… one might say, a burden on one's back… have been exposed… and even things in the planning stage… *(Waves his hand.)* They've all been recorded.

MME VYSHNEVSKY. But what is it, did somebody die?

YUSOV. No, Ma'am, it's a setback in life. *(He takes some snuff.)* In wealth and fame can occur an eclipse… of our feelings… we forget our poor brethren… pride, physical pleasure… Because of that we get punished for our affairs.

MME VYSHNEVSKY. I've known that a long time; only I don't understand why you're wasting your eloquence on me for no good reason.

YUSOV. It's close to my heart… Even though I don't have to answer for much in this business… still, to see it happen to such a high person! What is lasting?… When even a man's rank doesn't protect him.

MME VYSHNEVSKY. Happen to what high person?

YUSOV. We're in disfavor, ma'am.

MME VYSHNEVSKY. Go on.

YUSOV. There's been brought to light some alleged negligence, shortages of funds, certain irregularities.

MME VYSHNEVSKY. So?

YUSOV. So we're being brought to trial, ma'am... That is, I personally won't be especially accountable, but Aristarkh Vladimirych will have to...

MME VYSHNEVSKY. Have to what?

YUSOV. He'll have to answer for all his property and undergo trial for supposedly illegal procedures.

MME VYSHNEVSKY *(lifting her eyes)*. The atonement is beginning!

YUSOV. Of course, it's a fatal blow... They'll look for some pretext, and they'll probably find something. They're so strict now I suppose they'll dismiss me... I'll live in poverty without a crust of bread.

MME VYSHNEVSKY. I'm sure you're a long way from that.

YUSOV. But then there are the children, ma'am.

Silence.

I kept thinking on the way, in sorrow, why has God's visitation come upon us? It's because of pride... Pride blinds a man, clouds his eyes.

MME VYSHNEVSKY. Really now, what does pride have to do with it? It's simply for taking bribes.

YUSOV. Bribes? Bribes are of no great importance... lots of people have been subjected to them. There's no humility, that's the main thing... Fate is just like fortune... the way it's shown in that picture[13]... There's a wheel with people on it, it takes them up and then brings them down, they're elevated and then they're humbled, exalted and then nothing... So it's all a circle. You establish your well-being, you work, you gain property... You fly high in your dreams... and just like that you're naked!... There's an inscription below that wheel of fortune, and it reads like this... *(with feeling)*

> Marvelous is earthly man!
> Striving all his lifelong span,
> Happiness to him is dear,
> Yet to him is not this clear:
> Fate his course doth surely steer.

That's how you have to get down to the bottom of things! That's what a man has to remember! We are born with nothing, and that's how we'll go into the grave. What do we labor for? There's room for philosophy! What is our mind? What can it comprehend?

Vyshnevsky enters and silently passes into his study. Yusov gets up.

MME VYSHNEVSKY. How he's changed!

YUSOV. You should send for a doctor. A little while ago at the office he started feeling bad. Such a blow... for a man of noble feelings... how can he bear it!

MME VYSHNEVSKY *(rings. The boyservant enters)*. Go for the doctor. Ask him to come as fast as he can.

Vyshnevsky comes out and sits down in an armchair. Mme. Vyshnevsky goes toward him.

I heard from Akim Akimych that you had a misfortune. Don't take it too much to heart.

Silence.

You've changed completely. Do you feel bad? I sent for the doctor.

VYSHNEVSKY. Such hypocrisy! Such lowdown lying! Such meanness!

MME VYSHNEVSKY *(proudly)*. I'm not lying at all! I'm just sorry for you, as I'd be sorry for anyone in misfortune, nothing more, nothing less. *(She goes away and sits down.)*

VYSHNEVSKY. I don't want your sympathy. Don't be sorry for me! I'm dishonored, ruined! And why?

MME VYSHNEVSKY. Ask your conscience.

VYSHNEVSKY. You're a fine one to talk about conscience! You have no right to talk about it... Yusov! Why have I been ruined?

YUSOV. Life has its ups and downs... it's fate, sir.

VYSHNEVSKY. Nonsense, what fate! It's powerful enemies, that's why! That's what ruined me! Damn them all! They envied me my good situation. And why shouldn't they? In a few years a man rises to the top, gets rich, creates his own prosperity boldly, builds himself homes and summer cottages, buys up estate after estate, he's head and shoulders over them. So why shouldn't they be envious! A man goes to wealth and honors as easily as walking up the stairs. To overtake or at least catch up to him they need brains, they need genius. There's nowhere for them to get the brains, so they trip him up. I'm choking with rage...

YUSOV. Envy can move men to anything...

VYSHNEVSKY. It's not my downfall that makes me mad, no, but the triumph I'm giving them with my downfall. What talk there'll be now, what joy! Damn it all, that's what I won't be able to bear! *(He rings.)*

Anton enters.

Water!...

Anton gives him some water and leaves.

Now I want to have a little talk with you.

MME VYSHNEVSKY. What do you want?

VYSHNEVSKY. I want to tell you that you are a depraved woman.

MME VYSHNEVSKY. Aristarkh Vladimirych, we're not alone.

YUSOV. Would you like me to leave, sir?

VYSHNEVSKY. Stay! I'd say the same things in front of all the servants.

MME VYSHNEVSKY. Why are you humiliating me like this? You want someone to take out your spite on. It's not right!

VYSHNEVSKY. There's the justification for my words.

He throws an envelope and some letters. Yusov picks them up and hands them to Mme Vyshnevsky.

MME VYSHNEVSKY. Thank you. *(She looks them over convulsively and puts them away in her pocket.)*

VYSHNEVSKY. Yusov, what do they do with a woman who, despite all her husband's good deeds, forgets her duty?

YUSOV. Hmm…hmm…

VYSHNEVSKY. I'll tell you. They drive her out in shame! Yes, Yusov, I'm unfortunate, completely unfortunate, and I'm not alone. Don't you abandon me at least. No matter how high a man is placed, when he's in grief he still looks to his family for comfort. *(With spite.)* But what I find in my family is…

MME VYSHNEVSKY. Don't talk about your family! You never had one. You don't even know what a family is! Let me tell you, Aristarkh Vladimirych, all I've had to endure, living with you.

VYSHNEVSKY. For you there are no justifications.

MME VYSHNEVSKY. I don't want to justify myself, I don't need to. For a momentary passion I have borne much grief and a lot of humiliation, but believe me, I haven't complained against fate and cursed like you. I only want to tell you that if I'm guilty, it is towards myself alone and not towards you. You have no right to reproach me. If you had a heart, you would feel how you destroyed me.

VYSHNEVSKY. Ha, ha! Accuse somebody else for your behavior, not me.

MME VYSHNEVSKY. No, you. Did you really choose a wife? Remember how you courted me! I didn't hear a word about family life. You acted like an old flirt trying to seduce a young woman with gifts, looked at me with voluptuous eyes. You saw my aversion to you, and yet, despite that, you bought me with money from my parents, the way they buy slaves in Turkey. So what do you want from me?

VYSHNEVSKY. You're my wife, don't forget that! And I have the right to demand that you fulfill your duty.

MME VYSHNEVSKY. Yes, and your purchase, you didn't sanctify it with marriage, you concealed it with the mask of marriage. Otherwise it would have been impossible, my parents wouldn't have consented. But for you it was all the same. And later too, when you were already my husband, you didn't treat me as your wife; you tried to buy my caresses with money. If you saw I had any aversion to you, you came running with some expensive gift, and then you could come boldly, with a full right. So what could I do?... After all, you're my husband; I submitted. Oh! One stops respecting oneself. How one despises oneself! That's what you brought me to. But what happened to me later, when I found out that even the money you were giving me... wasn't yours, that you had gotten it dishonestly...

VYSHNEVSKY *(gets up)*. Be quiet!

MME VYSHNEVSKY. All right, I'll be quiet about that, you've been punished enough for it, but I'll keep on about myself.

VYSHNEVSKY. You can say what you want, I don't care. You won't change my opinion of you.

MME VYSHNEVSKY. Perhaps you'll change your opinion of yourself after I've spoken. You remember how I avoided society, I was afraid of it. And with good reason. But you insisted, and I had to give in. So there I was, completely unprepared, with no advice, no guide, and you took me into your circle with its temptation and vice at every step. With nobody to warn me or support me! All the same, by myself I came to see all the pettiness and all the depravity of your acquaintances. I watched out for myself. That was when I met Lyubimov in society, you knew him. You remember his open face, his bright eyes, how intelligent and pure he was! How ardently he argued with you, how boldly he spoke out about any lie or wrong! He said what I was already feeling, even if vaguely. I waited for your reply. You had none, you simply slandered him, behind his back thought up vile gossip, and you tried to lower him in public opinion. How I would have liked to intercede for him, but I didn't have the chance or enough cleverness. There was only one thing I could do... fall in love with him.

VYSHNEVSKY. So that's exactly what you did?

MME VYSHNEVSKY. So that's exactly what I did. I saw later how you destroyed him, how little by little you reached your goal. That is, not just you but everyone who found it useful. At first you armed society against him, saying that knowing him was dangerous for young people. Then you kept repeating that he was a freethinker, a harmful man, and you set his superiors against him. He was forced to leave the civil service, to leave his relatives, to leave here... and he died far away. *(She covers her eyes with her handkerchief.)* I saw all this, but I endured it. I saw how spite triumphed and how you still considered me the girl you had bought and who must be grateful and love you for your gifts. Out of my pure relations with him people made vile gossip, and ladies began to scandalize me openly, though secretly they were jealous of me. Young and old Don Juans started running after me without ceremony. That's what you brought me to, a woman able to understand the true meaning of life and to hate evil! That's all I wanted to tell you. You'll never hear any more reproach from me.

VYSHNEVSKY. And that's a mistake. I'm a poor man now, and poor men let their wives abuse them. They can do it. If I were Vyshnevsky as he was before today, I'd kick you out without another word, but now, thanks to our enemies, we've been cast out of the circle of decent people. In lower circles husbands quarrel with their wives, and sometimes they come to blows, and that doesn't scandalize anybody.

Zhadov enters with his wife.

Why are you here?

ZHADOV. Uncle, forgive me...

PAULINE. Hello, Uncle! Hello, Uncle! *(She whispers to Mme. Vyshnevsky.)* He's come to ask for a position. *(She sits down next to Mme. Vyshnevsky.)*

MME VYSHNEVSKY. What! Really! *(She looks at Zhadov with curiosity.)*

VYSHNEVSKY. You've come to laugh at your uncle!

ZHADOV. Uncle, perhaps I offended you. Forgive me... it was the enthusiasm of youth, the ignorance of life... I didn't have the right...you're my relative.

VYSHNEVSKY. So?

ZHADOV. I've come to feel what it means to live without support... without someone's helpful influence... I'm a married man.

VYSHNEVSKY. What are you trying to say?

ZHADOV. I live in a very poor way... For me there'd be enough, but for my wife, whom I love very much... Give me permission to work under you again... Uncle, take care of me! Give me a position where I... could... *(quietly)* acquire something.

PAULINE *(to Mme. Vyshnevsky)*. Some income.

VYSHNEVSKY *(bursts out laughing)*. Ha, ha, ha! Yusov! There they are, our heroes! The young man who shouted at every street corner about bribetakers, who talked about some sort of new generation, comes and asks us for a profitable position so he can take bribes! The wonderful new generation! Ha, ha, ha!

ZHADOV *(gets up)*. Oh! *(He clutches his chest.)*

YUSOV. You were young! So how could you talk sense! It was all nothing but words... Which is what they'll stay, just words. Life will tell. *(He takes some snuff.)* You'll give up that philosophy. The only bad thing is, you should have listened to smart people before, instead of getting rude.

VYSHNEVSKY *(to Yusov)*. No, Yusov, you remember the tone he took! How self-assured he was! What indignation towards vice! *(To Zhadov, becoming more and more excited.)* Weren't you the one who said that a new generation is growing up, educated and honest men, martyrs of the truth, men who would expose us and shower us with mud? Wasn't that you? I'll have to confess, I believed it. I hated you profoundly... I feared you. Yes, I'm not joking. And so how does it turn out! You are honest only until those lessons they drilled into you have lost their strength, honest only until you have your first encounter with need! So you've given me something to be happy about, I must say!... No, you're not worth hating. I despise you!

ZHADOV. Despise me, despise me. I despise myself.

VYSHNEVSKY. Certain people have taken for themselves the privilege of judging what's honorable! You and I've been put to shame because of them! They've put us on trial...

ZHADOV. What did you say!

YUSOV. People... are always people.

ZHADOV. Uncle, I didn't say our generation is more honest than others. There have always been and always will be honest people, honest citizens, honest officials; there have always been and always will be weak people. I myself am proof of that. All I said was that in our time *(He starts quietly and gradually gets worked up.)* society is little by little casting off its previous indifference to vice, you can hear strong cries against the evils of society... I said that an awareness of our defects is waking in us and that in this awareness there is hope for a better future. I said that public opinion is beginning to be formed... that among the youth a feeling of justice is growing, a feeling of duty, and it's growing, is growing and will bear fruit. If you won't live to see it, then we will, and we'll thank God for it. There's no reason for you to be happy about my weakness. I'm no hero; I'm just an ordinary, weak man. I have little strength of will, like almost all of us. Need, circumstances, lack of education in relatives, and corruption all around me can wear me down the way people wear down horses on the highway. But all I need is one lesson, even if it has to be like this... I'm grateful to you for it. I need just one meeting with a decent man to resurrect me, to help me stay firm. I can waver, but I won't commit a crime; I can stumble, but I won't fall. My heart has already been softened by education, it won't become coarse in vice.

Silence.

I don't know where to go from shame... Yes, I'm ashamed, ashamed that I'm here.

VYSHNEVSKY *(rising)*. Then get out!

ZHADOV *(meekly)*. I'll go. Pauline, now you can go to Mama's; I won't hold you back. I won't betray myself now. If fate leads me to nothing but black bread, I'll eat nothing but black bread. No comforts will tempt me, no! I want to keep the precious right of looking all men straight in the eye, without shame, without secret pangs of conscience. I want to read and see satires and comedies about bribetakers where I can laugh freely and openly. If my whole life consists of toil and deprivation, I won't complain... There's just one consolation I'll ask from God, one reward I'll look forward to. Can you imagine what that is?

A short silence.

I'll look forward to the time when bribetakers will fear the judgment of society more than that of the courts.

VYSHNEVSKY *(rises)*. I'll strangle you with my bare hands. *(He staggers.)* Yusov, I feel bad. Take me to the study. *(He goes with Yusov.)*

PAULINE *(goes up to Zhadov)*. Did you think I really wanted to leave you? I did it all on purpose. They put me up to it.

MME VYSHNEVSKY. Make it up, children.

Zhadov and Pauline kiss.

YUSOV *(in the doorway)*. A doctor, a doctor!

MME VYSHNEVSKY *(rising in her armchair)*. What is it, what is it?

YUSOV. Aristarkh Vladimirych has had a stroke!

MME VYSHNEVSKY *(crying out weakly)*. Oh! *(She sinks down in the armchair.)*

Pauline, in horror, squeezes up to Zhadov. Zhadov leans with his hand on the table and lowers his head. Yusov stands in the doorway, completely bewildered.

CURTAIN

NOTES

These notes and those for the other plays are based on those in A. N. Ostrovskij: *Polnoe sobranie sochinenii*, Moscow, 1973–1980.

1. From a song *(Vecherkom krasna devitsa…)* very popular at the beginning of the nineteenth century. Words by N. M. Ibragimov.

2. Collegiate assessor was a civil service rank bestowing the right of hereditary nobility. For contemporaries this would make comical Mme. Kukushkin's claim in Act Four, "With us nobility is inborn."

3. Before 1837 government officials could wear a mustache and beard. They were prohibited from doing so by the decree of Nicholas I dated April 2, 1837.

4. The decree of October 14, 1798 allowed their superiors to send office officials of nonnoble origin to the army for deviation from duty, negligence, or incompetence.

5. *Po ulitse mostovoi*, a very popular Russian dance tune, which had many recordings.

6. *"Ne staia voronov sletalas'!"* First line of Alexander Pushkin's poem *"Brat'ia razboiniki,"* published in 1825.

7. At that time a suburb of Moscow featuring various cheap amusements and outdoor festivals.

8. *"Luchina, luchinushka berezovaia!"* An old Russian folk song.

9. *"Matushka, golubushka, solnyshko moe…"* A very popular romance. Words by Nirokomsky (pseudonym) and music by A. L. Gurilev.

10. This would have been the Petrovsko-Razumovsky Park, where the Moscow nobility (primarily) went riding.

11. Obviously inspired by Cervantes' *Don Quixote*, which was available in an incomplete translation from French in 1769 and a translation from the original Spanish by K. P. Masalsky in 1838 and 1848-49.

12. Procurator's song from the comedy "Slander" (*labeda*, 1796) by V.V. Kapnist.

13. The reference is to a cheap popular print of 1820-21 entitled "Vanity of Vanities."

AFTERWORD

The basic background material for *A Profitable Position* (Dokhodnoe mesto) was provided by the experiences and impressions Ostrovsky gained during his seven-year service as a court clerk when he himself was in Zhadov's unhappy position.[1] Ostrovsky finished writing the play on December 20, 1856, and it was published in the No. 1 (March) 1857 issue of *Russian Colloquy (Russkaia beseda.)* Making a few cuts, the censor approved the play for performance, but he was officially overruled on the ground that the play accused government officials of being bribetakers and embezzlers. Before the play was officially banned, it was performed in some provincial theaters in 1857, but the first officially approved stage performance did not take place until September 27, 1863, in St. Petersburg, the Moscow premiere occurring on October 14, 1863.

In order to appreciate the place of this play in terms of Ostrovsky's playwriting development let us backtrack briefly. In his two early full-length plays *It's All in the Family* (1850) and *The Poor Bride* (1852) Ostrovsky had emphasized the dark side of social reality with endings that lacked any compensating consolation. This is especially true of *It's All in the Family*, which did not include a single morally positive main character. Though published in 1850 it could not be performed until 1861 and then only with a revised ending satisfactory to the censor. In the original ending the unscrupulous Podkhalyuzin had remained free and unpunished, but in the enforced revised ending he was arrested. The sorry business cost Ostrovsky his position in the civil service, and it certainly must have made him realize even more that to get his plays performed he would have to satisfy the censor.

Probably trying to find his way out of this painful predicament, though other factors were involved, Ostrovsky next wrote three plays, the so-called Slavophile plays *(Don't Sit in Another's Sleigh, Poverty's No Vice, Don't Live as You Please)*, in which he stressed the native goodness of basic Russian types while giving preference to indigenous traditions over foreign influences. Moreover, he made the endings morally respectable even though it necessitated sudden turnabouts of a deus ex machina nature. In his two-act play *Trouble Caused by Another*, published in 1856 just before *A Profitable Position*, Ostrovsky reached a compromise between the stark portrayal of a dark side of Russian reality and the idealized portrayal featured in the Slavophile plays. From then on, with the exception of primarily satirical plays, Ostrovsky's plays about contemporary life would portray both the seamy side of reality and morally good individuals protesting and/or struggling against the social evil oppressing them.

A Profitable Position oscillates between the business and social world of officialdom and the home life of officials and their families. This is so much the case that it would not be preposterous to consider the work two plays adroitly combined by Ostrovsky to give the impression of being one.

Established officialdom is represented by the hierarchical triumvirate of Vyshnevsky, Yusov, and Belogubov. Vyshnevsky, near the end of his life and career, understands only too well that some officials, himself included, could be answerable for corrupt practices. Yet he also cynically accepts corruption-tainted officialdom as too entrenched for someone like Zhadov to rebel against it, even if only verbally and in broad generalities.

Unlike Vyshnevsky, Yusov, one of Ostrovsky's great satirical characters, does not understand what's involved in the general scheme of things; he has profited so long from the present system that he without question accepts it as the best of all possible worlds. He does not consider the law to be above officialdom but rather its friend and ally. His only criticism of his boss Vyshnevsky, whom he much admires, is that he is "not at all strong in the law," a factor undoubtedly contributing to Vyshnevsky's ultimate downfall. Though Yusov accepts bribetaking as an innocent fringe benefit for officials in certain positions, the sky is not the limit, and an honorable official will never take a bribe without rendering the services expected.

Although Zhadov in terms of education is obviously more qualified for promotion than Belogubov, Yusov favors Belogubov because he has the "open mind" Zhadov lacks; that is, Belogubov is ready and willing to try to please his superiors. Moreover, the kindhearted Yusov will not discriminate against those handicapped by a lack of education, and he feels there is really no need for education since a good official can always find a brainy type to help out, as, for example, with spelling.

While the audience will consider Yusov criminal, he is not hypocritical in portraying himself to Mme. Kukushkin as a basically good man with nothing to be ashamed of. And in the delightful tavern scene when Belogubov, now ensconced in a "profitable position" and gratefully treating his mentor Yusov in celebration of his rise, has persuaded Yusov to let go and perform a solo dance, Yusov justifies his dancing: "I can dance. I've done everything in life that's prescribed for a man. My soul's at peace, my past doesn't wear on me. I've provided for my family—so now I can dance."

It is this self-righteousness and self-justification, the play suggests, that make Yusov more dangerous to society than Vyshnevsky. The Vyshnevskys are more apt to attract attention and be caught, but, more importantly, the Vyshnevskys might have misgivings and fears, whereas the Yusovs will have none, because their conscience is clean. They don't see their bribetaking as a cause of harm to individuals; on the contrary they even see it as a help to them, and they have come to assume that what is good for themselves and their loved ones is not against the general interest.

The home front supporting the amoral official world is for the most part represented by Mme. Kukushkin, her like-minded daughter, Julie, and eventually by the converted Pauline. Mme. Kukushkin is another of Ostrovsky's great satirical characters. A brilliant pragmatist, she knows exactly what she wants and how to get it singlemindedly. Her top priority is to marry off both daughters to officials who can give them the kind of idle and comfortable life for which she, like a good mother, has trained them.

Absolutely sure of herself and her beliefs, Mme. Kukushkin is never at a loss for words, sweet or abusive, but she also knows how to listen purposefully, and Yusov, a master in his own realm, is no match for her ingratiation. She finds Zhadov much more formidable, but her persistence prevails, and, with the help of Julie, she succeeds in alienating the married Pauline from him.

An important contribution Mme. Kukushkin makes to a better thematic understanding of the play is her attitude to bribetaking. Even though she is the widow of an official, the attention suddenly, for her, being given to bribe-taking astounds her, and she even claims that "bribe" is a new word: "Bribes! What kind of a word is that, bribes? They've thought it up themselves just to hurt good people. It's not bribes but gratitude!"

Mme. Kukushkin has known about bribetaking, of course, but she has managed to put it out of her mind for the very simple reason that it is of no interest to her. What matters to her is not the means but the end result, that the husband–official uses his position (She doesn't care how) to bring home the supplementary bacon. Indeed, the play itself is not primarily concerned with bribery per se (It has no bribegivers) but, as E. Kholodov points out, rather with the philosophy of self-interest.[2] It just so happens that officials find bribetaking a convenient means at hand to serve their interests, and it serves Mme. Kuku-shkin's interests to go along with this business, meanwhile reinforcing it with her own means, such as educating her daughters to reward their husbands with affection only if they measure up *comme il faut* and bring home what it takes.

Zhadov, Ostrovsky's most quixotic character, applies to reality precon-ceived standards which for him require no proof. A born preacher, he feels that he has only to proclaim such standards and they will be accepted. Whereas Don Quixote discovered his standards by reading books on chivalry, Zhadov found his at the university.

Nevertheless, in his more realistic moments Zhadov realizes how inef-fective he is. Just before capitulating to Pauline, he asks himself, "Why try to fight windmills!" His struggle is largely a matter of verbal, though not empty, gestures. For most of the play he does not yield to despair, maintaining his faith in man's goodness and intelligence, convinced or at least hoping that ulti-mately education and public opinion will bring about needed reform. At the end Vyshnevsky denounces Zhadov for betraying his (Zhadov's) ideals. How-ever, Zhadov has never abandoned them in principle and blames his wavering on personal weakness. At the same time, he was never quite so strong in his beliefs as his usual preachy stance would have suggested. He tells Vyshnevsky in Act One, "But I can't part with my convictions; they're my sole *consolation* in life" (italics mine). True, he does have faith in the power of public opinion to help bring about justice. But that faith is characterized by hope as much as certainty, the desired justice being projected into a future not near.

And yet, if I may qualify even more, Zhadov does demonstrate some heroism in his social context, and he suffers for his honesty both before and after his marriage. The main trouble is that in the system depicted by Ostrovsky Zhadov has no middle course open to him. As the scholar E. Kholodov so eloquently puts it, the play condemns "an existence, in which a man has to be a hero so as not to become a scoundrel."[3] The play begins and, to some extent, ends with Mme. Vyshnevsky's marital situation, easily the weakest element in the play, if only because she is so long-winded. Ostrovsky portrays Mme. Vyshnevsky sympathetically for her noble character and as a spiritual ally of Zhadov, but, for all that, her role is contrived and a bit confusing. Though her infatuation, while married, with the now-deceased idealist Lyubimov is believable enough in itself, Ostrovsky could not go into the matter sufficiently because Lyubimov was either a revolutionary or was considered such. He had probably been exiled as a dangerously liberal thinker, for Mme. Vyshnevsky at one point in the original version says that Lyubimov "died far away," words later deleted by the censor. While Lyubimov might have been used, then, as a complement to Zhadov, in actuality he is a distraction. As indeed in the overall pattern are Mme. Vyshnevsky and her domestic situation.

After four slow acts the final act comes as something of a blow to the audience. It starts with an unusually long soliloquy by Mme. Vyshnvesky but then suddenly shifts into a series of fireworks. Yusov informs Mme. Vyshnevsky that Vyshnevsky has been charged with malfeasance. Vyshnevsky, informed of Mme. Vyshnevsky's infatuation with Lyubimov, denounces her, provoking her spirited defense. Zhadov asks his uncle for a "profitable position," but when he learns that Vyshnevsky can no longer give it to him, he reverts to his idealistic stance, and Pauline makes up with him. The curtain falls with Yusov's announcement that Vyshnevsky, now offstage, has just had a stroke which at his age might be fatal.

The radical critic and writer Nicholas Chernyshevsky felt that artistically the play would better have ended with Zhadov's capitulation at the end of Act Four. I agree. The main burden of the first four acts is to show that Zhadov, mostly because of the strength of the opposition, has no real chance to initiate reform or even to live decently. Act Five largely turns the situation around. With regard to Zhadov we are basically back where we started, though, thanks to Ostrovsky's authorial omnipotence, things are even a bit better for Zhadov, since he suddenly has a wife apparently willing to forgo the good life, after all. Yet, in fairness to Ostrovsky, it is quite possible, in my view likely, that he wrote Act Five to appease the censor, judging that if the play had ended with Zhadov's capitulation, it would have spotlighted government corruption in a way the hypersensitive censorhip of the time would have considered too merciless. Ostrovsky may well have felt that he had no choice but to try to soften the play's basic impact.

The basic play (Acts 1-4) has a minuscule plot, proving, if proof be needed, that a good plot development is not a binding requirement for a play's success. As Pushkin's friend and fellow poet Baron Delvig said in relation to Pushkin's play, *Boris Godunov,* "Don't judge it by the rules but by the impression it makes on you." And Leo Tolstoy tacitly agreed, when he wrote to Ostrovsky, "This is a colossal thing because of its depth and power, its contemporary significance, and the irreproachable role of Yusov."

NOTES

1. In P. M. Nevezhin's recollections of Ostrovsky he noted that Ostrovsky more than once joked bitterly, "If I hadn't been in such a mess, I probably wouldn't have written *A Profitable Position.*" *A. N. Ostrovskii v vospominaniiakh sovremennikov,* 1966, 262.

2. E. Kholodov, *Dramaturg na vse vremena,* 1975, 340.

3. Ibid., 342.

AN ARDENT HEART

A Comedy in Five Acts
(1869)

CAST OF CHARACTERS*

PAVLÍN PAVLÍNYCH KUROSLÉPOV, a merchant of standing.

MATRYÓNA KHARITÓNOVNA KUROSLÉPOV, his wife.

PARÁSHA (her given name PRASKÓVYA is used on occasion), his daughter by his first wife.

NARKÍS, Kuroslepov's assistant at home.

GAVRÍLO (GAVRÍK, GAVRÍLKA, GAVREILUSHKA, GAVRYÚSHKA), Kuroslepov's assistant at the shop.

VÁSYA (VÁSKA, VÁSYENKA, VASÍLY) SHÚSTRY, son of a recently ruined merchant.

SILÁN (SILÁNTY), a distant relative of Kuroslepov. Yard keeper.

SERAPIÓN MARDÁRYICH GRADOBÓEV, Chief of Police.**

SIDORÉNKO, a police officer and Gradoboev's clerk.

ZHIGUNÓV (pronounced Zhigunóff), a policeman on general and sentry-box duty.

ARISTÁRKH (ALISTÁRKH, LISTÁRKH), a middle-class citizen.

TARÁKH TARÁSYCH KHLÝNOV, a rich contractor.

MAIDSERVANT.

GENTLEMAN, with a large mustache.

MIDDLE-CLASS CITIZENS: FIRST, SECOND, THIRD.

ROWERS, SINGERS, INVALID SOLDIERS, PRISONERS, DOMESTIC SERVANTS, KHLYNOV'S SERVANTS, PASSERS-BY, LABORERS, POLICEMEN, VARIOUS PEOPLE.

---

* Meanings which probably or possibly would be suggested to Ostrovsky's contemporaries: Kuroslepov—night blindness; Shustry—quick, lively; Gradoboev—city beater; Zhigunov—lasher; Khlynov—profiteer or scoundrel.

** "Chief of Police" is used here for the Russian term *gorodnichii*, chief official in Russian provincial towns from 1775 to 1862. The term has often been translated as "mayor", but I prefer to adopt the English term used by John L. Seymour and George R. Noyes in their translation of Gogol's *The Inspector*. The function of the *gorodnichii* was largely a police function, a function characteristic of Gradoboev in this play.

ACT ONE

A yard. To the spectators' right is a house porch with a door onto the room where Kuroslepov's assistants live. To the left is a wing in front of which are a fence section, bushes, a large tree, a table, and a bench. In the background is a gate. It is a summer evening, after seven. The action takes place about thirty years ago[1] in the provincial town Kalinov.[2] Gavrilo is sitting on the bench with a guitar. Silan is standing nearby with a broom.

SILAN. Did you hear something's missing?

GAVRILO. I heard.

SILAN. And that missing business is a load on me. Because of that, my friends, you assistants have got to toe the line with me, be home by nine, that's when I lock the gate. And if anybody's climbing over the fence at night, well he'd just better give it up because I'll grab him by the collar and straight to the master with him.

GAVRILO. When you want to, you can really be a character.

SILAN. It's my job. I could be told on, and who knows what he'd do? Right now I'm extraordinary mean, so mean, it's awful!

Gavrilo strums on the guitar. Silan silently looks at Gavrilo's hands.

Are you getting to it?

GAVRILO. I'm getting to it. *(He sings to his own accompaniment.)*

> Neither Papa, neither Mama,
> No one's home, nobody's here.
> No one's home, nobody's here.
> Through the window climb, my dear.[3]

SILAN. That's a grand song.

GAVRILO. It's really a wonderful song, you can sing it in all kinds of company. Only it goes awfully fast... you've got to watch sharp! See? It's not coming out right, what can you do!

SILAN. What I think, my friend, is you'd better give up on all this business.

GAVRILO. But why give it up, Silanty? Just think of all the work I've put into it.

SILAN. And what you've gotten out of it is a lot of pain and trouble.

GAVRILO. I don't mind the pain, but it's true there's been a lot of damage. Because the guitar's a delicate instrerment.

SILAN. All you have to do is up and smash it on the stove, and that's the end of it.

GAVRILO. That would be the end, my friend, the end. And all that money down the drain.

SILAN. On the stove, eh? And you know what the master's taken it into his head to do. No sooner does he set eyes on a guitar like this than he smashes it right then and there on the stove! It's really something!

GAVRILO *(with a sigh)*. Only it's not always on the stove, Silanty. He broke two of them on my head.

SILAN. That really must have been funny. We could hear the bang all through the house.

GAVRILO. It might have been funny for some people, but for me...

SILAN. You mean it hurt? Of course it would if he hit you with the edge...

GAVRILO. Even if it wasn't the edge... But I won't get after anybody for that, it's my own head, I didn't have to pay for it. But for those guitars I had to pay real money.

SILAN. And that's the honest truth. A head can ache and ache, and it'll heal up. But a guitar now, you won't heal that.

GAVRILO. You know what, maybe I should just clear out of here! So long as the master doesn't see me.

SILAN. How could he do that! He's asleep, as he ordinary is. He sleeps nights, he sleeps days. He's slept so much he doesn't understand a thing, doesn't see what's right under his nose. When he's just waked up, then what's really happened and what he's dreamed about, he gets them all mixed up, he just mumbles something. And then he gets straightened out.

GAVRILO *(sings loudly)*.

Neither Papa, neither Mama,
No one's home, nobody's here.

Kuroslepov comes out onto the porch.

SILAN. Stop that! I think he's coming out! He is! You better leave if you don't want trouble. No, better stay. Hide yourself somewhere here. He won't go beyond the porch, he's too lazy.

Gavrilo hides.

KUROSLEPOV *(sits down on the porch and yawns awhile)*. And why was the sky falling? So if it falls it falls. Or was I dreaming it? Just try and guess what's going on in the world—is it morning or evening? And no one about, damn 'em!... Matryona! Nobody home, nobody in the yard, the hell with 'em!... Matryona! That's when it's so horrible, when you don't know what's going on in the world... It's frightening. Was that a dream or what? There was a lot of wood stacked up, it seems, and devils. So I ask them, "What's the wood for?" And they say it's to roast sinners. Am I really in hell? Where did everybody disappear to? And how frightened I am today! And that sky, is it falling again?

It is, it's falling... Oh God! And now there's sparks. What if right now it's the end of the world! And no wonder! It could all easily happen because... there was a smell of tar somewhere, and somebody was singing with a wild voice, and there was a sound of strings or maybe a trumpet... I just don't understand.

The town clock strikes.

One, two, three, four, five *(he counts without listening)*, six, seven, eight, nine, ten, eleven, twelve, thirteen, fourteen, fifteen.

The clock stops striking after striking eight.

Is that all? Fifteen!... My God! My God! We've lived to see that! Fifteen! What we've lived to! Fifteen! And it's still not enough for our sins! What next! Should I go take a drink in any case? But then people say it's at just such a time that it's worse, that a man ought to go with a clean conscience... *(He shouts.)* Silanty, hey!

SILAN. Don't shout, I hear you.

KUROSLEPOV. Where did you disappear to? Just when this business is starting up...

SILAN. I didn't disappear anywhere. I've been standing right here, guarding you.

KUROSLEPOV. Did you hear the clock?

SILAN. Well, what about it?

KUROSLEPOV. It's a sign! Is everybody still alive?

SILAN. Who?

KUROSLEPOV. The people of the house and all Orthodox Christians?

SILAN. Come to your senses! Go wash up!

KUROSLEPOV. The springs haven't dried up yet?

SILAN. No. Why should they?

KUROSLEPOV. And where's my wife now?

SILAN. She went visiting.

KUROSLEPOV. At a time like this she should be with her husband.

SILAN. Well, that's her business!

KUROSLEPOV. Visiting! She's found a good time for it! It's all so terrifying.

SILAN. What is?

KUROSLEPOV. Everyone could hear how it struck fifteen.

SILAN. Whether it did or did not strike fifteen, the fact is that it's just after eight... exactly the time for you to eat supper and then back again to sleep.

KUROSLEPOV. You say it's time for supper?

SILAN. Yes, we've got to do that eatin'. If you get something like that going, you can't do without it.

KUROSLEPOV. Does that mean we're in the evening?

SILAN. Evening.

KUROSLEPOV. And everything's the way it always is? There's none of all that?

SILAN. Why should there be?

KUROSLEPOV. And I almost got frightened! What didn't I think up sitting here! I imagined that the end of ends was starting. And you know, it might not be far off at that.

SILAN. Why talk about it?

KUROSLEPOV. Have they left the church?

SILAN. Just now.

KUROSLEPOV *(starts to sing a bit of church music)*. But when... Did you lock the gate?

SILAN. I locked it.

KUROSLEPOV. I'm going to check up on you.

SILAN. Go take a little walk; it'll do you good...

KUROSLEPOV. You and your "go take a little walk"! It all comes from your not keeping watch. I've got to watch out everywhere. I'm missing two thousand rubles. And that's no joke! You save that up!

SILAN. And if you keep on sleeping, they'll steal everything.

KUROSLEPOV. I can see how sorry you are for your master's things! I haven't finished with you yet... just wait.

SILAN. All right! I'm shaking with fright! You don't have anything on me. I do my job, walk about all night long, and there's the dogs too... I could even take an oath on it. I don't see how a fly, let alone a thief, could get through. Where did you keep your money?

KUROSLEPOV. I didn't get to pack it away in the trunk. It was under my pillow, hidden in a stocking.

SILAN. So, you can judge for yourself who did it! If you hid it in your stocking, then give your stocking a good questioning!

KUROSLEPOV. You don't say! I ought to grab you by the hair the way our women rinse out clothes...

SILAN. You're not the man to do it!

KUROSLEPOV. And there's never enough wine either; whole bottles disappear.

SILAN. Then look for the man who's drinking it. God spared me that pleasure.

KUROSLEPOV. Who would steal it?

SILAN. It's really strange!

KUROSLEPOV. I'd think...

SILAN. So would I...

KUROSLEPOV *(in a singing voice)*. But when... So you say I should eat supper?

SILAN. It's the only thing to do.

KUROSLEPOV. Go order it.

SILAN. And what about the gate?

KUROSLEPOV Later. Now you...*(He uses a threatening gesture.)* Listen here! I don't give a hoot that you're some relative of mine. I want everything here, the doors, the locks, everything, to stay put. You guard it like the apple of your eye. I don't want to be ruined because of you.

SILAN. All right, that's enough! You've said your piece, so drop it.

KUROSLEPOV. Where are the assistants?

SILAN. Who knows?

KUROSLEPOV. If any of them don't come back in time, don't let him in; he can spend the night outside; just let in the lady of the house. And if any outsiders come, even if you know them very well, don't let them in on any account. I have an unmarried daughter I've got to think about too. *(He goes off into the house.)*

SILAN *(approaches Gavrilo).* Come out, it's all right!

GAVRILO. Is he gone?

SILAN. Gone. So now he'll eat supper and go back to sleep. And why does he sleep so much? It's because he has all that money! But I have to wear myself out all night long. He made his pile, but it's me who's got to guard it for him. Two thousand rubles. He can talk! Because I don't keep watch, he says. If you only knew how hard it is for me to hear reproaches in my old age! What I'd do if I laid hands on that thief! I'd really let him have it!... I think I could tear him to shreds with my teeth! Just let him show up now, and I'll go right at him with the broom... *(Catching sight of Vasya, who appears on the fence.)* Stop, stop! There he is! Wait, let him get down from the fence. *(He rushes at him with the broom.)* Help!

VASYA. What are you doing, what are you doing? Don't shout, you know me!

SILAN *(grabbing him by the collar).* So, I know you! Oh you! You really frightened me. But just why did you climb over the fence? Hel...

VASYA. Don't shout, please! I came for a little visit, it's awfully boring at home.

SILAN. If you have honorable intentions, you can come through the gate.

VASYA. The gate's closed, and if I knock, the master might hear.

SILAN *(holds him by the collar).* And just where has it been laid down that a man should go over the fence? Hel...

VASYA. Please, have a heart! After all, you know me. It isn't the first time, is it?

SILAN. I know you used to climb over the fence before, but that doesn't mean you always can. We weren't looking for anything before, but now two thousand rubles are missing. That's what comes of spoiling you!

VASYA. But I didn't steal them, you know that yourself. So what does it have to do with me!

SILAN *(shakes him by the collar)*. Nothing to do with you! Nothing to do with you! So, it's me alone who's got to answer for everybody else! Nothing to do with you people. All me! I'll make you sing another tune! Help!

GAVRILO. Look, you've tormented him enough.

SILAN *(to Vasya)*. Bow down.

Vasya bows down.

That's more like it! *(He takes him by the collar.)*

VASYA. But why are you grabbing me by the collar again?

SILAN. Just to be on the safe side. Tell me, is your father in good health?

VASYA. He's just fine, thanks.

SILAN. You see, I know why you came; only she's not home, she went visiting.

VASYA. Let me go!

SILAN *(holding him by the collar)*. She went visiting, my good friend. You just wait; she'll come back. She'll come back, and then you'll see each other, so there!

VASYA. Stop making fun of me. Why are you holding me by the collar?

SILAN. Here's why; shouldn't I perhaps take you to the master?

VASYA. Silanty Ivanych, are you a Christian?

SILAN *(releases him)*. Oh all right, God be with you. You can stay. Only it has to be on the up and up, for if you try anything, then it's your hands behind your back and straight to the master with you. Understand?

VASYA. How couldn't I understand?

SILAN. All right, so remember. I'd be held responsible. *(He goes off and strikes on the watchman's metal plate.)*

GAVRILO. How come we haven't seen you for so long?

VASYA. I was busy. And what wonderful things I've seen, Gavrik, things you wouldn't expect to see your whole life!

GAVRILO. Where was this?

VASYA. At Khlynov's.

GAVRILO. The contractor?

VASYA. Yes. Only he's given up contracting now.

GAVRILO. Does that mean you don't have any work at all now?

VASYA. What work! Everything's pulling me in different directions, so I don't feel like working. From all that money a man doesn't want to go out in the world; I've been spoiled...

GAVRILO. But whether you like it or not, you'll have to go to work when there's nothing left to eat.

VASYA. All right, if that's God's will, but for now I'm going to have a good time.

GAVRILO. Tell me, what unusual things did you see at Khlynov's?

VASYA. Miracles! He's living at his summer home now, in his grove. And what doesn't he have! In the garden he's put in bowers and fountains. He's got his own singers, and every holiday the regimental band plays. He got himself all kinds of boats and fitted out the rowers in velvet coats. He sits all the time on the balcony without his jacket but with medals hung all over him, and from morning on he drinks champagne. Around the house there's a crowd of people, all marveling at him. And when he gives the word to let people into the garden to look at all the wonderful things, then they wet down the paths in the garden with champagne. That's not life, it's heaven!

GAVRILO. But it really wasn't so long ago he was a peasant himself.

VASYA. Here's how his mind works. As soon as he gets some whim in his head he carries it out! He bought a cannon. What more could you want than that! You tell me. Eh? A cannon! What more could a man want on earth? What doesn't he have now? He has everything.

GAVRILO. But what's the cannon for?

VASYA. What do you mean, what for, are you crazy! With all his money it's something he has to have. As soon as he drinks a glass, right away they shoot the cannon; he drinks again, they shoot again. That way they know he's honored above everybody. Other people die never knowing such honor. If I could only live like that for just one day.

GAVRILO. How can people like us do that! You pray to God you can have a job all your life, a full stomach.

VASYA. He's got a gentleman with him too. He brought him from Moscow to look important, and he takes him along everywhere for that importance. That gentleman doesn't do a thing, and most of the time he doesn't say anything, just drinks champagne. And he gets a big salary just for his looks, just for having a very unusual mustache. That gentleman really has the life; a man could live like that forever.

GAVRILO. Oh Vasya, my friend! Who did you pick to be jealous of! Today that gentleman's given champagne to drink, but maybe tomorrow he'll be cursed out and sent packing. And he'll be lucky if he has some money on him, for if he doesn't he'll have to foot it all the way to Moscow. But you, even if you have only a copper in your pocket, at least you're still your own master.

VASYA. And he has still another adjutant, a man from around here, a man called Alistarkh.

GAVRILO. I know him.

VASYA. That one's just for thinking up things, how to do something different, how to have more fun drinking, just so it's not always the same old thing. He makes machines for Khlynov, decorates the flags, installs fountains in the garden, glues colored lanterns together. He made Khlynov a swan on the nose of the boat, just like a live one, and in the tower over the stable he put up a clock, one with music. He doesn't drink and doesn't take much money; that's why they don't respect him much. Khlynov says to him, "You have hands of gold, so go ahead and get yourself some money from me." "I don't want it," says Listarkh, "Because that money of yours is wholly unjust." "How dare you be rude to me," says Khlynov, "I'll send you packing." But Alistarkh comes right back at him, "Send me packing, I won't cry over it, I've had enough of you fools in my life." And it's as if they're chewing each other out. But Alistarkh isn't at all afraid of him; he's rude to him and tells him off straight to his face. And Khlynov even loves him for that. Of course, it has to be said that even if Khlynov has piles of money life is boring for him because he doesn't know how to spend that money for a good time. "If," he says, "I didn't have Listarkh, then I'd simply throw money around by the handful." So that's why he needs Listarkh, to do his thinking for him. For if he thinks up something himself, it's all a mess. Take not long ago, he got the idea of riding a sleigh through a field in the summertime. There's a village near there, and he got together twelve girls and harnessed them to the sleigh. What fun that was! He gave each girl a gold piece. But then all of a sudden he gets depressed. "I don't want to get drunk," he says, "I want to suffer for my sins." So he calls in the clergy and makes them sit down in the living room in proper order, all around, in the armchairs. He treats them and bows down to all of them. Then he makes them sing while he sits alone in the middle of the room crying his heart out.

GAVRILO. So how come you were at his place?

VASYA. Alistarkh invited me. They've done over this boat into their own kind of play boat.[4] It's a real boat, and it sails on the pond around the island. And on the island they have snacks and wine all ready, and Alistarkh acts the host, dressed up like a Turk. They played this game three days running, then got tired of it.

Narkis approaches.

NARKIS. I think I'll sit down with you for a bit. It doesn't matter that you're not really my set. *(He sits down.)*

VASYA *(not paying any attention to him)*. They go like pirates around the island a couple of times, and their leader keeps looking through his telescope. And then all of a sudden he lets out with a awful yell, and right away they land and are about to take plunder when the host bows to them and treats them all.

NARKIS. Just what kind of pirates were they, and where did they come from? That's what I'd like to know right now.

VASYA *(not listening to him)*. And the host speaks Turkish, everything just the way it's supposed to be.

NARKIS. There's also people who don't care to talk with other people, and for that they can get a good beating.

VASYA. And they're all dressed up in velvet, real velvet, Venetian.

NARKIS *(takes out a red silk kerchief, scented, and waves it)*. Maybe somebody else knows how to dress up too, so that even a merchant would sit up and take notice.

GAVRILO. You and your perfumes!

NARKIS *(showing a ring)*. And we can have sappires that maybe even merchants' children haven't seen. And about those pirates of yours, that's all going to come to light, because it's not permitted to hide them.

VASYA. Yes, and maybe you're a pirate yourself, who knows!

NARKIS. And for that kind of talk people like you can get a quick trial.

VASYA. When I was in Moscow I saw the play *The Bigamous Wife*,[5] and in it they shoot off a gun right from a boat. Nothing better than that.

NARKIS. I'll be going to Moscow, and I'll take a look. I'll look into it to see if what you're saying is right.

VASYA. And for this one actor they kept clapping and clapping their hands something awful!

NARKIS. Don't be in such a hurry to tell lies. I'll look into it. You might come out wrong.

VASYA. But our merchant, even though he's not an actor, does look more like a pirate.

NARKIS *(gets up)*. I can see you don't have any smart conversation here, so there's no point in my listening. Oh, by the way, I suppose I should tell you. I'm going to be a merchant myself one of these days. *(He goes off into the wing.)*

GAVRILO. Listen to the song I've arranged.

VASYA. Go ahead.

GAVRILO *(sings with the guitar)*.

> Neither Papa, neither Mama,
> No one's home, nobody's here.
> No one's home, nobody's here.
> Through the window climb, my dear!

SILAN *(from afar)*. Quiet down you, I think the master's coming...

Kuroslepov comes out onto the porch.

GAVRILO *(not listening, with great gusto)*.

> No one's home, nobody's here,
> Through the window climb, my dear!
> Stretched his hand the dear, dear boy,
> Whipped it was by Cossack lash.

Use the hallway, use the door,
Use the gate, the gate so new.

KUROSLEPOV *(comes down from the porch)*. Gavryushka! So you're the one who's booming away. What kind of a hubbub do you think you're making out here!

GAVRILO *(to Vasya)*. Oh my God! Quick, take the guitar and get into the bushes.

Vasya takes the guitar and goes into the bushes.

KUROSLEPOV. Who do you think I'm talking to! Are you deaf or something! Bring that guitar here right now!

GAVRILO. I don't have any guitar, Pavlin Pavlinych, may I die on the spot, no guitar, sir, I was just…

KUROSLEPOV. Just what, just what, you good-for-nothing!

GAVRILO. I was just doing it with my lips; really, Pavlin Pavlinych, it was with my lips.

KUROSLEPOV. Come here, come here, that's an order!

Vasya runs away with the guitar into the wing.

GAVRILO. What is this! I'm coming, sir!

SILAN. What it is is that he'll give you something of a thrashing, can't do without that, that's what he's the master for.

Gavrilo moves, step by step. Kuroslepov circles around him and wants to approach him. Gavrilo retreats, then runs onto the porch and into the house, Kuroslepov behind him. Someone knocks at the gate. Silan opens up. Matryona and Parasha enter. Silan, after letting them in, goes out through the gate. Matryona goes toward the porch. Gavrilo, disheveled, runs out and collides with her.

MATRYONA. Oh you! Right in the ribs! Right under my heart! You're going to get it from me and good, hold on there! *(She grabs him by the arm.)*

Parasha laughs.

What are you laughing at, what's so funny?

PARASHA. I felt like laughing, so I'm laughing.

MATRYONA. You snake! You're a snake! *(Dragging Gavrilo behind, she advances on Parasha. Gavrilo resists.)*

PARASHA. Better not come close if you know what's good for you.

MATRYONA. I'll lock you up, I'll lock you up in the store room. And that's final.

PARASHA. No, it's not final. There's a lot more for you and me to talk about. *(She leaves.)*

MATRYONA. That girl was born a snake! *(To Gavrilo.)* So where did you come from? Have you gone in for bumping people! Look what a mess you are! Looks like you got a beating, but it wasn't enough, that's for sure.

GAVRILO. You think that's a good thing, don't you, beating up people! A lot to be proud of! And do you know why it is they're always beating up people?

MATRYONA. Why is it? Tell me, why?

GAVRILO. It's from ignorance.

MATRYONA. From ignorance? Didn't he beat you enough? Let's go, I'll take you to the master again.

GAVRILO. But what is this, really now! Let me go! *(He tears himself loose.)* As it is, I'd like to drown myself because of you.

MATRYONA. Great! Parasha wants to drown herself too, so the two of you can do it together and get yourselves off our hands.

GAVRILO. Well, I know I'm nothing special, but why take it out on your daughter? Because of you she has no life at all. That's even rather mean on your part.

MATRYONA. You lowdown creature! How dare you talk like that to your mistress?

GAVRILO. You know, it's that ignorance in you that's making you so stormy.

MATRYONA. Shut up! I'm going to take away all your rights right now.

GAVRILO. What rights? I don't have any. And why should I shut up? I'll shout all over town that you're a tyrant with your stepdaughter. Put that in your pipe and smoke it! *(He leaves.)*

Narkis enters.

MATRYONA. Is that you, Narkis?

NARKIS *(churlishly)*. No, it's not me.

MATRYONA. How can you be so rude to me! The mistress desires to have a tender talk with you, she now has such a desire…

NARKIS. Is that so! Anything else?

MATRYONA. You're nothing but an ill-bred peasant.

NARKIS. So I'm a peasant. I don't make myself out to be a gentleman. Just because you took me when I was a coachman and made me into a merchant's assistant and steward, you think just like that I'm one of your gentlemen, how do you like that! But you get me that piece of paper that makes me a nobleman by birth, and then you can ask me for politeness.

MATRYONA. Why do you think in such an impossible way!

NARKIS. Maybe impossible, but that's how I am. I was ignorant, awkward, coarse, and that's how I've stayed. And it doesn't bother me at all because that's the way I like it.

MATRYONA. Why are you so cold with me today?

NARKIS. So I'm cold, that means I'm cold.

MATRYONA. But why?

NARKIS. No special reason. I've heard a lot about pirates.

MATRYONA. What pirates?

NARKIS. They've shown up in our parts... about a hundred and fifty of them. They go about in gangs through the woods and on the water in boats.

MATRYONA. But somebody's lying, they must be!

NARKIS. Who knows, maybe they're lying.

MATRYONA. So what about it? Are you afraid, perhaps?

NARKIS. Now what have you thought up! A lot I need to be afraid!

MATRYONA. What did you come for? Is there something you want?

NARKIS. At the moment I'm in very great need of...

MATRYONA. Of what?

NARKIS. Money.

MATRYONA. What money, what are you talking about!

NARKIS. The ordinary kind, what the government puts out. What did you think, play money? I'm not a child; I don't want to play with it. Give me a thousand rubles.

MATRYONA. You're out of your mind! It was just a little while ago...

NARKIS. Exactly, it was just a little while ago. Only if I'm stating a need, then that means I have a need. Because, since I want to be a merchant quickly, without fail, that means I must have a thousand rubles.

MATRYONA. You're a barbarian, a barbarian!

NARKIS. Exactly so, I'm a barbarian, you're right there. I don't take any pity on you.

MATRYONA. You're robbing me, you know.

NARKIS. And why shouldn't I rob you if I can? Why should I be such a fool to say no to my good luck?

MATRYONA. You're so greedy. Don't you have a lot already?

NARKIS. A lot or not a lot, but if I have this certain desire, then you should hand it over, no point in talking about it. Some joke that would be if I didn't take the money from you.

MATRYONA. Oh you...Merciful God!... what am I going to do with you!

NARKIS. We've had enough of this, it can't be helped! You should have thought about all that before...

MATRYONA. But where can I get you money?

NARKIS. That's not my problem.

MATRYONA. But do some thinking yourself, you blockhead, think!

NARKIS. A lot I need to do that! What's that to do with me! I'm to beat my brains out for you, how do you like that! Let the turkeys think. I've lived all my life without thinking; whatever comes into my head at the moment, that's it.

MATRYONA. You damn bloodsucker! *(She wants to leave.)*

NARKIS. Wait, don't go. I don't want any money. I was just joking.

MATRYONA. That's better.

NARKIS. What I really want is to get married to your stepdaughter, Parasha.

MATRYONA. After that aren't you really a filthy cur?

NARKIS. And along with it money, the dowry, the whole works.

MATRYONA. Ooh! Damn you! Your covetous eyes should be put out.

NARKIS. So do me a big favor and make the wedding soon. Otherwise I'll make a mess you'll never straighten out. Whatever my heart desires let it have! And please, don't keep me waiting. So there you have it, short and sweet! I'm not in the mood to talk with you any more. *(He leaves.)*

MATRYONA. He's bedeviled me, how he's bedeviled me! I've put a noose on my own neck. He's drained my soul right out of my body. My feet can't move. As if lightning struck me! If this girl could only be smashed down by a log somewhere I think I could make a vow to go on a pilgrimage all the way to Kiev.

Parasha comes out.

And where do you think you're running off to?

PARASHA. Go quick. Father's calling you.

MATRYONA. You go first, I'll follow you.

PARASHA. I'm no drummer boy, to march in front of you. *(She comes down from the porch.)*

MATRYONA. What are you aiming to do? You're not going to get your way; I won't let you hang around the yard at night.

PARASHA. Then in that case I'll go out on the street, since you've started the conversation. Even if there's no reason for it, I'll go out there. Go into the house, he's calling you, you've been told.

MATRYONA. Even if I'm torn in two, I'll have my way.

PARASHA. You've tormented me, tormented me to pieces. What do you want from me? *(She steps right up in front of her.)*

MATRYONA. What do you mean, what do I want? My first duty is to keep an eye on you!

PARASHA. Keep an eye on yourself.

MATRYONA. You can't lay down the law to me.

PARASHA. Nor can you lay down the law to me.

MATRYONA. I have to answer to your father for you, you trash...

PARASHA. There's no need for you to imagine what can't be. You don't have to answer for anything, you know that yourself, you're just worked up by hate. Why should it bother you if I take a walk in the yard? After all, I'm not married yet! That's the only fun we girls have, taking a stroll in the summer evening, breathing the open air. Can't you understand, out in the open, my own boss, doing what I please.

MATRYONA. I know why you've come out. It wasn't for nothing that Narkis was talking.

PARASHA. You should be ashamed to bring up Narkis.

MATRYONA. No, there's no…

Voice of Kuroslepov: "Matryona!"

Oh why don't you drop dead! You've worn me out! You're driving me into my grave!

PARASHA. Why are you tyrannizing over me? Even a wild beast in the woods has some feeling. Do you think we girls have an awful lot of freedom? Do I have much time that's my own? The truth is I'm always somebody else's, always owned by somebody else. When I'm young I'm supposed to work for my father and mother, then to get married and be my husband's slave, his absolute slave. So you want me to give you this little bit of freedom that's so precious, so short? You can take everything from me, everything, but I won't give you my freedom… I'll fight for that to the death!

MATRYONA. Oh, she's going to kill me! She'll kill me!

Kuroslepov comes out onto the porch. Silan comes in through the gate.

KUROSLEPOV. Matryona! Why must I keep calling you!

MATRYONA. Calm your daughter, calm her down! She wants to kill me.

PARASHA. You don't have to calm me down, I'm calm enough.

MATRYONA. What a family I've fallen in with, it's like hard labor. I'd have done better to stay an old maid with my father.

KUROSLEPOV. Now she remembers!

MATRYONA. They loved me there, they indulged me, even now they're all concerned about me.

SILAN. Shout louder. Almost the whole town is at the gate; maybe they think it's a fire.

KUROSLEPOV. Take a broom to her!

MATRYONA *(to Silan)*. God help you if you do! What I wouldn't do to you… *(To Kuroslepov.)* You're the one who spoiled your daughter, you! You people have one thing on your mind, you want to ruin me. Order your daughter to give in. I won't move from the spot.

KUROSLEPOV. Praskovya, give in.

PARASHA. But what am I supposed to give in to? I come out for a walk in the yard, and she gets after me. What does she think I am? Why does she disrespect me? I have more honor than she does! It's an insult to me, a bitter insult!

MATRYONA. Answer her, you hairy clown…

KUROSLEPOV. Silanty, I told you to take a broom to her!

MATRYONA. I'll take a broom to you! Tell me, sleepy peepers, is it my job to watch out for her or not?

PARASHA. There's no need to watch out for somebody who can watch out for herself! Don't say words like that to me!

KUROSLEPOV. All right, that's enough! Anyone would think we're at the bazaar! I told you to give in.

PARASHA. You too say, "Give in"? All right then, if that's what you want, I'll give in. *(To Matryona.)* Only here's what I'm going to tell you in my father's presence… it's for the last time, so remember what I said! From now on I'm going to go whenever and wherever I want. And if you try and stop me, I'll show you what it means to take freedom from a single girl. Daddy, you listen! I don't get much chance to talk with you, so I'll tell you right now. You people insulted me, a single girl. My conscience tells me not to quarrel with you, but I don't have enough will power to keep quiet. After this I'll keep quiet a whole year if need be, but this is what I'm going to tell you. Don't try to take away my precious freedom, don't dishonor my reputation, don't set a guard over me! If I want what's good for me, then I'll guard myself, but if you try and watch over me…it's not your place to watch over me! *(She leaves.)*

Kuroslepov, head lowered, follows after her. Matryona, following him, grumbles and curses to herself.

SILAN *(strikes the watchman's metal plate).* Keep watch!

ACT TWO

Decor of Act One. After nine o'clock. Towards the end of the act it is dark on the stage. Gradoboev, Silan, Sidorenko, and Zhigunov enter through the gate.

GRADOBOEV. Tell me, old fool, are the master and mistress still asleep?

SILAN. They must not be; they want supper.

GRADOBOEV. Why so late?

SILAN. They've been quarreling all the time. They cussed each other out for a long time, that's why they're late.

GRADOBOEV. And how is the case coming along?

SILAN. How should I know! Speak with the master.

GRADOBOEV. Sidorenko, Zhigunov, wait for me at the gate.

SIDORENKO and ZHIGUNOV. Yes, sir, Your Honor.

Gradoboev goes off into the house through the porch.

SIDORENKO *(to Silan, giving him a snuff box).* Have some snuff; it's scented with birch.

SILAN. With some ashes?

SIDORENKO. A little.

SILAN. And crushed glass?

SIDORENKO. I put in some, in proportion.

SILAN. But why should I take snuff, why take it, my friend? I've gotten old; nothing affects me, it doesn't get to me. Now if you could just put in more glass to give it some strength… shake a man up, that would be something! No, to get my spirits high it's got to reach my brain.

They go off through the gate. Parasha comes down from the porch.

PARASHA. It's quiet… nobody… And how my heart is yearning. Vasya's probably not around. There's nobody I can while away an hour with, nobody to warm my heart! *(She sits down under the tree.)* I'll sit down and think about how some live free, happy. And are there many of those happy ones? Even if there's not happiness, but just to live like human beings… There's a star falling. Where to? And where's my star, what's going to happen to it? Must I keep on putting up with things? Where does a person get the strength to put up with it all! *(She becomes pensive and then starts to sing.)*

> O thou freedom, mine so dear,
> Freedom dear, a maiden girl—
> The maid through market strolled.[6]

Vasya and Gavrilo enter.

GAVRILO. Did you come out for a walk?

PARASHA. For a walk, Gavryusha. It's stifling in the house.

GAVRILO. Right now's the best time to take a walk, Miss, and for talking with girls this is the most pleasant time for the heart. That's the way it is, Miss. It's like some kind of daydream or a dream of magic. From what I observe, Miss, you, Praskovya Pavlinovna, don't care to love me?

PARASHA. Listen, Gavryusha, you know a person can get fed up with all this! How many times have you asked me! You know I love somebody else, so why?

GAVRILO. That's so, Miss. I suppose even in the future I shouldn't have any hopes.

PARASHA. What's going to be in the future, my dear, only God knows. Is my heart really free? It's just that while I love Vasya there's no point in making a nuisance of yourself. You'd do better to keep an eye out that nobody comes. I want to have a talk with him…

GAVRILO. That's something I can easily do, Miss. Because from my feeling heart, if only in this little thing, I want to be pleasant to you. *(He goes off.)*

PARASHA. That's a good man! *(To Vasya.)* Vasya, when?

VASYA. Daddy's business is in rack and ruin.

PARASHA. I know. But after all, you're alive. We can live, that's all we need.

VASYA. That's true enough…

PARASHA. So what about it then? You know in our town there's an old custom of carrying off brides.[7] Of course, it's mostly done with the parents' consent, but a lot get carried off even without any consent. People have gotten used to it; there won't be any talk. There's only one thing bad, my father probably won't give us any money.

VASYA. Well, there you are!

PARASHA. But what's so important about that, my dear! You have hands; I have hands.

VASYA. I'd better get up my courage and come some time to bow down to your father.

PARASHA. Vasya, darling, I don't have much patience.

VASYA. But how would it be, really. Judge for yourself.

PARASHA. You're free to go about, but just think, darling, of the things I have to put up with. I'm telling you right out, I don't have the patience, I don't have it!

VASYA. Just a little more, Parasha. Put up with it a little more for me.

PARASHA. Vasya, what I said wasn't any joke, understand that! You can see, I'm trembling all over. When I say I lack patience, that means I won't have it much longer.

VASYA. Enough now! What are you trying to do, scare me!

PARASHA. A lot you're scared! You've gotten scared at my words, but if you could only look into my soul and see what's there! It's black there, Vasya, black. Do you know what goes on in a person's soul when patience is at an end? *(Almost in a whisper.)* Do you know what that is, my boy, the end, the end to one's patience?

VASYA. But my God!… What can I do! Don't you think I'm sorry?

PARASHA *(squeezes up to him).* Then hold me, hold me tight, don't let me go. The end to patience is either the water or the noose.

VASYA. There there now. As soon as our business affairs get a bit better then I'll go straight to your father. And if that doesn't work out we'll go ahead without his consent.

PARASHA. But when, when? Say the day! I'll stop living till that day. I'll make my heart die; I'll squeeze it with both hands.

VASYA. All that's as God wills. We have some receipts, some old debts, to collect; we have to go to Moscow…

PARASHA. But didn't you hear what I said? Do you think I'm fooling myself, just thinking up things? *(She cries.)*

VASYA. Come now, really! What's the matter with you!

PARASHA. Didn't you hear me at all? Was it just for nothing that I tore my heart from my breast for you? It hurts me so, it hurts! I'm not just babbling nonsense! What kind of man are you anyway? A good-for-nothing, are you? A word and an act, with me they're the same thing. You're leading me on, leading me on, but for me it's a matter of life and death. For me it's unbearable torture, I can't stand it another hour, and you come at me with, "When God wills, and we have to go to Moscow to collect debts!" Either you don't believe me or you were born such no-good trash that you're not worth looking at, let alone loving.

VASYA. But what's gotten into you? All of a sudden...

PARASHA. Oh God, why this punishment! What a boy, what a crybaby I'm stuck with! You talk as if you're being put upon. You look at me as if you're stealing something. Or is it possible you don't love me, that you're deceiving me? It makes me sick to look at you, it only makes me lose heart. *(She wants to go.)*

VASYA. Wait, Parasha, wait!

PARASHA *(stops)*. So then! You've finally decided something. Thank God! It's about time!

VASYA. But why are you going off angry like this? Is that the way to say good-bye? Really now! *(He embraces her.)*

PARASHA. All right, say something. Oh my darling boy!

VASYA. So when can I come see you? We could have a talk, a good talk.

PARASHA *(pushes him away)*. I thought you meant business. You're worse than a girl, get lost! It's clear I have to look out for myself. Never again will I put my hopes in other people. I'll make a pledge, to do whatever I decide for myself. At least I won't have anyone to complain about. *(She goes off into the house.)*

Gavrilo comes up to Vasya.

GAVRILO. Did you get to talk with her?

VASYA *(scratching the nape of his neck)*. I talked with her.

GAVRILO. How pleasant it must be in weather like this, in the evening, to talk with a girl about love! What does a man feel at such a time? I think that it must be like music playing in his soul. As a bystander I was glad you were talking with Praskovya Pavlinovna. How did it go for you?

VASYA. It was all right! She's just a bit angry today.

GAVRILO. Anyone would get angry from the kind of life she has. Just don't cause her any grief! Put me in your place and if she said to me, "Dance, Gavrilo," I'd dance... go to the bottom of the river, I'd go to the bottom. Whatever you want, my dear, whatever you want. Tell me, Vasya, what's the secret? Why do girls love one fellow while they can't love another for anything in the world?

VASYA. The fellow has to look impressive, be handsome.

GAVRILO. Yes, yes, yes. That's it, that's it.

VASYA. That's the first thing. And the second thing is he has to know how to talk.

GAVRILO. What should he talk about, my friend?

VASYA. Anything at all, just so he's free and easy.

GAVRILO. But with me, friend, as soon as I like a girl, right off she becomes dear to me and I start to feel sorry for her. And that's the end for me, all the free and easy talk is gone. Even if a girl has good parents, for some reason or other I'm still sorry for her. But if she has bad parents, then it stands to reason every second my heart aches for her for fear somebody will do her some wrong. And at night I get to thinking that if I got married how much I'd protect my wife. How I'd love her and do everything in the world for her, not just what she'd like but even more, how I'd try to make things pleasant for her in any way I could. That would make me glad because so many of our women are put down and neglected; there isn't any man, even the most worthless, who doesn't consider a woman lower than himself. So I'd manage to make at least one woman happy. And I'd be glad in my heart that at least one woman would be living to her delight without being hurt.

VASYA. What can anyone make of all this? Why are you thinking up such stuff? What will it lead to? I can't make head or tail of it.

GAVRILO. What don't you understand? I've made it all clear to you. But here's the bitter pill I can't swallow. Here I feel the way I do, and I'll end up with some piece of trash, a girl not worth loving, but I'll love her anyway. While scalawags like you get the good ones.

VASYA. Look, do you say this nonsense to the girls or not?

GAVRILO. I started to, my friend, I tried to, only I'm so shy I can't get any of it out right, all I do is mumble something. And then I get all embarrassed…

VASYA. And what kind of answer do they give you?

GAVRILO. What you'd expect, they laugh.

VASYA. And that's because that kind of talk is low and common. You've got to say something inspired. When do you think Parasha fell in love with me? I'll tell you. We had a party one night, only I'd gotten a little drunk the day before, and that morning I'd had an argument with my father, so all day long I'd been in a bad mood. I come to the party, and sit there quiet as if I'm mad and upset by something. Then all of a sudden I take up my guitar, and since I'm feeling so bad from arguing with Daddy, I sing this song with a lot of feeling:

> O raven black, why winds your flight,
> Why o'er my head your plumage soars?
> Upon your prey you'll ne'er alight;
> I'm not your friend, no, I'm not yours!

Just look beyond that bush so green!
Keep watch lest something loudly roars;
My pistol's loaded, barrel's clean!
I'm not your friend, no, I'm not yours![8]

Then I stopped with the guitar and went home. She told me later, "That's when you shot right through my heart!" And it's no wonder because I had some heroism in me. But what is it you're saying? Some kind of gloomy words that aren't interesting at all. But you wait, one of these days I'll teach you how to talk with those girls and what sort of mood to be in. What you're doing now is just a waste of time. Now I've got to find my way out of here! It's no good going past Silan, I'll go over the fence again. Good-bye. *(He goes toward the fence.)*

On the porch appear Kuroslepov, Gradoboev, Matryona, and the maidservant.

GAVRILO. Where are you going! Come back! The master and mistress came out, they'll see you, danger! Let's hide in the bushes till they leave.

They hide in the bushes.

KUROSLEPOV. Serapion Mardaryich, let's you and I have a drink now under the tree. *(To the maidservant.)* Serve us something under the tree.

GRADOBOEV. Let's have a drink under the tree.

MATRYONA. Why can't you two stay still in one place!

KUROSLEPOV *(to his wife)*. Scat, cat, under the bench! *(To Gradoboev.)* So tell me how it was you fought with all those Turks.

GRADOBOEV. The way I fought was very simple. And how many forts we took from them!

MATRYONA. You couldn't be telling lies, maybe?

KUROSLEPOV. Scat cat, I just told you!

MATRYONA. Why do you keep on with that crazy cat business?

KUROSLEPOV. Don't let it get to you, Serapion Mardaryich, God have mercy! Just don't look at her, turn your back on her, let her howl at the wind. So tell me how you took those forts.

GRADOBOEV. We took them with our hands. Your Turk is very brave, but his spirits don't stay up long, and he doesn't understand his military oath, how he's supposed to keep it. So when he stands sentry duty they straightaway chain him to a cannon or something so he won't run away. But when they first come out of the fort that's the time to stay away from them; that's when they each take a glass of opirum.

KUROSLEPOV. Opirum? What's that?

GRADOBOEV. How can I tell you? It's a lot like drying oil. He takes that, and right away he has all kinds of courage. Don't fall in with him then, he'll rip you apart with his teeth. But we found a way to handle them. As soon as they roll out of their fort in one big pile and they start yelling in that lingo of theirs, that's when we beat a retreat. We keep on retreating and leading on those Turks more and more till that courage of theirs wears off, so that after we've led them a long ways all their brave spirit has flown away. Now our Cossacks come riding in from the sides and chop those Turks up. Here is where you can take that Turk with your bare hands, and on the spot he'll yell, "Aman!"

KUROSLEPOV. He doesn't like all that! But what's that "aman" business? What's that for?

GRADOBOEV. It's their word for "mercy."

MATRYONA. You say "mercy," but I've heard that some don't show any mercy at all.

GRADOBOEV. You've heard the ring of a bell, but you don't know where it is.

KUROSLEPOV. Do me a favor, don't encourage her bad habits. Don't listen to her, let her talk to herself. If you give her a bit to latch onto you'll regret it the rest of your life. All right, so here we are now after that battle with the Turks, and we can have a drink.

GRADOBOEV. It's the usual thing!

They sit down and pour their drinks.

That's the kind of police chief I am! I tell you about those Turks, I drink vodka with you, I look at all your ignorance and don't make anything of it. So then, am I not like a father to you, what do you say?

KUROSLEPOV. No question about it.

MATRYONA. Wouldn't you like some pie? Eat it and enjoy it, Scorpion Mardaryich.

GRADOBOEV. Oh merciful God, where did you get that Scorpion! You're the scorpion, I'm Serapion.

MATRYONA. Why take it out on me? I didn't christen you! Is it my fault, what they named you? No matter how I twist my tongue it always comes out that same old scorpion.

GRADOBOEV. Look, dear lady, I think it would be a good thing if you go take a look at what's going on in the house. It's a lot better when you see to things yourself.

MATRYONA. Stop trying to play the devil's tricks on me! I'm no stupider than you even if I haven't been in Turkey land. I can see you want to drive me away, so now I'm going to stay.

KUROSLEPOV. Don't pay any attention to her! What's the attraction! I don't understand it... Talking with a woman is the worst thing you can do. If only I didn't have this money business! Drink up.

They drink.

GRADOBOEV. So what about that money of yours? What are you going to do about it?

KUROSLEPOV. No use crying over spilt milk.

GRADOBOEV. Where did you keep the money?

KUROSLEPOV. I kept it in the closet, it's so dark in there. Besides me and the wife nobody ever goes there.

GRADOBOEV. There's nobody you suspect?

KUROSLEPOV. Why sin? I don't suspect anyone.

GRADOBOEV. Well, we've got to have some interrogating.

MATRYONA. Of course, how could you do without your in terror hating!

GRADOBOEV. Has to be done.

MATRYONA. And I'm supposed to let you carry on your disgraces in my home.

GRADOBOEV. It's not likely we'll ask your permission.

MATRYONA. I know why you need that in terror hating, what it's all for.

GRADOBOEV. Of course you know, a smart woman like you. I have to justify myself or people might say there's been a robbery in the town and the chief of police didn't do a thing about it.

MATRYONA. Really! It's not for that at all but simply because you're a greedy man.

GRADOBOEV. You don't say!

KUROSLEPOV. Turn your back on her!

MATRYONA. All you get isn't enough for you...

GRADOBOEV. That's true, it isn't enough. You know what kind of salary I get, and I have a family too.

MATRYONA. So I'm right you are a greedy man! You were born a scorpion, and a scorpion you still are.

GRADOBOEV *(tries to frighten her)*. You and I are going to end up quarreling! I warned you not to call me a scorpion! I have the rank of captain, and I've got medals. I'll either fine you for disrespect or throw you in the clink!

KUROSLEPOV. Give it to her good!

MATRYONA. In the clink? Are you in your right mind?

GRADOBOEV. And besides that I'll challenge you to a duel.

MATRYONA. And now you've really frightened me! You can only fight with women! It's no great sin I called you "scorpion." No matter what you're called, you still want money.

KUROSLEPOV. Don't have anything to do with her! For a long time now I haven't talked with her about anything, a very long time because I just can't. All I tell her is: give it here, take it, off you go... nothing more than that.

MATRYONA *(to Gradoboev).* You have your in terror hating, but I have my in terror hating too. I'll lock the gate and let loose the dogs, and then you'll have an in terror hating. What you really ought to do is catch those pirates, and you go on talking about in terror hating...

GRADOBOEV. What pirates?

KUROSLEPOV. Don't pay any attention to her!

MATRYONA. About a hundred and fifty men sailed in from the Bryn woods.[9]

GRADOBOEV. Along the dry shore... And just where did you see them?

KUROSLEPOV. Stop talking to her, better be quiet, or she'll spout such nonsense you'll only be able to calm her down with the fire hose.

GRADOBOEV. You're the one who should stop her.

KUROSLEPOV. I've tried, but that's even worse! There's only one thing to do. Give her free rein, let her jabber away whatever she wants, but don't listen or answer. Then she gets tired and stops.

They drink.

MATRYONA. Those pirates are plundering Christian folk, but some people here can take it easy and drink their vodka.

GRADOBOEV. Where are they plundering? Tell me that! And who's been plundered?

MATRYONA. How should I know? I'm no detective. They're plundering people in the woods.

GRADOBOEV. Then that's not my jurisdiction but the district police inspector's.

KUROSLEPOV. What can you expect from her? I'm telling you it's just impossible to talk with her. You can try if you want, but I guarantee that after half an hour you'll either go out of your mind or start running up the walls. You'll kill somebody, a stranger, a man completely innocent. I'm talking from experience.

GRADOBOEV. So I see it's time to bring you a little gift. It's something I bought in Bessarabia from a Kirghiz Cossack.

KUROSLEPOV. Sounds very nice!

MATRYONA. What new brainstorm is this?

GRADOBOEV. It was braided in the horde, and the handle is mounted in silver with niello decoration. But I won't begrudge it for a friend. And how useful it can be!

MATRYONA. You people are so smart! Your gift is a whip! That whip of yours costs a lot, only there's nobody to whip, because I'm worth more than both of you put together, let alone your whip. Go ahead, bring your whip! We'll take it! It might come in handy to use on some lout of a guest.

GRADOBOEV. Which one of your fences leads onto the open land?

KUROSLEPOV *(pointing)*. That one.

GRADOBOEV. We'll have to measure how far it is from the house.

KUROSLEPOV. What for?

GRADOBOEV. To do things in order.

KUROSLEPOV. In that case, all right.

GRADOBOEV. Let's count the steps, you from the house and me from the fence, then we'll come together. *(He goes off toward the fence.)*

KUROSLEPOV. Here we go. *(He goes off toward the house.)*

MATRYONA. Step away, you two. You're lucky it's dark so nobody will laugh at you.

GRADOBOEV *(comes from the fence)*. One, two, three...

KUROSLEPOV *(comes from the house)*. First, second, third... wait a minute; I'm off course, let's start again.

Each goes back to his former place, and gradually they approach each other.

GRADOBOEV *(stumbling onto Vasya)*. Stop! Who's this? *(He grabs Vasya by the collar.)* Sidorenko! Zhigunov!

KUROSLEPOV *(stumbling onto Gavrilo, who trips him and runs away.)* Oh, he's killed me! Oh, he's killed me! Help! Grab him!

Silan runs in, followed by the two policemen and some laborers.

MATRYONA. Oh, the pirates! Help! They're killing people!

SILAN. Where are they?

MATRYONA. Over there in the bushes. They're killing the master! Oh, help!

GRADOBOEV *(to the policemen)*. Tie him up, twist the cord on him, the robber! So you want to steal, you want to steal, eh? And in my town at that? Oh ho ho!

The policemen tie up Vasya.

SILAN *(grabbing Kuroslepov)*. No, you can sing any tune you want, but this time I've got you! It's my hands you've fallen into! Why should I suffer just because of you and be under suspicion...

KUROSLEPOV. Who do you think you've got, who? It's your master, that's who! Watch what you're doing.

SILAN. None of your tricks! You can't fool me! I'm not getting into trouble because of you.

GRADOBOEV *(to Silan)*. Drag him over here! Somebody get a light!

SILAN *(to a yardkeeper)*. Run into the assistants' room and bring a lantern.

The laborer leaves.

KUROSLEPOV. So you're in cahoots with the robbers! You're against your master, and a relative at that!

MATRYONA. Are there many pirates there?

SILAN. No one'll get away, they're all here. Hold them, brothers. Where did I put my rope? *(He puts his hand into his boot.)*

MATRYONA. All? A hundred and fifty! Help! They'll make mince meat of everyone, and then they'll get to me. *(She falls onto the bench.)*

GRADOBOEV. Tie them up! Oh ho ho! And in my town! You couldn't find another place!

KUROSLEPOV. Hold on, just let me free my hands, you'll get a lot of...

The laborer brings a lantern and puts it on the table.

GRADOBOEV. Bring them here. We'll have the questioning right now. Ooh, am I tired! That's what our work is like! *(He tries to sit down on the bench.)* Now what! Something soft here! A dead body? *(He feels with his hands.)* More trouble! What a life! Not a moment's rest.

MATRYONA. Oh, now they've gotten to me!

GRADOBOEV. Ah, that woman! You again? *(He takes her by the arm.)*

MATRYONA. Whatever you do, don't kill me and don't touch my white body!

GRADOBOEV. All right, a lot anyone would want to do that! Well, I never! Get into the house you, that's an order! *(He stamps his feet.)* What right do you have to interfere with the due process of law? *(He sits down on the bench.)* I'm carrying out my duties, I'll have you arrested right now.

Matryona leaves.

SILAN *(drags Kuroslepov with the help of the other yardkeepers)*. Here we are, Your High... Oh hell! It really is him, it's the master.

KUROSLEPOV. Are you people crazy! *(He tears himself away and grabs Silan by the collar.)* Serapion Mardaryich! Chief of Police! Try him! I beg you, try him right now! *(To Silan.)* You ought to get every punishment in the book because of what you've done to a merchant who's been exalted by society for his donations and his splendor... Your provider too... and you tied his hands in public, that's what you did to me! Now all my honors are as good as nothing...

GRADOBOEV. Don't worry! Nobody's going to get away. Sit down.

SILAN. Who'd have thought it? How do you like that! And you were scolding me for not keeping a good watch! Well, I was doing it, wasn't I? As much as was in me, and it wore me out. And see how unharmed you are! Besides… it wasn't really my fault, it was dark.

GRADOBOEV. All right, you people can straighten that out later. Bring the real thief here.

The policemen bring Vasya.

Who are you?

KUROSLEPOV. Why it's Vasya!

GRADOBOEV. So why, my dear friend, have you gone in for stealing?

KUROSLEPOV. Yes, he has to be the one, because his father's business is ruined…

GRADOBOEV *(to Kuroslepov)*. You want to do the questioning? I haven't been doing my job perhaps? Then you put on my uniform, and I'll put in for retirement.

KUROSLEPOV. All right, you don't have to get mad!

GRADOBOEV *(to Vasya)*. So how about it, dear friend?

VASYA. But please, Serapion Mardaryich! You can't say you don't know me and my father!

GRADOBOEV. Hold on there! You just answer my question. Why is it you've gone in for stealing? Did you take a liking to the trade? Or did you find it very profitable?

VASYA. But please, I, to tell the truth, came to pay a visit, and I naturally wanted to hide from Pavlin Pavlinych, because he always goes after my hair… From childhood up I've never had any desire to steal… Even if it's some little thing, if it's somebody else's, I don't want it.

GRADOBOEV. Are you in this business alone or is somebody in it with you?

VASYA. I don't care what you say, I'm not in this business, sir.

KUROSLEPOV. Really now! What kind of trial is this! Do you expect him to confess? And even if he does, the money's gone! Where does it ever happen, and especially among us, that stolen money's been found! So there's no point in searching and nothing to have a trial about.

GRADOBOEV. No, don't talk like that! You'll answer for it!

KUROSLEPOV. What's there to answer for! You find the money, then I'll answer for it.

GRADOBOEV. Don't get me worked up! Don't aggravate me! If I set out to find that money, I'll find it. Now you've touched me to the quick.

KUROSLEPOV. Go on, look for it! If you find it, you'll be right, and I'll be wrong. But what we can do is just send him off as an army recruit from the commune. He and his father are ruined in business, so he's loitering around with no work… so that's the end of the matter. We'll send him off this week, but meanwhile he can stay in jail as a suspect.

GRADOBOEV. Good enough. He can stay there meanwhile. *(To the policemen.)* Take him off to jail.

VASYA. But please, what for!

GRADOBOEV. March! No back talk!

The policemen take Vasya away.

KUROSLEPOV. You should pray more… *(To the workers.)* Go back to where you belong, why are you standing there with your mouths open!

Silan and the workers leave.

GRADOBOEV. Do you think someone else was in on it with him?

KUROSLEPOV. Probably one of my own people. I'd say Gavrilka! Well, I can settle with him myself.

GRADOBOEV. So the business is all finished?

KUROSLEPOV. All finished.

GRADOBOEV. Well!

KUROSLEPOV. Well what?

GRADOBOEV. If the business is all finished, what comes next?

KUROSLEPOV. What?

GRADOBOEV. Merci.

KUROSLEPOV. What's that merci?

GRADOBOEV. You don't know? That means "I humbly thank you." Understand now? Do you really think I should go looking for that money of yours for nothing?

KUROSLEPOV. But you didn't find it.

GRADOBOEV. You want me to find it yet! If I had found it, I wouldn't be talking to you this way. Do you think I'm a little boy, to go about nights catching robbers at the risk of my life! I'm a man who was wounded!

KUROSLEPOV. But after all, you just happened to be coming by and dropped in for a drink of vodka.

GRADOBOEV. Vodka is vodka, and friendship is friendship, but don't you lose sight of proper order! You know you wouldn't sell anything without a profit. Well then, I've worked out my own system of getting a benefit from each case. So you give me a benefit! If I indulge you, the others will take liberties too. You eat, and I want to eat too.

KUROSLEPOV. Well, all right then, maybe tomorrow…

GRADOBOEV. Feel welcome to drop in for a cup of tea, only make it early.

KUROSLEPOV. All right, I'll drop in.

GRADOBOEV *(gives him his hand.)* So long. Send Silan to me tomorrow. I have to question him. *(He leaves.)*

KUROSLEPOV *(loudly).* Gavrilka!

Gavrilo sings loudly by the window: "Neither Papa, neither Mama."

You're off-key, you can't fool me! Gavrilka!

Gavrilo enters.

GAVRILO. If you're going to grab me by the hair again, then you might as well fire me!

KUROSLEPOV. In fact I'll fire you right now. Silanty! Silanty! Hey!

Silan enters.

Throw his trunk out on the street, and throw him out too.

GAVRILO. But where can I go at night?

KUROSLEPOV. What's that to do with me! My house isn't a home of charity for undeserving people. If you don't know how to live, then off you go, good riddance.

GAVRILO. But you owe me a hundred and fifty rubles in back wages.

KUROSLEPOV. Big deal, a hundred and fifty rubles; I've lost two thousand. A hundred and fifty! Or do you want to go to prison?

GAVRILO. But what's going on? I'm a poor man!

KUROSLEPOV. It's exactly the poor people who steal.

GAVRILO. Give me my money! I don't want to die from hunger.

KUROSLEPOV. Try and get it from me. Oh, these damn people! Here I wanted to have supper, but now I don't feel like it any more. And he talks about dying from hunger... and a hundred and fifty rubles! I wouldn't let you give me a thousand rubles for this confusion. Come with me, Silanty, I'll give you his papers. *(To Gavrilo.)* You stay here and you'll end up in prison. *(He goes off with Silan.)*

GAVRILO. What a bolt from the blue! Oh Gavrilka, where can you go now! Wherever you show up they'll say you were kicked out for stealing. It's shame on my poor head! I've lost everything and been slandered too. What can I do now? A straight line, out the gate and into the water. Right to the bottom, up come the bubbles. Oh, oh, oh!

(Silan comes out.)

SILAN. There's your papers. You're free as a Cossack now. Myself, I think it's for the best. Want me to gather your belongings for you?

GAVRILO. Please, get them for me, friend. I don't have much stuff, it can go into one bundle; right now I feel helpless. But don't forget the guitar. I'll sit on this pile while I wait.

Silan leaves. Gavrilo sits down on a pile. Parasha comes out.

PARASHA. Daddy's carrying on something fierce. What terrible thing happened to you?

GAVRILO. I can't make it out. I've been fired altogether.

PARASHA. What do you mean, altogether?

GAVRILO. By altogether I mean that I don't have a kopeck. All that work for nothing, and I'm off to the four winds.

PARASHA. You poor boy!

GAVRILO. Even so it's not too bad for me, but they're sending Vasya into the army.

PARASHA *(with horror).* The army?

GAVRILO. He's in jail now, but in a few days they'll send him off.

PARASHA. No! What did you say! Because of me they'll make him a soldier?

GAVRILO. It's not because of you but because they found him here in the yard and falsely supposed he's the thief, that he'd stolen that money.

PARASHA. But it's all the same, the same thing, because it was for me he came here. Because he loves me! Oh Lord! How awful! He came to see me, and so they're sending him into the army, away from his father and away from me. His old father will be left all alone, and they're driving Vasya away, driving him away! *(She cries out.)* Oh how miserable I am! *(She grabs her head.)* Gavrilo, stay here, wait for me a minute. *(She runs off.)*

GAVRILO. Where's she going? What's the matter with her? Poor girl, the poor thing! Here she is with her father and mother, but she's just like an orphan! She always has to look out for herself. There's nobody to sympathize with her in her orphan maiden grief. How could a man not love her! Oh how it all hurts; my tears are choking me. *(He cries.)*

Silan comes out with a bundle and guitar.

SILAN. Here's your hat. *(He puts it on him.)* Here's your bundle, and here's your guitar. And so, my friend, good-bye. Don't think badly of me; think well of me.

Parasha comes out in a cloak and with a kerchief on her head.

PARASHA. Let's go, let's go.

GAVRILO. Where, where are you going? What is this!

PARASHA. To him, Gavrilushka, to my dear boy.

GAVRILO. But you know he's in jail. How can you, what are you doing!

PARASHA. I have some money, look! I'll give it to the guards, and they'll let me pass.

GAVRILO. You can do that in the morning, but where are you going to spend the night? *(He bows down at her feet.)* Stay here, my dear girl, stay here.

PARASHA. I'll spend the night with my godmother. Let's go! Let's go! There's nothing to discuss.

SILAN *(to Parasha).* You want to see him beyond the gate, is that it? All right, see him there. That's a kind thing to do. He's all alone in the world.

PARASHA *(turning toward the house, she looks at it silently for some time).* Good-bye, home of my childhood! How many tears I've shed here. Good Lord, how many tears! And now you'd think at least one little tear would drop, for after all I was born here, and it was here I grew up... It wasn't long ago I was a child, and then I thought there was nothing in the world nicer than you, my home, but now I don't care whether I ever see you again. You can go to the devil, my maiden prison! *(She runs off, Gavrilo following.)*

SILAN. Wait! Where are you going? *(He makes a gesture of helplessness.)* It's none of my business! *(He locks the gate.)* What a life! Nothing but punishment! *(He strikes the watchman's metal plate.)*

ACT THREE

Square at the town exit. To the left of the audience is the police chief's house with a porch. To its right is a jail with iron bars in the windows; at its gate an invalid soldier stands guard. Straight ahead is the river and a dock, beyond which is a rural view.

Aristarkh is sitting on the dock, fishing with a rod. Silan approaches and looks on silently. A crowd stands near the porch of the police chief's house.

ARISTARKH *(not noticing Silan).* Just see how clever he is, oh, he's the sly one! But you just wait, I'll outsmart you yet. *(He takes out the rod and adjusts the hook.)* You're tricky, but I'm trickier. A fish is tricky, but man is very wise, by God's will... *(He casts the line.)* To man such cleverness was given that he is master of everything, what's on land and beneath the land and in the waters... Come here! *(He pulls up the rod.)* What? You got caught? *(He takes the fish off the hook and puts it into a fish pond.)*

SILAN. That's the way to catch them!

ARISTARKH *(turning around).* Greetings, Silanty!

SILAN. When you cast a spell like that... really... You know a lot of all that spell business, but I don't know it yet, so I don't catch the fish.

ARISTARKH. What spell?

SILAN. It's a prayer, they say, or something, some kind of words. I've heard them, but didn't understand. But the fish come when they hear them.

ARISTARKH. No, Silanty, what spells! I was just talking to myself.

SILAN. So what! If you know the right words, that makes it even better... It's like prayers... You say the words with nothing special in mind.

ARISTARKH. Did you come to do some fishing too?

SILAN. Fishing! I'm here to see the chief of police.

ARISTARKH. What for?

SILAN. At home everything's an awful mess. It's as though Khan Mamay passed through... Some money's disappeared... that's the first thing. Then your god-daughter's run off.

ARISTARKH. That's not surprising! Anyone would want to leave there. Where'd she go?

SILAN. She's with her godmother, I dropped in there. She told me not to let her father know... As if I'd want to do that.

ARISTARKH. But what about the money? Who could have taken it?

SILAN. You tell me! That thief committed one sin, but our master has committed ten; how many people he's slandered! He kicked out Gavrilo, and right now Vasya Shustry is being held in jail awhile.

ARISTARKH. In jail? No! That's a sin!

SILAN. Sin is right... They've committed more sins than there's grains of sand on the seashore.

ARISTARKH. So what's to be done? We've got to get Vasya out of this. Who got him in jail? The master?

SILAN. The master! He has the power, so he can do crazy things. Has the chief of police waked up yet?

ARISTARKH. Go find out.

SILAN. Why go? He'll come out on the porch himself. He sits on the porch all day, looking at the road. And what a sharp eye he has for anybody without papers! Even if you had a hundred men all bunched up together, right away he'd look at his man and wave him over: "You just come here, my dear friend!" That's the way things are here. *(He scratches the back of his head.)* But I suppose I'd better go. *(He goes toward the police chief's house.)*

ARISTARKH. What goings-on in our town! What inhabitants! They might as well be Samoyeds! But even the Samoyeds must have better manners. What a crazy state of affairs! Oh my! God bless us! *(He casts the rod.)*

Gradoboev comes out in his dressing gown. He has on a military cap, holds a cane and a pipe. Sidorenko is with him.

GRADOBOEV *(sitting down on the porch steps).* "To God above it's high, our Tsar on earth's not nigh." Have I spoken the truth?

VOICES. Yes, Serapion Mardaryich! Yes, Your Honor!

GRADOBOEV. But I am near to you, and that means I'm your judge.

VOICES. Yes, Your Honor! That's true, Serapion Mardaryich.

GRADOBOEV. So then, how do you think I should try you now? If I should try you by the laws...

FIRST VOICE. No, why do that, Serapion Mardaryich!

GRADOBOEV. You speak when you're asked, and if you start interrupting, I'll give it to you with the cane. So, if I should try you by the laws, then we have a lot of laws... Sidorenko, show them how many laws we have.

Sidorenko goes off and returns quickly with a whole armful of books.

That's how many laws! That's just what I have, but there's a lot more in other places! Sidorenko, put them back in their place.

Sidorenko goes off.

And the laws are all strict. In one book they're strict, in another stricter yet, and in the last strictest of all.

VOICES. That's true, Your Honor, exactly so.

GRADOBOEV. So, my dear friends, what do you want? Should I try you by the laws or the way I like, as God puts it in my heart?

Sidorenko returns.

VOICES. Judge as you like; be a father to us, Serapion Mardaryich.

GRADOBOEV. All right, fine. Only don't make any complaint, for if you do make a complaint... Well, then...

VOICES. We won't, Your Honor.

GRADOBOEV *(to Zhigunov).* Are there any prisoners?

ZHIGUNOV. We picked some up last night, Your Honor... for disorderly conduct... two tailors, a shoemaker, seven factory workers, a clerk, and a merchant's son.

GRADOBOEV. Lock up the merchant's son in the store room and tell his father to come and get him out and bring the ransom. Let the clerk go, and as for the others... Do we have any work to be done in the vegetable garden?

ZHIGUNOV. Yes. We need two men.

GRADOBOEV. Then pick out the two healthiest-looking ones and pack them off to the garden. The others can go back to jail; we'll decide about them later.

Zhigunov goes off with the prisoners.

Do we have any other cases? Come up one at a time.

FIRST MIDDLE-CLASS CITIZEN. Here's some money for your Honor, on a promissory note.

GRADOBOEV. Fine, very good, one business off my shoulder. Sidorenko, put it in the table drawer. *(He gives the money to Sidorenko.)*

SIDORENKO. We have a lot of this money piled up, Your Honor. Shouldn't we send it off in the mail?

GRADOBOEV. Send it off! What new fashion is that! It's our job to collect it, and we've collected it. If somebody needs that money, then let him come himself for it, and we'll give it to him. And you want us to send it, Russia's a big country! And if a man doesn't come for it, that means he doesn't need it very much.

The second middle-class citizen comes up.

What do you want?

SECOND MIDDLE-CLASS CITIZEN. This is a promissory note. The man won't pay.

GRADOBOEV *(taking the promissory note)*. Sidorenko, stick it behind the mirror.

Sidorenko goes off.

SECOND MIDDLE-CLASS CITIZEN. How come you're sticking it behind the mirror?

GRADOBOEV. And where else should I put it? Do you want me to frame it? Yours isn't the only one I have there. There's about thirty of those promissory notes stuck there. If sometime I run into your debtor I'll tell him to pay up.

SECOND MIDDLE-CLASS CITIZEN. But if he...

GRADOBOEV. But if he... but if you give me any more of your lip, then you'll see. *(He shows his cane.)* Clear out! *(Catching sight of the third middle-class citizen)* So, my dear friend, you're here! Debts to pay, you don't have money, but for getting drunk you do. The promissory note against you has been stuck there behind the mirror going into the second year now. It got moldy a long time ago, but you keep on getting drunk. Go into the entry and wait. I'm going to put a promissory note on your back, and I'll take out a payment with my cane.

THIRD MIDDLE-CLASS CITIZEN. Show God's mercy, Your Honor! You know our means... show mercy!

GRADOBOEV. So be it, I'll show you mercy, beat it! *(Noticing Silan.)* Hey, you there! Follow me inside. You and I'll have a long conversation. *(To the others.)* Well, God go with you. I don't have the time to try you now. Anyone who has to, come back tomorrow. *(He goes off with Silan.)*

All disperse. Gavrilo enters with a cloth sack on his shoulder.

ARISTARKH. Ah! The man who was kicked out. Hello!

GAVRILO. So you heard?

ARISTARKH. I heard.

GAVRILO. Where is righteousness?

ARISTARKH. You really don't know? Lift up your head.

Gavrilo lifts his head.

That's where it is.

GAVRILO. I know. But where should we look for justice?

ARISTARKH. Justice is over there! *(He points to the police chief's house.)*

GAVRILO. But what if I want true justice?

ARISTARKH. If it's true justice you want, then wait. There'll be true justice too.

GAVRILO. Will it come soon?

ARISTARKH. Well, not too soon, but when it comes it'll be good. It'll judge everybody, the judges and the judged, those who gave an unjust judgment and those who didn't give any.

GAVRILO. I know what it is you're talking about.

ARISTARKH. So you know, why ask? Are you wearing that sack or going on a trip?

GAVRILO. I'm going on a pilgrimage.

ARISTARKH. A pleasant trip! Where to?

GAVRILO. To a hermitage.

ARISTARKH. Alone?

GAVRILO. No, there's a lot of us, and your goddaughter too.

ARISTARKH. The one who ran away? They must be looking for her at home.

GAVRILO. No, her godmother sent word that they'd gone off on a pilgrimage and not to look for her. And who's going to cry for her over there? Her stepmother will be glad she's gone, and it won't make any difference to her father since he's lost all understanding. He won't give me my back pay, a hundred and fifty rubles.

The chief of police and Silan come down from the porch.

GRADOBOEV. I'll go crazy with this damn business; I can't sleep nights now. It's as if somebody stuck a nail in my head. But I'll get to the bottom of it. *(To Silan.)* Now you just speak some sense, you dummy!

SILAN. I won't say a thing, so there. It would be a great sin. This is a mixed-up business! Yes! Mixed up! Terribly mixed up!

GRADOBOEV. Well, and the master, before Vasily, did he suspect anybody then?

SILAN. His eyes were bloated, I say, bloated, all dimmed over. He can't see what's real, and because of his craziness, he just spouts nonsense.

GRADOBOEV. I'll take you in hand. I'll put you in prison.

SILAN. Just look! He's thought and thought, and come up with something new. All from a great mind!

GRADOBOEV. Who do you think you're being insolent with! You watch out who you're being insolent with!

SILAN. This is all stupid and has nothing to do with anything.

GRADOBOEV. I can see you haven't been in jail for a long time.

SILAN. Because that's not where I belong.

GRADOBOEV. Be quiet!

SILAN. I'm quiet.

GRADOBOEV. I'll make you talk, brother! *(Advancing on him)*. Who stole it?

SILAN. If you try to scare me… then I don't know a thing… that's what I'll say over and over again… You can burn me with fire… So that's how it is. I'm telling you, you can look for an answer from a stone quicker than from me.

GRADOBOEV. You people are all barbarians! But you're sure it wasn't Vaska?

SILAN. How should I know? Vaska is small fry, you can pester him any way you want, but all the same, he has a soul, it has feelings.

GRADOBOEV. And it wasn't Gavrilka either?

SILAN. That again is not my business. Gavrilka is an honest man no matter how you twist him. And do you think he has a miserable penny to his name? Not at all! But compared to some others he has a conscience… He has enough of that.

GRADOBOEV. So, then it comes down to you?

SILAN. To me? I don't know a thing, that's the long and short of it!

GRADOBOEV. All right then, to prison you go. There's no point in talking with you any more.

SILAN. Even if you put me in prison it won't change anything. So there… *(Decisively.)* I don't know a thing… How could you try to scare me, an old man!

GRADOBOEV *(running up to him and showing his fists)*. But I'm not trying to scare you. I'm using tenderness with you, do you understand, tenderness.

SILAN. But even with tenderness…

GRADOBOEV. You know, if you help me, I'll seal the deal with something nice… say, ten or fifteen rubles.

SILAN. It would be easier for you to get a stone priest to give you iron communion wafers than…

GRADOBOEV. Not another word, you scoundrel! Show respect for the town's chief official.

SILAN. What do you mean, respect? I'm showing it, my hat's off.

GRADOBOEV. Listen! *(He whispers into Silan's ear.)*

SILAN. Yes!

GRADOBOEV. Often?

SILAN. Almost every night.

GRADOBOEV. Well, listen. *(He whispers.)* You give the sign right away. Shout.

SILAN. I'll do it!

GRADOBOEV. Only not a word to anyone or you'll hear from me!

SILAN. All right…

GRADOBOEV. So go!

SILAN. Good-bye. *(He leaves.)*

Gavrilo approaches.

GRADOBOEV *(seeing Gavrilo)*. And what are you doing here, my dear friend, loitering?

GAVRILO. Your Honor, I don't have a job any more, sir.

GRADOBOEV. That's bad. It's the man without a job who ends up a scoundrel.

GAVRILO. Serapion Mardaryich, none of this is my fault. And it isn't just that I don't have a job; I don't have a single kopeck.

GRADOBOEV. That's even worse! Now you and I have an extra sorrow. My friend, I'll have to look after you as if you're my own son.

GAVRILO. Don't abandon me.

GRADOBOEV. I won't abandon you. I'll keep both eyes peeled on you so you won't steal a thing. For it's when a man doesn't have a kopeck in his pocket that he looks at other men's goods, that's when his hands itch. And people like that are dear to my heart.

GAVRILO. What do I want with other people's goods! It's my very own that's not being given me.

GRADOBOEV. Not being given?

GAVRILO. The master kicked me out but didn't pay me.

GRADOBOEV. He kicked you out? The robber! So what do you want me to do with him at this point?

GAVRILO. Show God's mercy to me.

GRADOBOEV. I'll do it. You wait till your master comes and ask him for a settlement in my presence. Then I'll get satisfaction from him.

GAVRILO. And will that turn out good for me, Your Honor?

GRADOBOEV. I don't know, my friend. Here's what I think will happen. The master will curse you out, but you'll insist. Then he'll give you a good thrashing, and I'll add to it.

GAVRILO. Then how can I get the money from him, Your Honor?

GRADOBOEV. What does that have to do with me? Any way you want!

GAVRILO. So I'm supposed to die of hunger?

GRADOBOEV. So you're supposed to die. But who knows, maybe he'll give it to you.

GAVRILO. No, he won't give it. Not unless you order him to.

GRADOBOEV. Order him to! But first think of this, whether you're such a high and mighty bird that for your sake I should have a quarrel with your master. I'm not about to grab him by the collar or reprimand him with the cane, the way I do with you. If I go and intercede for some merchant's assistant what will all the masters say! The assistants aren't going to send me any flour, or any oats for my horses. Are you assistants going to feed me? So, hasn't your desire to go to court just passed away? If it hasn't, you just wait, my friend, you just wait!

GAVRILO. I think I'd better…

GRADOBOEV. Exactly, you'd better… get going, and quick, or else I'll give orders to detain you.

GAVRILO (stepping away and bowing). I'm going…

GRADOBOEV. Go!

Gavrilo goes off quickly.

Stop him! Ha-ha-ha!

Gavrilo runs away and hides behind a corner.

Ah, work, work! Now for the sake of order I've got to go down to the market! (He shouts.) Sidorenko!

Sidorenko appears in the doorway.

SIDORENKO. Would you like something, Your Honor?

GRADOBOEV. Bring a sack and catch up with me. I'm going to the market. (He leaves.)

Sidorenko runs after him with a sack. Gavrilo and Parasha enter. She is dressed as a pilgrim. Aristarkh goes up to her.

ARISTARKH. Why, my beauty, are you wandering about town?

PARASHA. Godfather, how could I get to see Vasya?

ARISTARKH. Why bother with him? Leave him alone!

PARASHA. No, Godfather, that's impossible. It's because of me he's there, but he's innocent. I'll tell you the whole mess right away; I don't have to feel ashamed with you. He came to see me, but they took him for a thief.

ARISTARKH. I see! Yes, it's a bad business all right! But you're the daughter of a rich father; probably somebody would take notice.

PARASHA. It doesn't matter! They won't recognize me. You see how I'm dressed and I'll cover my face with my kerchief. And even if they do recognize me, what's the harm! I'm not a rich father's daughter any more; now, Godfather, I'm a soldier's wife.

ARISTARKH. What's that, what did you say? Wife of a soldier?

PARASHA. That's right! *(She undoes the bundle in the kerchief.)* I'll marry him for sure in a few days, and if somebody stops me, then I declare ahead of time that I'll do something shameful, I'll go off to him in the barracks. *(She gives him money.)* Here, take this money and give it to the soldiers on guard.

ARISTARKH. Are you out of your mind! Good heavens!

PARASHA. But what's the matter! What are you afraid of? Am I not responsible for myself? Don't be afraid! Why! My conscience is compelling me so this must be necessary. People have treated him badly, taken everything from him, everything... separated him from his father. Really! He loves me, and this might be all he has left in the world, so why should I take this last joy from him? Why should I be proud before him? Is he worse than I am? In any case, I wouldn't stay single, you know that. They'd marry me off, Godfather. Do you think it would be easier for me to try and please some drunken merchant against my will? Not only wouldn't I want to, but I even think I could murder him with a knife! But here there's no sin, it's for love.

ARISTARKH. Well, I can see nobody's going to outargue you. What can anyone do with you! But what do I need with your money? I have money of my own, and you may need yours. *(He gives back the money and goes off into the jail.)*

GAVRILO *(putting his sack onto his shoulders).* Are we going to set off soon?

PARASHA. As soon as I get to see Vasya.

GAVRILO. All right, you two see each other. Aristarkh and I'll keep watch so nobody sees you.

Aristarkh comes out.

ARISTARKH. The prisoners are going for water now, and they're going to let him out with them.

Two prisoners come out carrying a tub, and they pass by on their way to the river. Behind them come Vasya and a soldier. Aristarkh and Gavrilo go off to the dock.

PARASHA *(bows).* Hello, Vasya.

VASYA *(completely overwhelmed).* How did you get here? Oh God! This makes it even harder for me! *(He wipes away tears.)*

PARASHA. It's all right, Vasya, it's all right! Don't cry! *(She embraces him.)* I left home for good, now I can be with you the rest of my life. However you live, I'll live.

VASYA. How can that be?

PARASHA. I'll marry you, we'll get married... it's all right, don't cry... He's my husband, I'll say, I can't be separated from him, I'll say... don't pull us apart, I'll say, you'll do better to give us a church wedding.

VASYA. Thank you! *(He kisses her.)*

PARASHA. Well, that's settled. Now let's talk about our life, Vasya, my darling Vasya!

VASYA. Let's talk about it.

PARASHA *(squeezing up to him)*. In the army they'll beat you a lot.

VASYA. I'll try hard.

PARASHA. Try, Vasya, try! And here's what to do. As soon as you've gotten all your training and been transferred from the recruits to a regiment and you're a real soldier, then you ask the chief himself, whoever's the most important, to send you to the Caucasus and straight into combat!

VASYA. What for?

PARASHA. And you try to kill as many as you can, as many of the enemy as you can. Don't spare yourself at all!

VASYA. But what if I'm the one to get...

PARASHA. Well, all right, we all have to die sometime. At least I'd have something to cry about. I'd have real grief then, a most solemn grief. But you just stop and think. If you don't ask for combat duty and they transfer you to garrison duty, you'll start getting spoiled... you'll steal from the vegetable gardens... what kind of life would I have then? The worst of all. It wouldn't be grief, but it wouldn't be happiness either; it would be a low and vile life. My heart would be in anguish just looking at you.

VASYA. I imagine they'll send me to the guards, to St. Petersburg.

PARASHA. All right, fine, still combat duty would be better. Just imagine. If God helps you, they'll promote you for your bravery to officer, and you'll get a leave. You and I'll come to this very town, and we'll walk around arm in arm. Then let these villains take a look at us. *(She embraces him.)* Eh, Vasya? Maybe you and I, to make up for all our trouble, will live to see such joy.

VASYA. Why not, what's so surprising, if a man has courage...

PARASHA. So, Vasya, I'm going to a hermitage now, and I'll pray to God for you. I'll pray all day, Vasyenka, all day long that God grant us everything you and I have thought of. Could my sinful prayer really not reach Him? Where could I go then? People are treating me badly... *(She cries.)* Here's what, Vasya. I'll come see you tomorrow. I'm living with my godmother now, and I won't go back home for anything! As soon as I stepped over the threshold, could you believe it, I felt I'd rather go through fire than go back there. When I'm there

I feel cold, as if there's no light and there's somebody to hurt you in every corner, it's as if I'm being cursed there forever and ever, and I'm full of anguish. It's just as if I'd been thrown into a pit, a pit. *(She becomes pensive.)* But never mind, Vasya, you take courage and get ahead of those others...

SOLDIER. Hey, you! It's not permitted to talk with prisoners.

VASYA. Just a minute, soldier, just a little bit longer. *(To Parasha.)* You seem like some angel from heaven now...

PARASHA. So, my dear, good-bye for now.

VASYA *(kisses her)*. Good-bye. *(He kisses her.)*

Parasha goes off and bows from afar. Vasya goes toward the gate with the soldier.

PARASHA *(to the soldier)*. Oh wait, soldier, wait!

The soldier and Vasya stop.

Vasya, here is a little money for you, even if it's just to buy a little loaf of bread. Good-bye, darling.

VASYA. But that's enough now!

SOLDIER. Let's go! What do you think this is! It's not permitted!

PARASHA. All right, God be with you!

Vasya and the soldier go off. Parasha looks after him for some time.

Wait, soldier, wait!

Aristarkh and Gavrilo approach.

GAVRILO. Let's go quickly. The pilgrims have just left town.

PARASHA. Stay away from me! *(She walks to the jail, looks at the windows, then sits down on the bench by the gate and sings.)*

> I see my friend off far away,
> A man exiled he's gone to stay.
> I go with him, we both go down
> To stony Moscow, mother town.
> The merchants there at us did stare,
> Who says good-bye, what kind of pair?
> Not brother's sister, husband's mate?
> Or some brave lad's most pretty Kate?[10]

(She wipes away the tears and comes to Gavrilo.) All right, let's go. Don't be mad at me.

GAVRILO *(giving her a staff)*. How could I be! Here's a staff I picked out for you.

PARASHA *(takes the staff)*. I have to start a new life, Gavryusha. And it's hard for me. You can say what you want, Gavryusha, but women don't have the strength of men.

GAVRILO *(through tears)*. There's some carving on the staff. It's very pretty!

ARISTARKH. Go, Parasha, go! The chief of police is coming with your father.

PARASHA. Good-bye, Godfather!

Parasha and Gavrilo leave.

ARISTARKH. She's not my daughter, but I feel so sorry for her, so awfully sorry!

The police chief, Kuroslepov, and Sidorenko enter. Sidorenko has some sacks.

GRADOBOEV *(to Sidorenko)*. Tell them to get some refreshments ready.

Sidorenko goes off.

KUROSLEPOV. You find her for me! That's your first order of business! That's why you're chief of police here.

GRADOBOEV. Don't you teach me. I know my job and why I have it. It wasn't you who made me chief of police, and you have no right to tell me what to do.

KUROSLEPOV. If you're going to let people run away and not pay any attention whatsoever…

GRADOBOEV. What do you mean, run away? She went off on a pilgrimage with her godmother.

KUROSLEPOV. A pilgrimage?

GRADOBOEV. There, you see? I know more about it than you do. That's why I'm chief of police, that's why I've been honored with an official position. But you're a peasant, and it's a peasant you'll stay for ever and ever.

KUROSLEPOV. But how could she go without asking?

GRADOBOEV. Who was there to ask? Her stepmother wouldn't let her go, and you sleep all day. But she has some energy.

KUROSLEPOV. Anyway, when she comes, you send her to me with a guard…

GRADOBOEV. A guard?

KUROSLEPOV. On a rope.

GRADOBOEV. A rope too?

KUROSLEPOV. We'll lock her upstairs so she can't get out.

GRADOBOEV. Just what kind of people are you? Why do you enjoy doing every shameful thing? Others are ashamed of doing shameful things, but for you it's the greatest pleasure. Do you have any understanding of what honor is or not?

KUROSLEPOV. What honor is? I've made my bundle, there's honor for you. The more money you have, the more honor you have.

GRADOBOEV. Well, the peasant will show himself! You're coated with ignorance, like a tree with bark. And that bark couldn't be broken even with a cannon.

KUROSLEPOV. So what!

GRADOBOEV. His daughter, unmarried, and he wants her led by a guard on a rope.

KUROSLEPOV. It's because of… it's for her lack of respect… so she should feel…

ARISTARKH. Poor thing!

KUROSLEPOV. Who's that? Who was that talking?

GRADOBOEV. It's Aristarkh, your daughter's godfather.

KUROSLEPOV *(to Aristarkh)*. Who is that poor thing you're talking about?

ARISTARKH *(bowing)*. Good day, honored sir.

KUROSLEPOV. No, who's that poor thing?

ARISTARKH *(with a sigh)*. A little fish.

KUROSLEPOV. So why is it a poor thing?

ARISTARKH. Because a big fish treats it badly.

KUROSLEPOV. You and your fish. But if you're getting too big for your breeches, then…

GRADOBOEV. You've said enough already; you're not going to add anything that makes sense.

KUROSLEPOV. And when was it you became godfather to my child? It was when I didn't have money.

GRADOBOEV. Let's go, let's go. There's refreshments waiting for us. *(He leads Kuroslepov away.)*

ARISTARKH. Why do I like to catch pike? Because it harms the other fish. It's a big fish with teeth, so it grabs. A poor little fish can flounder and flounder about, but there's no way it can get away from the pike!

A song is heard in the distance.

What's that? Our people? They came at a good time.

A boat approaches. In it stands Khlynov without a jacket, his arms akimbo. Also in it are six rowers and a gentleman with a large mustache.

Why are you people carrying on like hooligans, you're frightening the fish! *(To Khlynov.)* Look at you, you've been getting drunk since morning. A man can't hide from you anywhere.

Khlynov and the gentleman with the mustache are helped out onto the dock.

128

KHLYNOV *(importantly)*. How can you talk like that, brother! The river's not prohibited to anyone.

ARISTARKH. Come here, brother, over here. *(He leads Khlynov to the front of the stage.)* If you want to be a merchant to make people sit up and take notice, then stop pouring champagne on the sand! Nothing's going to grow there.

KHLYNOV. All right, brother, cut it short! I don't have time now to listen to your sermons…

ARISTARKH. Look, do at least one good deed. Then people will start talking about you. Then you'll show yourself to good advantage.

KHLYNOV. I can do anything…

ARISTARKH. Do you know Vasily Shustry? He's in jail, but he's innocent. You take him out on bail.

KHLYNOV. That's of no consequence! Speak faster brother! You can see I don't have much time.

ARISTARKH. He's being sent into the army simply out of spite, but you can buy him off; he'll earn the money back for you. You can hire a volunteer replacement for him or you can buy an exemption.

KHLYNOV. This is such a worthless business you're bothering me with, brother.

ARISTARKH. A man is being ruined unjustly, and he calls it a worthless business.

KHLYNOV. You're not making any sense to me, brother. What kind of honor is it for me to buy him off! All those words of yours aren't worth a thing. But this is what is all adds up to. Since Vaska has begun to understand very well how to play the tambourine and since, for that very reason, he gives me a lot of pleasure, that means I'll settle this business in a second. Because, if I take a liking to somebody, don't anyone dare touch him.

ARISTARKH *(with a bow)*. Fine, as you wish, as you wish. Just don't let them do him any harm.

KHLYNOV. How dare you give me orders! At home we can talk things over, but in town you're no comrade of mine. Keep your distance, move back! *(To the gentleman.)* Sir, Your Honor, let's go to the chief of police.

ARISTARKH. And you don't have your jacket! That's how to go visiting!

KHLYNOV. You heard me, keep your place! To the rear table, with the musicians! And keep all those sermons to yourself; we don't find them very interesting.

GENTLEMAN. I'm not going, it's not proper, it's ill-bred.

KHLYNOV. According to my understanding, it's just your pride.

GENTLEMAN. It's not pride at all, mon cher, what do I have to be proud about? But it's just not proper. You know I don't like this trait in you. You'll have to excuse me.

KHLYNOV. Yes, sir. And what is this trait, may I ask?

GENTLEMAN. Your swinishness!

The chief of police and Kuroslepov come out. Sidorenko is in the doorway.

KHLYNOV. Governor of our town! *(He bows.)* Colonel, sir, we have come to pay Your Honor a visit! Our respects to Pavlin Pavlinych, our merchant leader. *(To the gentleman.)* Sir, look at them, our authorities! Colonel Gradoboev and Mr. Kuroslepov, most worthy... worthy merchant. But for you and me this doesn't matter, for we can be free and easy...

GRADOBOEV. Mr. Khlynov, you're carrying your wild pranks too far!

KHLYNOV. Colonel, sir, you are absolutely right; there's been more than enough of our wild pranks. Colonel, sir, please set a fine on me for my wild pranks, set a fine! Whenever I do something very bad, you say straight off, "Khlynov, a fine!" Please take the money, Colonel, sir.

KUROSLEPOV. Why are you putting on all this show?

KHLYNOV. And why shouldn't I put on a show, Mr. Kuroslepov? My whole arsenal's full of show. Gentlemen authorities, please give me an answer. Why are you holding Vaska Shustry?

GRADOBOEV. All right now, Mr. Khlynov, putting on a show is one thing, but don't go meddling in other people's business or else I'll put some limits on you.

KHLYNOV. It's not other people's business at all, because at present I have need of him.

KUROSLEPOV. And we don't like pranks in our town either.

KHLYNOV. If it's a question of his pranks, I'll answer for him. I'll bail him out right now.

KUROSLEPOV. He's going into the army from the commune. We find a place for everybody.

KHLYNOV. I'll arrange for a replacement, Mr. Chief of Police; please release Shustry to me on bail. If gratitude is in order, we won't let that hold things up. *(He searches in his pocket.)*

GENTLEMAN. That's enough, how can you!

KHLYNOV. Shhh, not a word! Colonel, sir, please, you set the amount yourself.

GRADOBOEV. Sidorenko, go tell them to release Shustry.

SIDORENKO. Yes, sir, Your Honor! *(He goes off.)*

KHLYNOV. Gentlemen, please come and eat with me at my summer home. I most humbly beg you, eat my cabbage soup and porridge! And maybe we'll scrape up some fish, some sterlet. I hear they've gotten tired of staying in the fish ponds; they've been asking for some time to be put into fish soup. We'll drum up some wine too, I have a bottle around somewhere. And the servants won't be idle; they'll go down to the cellar and drag up a dozen or two bottles of champagne. Since you're authorities, we'll drink to your health along with a shot from the cannon, and we'll set people in the garden to shout hurrah. You're welcome, gentlemen!

GRADOBOEV. When you talk sense like that, it's a real pleasure to listen to you.

KUROSLEPOV. My wife will be expecting me, she might dream up something.

KHLYNOV. We'll send your spouse a dispatch; we'll supply an express messenger.

Sidorenko leads in Shustry.

KHLYNOV *(to Vasya)*. Know the proper customs! How awfully ignorant you are, brother! Bow down to the town's governor!

Vasya bows to Gradoboev.

To his worthy honor!

Vasya bows to Kuroslepov.

To me!

Vasya bows to Khlynov.

Get into the boat and take the tambourine!

Vasya gets into the boat.

Gentlemen, please!

All get into the boat.

Aristarkh, take the rudder!

Aristarkh takes his position by the rudder.

Canteen keeper! Do your business!

One of the rowers gives him a flask of vodka and snacks to go with it.

Please, gentleman, something for the trip, so we can go in boldness.

All drink and eat.

Aristarkh, brother, watch out for the shallows and the rocks under water. As soon as you see a dangerous place, tell us so at that very moment we can take something for our insides to give us courage. We're off! Start! Vaska, strike up the tambourine!

A song. They sail off.

ACT FOUR

SCENE I

Garden at Khlynov's summer home. Entrance to the house is at the left. Gradoboev, Kuroslepov, Khlynov, the gentleman, and Khlynov's servants are coming out of the house.

KUROSLEPOV. That's what I call a treat! God only help me survive it. That's the way you could pay respects to the governor general himself. I must say it does you honor!

KHLYNOV. And why do we struggle if not for honor? That's the one thing we hold to.

KUROSLEPOV. So, then, it's good-bye; my horses have come for me. They'll take me home now.

KHLYNOV. Hold on now, you can't leave just like that. You've got to have a last drink for the road. *(To a servant.)* Hey, brother! Go see if we have any wine. I think some could be found.

The servant leaves.

GRADOBOEV. You people drink. I've had enough.

KHLYNOV. Colonel, sir, we have a saying: a guest is a prisoner.

GRADOBOEV. You've already made me enough of a prisoner.

The servant brings in a bottle of champagne.

KHLYNOV. Town governor! My respects! Brave warrior! Don't wound your host, don't dismay the merchant Khlynov. *(He gives him a glass.)*

GRADOBOEV. No, that's an old trick. A man can't drink all the wine you have. Drink it yourself.

KHLYNOV. Colonel, sir, if you would like to see whether your citizens behave correctly, we'll show you straight off. *(To Kuroslepov.)* O leader, sir, I beg of you! *(To the gentleman.)* Sir, save the situation!

They drink.

It all seems right and proper. *(He shows Gradoboev a glass.)* Because I like things to be exactly right in my house. *(To the servant.)* Guess what we want, brother, guess what we want.

SERVANT. It's ready sir. *(He serves another bottle.)*

KUROSLEPOV. No, really, you'll have to excuse me, or else I won't make it home, I'll fall out of the carriage.

KHLYNOV. We'll send somebody with you.

KUROSLEPOV. You're stubborn, but I'm even more stubborn. You can kill me, but I won't drink any more. I did you the favor, let it stop there. Besides, you should see the dreams I've started having. Lord! Always wild animals, and they have trunks, always grabbing at you and catching you, and with the sky falling... Good-bye, I'm going. *(He starts off.)*

KHLYNOV. Don't forget us!

KUROSLEPOV. Your humble guest. *(He leaves.)*

KHLYNOV. Hey, boys! Put Mr. Kuroslepov into his carriage. And if he doesn't prove to be a real fortress, then one of you sit opposite him and hold him by the shoulders till he gets home. *(He wants to go along.)*

GENTLEMAN. You stay here with the colonel. I'll see him off. *(He goes off. Several follow him.)*

KHLYNOV *(with a glass on a tray)*. Colonel, sir, you first!

GRADOBOEV. I'm not going to! Am I speaking to you in Russian or not?

KHLYNOV. I have a rule, sir. If a man won't drink up, then we pour it on his head.

GRADOBOEV. A lot I need to know your rules. You have a rule, but I have a cane.

KHLYNOV. You won't win, Colonel, sir; we'll pour it on you. I'll make a bet with you on it.

GRADOBOEV. You just try! What I'll do to you!

KHLYNOV. You won't do a thing to me, that's how I understand it.

GRADOBOEV. You'll get such a sentence there won't be room for you in Siberia.

KHLYNOV. I'm not frightened, Colonel, sir; don't try to scare me! Really, you better not try to scare me! Because that only makes it worse. And would you like to make a bet I'm not afraid of anything? I'll reason it out good and clear for you right now. Let's just suppose you do something bad to me. At that very moment I go straight to the governor general himself. And the very first word from His Excellency will be this: "You, Khlynov, are doing all kinds of disgraceful things!" And I'll answer, "I do those disgraceful things, Your Excellency, because of the way I was brought up, lots of beatings but no good from them. I've heard that your fire brigade needs to have some repairs made, and that's a matter I can take care of without charge." "So," he'll say to me, "Is it true that you have a violent disposition?" "It's violent, Your Excellency, I don't like my disposition myself, I'm a wild beast. And the jails are in bad shape too, Your Excellency. Next thing you know the prisoners will escape. That too is something I can take care of without charge." So there you have our policy, Colonel, sir. But that's not all. From him I'll go to his wife. "Wouldn't it give you pleasure, dear lady, if I built a house in town for the orphans, as a donation?" Because not only can I see her whenever I want, but I've even had tea and coffee with her there, and rather offhanded too. So that's how it is, Colonel, sir, and what it all comes down to is that it's not very profitable for chiefs of police to quarrel with me. They might frighten other people, but for me they're nothing at all. So you better not try passing sentence on me, for I can outsmart you straightaway. You better just fine me for my disgraceful acts a hundred rubles in silver. *(He offers the wine.)* Please, don't stand on ceremony!

GRADOBOEV *(takes the glass).* You leper you! I wasn't so afraid of the Turks as I'm afraid of you devils! It's against my will that I'm drinking for you, you barbarian. When will you choke on your damn wine!

KHLYNOV. All this, Colonel, sir, has been done for your benefit... If sometimes it seems a lot to take, at other times it can happen to be even more...

GRADOBOEV. Happen! This happens with you every day.

KHLYNOV. Maybe so. But if it's done with prayer and, the main thing, nobody tells on me... what harm can there be!

GRADOBOEV. Good-bye! You're not going to tempt here again soon.

The gentleman returns.

KHLYNOV. But why is that, sir! And here we were hoping you'd be our constant guest. *(He takes out his wallet.)* Allow me! *(He gives him three one-hundred-ruble notes.)* Consider this a fine.

GRADOBOEV. Oh you, you shouldn't do that!

KHLYNOV *(embraces him and forces the money into Gradoboev's pocket).* It's impossible not to! I can't let you go without a present. We too understand very well what your job is like.

GRADOBOEV. You've broken me, you devil.

KHLYNOV. It's not your fault, so please don't worry about it, because it was forced on you.

GRADOBOEV. Well, good-bye. Thank you.

They kiss.

KHLYNOV. You people there! See off the town governor. Stand at attention.

All but the gentleman leave. Vasya enters.

GENTLEMAN. Well, how's your business coming along?

VASYA. I got the exemption, but I don't know about Mr. Khlynov... He...

GENTLEMAN. He'll pay the money.

VASYA. You think he'll really pay?

GENTLEMAN. He'll pay all right, only he'll make a clown out of you.

VASYA. But why should I make a fool of myself!

GENTLEMAN. You mean you don't want to? You'd rather go into the army?

VASYA. Of course.

GENTLEMAN. No, you have to be joking! I've seen enough people of your stripe. You're just not the soldier type; your knee joints aren't firm. You're made to be a clerk, to curl your hair and grease it, dangle a bronze watch chain, copy tender poetry in a notebook, that's what you're made for. You're just no good for the soldier life. But here comes Khlynov himself; talk with him.

Vasya steps back timidly. Khlynov and several servants enter.

KHLYNOV. They've gone. Well, here I'm left, my friend! Because of all my money I have to die of boredom.

GENTLEMAN. You're bored of your own free will!

KHLYNOV. But what am I supposed to do? Run up and down? Look at you in wonder? See what kinds of patterns you've got on you?

GENTLEMAN. In the first place, you be more careful how you express yourself. And in the second place, you have Aristarkh for that, to think up distractions for you.

KHLYNOV. Yes, and he probably hasn't thought up a thing. I told him a little while ago: sit, brother, don't move, think up something for me to do tonight. *(To a servant.)* Where's Aristarkh?

SERVANT. Here, in the garden. He's lying under a tree.

KHLYNOV. Thinking?

SERVANT. No, he's playing a pipe; he wants to attract the hawks.

KHLYNOV. He was told to think, and he's playing a pipe. Call him here right now.

The servant leaves. Khlynov, catching sight of Vasya, sits down in an armchair, sprawls out, and speaks with a tone of importance.

So, you're here! Come here, I want to talk with you. Because I, brother, in view of your poverty, wish to be your benefactor,

Vasya bows.

and about that very matter I want to ask you what your thoughts are.

VASYA. We got the exemption, sir.

KHLYNOV. And what might be the going rate on such documents?

VASYA. You mean the price, sir?

KHLYNOV. Look, brother, you should have understood that right off. I can't repeat things ten times for every no-account fellow.

VASYA. Four hundred rubles, sir.

KHLYNOV. And exactly where were you hoping to get that money from?

VASYA *(bowing low)*. Don't abandon me, Tarakh Tarasych!

KHLYNOV. Do you imagine, brother, that your bows are worth an awful lot?

VASYA. God will provide. Daddy and I'll get ourselves straightened out, and at that time and with our gratitude you'll be...

KHLYNOV. How dare you, brother, and at my own summer home, say such things! Do you think I'm your equal, that you can pay me back money? You want to borrow from me maybe, like friends? When I look at you, brother, I can see you don't have any education at all! You've got to wait, to see what kind of mercy I might want to show. Maybe I'll forgive you this money or maybe I'll make you turn a somersault and call it quits. How can you know my soul when I don't know it myself, because it all depends on what kind of a mood I'm in.

VASYA. It's all as you will, Tarakh Tarashch, but right now I'm as good as dying.

KHLYNOV. That's the tack you should have taken in the first place... submission... Now then, brother, here's what I've decided. For me four hundred rubles isn't worth spitting on, but for that money you'll work for me one year, at any task I pick for you.

VASYA. Tell me what it'll be, Tarakh Tarasych; I'll explain why. Daddy knows a lot of people, we're upper class in the town, and we're merchant class too...

KHLYNOV. When you're with Mr. Khlynov, brother, you'll be the leader of the chorus. That's the rank and class you'll have with me.

VASYA. But Tarakh Tarasych, I'll be shamed in front of my friends.

KHLYNOV. If you're going to be shamed, brother, then I won't force you. You can go into the army.

VASYA. Please, Tarakh Tarasych, let me think about it!

KHLYNOV. Once again you end up a fool and ignoramus! Did you just become a senator, that you suddenly feel like thinking! It's for clever people to do the thinking. But if you want to think, brother, then I'll have them take you back to jail. You can think better there.

VASYA. No, how can you say that, Tarakh Tarasych, don't ruin my youth. Whatever you want, let it be.

KHLYNOV. It didn't take you long, brother, to do your thinking.

Aristarkh enters.

Where have you been, brother...

ARISTARKH, Now you just hold on, you disgusting man! *(To the servants.)* When you people stagger about drunk in the garden, then watch out you don't fall into the trap I set there, it's for skunk. And the household servants too! They're no worse than the master. And I have a snake there under the tree.

KHLYNOV. What do you have a snake for? How stupid can you get, brother! It will bite somebody.

ARISTARKH. That shows how smart you are. It's a paper kite, we call it a snake. I glued it together and set it there to dry.

KHLYNOV. For what purpose?

ARISTARKH. We'll put it up at night with a lantern, from a boat. And to that boat I'm attaching a kind of contraption. It works by hand, and I've ordered wheels for it; it'll be something like a steamship.

KHLYNOV. But how about it, brother, I told you to think up how I'll spend the time tonight.

ARISTARKH. I've already thought it up, let me tell you. *(He takes a chair and sits down.)* Listen! Not far from here there's a gentleman by the name of Khvatsky. He used to have a good estate, only he ruined it trying out all kinds of things. He broke up his house, took apart all the stoves and partitions, and he made a theater of it; he himself lives in the bathhouse. He bought a lot of scenery, all kinds of costumes, wigs, headpieces to show baldness, all sorts of things. Only he didn't have anyone to act or look at this theater. Now he needs money badly, because he planted potatoes in all his fields, wanted to make starch out of them, but his crop was frostbitten, and it stayed in the ground. So now he wants to go to Astrakhan to make fish glue, and he'd sell his whole theater for almost nothing.

KHLYNOV. But brother, why are you preaching us this long sermon?

GENTLEMAN. Wait, I think I can see some sense in this.

ARISTARKH. Of course there is; I'm not about to talk for nothing. Listen, you disgusting man, to what comes next. I'll go and buy all his costumes from him. And at night we'll dress up all our people like robbers; he has big hats, with feathers. Our robbers won't be Russian ones but the kind they have in the theater; I can't describe them to you; what I don't know I don't know. And we'll dress up too; I'll be a hermit…

KHLYNOV. But why a hermit?

ARISTARKH. Is there anything you understand! If I say something, that means I know what I'm talking about. Robbers always have a hermit with them; that makes it more fun. And we'll all go out into the woods, to the great highway, near where the hut is. We'll dress up the gentleman as the chief, because he has a stern look anyway, and then there's his mustache. We'll dress you up as a robber too, only we won't have to disguise you very much; you look like a robber as it is, and in the woods at night you'll be perfect.

KHLYNOV. Careful, brother, don't you go forgetting yourself!

ARISTARKH. We'll whistle in the bushes, and we'll stop people going by and take them to the chief. We'll give them a good fright, then we'll get them drunk and let them go.

GENTLEMAN. That's a great idea.

KHLYNOV. Not bad, we'll do it. A very interesting business. So you go ahead with it while I take a little nap. *(He goes off.)*

GENTLEMAN. First we'll have a rehearsal with our people. This is going to be a great prank, noble and pleasant. Yes, devil take it, this is going to be funny, and just when I was dying of boredom. *(He leaves.)*

Vasya approaches Aristarkh.

VASYA. Aristarkh, I've thrown in my lot with Khlynov.

ARISTARKH. That's your business.

VASYA. But I still wonder about it! Sometimes I think, wouldn't it be better to be a soldier! And if things weren't so hard, I'd do it right now... because I have a heroic spirit...

ARISTARKH. So you and your heroic spirit have become a clown.

VASYA. It couldn't be helped. It's awful! But if I dared to, I think I could do some great deeds.

ARISTARKH. That's enough talk! How could you do anything! You've just eaten too much white bread. You have almost no spirit at all, so what's the point in bragging! Heh, heh, heh! You're a small piece of goods, sewn together with bast! All your life you've been feeding on bits and pieces, never seeing a big piece of anything, all the time trying to bolster yourself up so people won't think you're low class. You're always thrashing about, on the move, afraid you might be caught lying in the mud.

VASYA. It may be true...

ARISTARKH. When you're young and still have your strength and are still worth something, it somehow doesn't seem right for you to be turning somersaults. Of course it's really none of my business, but the words came to mind, and I said them.

VASYA. That's true enough. But what worries me is what Parasha will say if I stay leader of the chorus with Khlynov! But then what should I care what people think! If she loves me, she should think the way I do. Whatever's best for me. So why cry over it? A man's got to look out for himself, right, Aristarkh? And I'll be a dashing singer too.

He goes off with Aristarkh.

SCENE TWO

Clearing in a forest. On the left is a small wicker shed for hay. Near the shed, on the side facing the audience, a board has been put on two stumps to serve as a bench. On the right are two or three stumps and a felled dry tree. In the background trees are everywhere, and beyond them are visible a road, beyond the road fields, and in the distance a village. The sun is setting.

NARKIS *(off stage).* Who-oa-oa! Damn you! Where've I gotten to? It's all thicket! It's not a matter of getting through with a horse, you can't even get through on foot! *(He comes out on the stage.)* How did I end up in such a mess! I must've dozed off. *(He stops.)* What little hut on chicken legs is this? It's a shed! Ah, this is the second time I've come to the very same place. I've gone in a circle! It's the doings of evil spirits! May this place be holy! But how could I have circled round, it's still light. No, I must've dozed off. And it's no wonder, the drinking I did with those peasants! What did I drink? God help me remember. Two glasses, then half a glass, and two cups of tea, then another half glass, then a glass. But why keep count, to your health! I'm one that can manage it, for me it's like water, though there's some people couldn't handle that much water. Keeping count's a sin; they say you can get thin from keeping count... Altogether it's only three miles to home, but I'm just not getting there. I'll lead the horse out onto the road and give it the whip, then we'll be home in no time. If not, it will be embarrassing! The master sent me on business, and I got lost. People might even think I'd been drunk. *(He goes off.)*

Out of the woods in marching formation come Khlynov, wearing a Spanish cloak over his waistcoat and also a velvet hat with feathers; Aristarkh dressed as a Capuchin; the gentleman; behind the gentleman Khlynov's men paired off in various costumes, Vasya among them. Two baskets with drink and food are being carried in the rear.

KHLYNOV. Forward, march! *(He wants to go out onto the road.)*

ARISTARKH *(stopping him).* Wait, you disgusting man! Where do you think you're going?

KHLYNOV. Someone just went by, brother.

ARISTARKH. Well, so what?

KHLYNOV. Shouldn't I look into it?

ARISTARKH. It's still too early to go out of the woods, it's too light. *(He looks at the road.)* I can tell you right now who went by. That's Narkis, Kuroslepov's assistant, on his master's wagon. They sent him somewhere, and there he is rocking back and forth, must have dozed off! Where is the crazy man headed for! Oh well, the horse knows, it'll get them onto the road.

KHLYNOV. You got this business started, brother, so get it organized.

ARISTARKH. Everybody stop here! This will be our halting place. *(To the gentleman.)* Sir, and you landowner Khlynov, you two sit down on the bench behind the shed, no one can see you there from the road; somebody take the baskets into the shed.

KHLYNOV. Canteen keeper, prepare a snack, brother, so we can stay sober.

He and the gentleman sit down on the bench.

ARISTARKH. Now we'll split up. You two go to the little hill, you two to the bridge, and hide well behind the bushes; don't go to the country road; only peasants and pilgrims go there. If you see someone going by on foot or by horse, first let them go by, then whistle. And the rest of you sit down near here in the bushes. Only sit and don't make any noise, don't sing any songs, don't play heads or tails, don't get into any boxing matches. When I whistle, then come out. *(He goes up to Khlynov.)*

KHLYNOV. Why, brother, are we just sitting here? Your first concern is to keep me occupied. As soon as I don't have anything to do, I can get bored and fall into sadness. And when I'm sad and bored, brother, bad thoughts come into my head, and from that I can suddenly grow thin.

ARISTARKH. But why be bored! It's so quiet here! I hate to leave the woods, it's such a wonderful evening!

KHLYNOV. What's a wonderful evening? What's good about it? What can you understand, brother? The pleasant thing about a summer evening is that it's easy to drink champagne, because the weather's cool. But without the champagne what good's the evening? *(To the gentleman.)* Sir, shouldn't we break into a bottle?

A whistle.

ARISTARKH Wait! *(He whistles.)*

Khlynov's men come out of the woods.

Quiet!

NARKIS *(off stage)*. Whoa-oa-oa! Damn you! I wish a wolf'd eat you up! Where've you brought me! Whoa-oa-oa!

ARISTARKH. I'll go take a look. *(He goes to the bushes and returns.)* It's Narkis, he's lost in the woods. *(To Khlynov.)* There's a good catch for you!

NARKIS *(off stage)*. It's really weird! I just can't get out of here no matter what I do. I've got to pull the devil back by his tail. Where'm I stuck this time? I'll have to look around.

ARISTARKH *(to the men)*. Surround him, and when I give the sign, grab him and bring him here.

Narkis comes on stage. Khlynov's men come from all sides.

NARKIS *(looking around)*. How about that! The shed! Here I am again, for the third time. Good for me! Now isn't that the work of the devil! No, you can say what you want, but the business is clear enough. It's when it gets dark I get frightened. It's *him* playing jokes, it's the devil come out now; when it gets dark he comes out; he never comes out when it's light, that's not for him, he can't then… Well, let him have his little jokes, just so I don't see him. They say his looks strike so, no man dares look straight at him! Now when am I going to get home? No, I'm fed up with all this! This time I'll lead the horse by the bridle, and I won't doze off. Just so long as *he* doesn't come at me, for if he does, I think I'd even leave the horse. No, I'll be home soon, I'm no coward. Of course, if he suddenly popped up in front of me, then I might be frigh… *(He goes toward the horse. At a sign from Aristarkh one of Khlynov's men bars the way to Narkis.)* There he is, it's *him!*… How do you like that! Speak of the devil! I'll just go another way and not look at him. *(He goes in another direction. Another man bars his way.)* There's another one, really! *(Aristarkh comes out from behind the shed and gives the sign to take him.)* A third one! The wood's full of them! But that one must be the real one! I'm not drunk any more. Should I shout or not? But what's the good of shouting? Besides the wood demon no one's going to answer. *(He waves his hand at Aristarkh.)* May this place be holy. *(He whispers.)* Didn't work! It's the end of me.

Servants take him by the arms and lead him to Khlynov. Others bring wine and a glass. The gentleman signals him to drink.

You mean I'm supposed to drink? Is it some kind of poison? Will it make me explode?

The gentleman nods no.

Is your word good? All right, I'll drink it. *(He drinks. They pour him some more.)* So, more? The first went off good enough. I'll try another. *(He drinks.)* Thank you. Now allow me to ask you, are you people, more or less, or something else?

GENTLEMAN *(in a deep voice)*. We're robbers.

NARKIS. Robbers? You don't look like it. You look more like those you shouldn't mention at night but only in the daytime, especially that one there. *(He points at Aristarkh.)* This is really scary, especially in the woods and at night.

ARISTARKH. Tremble!…

NARKIS. But I'm trembling already. I'm trembling all over.

GENTLEMAN. We come from foreign lands.

NARKIS. You do? You just came? Say, do you spend your time murdering people?

GENTLEMAN. No.

NARKIS. That makes me feel better. You know, that's a good thing, that you don't kill people. And do you rob a lot?

GENTLEMAN. No.

NARKIS. What do you mean, no? But why don't you rob? You're making a mistake there. You're from foreign lands, you don't know our people. Our people's a simple, peaceable, and patient people. I'm telling you, you can rob it. There's even a lot of people who don't know what to do with all their money. That's right. Take Khlynov, for example, why not rob him! It might even make him feel better.

KHLYNOV. Brother, how can you...

ARISTARKH *(sternly)*. Quiet!

NARKIS *(to the gentleman)*. Tell you what, kind friend, have them bring another little glass. Without that I'll be shivering from fright.

The gentleman nods his head.

After that you can do what you want with me. I'm sure your wine is imported, but what they sell us, kind friend, is a fraud. *(They bring the wine; he drinks it.)* You say you don't rob?

GENTLEMAN. We don't rob.

NARKIS. Then what do you do with us?

GENTLEMAN. We take people, make them drink, and let them go.

NARKIS. That's very good. That's wonderful.

ARISTARKH. You like that?

NARKIS. Couldn't be better. It's unheard of; if somebody told me, I wouldn't believe it.

GENTLEMAN. Would you like to join our band and be our kind of robber?

NARKIS. Your kind of robber? What's it like? Are you a collective artel or do you have a boss and salary?

GENTLEMAN. There's a salary.

NARKIS. Do you eat your own grub or the boss's?

GENTLEMAN. The boss's.

NARKIS. That's a good setup. I'd join you with the greatest of pleasure, only here's the thing, my friend...*(Looking around at Khlynov's men.)* What are they standing there for! Send them away, don't worry, I won't go away. We'll sit on the grass, I like good company.

Aristarkh makes a sign, and the men disperse. Narkis, Khlynov, the gentleman, and Aristarkh sit down on the ground.

The thing is, my only friend, I don't know what to call you...I'd really like to... but I won't be coming with you.

GENTLEMAN. Why not?

NARKIS. Because I have the life now... do I have the life! It's the berries! Like that I could live forever, everything top grade. I have a stupid master; he sent me to come to terms with the peasants on farming out the meadows, but I don't have much respect for him. With his wife, though, I'm in love and perfect agreement.

142

ARISTARKH. I don't believe it.

NARKIS. It's the honest truth. I don't say things for nothing. I get fed and the rest... everything... that's where I'm going right now... come be my guest! While you're there first thing I'll call for wine, brother, all kinds, red, white, and rum... all kinds. And next I'll say, bring me a thousand rubles! In the shake of a lamb's tail! And she'll bring it.

ARISTARKH. You're making it up!

NARKIS. It's true! Wouldn't be the first time! She'd bring me two thousand if she could swipe it easily from her husband. It's just awful how much she loves me! I'm telling you, my only friend, there's no words to tell how much she loves me. Now take not long ago, she brought me two thousand with her very own hands. And then and there, my only friend, I put it in a box under my pillow... I turn the key, and the key goes onto my cross. So now when I get there I'll tell her to bring me a thousand, and into the box and click with the key. Because, kind friend, I want to set myself up as a merchant. That's how I think of myself, what I need. And that's how it is, dear friend...

ARISTARKH. Looks like you love her, right?

NARKIS. It's not exactly that I love her; it's just that, the way I feel about things, it's all useful to me.

ARISTARKH. So be it! I'd like to go with you, but we get as much wine as we want. *(He beckons to one of the men.)* They'll help you lead your horse out. *(To the man.)* Give him lots to eat and drink, *(quietly)* then lay him in the wagon and see him to town. *(To Narkis.)* Go with him, he won't do you any harm.

NARKIS. Thanks for your company. *(He leaves.)*

ARISTARKH *(to Khlynov)*. What about it, are you satisfied? Every cloud has its silver lining. Now I'll explain all this to the chief of police so innocent people won't suffer because of that scoundrel.

KHLYNOV. It'd be a good thing now, brother, if we could catch some nobleman, to drink some champagne with him.

GENTLEMAN. Or some young lady, one well brought up, one from an institute for young ladies!... I'd fall on my knees before her right away, and I'd act out some scene from a tragedy.

ARISTARKH. Let's go out on the highway; we might run into somebody there. But we're out in the country here. Look, there come some pilgrims.

Pilgrims pass along the road.

KHLYNOV. We can't have any fun with people like that, brother, it's just a waste of time.

They go off. Parasha and Gavrilo appear on the road.

143

PARASHA. I'm so tired! I don't have any more strength! I can't move from the spot, I won't make it to the next town.

GAVRILO. Rest a minute, Praskovya Pavlinovna. Sit down here in the clearing, on the logs. Don't sit on the grass, there's dew. We'll rest a bit and then catch up with the others, it's still early. We'll reach the town before ten.

PARASHA. Let's stay awhile, I can't go on, I just can't!

GAVRILO. It's not so much the road as your feelings.

PARASHA. I'm falling, I'm falling.

GAVRILO. Please, let me hold you by the elbow. (*He leads her to the logs.*)

PARASHA. I'm just tired, but after I've prayed I'll feel better. I don't know how to thank you. Without you I'd have never made it here.

GAVRILO. But you know I had to come myself...

PARASHA. No, don't say that, I know you came just for me. My head... and my legs and arms feel as though they don't belong to me, it's as if I'm unconscious. And there's a noise in my head, but I don't feel any pain, and I feel so good, and it's so pleasant, and I'm imagining something... only what is it? There's some noise, a kind of noise, like a stream over the rocks or a mill... I feel faint, Gavryusya, I feel faint!

GAVRILO. But what's the matter, my dear! I'll go get some water, there was a spring here somewhere.

PARASHA. Go, go!

Gavrilo goes. Whistles sound in various places. He comes running back.

GAVRILO. Somebody's whistling.

PARASHA. What? I don't hear anything.

GAVRILO. Somebody's whistling in the woods.

PARASHA. Well, it doesn't matter, they're just having fun... Go.

Gavrilo goes off. The whistling intensifies. The gentleman comes out of the bushes and, catching sight of Parasha, runs up to her. She looks at him in fright. Khlynov's men appear in several places.

GENTLEMAN. O beauteous one! At last I've found thee. (*He takes her by the hand.*)

Parasha wants to escape, but her strength abandons her. The gentleman supports her, embracing her with one arm.

GAVRILO (*grabbing a large branch, he throws himself at the gentleman*). Don't touch her! I'll die on the spot, but I won't let you touch her!

The gentleman shoots from his pistol; Gavrilo falls.

PARASHA. Oh, he's killed, he's killed! *(She covers her face with her hands.)*

GAVRILO *(getting up and feeling himself)*. No, I seem to be alive. I must have fallen from fright. It deafened me. But what's going on, good Lord! *(He gets up.)*

The gentleman makes a sign. Men run in and carry Gavrilo off.

GENTLEMAN. You don't recognize me? Oh I've loved you a long time. Why have you made me so unhappy? I left the world of people and ran off to the woods to get together a band of robbers. At last you're in my arms. You will be mine. Oh!...

PARASHA *(tries to push him away)*. No, no! Vasya, Vasya!

GENTLEMAN. Would you like some brocade? Velvet, diamonds? They're all yours. Only love me.

PARASHA *(tries to free herself, but her strength diminishes)*. Oh no, no! I don't want them, I don't want anything! Let me go! Have pity on me... I beg you, I implore you, have pity on me! *(Almost in a whisper.)* I don't belong to myself now. I belong to somebody else, I belong to Vasya... Vasya, Vasya! *(She faints.)*

The gentleman places her on the bench by the shed and supports her. Khlynov and Aristarkh enter.

KHLYNOV. What's all that shooting?

GENTLEMAN. Come quick! See what a beauty I've found! She must have gotten a big fright, she needs some help.

KHLYNOV. That girl's first-rate, brother. You have my approval.

ARISTARKH *(running up)*. Oh you barbarians! This is my goddaughter Parasha, Kuroslepov's daughter. *(To Khlynov.)* Send for a carriage right away, I'll take her home.

Khlynov sends one of his men.

(To the gentleman.) And you, sir, really found someone to take advantage of. You clearly have the mind of a small child. Give her to me, you bandits, she's too good for you drunkards! Stay away you, stay away! *(He sits down on the bench next to Parasha and fans her with a kerchief.)* Get some water! *(Some men run for water.)* How dared you touch her with your dirty paws! Her a dove and you little better than devils. Great joke! And to think I, stupid fool that I was, wanted to give you some amusement! I should know by now you can't play a single trick without hurting somebody. Your greatest joy is to harm people who're poor and defenseless. *(They bring some water; he pours several drops on her head.)* As if this girl hadn't been hurt enough, you have to go and add your bit. They pestered her to death at home, somehow or other she got away...

Parasha gradually comes to and listens.

and she went off to pray to God, to ask Him for protection… So her father, sleepy eyes, being egged on by her stepmother, told the chief of police this morning to catch her and shame her by having her led on a rope by a guard through the town. Then he'd lock her up in the store room for half a year, maybe even a year.

PARASHA *(rises and talks as if in a delirium).* Through the town with a guard? In the store room? Where is he, where's the head man here? Let's go! Let's go together! I'll go with you…

GENTLEMAN AND ARISTARKH. Where? Where?

PARASHA. To the town, to the town! I'll go myself…*(With a shout.)* They can't abuse me! They can't make me stay in the store room! I'll set fire to my house at all four corners. Let's go! I'll lead you, I'll lead you straight there. Hand me something!… A gun… fire, fire again. *(She weakens.)*

ARISTARKH. Parasha! What's the matter! God be with you! It's me, your godfather. *(He takes off his hood.)*

PARASHA *(looks at him).* Godfather?

ARISTARKH. Yes, yes, your godfather! Aristarkh. Recognize me now? We were playing a joke. That there's the contractor Khlynov! Have you heard of him? An ugly type. But he can't help it; he has a lot of money and has to amuse himself.

PARASHA. But where's Gavrilo?

ARISTARKH *(turning around).* Where's Gavrilo?

ONE OF THE MEN. He got away from us and ran away.

ARISTARKH. Now he'll go running to town and get everybody there upset. But it doesn't matter, with the horses we'll get there first. You know, Parasha, Khlynov paid to keep Vasya out of the army.

PARASHA. Paid for him?

KHLYNOV. I paid four hundred silver rubles.

ARISTARKH. But where is that Vasya? He was with us.

Vasya comes out of the grove.

PARASHA. Vasya! Vasya! *(She throws herself on his neck.)*

VASYA. What are you doing? It's not right with people around.

PARASHA. You're free?

KHLYNOV. I've made him my singer now.

PARASHA *(stepping back).* Singer?

VASYA. So what, a man has to do something for his bread.

KHLYNOV. For that money I paid out I've taken him into bondage for a year.

PARASHA *(with fright)*. Bondage?

ARISTARKH. What a thing to brag about! Benefactor! Making clowns out of people.

KHLYNOV. And suppose I do make them clowns, brother, who's going to stop me? He's bankrupt, and for my money I can make him work at anything I want, and that's what he'll want. I hired him as a clown, so a clown he is. Vaska, keep your distance! To the rear table! Young lady, would you like some entertainment? I can order a gay song for you right now. Hey, people! Vaska, get your tambourine, step lively!

Vasya goes off.

PARASHA *(with tears)*. Vasya! Vasya!

VASYA *(going towards her)*. What is it?

PARASHA. Vasya, why did you take that money?

VASYA. What should I do, go into the army?

PARASHA. Yes, yes. I was already praying about it... I had committed myself to that. Yes, yes, into the army. It would have been a shame, but it would have been honest... You know, we had decided, we'd agreed on it, you wanted to... did you really... did you really...

KHLYNOV. Vaska, know your place!

Vasya goes off.

PARASHA. Did you really... turn coward?

Vasya is given the tambourine; he takes it silently.

Answer! Answer me! Did you turn coward? Did you get frightened?

Vasya shakes the tambourine angrily.

Such a handsome boy, such a brave young lad, and he turned coward. And there he stands with the tambourine! Ha, ha, ha! It's that that hurts. What am I? What am I? He's a song and dance man, so what does that make me? Somebody take me away! I lived just for him, for his sake I put up with things. I, the daughter of a rich merchant, wanted to be a soldier's wife, to live in the barracks with him, but he!... Oh, Godfather! It's so hard for me... I need courage!... I need courage... but I don't have it. I've been beaten down by fate... beaten down... and he... he has finished me off. *(She falls into Aristarkh's arms.)*

ARISTARKH. Bring the horses quick! God grant we can get her there alive! You poor thing, you poor martyr!

ACT FIVE

Scenery of Act One. It's ten p.m. Matryona comes down from the porch and walks in the yard. A little later Kuroslepov comes out onto the porch. Silan is at the gate.

KUROSLEPOV. Matryona!

MATRYONA. What next! I have to babysit him like a little boy. Seems he's waked up, his eyes are open.

KUROSLEPOV. Come here!

MATRYONA *(turning)*. Well?

KUROSLEPOV. Why do you leave me alone! It's nighttime...

MATRYONA. If it's nighttime then go to sleep! What more do you want?

KUROSLEPOV. It's time to sleep, that's right... but I'm troubled... where's Narkis?

MATRYONA. Don't worry, he'll turn up. Narkis isn't a needle; you lose that and you won't find it right away.

KUROSLEPOV. But what's going on? How could he do such a thing! I ought to throw him out by the neck. Sent on his master's business, and I gave him orders...

MATRYONA. And if he's home?

KUROSLEPOV. Then why doesn't he show himself?

MATRYONA. And what if he's asleep! He's a human being, or isn't he?

KUROSLEPOV. What you're saying is he's drunk.

MATRYONA. And were you sober when you came home from Khlynov's? A servant sitting there in front of you holding you up by the shoulders. And in the daytime too, through the town.

KUROSLEPOV. Everybody knows I'm the master. But what's he?

MATRYONA. What the master's like his people are like. Who sets the example if not the master?

KUROSLEPOV. Don't try to pull the wool over my eyes! I'm not in my second childhood yet. When a man's sent on a business, should he give an accounting or not? Speak, should he?

MATRYONA. As if tomorrow's not going to be a day for you! You two can talk things out then. Let's hope they're not affairs of state.

KUROSLEPOV *(with horror)*. Matryona! Matryona!

MATRYONA. What's the matter with you?

KUROSLEPOV. Look up! Look!

MATRYONA. Oh! How sudden you are for us women, Pavlin Pavlinych! How frightening you can be! We women are so weak any little thing can grow to anything! Some day you'll turn me into a monster. My heart sunk. I'm hardly alive, I feel empty.

KUROSLEPOV. Look up there! I'm telling you!

MATRYONA. What for?

KUROSLEPOV Is it falling?

MATRYONA. What falling, you nut?

KUROSLEPOV. The sky.

MATRYONA. All right, that's enough! Now you've said it, let it go at that. Go to bed! You've worn me out! They ought to tie you up and put you in the crazy house! How can the sky fall when it's fixed firm? That's what they call it, the firmament! Go to bed! Go without arguing. With you there's not a moment's peace.

KUROSLEPOV (going off). Then to bed it is. I'm off.

MATRYONA. What's that you're hiding in your boot?

KUROSLEPOV. Money.

MATRYONA. Is it a lot?

KUROSLEPOV. Add a ruble, and it'll be six hundred and forty.

MATRYONA. You lose that from your boot, and you'll start another hullabaloo.

KUROSLEPOV. No, do you know where I'm going to put it now? In the bedroom there's a bag with nuts, so I'll put it under the nuts, on the very bottom, and it can stay there till tomorrow. It'll be safer there, in those nuts. (He goes off.)

MATRYONA. Silanty!

SILAN (approaching). What do you want?

MATRYONA. How's Narkis?

SILAN. He's all right, he's come around. He's combing his hair now.

MATRYONA. But where was he?

SILAN. Are there only a few places for him? He goes where he wants! He was bargaining with the peasants, the whole community there.

MATRYONA. Then what?

SILAN. The same old thing. The peasants don't have a duma or senate building. They have only one building for judging their community business.

MATRYONA. So that's what it was!

SILAN. What else? It's been the custom, and they're not about to change it. So you figure it all out for yourself since he's got a weakness for the stuff. But there he is now, Narkis himself. (Silan goes off from Matryona and out through the gate. Narkis enters.)

MATRYONA. You're debauched, you're just a debauched man! You wait, you're going to get if from the master.

NARKIS. I'm not awfully afraid. Don't try to scare me. I've just seen horrors a lot worse than that, and I didn't get scared. If you'd seen all that horror I'd like to see what you'd say. One of them had on such boots, just from the boots alone you'd have been scared stiff. And you should have seen the hats! All with feathers. And one had a cloth bag on his head.

MATRYONA. When a man goes on a spree like you there's nothing he can't dream up. Enough to talk about for two days.

NARKIS. I ought to know whether I dreamed it or not. Even if it didn't scare me much, I'm still a bit shaken up. What I need now is a good remedy.

MATRYONA. What kind of remedy?

NARKIS. A bottle of rum, or better two…That'll warm me up for the night.

MATRYONA. Lime blossom would be better for you.

NARKIS. More nonsense! And why shouldn't I drink a little rum? My belly has an awful need for some dampness. I told you, rum. I know my constitution better than you.

MATRYONA. But where can I get rum?

NARKIS. Look for it! Since you won't find it in the dark, light a lantern.

MATRYONA. This world has never created a man mean as you.

NARKIS. And while you're at it, along with that rum grab me off a thousand rubles. By my count what I'm lacking now is exactly a thousand.

MATRYONA. No, no, no! Not for anything! Don't even talk about it!

NARKIS. I'm not talking about it, I'm just telling you in plain language. If you don't do it then I won't let you come to me, not even to the threshold. And tomorrow, when I give my accounting to the master, I'll tell him all about your doings, the whole business.

MATRYONA. And aren't I the one who's been doing favors everywhere for your ugly mug? Don't you have any pity for your benefactor?

NARKIS. How many times have I told you there's no pity in me? Don't ever pin your hopes on pity from me.

MATRYONA. Oh, you've destroyed me, you've destroyed me!

NARKIS. Now look, speak quieter, don't make a scandal before you have to.

MATRYONA. But where can I get so much money?

NARKIS. Well, if there's a little lacking, I'll forgive you.

MATRYONA. And how can I come to you? What if Silanty sees me?

NARKIS. Here's what to do. Take your husband's long cloak or overcoat and put it on, then his hat on your head. If Silanty sees you, he'll think it's the master himself come to bawl me out. And I'll go heat up the samovar so I can have something warm…

He goes off into the wing, and Matryona goes into the house. Silan enters through the gate.

SILAN. They've left each other and gone their ways. That's something new! And the chief of police is waiting out there. I'd better go and tell him to go home. You've been out enough nights, I'll tell him. Go home, I'll say, poor old man, go home. What a job they have! You have to be sorry for the man! The master is asleep, but the chief of police has to protect him. And who is it he's protecting? What kind of man? And yet they make all those demands. They tell him, "You weren't watching out; you failed again." The master needs his rest but why? What's he done, overworked himself? He's filled himself up with food and drink, and then it's plop on his feather bed like some log or stump. He never had any army service, never wore himself out in campaigns from beginning to end, never looked at the cup of death. So there he lies like a boar and says, "You guard me from misfortune!" No, they can say what they want, but I'm sorry for our old chief of police. In the first place, he's old, and then he was wounded...

Matryona comes out in an overcoat and hat.

What wonder is this! The master came out! I can't get over it, because at this time you can only get him up with a lever or a pulley. *(He goes up to Matryona.)* What do you want? Can't you sleep? Don't worry, I'm here.

MATRYONA *(changing her voice)*. Go outside the gate. There's nothing you haven't seen here.

SILAN. Outside the gate? I was outside the gate.

MATRYONA. Get going, I told you.

SILAN *(to himself)*. Aha! So that's it! *(To Matryona.)* I'm going, I'm going, master. I'll stay all night by the gate... don't worry about a thing. *(He goes to the gate. Matryona goes in to Narkis.)* No, you're playing tricks! You can't fool me. You take short steps, and your feet are mixed up. What does she have in her hands? Some sort of bag. She must be carrying nuts to Narkis, so they can enjoy themselves. *(He goes to the gate and opens it.)*

Aristarkh and Parasha enter.

SILAN. How did you get here?

ARISTARKH. A magpie brought us on its tail. Did she go by?

SILAN. Who? Move on, brother, move on. You don't have any business here. Whatever there is is between the master and me. We don't have to blow a trumpet.

ARISTARKH. Don't put on airs with me! The chief of police sent me. We're looking for a witness.

SILAN. Then why didn't you say so! She went by, brother, she went by. *(To Parasha with a bow.)* You've been to prayers?

PARASHA. God sent His mercy, Silanty.

ARISTARKH *(to Parasha)*. You go now, my beauty, into your little nest, and don't worry about a thing, I'll answer for you with my life. There's going to be trouble, only not for you. Don't be mad at your father. It wasn't so much from spite as his weakness. What can you do when the wife rules the roost! But as for that villain, God willing, we'll curb her tongue.

Parasha goes off into the house.

SILAN *(loudly)*. Keep watch!

Gradoboev, Vasya, Sidorenko, some policemen and invalid soldiers enter.

GRADOBOEV *(to Sidorenko)*. Station your command at the windows, the doors, and the gate so even a fly can't get by. Oh ho ho! So I can't find stolen money! Can't find stolen money! I'll show him how I can't find it. I'll find his money and stick his nose in it. Look, I'll say, look! I can't find it? Do you see it now? And now, so you won't go on insulting old and deserving officers, I'll just put this here money in my pocket. Sidorenko, do you have those papers with you, to write the decree?

SIDORENKO. I have them, Your Honor.

GRADOBOEV. Are the witnesses here?

SIDORENKO. They're behind the gate, Your Honor.

GRADOBOEV *(to Silan)*. Now you bring us your master.

SILAN. You mean wake him? But what good's that? When he's just waked up he's crazy!

Kuroslepov comes out onto the porch.

But there he is himself…Now you can do what you want with him…

KUROSLEPOV *(on the porch)*. That's nuts for you! Matryona, Matryona, you haven't seen where the nuts are, have you? *(He looks up.)* Oh Lord! It's falling again! There, there… No, it's not falling, but it's as if cut in two…

SILAN *(to Gradoboev)*. You hear what he's saying.

KUROSLEPOV. Matryona! Silan! Hey! Anyone alive here!

Matryona appears in the doorway of the wing.

SIDORENKO *(barring her way)*. It's not permitted!

MATRYONA. Aie! *(She goes off into the wing.)*

KUROSLEPOV. So, somebody's getting killed. Just try and live here. Stealing in the house and robbing outside. It's clear the last days have come, that crack in the sky had a reason.

GRADOBOEV. That's enough of your forecasting! Come here, we've been waiting for you a long time.

KUROSLEPOV. What kind of man are you?

GRADOBOEV. Come down, I tell you! We don't have time to waste.

KUROSLEPOV. Ah! So it's you! Well, now I feel a lot better. But it's happened again, brother... a whole bag of nuts.

GRADOBOEV. It'll be found.

KUROSLEPOV. Yes, that's what you always say, it'll be found, but nothing ever gets found. You promised...

GRADOBOEV. Well, I have news for you. Your money's been found, only it's awkward to take it.

KUROSLEPOV. How come?

GRADOBOEV. You'll see for yourself! Let's go together.

KUROSLEPOV. Let's go.

GRADOBOEV. Zhigunov, bring your command. Forward, march!

Zhigunov and several soldiers march into the wing.

KUROSLEPOV. Stop!

GRADOBOEV *(to Zhigunov)*. Halt!

KUROSLEPOV. There's something I want to ask you, to put my mind at rest... Look up.

GRADOBOEV. I'm looking.

KUROSLEPOV. Did the sky crack? Is it a little on the slant?

GRADOBOEV. What do you think I am, an astronomer or something? I'm busy up to my neck without that. If it's cracked, let them fix it. What does that have to do with us! March!

The door to the wing opens. Matryona appears in an overcoat and hat.

SIDORENKO *(not letting her by)*. Not permitted.

KUROSLEPOV. Now my death has come! Whatever wonders happened to me before, this never did. No, it's clear enough, my friend, no matter how hard I try, I can't get away from it all. Because, look! Here I am with you, but over there, on the threshold, there I am again.

Matryona, catching sight of her husband, disappears into the wing.

GRADOBOEV. You'll see more than that, just wait! March!

Zhigunov and the soldiers go off into the wing, Gradoboev and Kuroslepov following.

ARISTARKH *(to Vasya)*. Now, Vasily, your affairs are taking a turn for the better.

VASYA. And I'm going to be strict with him, because he shouldn't dare put me to shame! I'll get even with him for taking away my honor... He would have put me in the army, and all because of him I'd have been in bondage. But now, the way things have worked out, I can be bold and demand his daughter. We may be little people, but what right does that give him to stain our name! No, now he can give me his daughter. Everybody knows I climbed over the fence to see her, you can't keep that a secret in our town. So what it means is, I'm her fiancé. That's the custom with us.

ARISTARKH. Do what's best for you, brother.

VASYA. For I'm a man with character, Aristarkh, a lot of it. And people like us aren't going to let anyone step all over us.

Out of the wing come Gradoboev; Kuroslepov; Matryona; Narkis, bound; Zhigunov and the soldiers.

GRADOBOEV *(to Kuroslepov)*. Do you understand now?

KUROSLEPOV. Why shouldn't I understand? I wasn't born yesterday. Well, Matryona Kharitonovna, what do you have to say for yourself?

MATRYONA. Do you think I did it of my own free will? You can see yourself, it was the devil mixed me up. The whole blame should be put on him. He mixed me up, mixed me up, that's what it was... No matter how hard I fought against him, no matter how I asserted myself, you can see how strong he is... He can rock mountains, let alone us sinners in our weakness.

KUROSLEPOV. Is that so? Mountains... Yesterday you were preaching at us that at your father's it was better than anywhere, that they do all kinds of things for you there, so now you can just go hotfooting it to him!

MATRYONA. Of course. And I ought to enter a complaint about you. Who is there here to stand up for me! At least I can complain to my father that you put me to shame. Since you've been a scoundrel to me all my life here, what more could I expect from you? And what's more, we'll take you to court for a big trial.

KUROSLEPOV. That's not so frightening. For now you ought to hide your nose in your pillow for shame. And tomorrow, as soon as it's light, we'll send you off.

Matryona goes off.

GRADOBOEV. That's how to do it, good for you.

KUROSLEPOV *(to Narkis)*. And what do you say about it?

NARKIS. A fat lot I care.

KUROSLEPOV. You're not going to be praised for that.

NARKIS. Well, whatever happens, at least I've had some fun. It's a shame I didn't join up with those robbers! That's my real calling.

GRADOBOEV. So then, what are we going to do with him? Make a decree and get the business started in proper form?

KUROSLEPOV. What for, why dirty up your paper? Tell them to take him to jail. We'll put him in the army instead of Vaska, and that's the end of it!

GRADOBOEV. Sidorenko, take him to jail and let the witnesses go. Hey you, soldiers! March home!

They go off, taking Narkis with them.

VASYA. But really, what is all this! Why were you against me when I was innocent all the time? Do you think that's good, to wrong me like this!

KUROSLEPOV. I did wrong, brother! I was in too much of a hurry. You'll have to be in the army, only not right away. Well, all right then, since you're innocent, you can have fun for a while, till your turn comes.

GRADOBOEV. So, I have your money here, you and I'll divide it up tomorrow. You remember our conversation, how you insulted me, and we'll settle that then. But right now it would be a good thing to wet our whistle after our labors, drink a toast to what we've recovered.

KUROSLEPOV. Silanty, tell them to bring champagne.

Silan goes off.

GRADOBOEV. So now you'll lead a normal life, your daughter in charge of the household, and you be sure to take a good son-in-law into the house.

KUROSLEPOV. Daughter! My daughter ran away.

GRADOBOEV. That's something you saw in a dream.

KUROSLEPOV. What's that again!

ARISTARKH. It was a dream, Your Excellency.

KUROSLEPOV. What are you talking about!

Silan enters.

Where's my daughter?

SILAN. Where should she be! As everybody knows, she's home.

Parasha enters with a bottle of champagne and a glass on a tray.

Here she comes now with something to drink.

KUROSLEPOV. Wait! (*He leads Gradoboev aside.*) Listen, be my friend, I beg you with tears in my eyes, tell me honestly: have I gone absolutely crazy or is there a spark of sanity left inside me? If I'm absolutely crazy, then you better put me behind bars so I won't mix with people.

GRADOBOEV. Look me in the eye! No, it's too early for you yet behind bars, you can still have some fun. I'll tell you when.

KUROSLEPOV. Well, all right. *(To Parasha.)* Serve our guests. You'd better get used to being lady of the house.

Parasha pours a glass and gives it to Aristarkh.

That just shows how little you know. Serve people in order of rank.

PARASHA. I don't know those ranks of yours, I'm serving first the one who loves me most. If I'm lady of the house then don't give me lessons. *(She serves Gradoboev.)*

GRADOBOEV *(drinks).* Really, brother, you ought to marry her off, it's time. Everything tells me it's time.

Parasha serves her father.

KUROSLEPOV. Do you want to get married?

PARASHA. Why not! Only I'll tell you ahead of time, so we won't have an argument! Give me the man I love myself. Don't you try forcing me against my will! For if I get married against my will, then, with the kind of heart I have, don't expect any good from it.

GRADOBOEV. So that's what she's like! I say, marry her off quick!

A loud knock at the gate.

SILAN. Now who! *(He opens up.)*

Gavrilo runs in.

GAVRILO *(not noticing Parasha).* Good Lord! I'm exhausted! Pavlin Pavlinych! I'm all out of breath! There's trouble!

KUROSLEPOV. What happened, did you break loose from the gallows?

GAVRILO. Worse than that! They took her away, they took her out of my hands!

KUROSLEPOV. Who?

GAVRILO. Your daughter, your Praskovya Pavlinovna! I was running to help her, but he took a shot at me with a pistol. But that doesn't matter! I'd gladly give my life for her, but he didn't kill me, he didn't kill me.

KUROSLEPOV. I can see he didn't kill you.

GAVRILO. I organized two villages, and we searched the whole woods, but there wasn't anyone, he'd carried her off. They took her out of my hands, out of my hands… Pavlin Pavlinych! *(He bows.)*

KUROSLEPOV. Now what should I do with him? Try water from the tub on him?

GAVRILO. Oh God, my friends! It was an evil fate that made me take her along, fool that I was! What for me was dearer than anything in the world, what I would guard like the apple of my eye... I think I could spend all day just blowing every speck of dust off her. And here just like that they took her from me...

KUROSLEPOV. Well, Gavrilka, I can see you and I'll have to be chained together!

GAVRILO. You forgive me, for God's sake! I just ran in to tell you, and so for me there's only one thing left...From the bridge, from the bridge! From the very middle and with a rock. Forgive me, Orthodox Christians, if in some way there's somebody I've... *(Catching sight of Parasha.)* Oh! *(He wants to run away.)*

SILAN *(stopping him)*. Hold on there! Where are you going? That's quite a joke, your bridge there!... Some calamity you thought up! But I'm not going to let you... There's no good in that, believe me.

Aristarkh goes up to Gavrilo and whispers in his ear.

PARASHA. It's all right, it'll pass off. He's unhappy because they took away his job. *(She serves Gradoboev.)* Please!

KUROSLEPOV. You ought to have another bottle brought for us.

PARASHA. It'll be brought right away. Silanty! Get a bottle from the hallway.

Silan goes off.

Just now I began to say something, but I didn't finish. *(To her father.)* You give me your absolute promise you won't make me marry somebody who's not dear to me.

GRADOBOEV. Yes, and we'll be witnesses.

KUROSLEPOV. I'll give it to you right now if you want. Tell me the man you love, and you can marry him.

PARASHA. The man I love? Tell you that? Well, all right, I'll tell! *(She takes Vasya by the hand.)* Here's the man I love.

GAVRILO *(wipes away tears)*. Well, thank God!

VASYA. Yes, now you can speak right out.

PARASHA. And now I will speak right out. *(To her father.)* Here's how much I love this man. When you wanted to send him into the army, even then I wanted to marry him, I wasn't afraid to be a soldier's wife.

GAVRILO. That's good, everything's fine now.

PARASHA. And now, when he's free, and I have the money, and there'll be a dowry, and nobody to stop us...

GAVRILO. God grant it!

PARASHA. Now I'd marry him only I'm afraid he'd leave his wife to become a dancer. So I won't marry him even if you cover me with gold from head to foot. He couldn't manage to take me when I was poor, so he won't when I'm rich. But here is the man I'm going to marry. *(She takes Gavrilo.)*

GAVRILO. No, no, Miss! You made a mistake. That's not it at all, Miss.

PARASHA *(to her father).* If you won't give me to him, then we'll run off and get married. He doesn't have any money nor do I. But we won't let that frighten us. We'll manage somehow. At least we could deal in rotten apples at bazaars, but we won't go into bondage to anybody! But what means most to me is to know for sure that he'll love me. I saw him for one day, but I'll entrust myself to him for the rest of my life.

GAVRILO. But that's impossible, how can you say that!

PARASHA. And why is it impossible?

GAVRILO. What kind of a match am I for you! Am I really an honest-to-goodness man, like the others?

PARASHA. And why aren't you an honest-to-goodness man?

GAVRILO. That's how it is, Miss, I'm not a complete man. I've been grabbed a lot by the back of the neck, from the very start to this very day, so I've a lot of feelings knocked out of me, the kind a man ought to have. I can't walk straight ahead, can't look people in the eye, can't do anything.

GRADOBOEV. That's all right. You'll get straightened out after a while.

KUROSLEPOV. Well, all right then, marry Gavrilka. There'll be more honor in the house than there's been so far.

PARASHA. Thank you, Daddy, for remembering me, a poor orphan. It's been many years now, but this is the first I can bow to you with the feeling a daughter ought to have. For a long time I've been a stranger to you, but it wasn't my fault. I don't want to force my love on you, but if you want my love, then try to cherish it. Godfather, we'll take you on as assistant in place of Narkis. You can move in tomorrow.

Silan brings some wine.

KUROSLEPOV. You didn't even ask me.

PARASHA. If it's something I don't know about, I'll ask, but if it's something I know about, why should I ask?

KUROSLEPOV. Well, all right, you do the managing, you do the managing.

PARASHA *(serving the wine).* Please!

GRADOBOEV. Congratulate the bride and groom!

KUROSLEPOV. So, children, may God grant you a better fate than ours.

GAVRILO. We humbly thank you, sir. *(To Parasha.)* But is this all really true, Miss?

GRADOBOEV. Now that we've drunk to it, that means it's all settled.

KUROSLEPOV. How many days are there in this month, thirty-seven or thirty-eight?

GRADOBOEV. Whatever it is, it seemed like a long month.

KUROSLEPOV. It was long all right.

GRADOBOEV. But why keep count! No matter how many days it adds up to, you still have to live to the next month.

KUROSLEPOV. Yes, of course, you have to. Only it's been an unlucky month for me. What'll the new one be like? What only didn't happen to me this month! Money stolen, people not paying their debts; yesterday I thought the end of the world was here, today the sky kept falling, and twice I dreamed I was in hell.

GRADOBOEV. Did they judge you worthy of acceptance?

PARASHA. Well, dear guests, I can see it's Daddy's bedtime. He's already begun to say this, that, and the other.

GRADOBOEV. Well, good-bye. When's the betrothal going to be?

PARASHA. Give us a little time to put things in order, and we'll send out invitations. Good-bye, Godfather. Good-bye, Vasya. Don't be mad at us, visit us.

All leave.

(To her father.) So, good night, Daddy. Sleep, and God be with you! And now I've lived to see beautiful days, now I'm going to stay out in the open all night long with my darling under our little tree, and I'll tell him openly whatever I, a young maiden, want to say. He and I'll chirp together like the swallows till the clear dawn itself. Then the little birds will wake up, and they'll start chirping their way, it'll be their turn, and then we'll part and go home.

She embraces Gavrilo. They sit down on the bench under the tree.

CURTAIN

NOTES

1. F.A. Burdin, a friend of Ostrovsky and an actor in St. Petersburg, was responsible for the predating of the play's action. The censor felt that the portrayal of the chief of police had too much contemporary relevance. Burdin managed to get the play through censorship by predating the action on his own, notifying Ostrovsky later. We need not take too seriously the fact that the office of gorodnichii (chief of police) was abolished in 1862, and we can safely assume that the play reflects the recent past relative to 1869. It is of incidental interest that the play reflects a certain amount of social change in the decade following Ostrovsky's writing of *The Thunderstorm*. See next note.

2. Kalinov is a fictitious place. Ostrovsky used the same place name for his earlier play *The Thunderstorm* (written in 1859, published in 1860).

3. A folksong with several variants, dating as early as 1799.

4. Described is a dramatization of an old Russian folksong "Down Mother Volga" *(Vniz po matushke po Volge)*. The actors are ataman (Cossack chief), pirates, a rich landowner and his family. This dramatization has been dated as early as 1814.

5. A play *(Dvumuzhnitsa*, 1832) by Alexander A. Shakhovskoi (1777-1846).

6. A variant of a folksong recorded by T.I. Filippov *(40 narodnykh pesen,* Moscow, 1882).

7. Ostrovsky had noted such a custom in the town Torzhok (considered by some a model for the fictional town Kalinov) when he participated in an ethnological expedition in the upper Volga valley in 1856-57.

8. A romance in the repertory of tavern guitarists. Recorded as early as 1839.

9. At one time brigands took refuge in the Bryn woods, dense woods along the Bryn River in Kaluga Province.

10. From the song "Don't rage, stormy winds" *(Ne bushuite, vetry buinye)*.

11. As the text suggests, it was possible for a recruit to avoid army service by hiring a volunteer replacement or by buying an exemption from the government.

AFTERWORD

Ostrovsky probably began work on *An Ardent Heart (Goriachee serdtse)* in the summer of 1868, finishing it in December of that year. It was published in the No. 1, 1869 issue of *Fatherland Notes (Otechestvennye zapiski)*.

The play premiered in Moscow on January 15, 1869, with only moderate success. The St. Petersburg premiere on January 29, 1869, enjoyed no success and was followed by only a few performances there. Its failure was a crushing disappointment for Ostrovsky. The play's greatest success came with Stanislavsky's memorable staging in 1926, which highlighted the play's satirical strain with abundant grotesquerie and high jinks.

Ostrovsky wished to revise the play for his collected works but did not manage to do so.

An Ardent Heart has two basic themes, which Ostrovsky combines with some skill, though ultimately, in my assessment, unsuccessfully. The more obvious one, because of the title, is that of Parasha, the young woman of the ardent heart. When Parasha loves, she commits herself fully, though eventually even she has to give up on the unworthy Vasya. Her independent spirit is as prominent as her loyalty in love. She is ready, almost eager, to fight and to endure privations for the freedom to marry the man of her choice. All of which stirs us with sympathetic admiration.

All the same, it seems to me, Parasha's revolt (as some have considered it) is not nearly so lasting or deep as that of the generally outwardly passive Katerina Kabanov of *The Thunderstorm,* who invites comparison if only because both women's oppression takes place in the same fictional town of Kalinov. Katerina, partly because she is married, feels hemmed in and oppressed by an entire way of life sanctioned or permitted by a society largely hostile or indifferent to her. Whereas Parasha has no real problem with society in general. Parasha's problem is her stepmother, Matryona, who would deny to Parasha the freedom customary in that locale for unmarried young women to circulate (paradoxical as that perhaps might seem in view of the general confinement of married women). In this regard, then, Parasha is not a rebel but a conservative who insists only on rights approved by society. And when that obstacle (Matryona) is removed, Parasha quickly adapts to the domestic situation, formally asking her father's consent to her marital choice.

While basically we are to take Parasha seriously, it strikes me that there is also some undercutting that suggests a possible parodying of true love struggling against odds. The dialogue between Parasha and her two suitors, especially with Vasya, at times verges on naive silliness, such as when Parasha urges Vasya to volunteer for dangerous combat to earn glory. It is clear that Ostrovsky wanted this trio to be folksy: their associations with folk music help them to gain the audience's sympathy vis-a-vis the mostly negative characters of Kuroslepov, Gradoboev, Khlynov, Matryona and Narkis. While Vasya proves unworthy of Parasha, he is not really evil, but weak.

Aristarkh, though he serves Khlynov, is certainly on the side of the angels in his sentiments, but he knows his place and, while preserving a limited self respecting independence, will not stick his neck out because he is sure it will do no good.

The real strength of the play in the history of its performance (and in my view also in the reading of it) has been the social theme, specifically the theme of corrupting power as embodied in Kuroslepov, Gradoboev, and especially Khlynov. Each in his own way not only exercises some degree of power but revels in it (Kuroslepov revelling less than the others). The power of Kuroslepov and Khlynov is fueled by money, which, incidentally, is a constant concern in Ostrovsky's plays.

Kuroslepov at this stage is generally no longer a threat to anyone, since in his dotage he has largely withdrawn to a somnolent state amounting to quasi-vegetation. Nevertheless, power over those in his domain is at his constant disposal, and he does not hesitate without any proof of guilt to have Vasya sentenced to army duty on mere suspicion, nor to send Gavrilo packing without back wages simply because Gavrilo is associated with Vasya. While Kuroslepov is upset by the theft of his money (a loss he can easily afford), he is not a miser. It is not the glitter of money but the status it gives which matters to him. When Gradoboev asks Kuroslepov if he knows what honor is, Kuroslepov replies, "What honor is? I've made my pile, there's your honor. The greater the capital, the greater the honor."

Gradoboev is a shrewd sadist who enjoys exploiting his power derived from his authority as chief of police. In his domain the law is basically irrelevant since he himself is the law. Take the oft-noted dispensation of group "justice" in Act Three. Gradoboev starts off with a familiar proverb ("To God above it's high/Our Tsar on earth's not nigh") indicative of how legally vulnerable were those in the provinces, which were mostly free of any ongoing central supervision. After scaring the people with books of law statutes, Gradoboev, sure of the answer, asks them, "So, my dear friends, what do you want? Should I try you by the laws or the way I like, as God puts it in my heart?"

However, Gradoboev is properly submissive with those more powerful than he is. When he tries to match himself with Khlynov in Act Four it is simply because he doesn't yet realize how powerful Khlynov is. And Gradoboev ingratiates himself with Kuroslepov, being on his side no matter what, because Kuroslepov can reward him financially. Although, to do him justice, he does display a certain proper dignity with Kuroslepov, feeling that the gratuity for special services is only proper—and most likely his salary is inadequate.

Khlynov was undoubtedly modeled on a well-known contemporary, G. I. Khludov, who performed weird stunts and even had a gentleman with a mustache in his entourage. Khlynov was originally a peasant and in terms of culture still is. A nouveau riche, he now goes all out for self-indulgence, showing off or doing whatever happens to suit his whim at the moment. Still, happiness eludes him. In his attempts to escape his empty spiritual self or his melancholic spells he has to seek help from outside himself.

But what Ostrovsky emphasizes is not Khlynov as an emotionally pathological individual but rather his danger in society. Khlynov knows that in his milieu his wealth guarantees that to him all is permitted. He makes it crystal clear to Gradoboev, the representative of the law, that he, Khlynov, is above the law and has foolproof ways to bribe the governor and the governor's wife too. Boorish and ignorant though he be, however, Khlynov does have native intelligence; he did not rise from peasant to rich contractor by sheer chance. This intelligence in the service of his self-centered form of madness makes him even more dangerous.

Obviously negative characters, Matryona and Narkis can probably be dismissed simply as melodramatically black villains with no redeeming traits.

The plot is more intricate and has more suspense than in most of Ostrovsky's plays, though the suspense is largely concentrated in the events at the end. That said, much of the play is slow-moving with a good deal of sociological stamping in place.

The ending is for Ostrovsky a rare happy one, without the usual disturbing undertone of near tragedy averted in effect by sheer chance. To be sure, chance saved the situation for Parasha, but the saving events occur in the penultimate act, and their very fairy-tale nature influences us not to worry very much from then on. At the end the virtuous Parasha and the reluctant knight in shining armor, Gavrilo, receive their just reward, each other, and presumably live happily ever after.

The play seems overcrowded and it remains a question whether the vaudeville humor is helpful or harmful, even if Stanislavsky's exploitation of the play's comic elements made his production a sensational success at the box office. The entire forest scene, which strikes me as both melodrama and parody of melodrama, is quite contrived, a play within a play to usher in the denouement. It is cleverly done, but basically it's an extended deus ex machina device.

Nevertheless, despite its imperfections, put in perspective *An Ardent Heart* is rightly considered a strong play, mainly because of its convincing satirical portraits of Kuroslepov, Gradoboev and Khlynov.

WITHOUT A DOWRY

A Drama in Four Acts

(1879)

CAST OF CHARACTERS*

KHARÍTA IGNÁTYEVNA OGUDÁLOV (MME. OGUDALOV). A middle-aged widow. Dressed elegantly but daringly, not in keeping with her age.

LARÍSA DMÍTRIYEVNA OGUDÁLOV. Mme. Ogudalov's unmarried daughter. Dressed richly but modestly.

MÓKY PARMÉNYCH KNÚROV. One of the entrepreneurs of the time. Elderly, rich.

VASÍLY DANÍLYCH VOZHEVÁTOV (VÁSYA). A very young man. One of the representatives of a rich trading firm. Dressed in Western European style.

YÚLY KAPITÓNYCH KARANDYSHÓV (pronounced Karandyshóff). Young official of modest means.

SERGÉY SERGÉYICH PARÁTOV. An imposing gentleman shipowner. Over thirty.

ROBINSON.

GAVRÍLO. Club bartender and owner of a coffee house on the boulevard.

IVÁN. Waiter in the coffee house.

ILYÁ. A gypsy.

MANSERVANT of Mme. Ogudalov.

YEFROSÍNYA POTÁPOVNA. Aunt of Karandyshov.

GYPSY MEN and WOMEN.

---

* Meanings which probably or possibly would be suggested to Ostrovsky's contemporaries: Ogudalov—swindler; Knurov—boar; Vozhevatov—pleasant, polite; Karandyshov—short stature; Paratov—strong and fast (in connection with dogs and horses).

Robinson would certainly suggest Robinson Crusoe, especially in the play's context. Near the end of Act One Paratov says that Robinson's real name is Arkády Shchastlívtsev and that he is an actor from the provinces. Ostrovsky's contemporaries would have recognized him immediately as a character in Ostrovsky's earlier play *The Forest* (1871), where he was a vagabond ex-actor who had played comic roles. Shchastlivtsev suggests "happy," and Arkady is derived from the Greek place name Arcadia, traditionally symbolizing rustic bliss. Neputóvy (Robinson's friend, who is merely mentioned) suggests "dissolute." Neputovy was also the name of a character in an earlier Ostrovsky play, namely *At the Jolly Spot* (1865).

Especially significant is the fact that Mme. Ogudalov's first name Kharita as well as her father's first name Ignat (as is evident from her patronymic Ignatyevna) were often names of gypsies.

ACT ONE

The action takes place in the present [1878], in the large town of Brya-
khimov[1] on the Volga.

A boulevard on the high bank of the Volga, with an open area in front of
a coffee house. On the right of the actors is an entrance to the coffee house. On
their left are trees. In the background is a low iron railing, beyond it a sweeping
view of the Volga. with its forests, villages, etc. In front of the coffee house are
tables and chairs: one table on the right, close to the coffee house, another on
the left.

Gavrilo is standing in the doorway of the coffee house. Ivan is tidying up
the furniture.

IVAN. Not a soul on the boulevard.

GAVRILO. It's always like that on holidays. We keep to the old ways here. After late
mass everybody puts away meat pie and cabbage soup, then they treat their
guests with hospitality, and after that it's seven hours of rest.

IVAN. What do you mean, seven! More like three or four. Anyway, it's a good custom.

GAVRILO. And then about vesper time they wake up and drink tea till they're
bored stiff.

IVAN. Bored stiff! What's there to be bored about?

GAVRILO. You just sit down by the samovar and drink boiling hot tea a couple
of hours, then you'll find out. A man gets all covered over with sweat, and
he starts to get bored... So that's when he says good-bye to his tea and drags
himself out on the boulevard for some fresh air and a walk. This is the time
when the high-class folk take their walk; look, over there you can see Moky
Parmenych Knurov, stretching his legs.

IVAN. Every morning he paces back and forth on the boulevard, as if he'd made a
vow. Why does he go to so much trouble?

GAVRILO. For the exercise.

IVAN. But what's the exercise for?

GAVRILO. To work up an appetite. He needs the appetite for dinner. You should
see the dinners he has! Do you think he could eat dinners like that without
exercise?

IVAN. Why is he so quiet all the time?

GAVRILO. "Quiet"! You're really something... How can you expect him to go on
carrying conversations when he has all those millions! Who's he supposed to
talk with? There's only two or three people in town he can talk with, so he
keeps quiet. And that's why he doesn't stay here very long, wouldn't stay at all
if he didn't have business. For talking he goes to Moscow, to St. Petersburg,

and abroad too; he has more elbow room there.

IVAN. There comes Vasily Danilych from over the hill. He's rich too, but he talks a lot.

GAVRILO. Vasily Danilych is still young, still on the timid side, but when he gets older he'll act like God too.

Knurov enters from the left and, not paying any attention to the bows of Gavrilo and Ivan, sits down at a table, takes out a French newspaper from his pocket, and reads it. Vozhevatov enters from the right.

VOZHEVATOV *(bowing respectfully).* Moky Parmenych, I have the honor of greeting you!

KNUROV. Ah, Vasily Danilych! *(He holds out a hand.)* Where did you come from?

VOZHEVATOV. From the dock. *(He sits down.)*

Gavrilo comes closer.

KNUROV. Were you meeting somebody?

VOZHEVATOV. I was supposed to but didn't. I had a telegram yesterday from Sergey Sergeyich Paratov. I'm buying a steamboat from him.

GAVRILO. It's not the *Swallow,* Vasily Danilych?

VOZHEVATOV. Yes, it's the *Swallow.* What about it?

GAVRILO. It goes fast, it's a strong boat.

VOZHEVATOV. But Sergey Sergeyich let me down, he didn't come.

GAVRILO. You were expecting him to come on the *Flier,* but maybe he'll come on his own boat, the *Swallow.*

IVAN. Vasily Danilych, there's another boat coming down the river.

VOZHEVATOV. A lot of boats sail the Volga.

IVAN. That's Sergey Sergeyich coming.

VOZHEVATOV. You think so?

IVAN. It looks like him, sir... The paddle boxes on the *Swallow* stand out a lot.

VOZHEVATOV. That means you'd be making out paddle boxes at five miles.

IVAN. I can make them out at seven miles, sir... And it's coming fast, it's clear the owner's with it.

VOZHEVATOV. And how far is it?

IVAN. It's come out from behind the island. It's making a lot of headway, a lot.

GAVRILO. You say it's making a lot of headway?

IVAN. A lot. An awful lot! It runs faster than the *Flier,* they've timed it.

GAVRILO. It's him, sir.

VOZHEVATOV *(to Ivan).* You tell us when they start coming aside.

IVAN. Yes, sir… I suppose they'll shoot from the cannon.

GAVRILO. They're sure to.

VOZHEVATOV. What cannon?

GAVRILO. He has his own barges anchored in the middle of the Volga.

VOZHEVATOV. I know.

GAVRILO. One barge has a cannon. Whenever somebody meets Sergey Sergeyich or sees him off they always fire a salute. *(Looking beyond the coffee house.)* There's one of Chirkov's carriages going for him now, sir. They must have let Chirkov know he'd be coming, for Chirkov himself is on the box. That's him they're going for, sir.

VOZHEVATOV. But how do you know it's for him?

GAVRILO. They've got four pacers lined up, it's really for him. Who else would Chirkov make up four horses for? It's even scary to look at them… they're like lions… all four with snaffle bits! And the harness, the harness! They're going for him, sir.

IVAN. And there's a gypsy sitting on the box with Chirkov, he has a fancy Cossack coat on, and his belt's so tight he could snap in two.

GAVRILO. They're going after him, sir. It couldn't be anyone else with four horses like those. It's him, sir.

KNUROV. Paratov lives in style.

VOZHEVATOV. Whatever else, he has plenty of style.

KNUROV. Are you buying the boat cheap?

VOZHEVATOV. Cheap, Moky Parmenych.

KNUROV. Yes, of course; otherwise, what's the advantage of buying? Why is he selling it?

VOZHEVATOV. I suppose he doesn't find any profit in it.

KNUROV. Of course, how could he! That's no business for a gentleman. But you'll make a profit, especially if you buy it cheap.

VOZHEVATOV. It suits our purpose; we have a lot of cargo down the river.

KNUROV. Maybe he needs the money… he's a great spender, you know.

VOZHEVATOV. That's his business. We have the money ready.

KNUROV. Yes, with money a man can do business. *(With a smile.)* A man who has a lot of money, Vasily Danilych, that man's in good shape.

VOZHEVATOV. How could he be in bad shape! You yourself know that better than any one, Moky Parmenych.

KNUROV. I know it, I know it.

VOZHEVATOV. Moky Parmenych, couldn't we have a cool drink?

KNUROV. What do you mean, it's still morning! I haven't eaten yet.

VOZHEVATOV. That doesn't matter, sir. There was an Englishman, a factory director, and he told me that if a man has a cold it's a good idea to drink champagne on an empty stomach. And yesterday I caught a little cold.

KNUROV. How could you do that? We're having such warm weather now.

VOZHEVATOV. I caught cold from the drink itself; they served it up very cold.

KNUROV. No, what's the good of that? People will see us, and they'll say: it's hardly morning yet, and they're drinking champagne.

VOZHEVATOV. But so people won't say something bad, we'll drink tea.

KNUROV. Tea, that's another matter.

VOZHEVATOV *(to Gavrilo).* Gavrilo, bring us some of my tea, you understand?... Mine!

GAVRILO. Yes, sir. *(He goes off.)*

KNUROV. Do you drink a special kind?

VOZHEVATOV. It's really champagne, but he'll pour it into teapots and serve it in tea glasses with saucers.

KNUROV. That's smart.

VOZHEVATOV. Necessity is the mother of invention, Moky Parmenych.

KNUROV. Are you going to Paris, to the exposition?

VOZHEVATOV. After I've bought the boat and sent it down the river for cargo, then I'll go.

KNUROV. Me too one of these days. I already have somebody waiting for me there.

Gavrilo brings a tray with two teapots containing champagne and two glasses.

VOZHEVATOV *(pouring).* Have you heard the news, Moky Parmenych? Larisa Dmitriyevna is getting married.

KNUROV. Getting married! You can't mean it! Who to?

VOZHEVATOV. Karandyshov.

KNUROV. What kind of nonsense is that! It's insanity! What's Karandyshov! You know he's no match for her, Vasily Danilych.

VOZHEVATOV. Of course he's no match! But what can they do, where can they find a husband for her? After all, she doesn't have any dowry.

KNUROV. Even girls without a dowry can find good husbands.

VOZHEVATOV. Times have changed. There used to be enough eligible bachelors, even for girls without a dowry. But now there's just enough for girls with a dowry, no extras for those without. Do you think Kharita Ignatyevna would marry her daughter off to Karandyshov if she could find anyone better?

KNUROV. She's a resourceful woman.

VOZHEVATOV. She can't be Russian.

KNUROV. Why not?

VOZHEVATOV. She's so energetic.

KNUROV. How could she make such a mistake? The Ogudalovs have a respectable family name, and just like that a marriage to the likes of Karandyshov!... And with all her cleverness... their house is always full of bachelors!...

VOZHEVATOV. The men all go to her house because it's so much fun there. Her daughter's pretty, plays different instruments, sings, has a free and easy manner, all that attracts them. But getting married to her is something to think about.

KNUROV. The other two daughters got married off.

VOZHEVATOV. They got married off all right, but you should ask them how sweet their life is. The oldest girl was taken away by some mountaineer, a young prince from the Caucasus. What fun that was! When he first saw her, he started to shake all over, he even began to cry. He stayed near her for a couple of weeks, he'd hold on to his dagger, and his eyes flashed so that nobody else came close. So they got married and went off, but they say he didn't even get her to the Caucasus, that he killed her on the way from jealousy. The other girl got married too, to some sort of foreigner, only later it turned out that he was no foreigner at all but a card shark.

KNUROV. Madame Ogudalov wasn't dumb the way she figured it out. She doesn't have any money and can't give a dowry, so she keeps open house and receives everybody.

VOZHEVATOV. She likes to have fun herself, but she just doesn't have the means for such a life.

KNUROV. Then where does she get the money?

VOZHEVATOV. The suitors pay. If a man likes the daughter, than he shells out. Later on the mother will want money from the groom to pay for the dowry, only he shouldn't ask for the dowry.

KNUROV. Well, I don't think it's just the suitors who pay for it. Take you, for example. It must cost you a pretty penny to visit the family so often.

VOZHEVATOV. It won't ruin me, Moky Parmenych. What's a man to do? He has to pay for his pleasures, they don't come free. And being in their home is a great pleasure.

KNUROV. It really is a pleasure, you're right there.

VOZHEVATOV. And yet you yourself are almost never there.

KNUROV. It's awkward; there's so much riffraff there. You run into them later and they exchange greetings, then worm their way into a conversation. Karandyshov is one of them. What kind of an acquaintance is he for me!

VOZHEVATOV. Yes, their home is like a bazaar.

KNUROV. So what's the good of it? One fellow goes up to Larisa Dmitriyevna with his compliments, another with tender remarks, and they buzz away so you can't get in a single word with her. I'd like to see her more often when she's alone, without any interference

VOZHEVATOV. Somebody ought to marry her.

KNUROV. Marry her! Not everybody can, and not everybody even wants to. Me, for example, I'm a married man.

VOZHEVATOV. Then there's nothing to be done. The grapes are pretty but not for picking,[2] Moky Parmenych.

KNUROV. You think so?

VOZHEVATOV. That's the way it seems. They don't follow those procedures. There were a few times when they could have, but they weren't tempted. It's got to be marriage even if that means Karandyshov.

KNUROV. But it would be nice to make a trip to the Paris exposition with a girl like that.

VOZHEVATOV. Yes, that wouldn't be boring, a pleasant trip that. What plans you have, Moky Parmenych!

KNUROV. And you've never had any plans like that?

VOZHEVATOV. How could I! I'm green at such things. I just don't have any boldness with women. You know, I was brought up in a terribly moral, old-fashioned way.

KNUROV. Oh come now! Your chances are better than mine; you have youth, a big thing. And you won't begrudge the money; you're buying the boat cheap, so you can take it out of the profits. Still, you must realize it would cost you as much as the *Swallow.*

VOZHEVATOV. Every piece of goods has its price, Moky Parmenych. I may be young, but I won't overdo it. I won't give any more than I have to.

KNUROV. Don't guarantee it! At your age it wouldn't take much to fall in love, and then we'd see what calculations you'd make!

VOZHEVATOV. No, Moky Parmenych, somehow or other I don't notice that sort of thing in myself.

KNUROV. What sort of thing?

VOZHEVATOV. What they call love.

KNUROV. That's commendable, you'll make a good merchant. All the same, you're a lot closer to her than the others.

VOZHEVATOV. But what does my being close to her amount to? Sometimes I'll pour her an extra glass of champagne when her mother's not looking, learn a song from her, bring her novels, the kind they don't give girls to read.

KNUROV. In other words, you're corrupting her a little.

VOZHEVATOV. What's that to me! After all, I'm not forcing myself on her. Why should I worry about her morals? I'm not her guardian.

KNUROV. I just can't get over it. Does Larisa Dmitriyevna really have no other suitors besides Karandyshov?

VOZHEVATOV. She had some, but she's terribly naive.

KNUROV. Naive, how? You mean she's stupid?

VOZHEVATOV. She's not stupid, but she's not shrewd at all, she doesn't take after her mother in that. Her mother's always shrewd and full of flattering, but she for no reason at all will suddenly come out with something she doesn't have to.

KNUROV. You mean the truth?

VOZHEVATOV. Yes, the truth. But that's something that young women without a dowry just can't do. If she likes somebody, she doesn't hide it at all. Last year Sergey Sergeyich Paratov showed up, and she couldn't see enough of him. He kept coming for a couple of months, beat away all the other suitors, and then he flew the coop. Nobody knew where he disappeared to.

KNUROV. Whatever possessed him to do that?

VOZHEVATOV. Who knows? He's a hard one to figure out. But you should have seen how she loved him, she almost died from grief. How sentimental she was! *(He laughs.)* She set out to try and catch up with him, but her mother got her at the second stop and brought her back.

KNUROV. And were there any suitors after Paratov?

VOZHEVATOV. Two came from somewhere. One was an old man with the gout. Then there was a manager for some prince or other; that manager had gotten rich, but he was always drunk. Larisa didn't want to have anything to do with them, but she had to be nice to them, Mama's orders.

KNUROV. Her lot is not a happy one.

VOZHEVATOV. No, it's even absurd. Sometimes there were a few tears in her eyes, and you could see she was about to cry, but Mama told her to smile. And then a cashier turned up. He threw his money all about, enough to cover Kharita Ignatyevna with it. He won the field over everybody, but he didn't strut for long, they arrested him at his home. What a great scandal that was! *(He laughs.)* For about a month the Ogudalovs couldn't go anywhere. It was then that Larisa told her mother point-blank, "We've put up with enough of this shame. I'll marry the first one who comes along, whether he's rich or poor. I'm not going to be choosy." And up pops Karandyshov with his proposal.

KNUROV. Where did this Karandyshov come from?

VOZHEVATOV. He's been hanging around their house a long time, about three years. They didn't chase him away, but they didn't show him much respect either. When the lull set in and there weren't any rich suitors in sight they held onto Karandyshov and gave him some invitations so the house wouldn't be empty. But when some rich guy dropped in, it was simply pitiful to look at Karandyshov. They didn't even talk to him or even look at him. And there he sat in his corner, playing his different roles, throwing out savage looks, pretending to be in despair. Once he wanted to shoot himself, but nothing came of that, he just made everybody laugh. And here's the funny part. Once they had a costume party, and Paratov was there. So Karandyshov dressed himself up as a highway robber, took an axe in his hands, and threw wild looks at everybody, especially Sergey Sergeyich.

KNUROV. Then what?

VOZHEVATOV. They took his axe away from him and told him to change his clothes or else he'd have to leave!

KNUROV. What it all means is, he's being rewarded for being faithful. He's happy, I'm sure.

VOZHEVATOV. Happy and then some, glowing like an orange. It's so funny! He's really a nut. What he ought to do is marry her as soon as he can and take her away to his little estate till the talk dies down. The Ogudalovs would like that. But instead he drags Larisa along the boulevard on his arm with his head raised so high he'd run right into you if you didn't watch out. And then for some reason he's taken to wearing glasses, but he never used to wear them. When he bows he hardly nods his head, and he's taken on a certain air. Before you'd hardly hear a word out of him, but now it's always, "I this, I that, I want, I wish."

KNUROV. He's like the Russian peasant. It's not enough fun just getting drunk. He has to act high and mighty so everybody takes notice. So he gets up on his high horse, and they give him a thrashing or two. Then he's satisfied and goes off to sleep.

VOZHEVATOV. Yes, I suppose that's the sort of thing Karandyshov has to go through.

KNUROV. Poor girl! She must suffer just looking at him.

VOZHEVATOV. He got the idea of decorating his apartment, and here's what he dreamed up. In his study he put up a cheap tapestry on the wall, and he hung up daggers and pistols from Tula. That would be no surprise if he were a hunter, but he's never held a gun in his life. So he drags you to his place and shows it all off to you, and you have to praise him for it or he'll take offense. He's a proud man, envious too. He ordered a horse from the country, some nag or other with different colors, and he has a little coachman who wears a coat handed down from a big coachman. And with that camel he takes Larisa Dmitriyevna driving; he sits there so proudly, as if he were driving with a thousand trotters. He walks up from the boulevard and shouts to the constable, "Have them bring my carriage!" So that carriage of his comes driving up with all its music, the screws and nuts all jangling out of tune, and the springs shaking as if they're alive.

KNUROV. I'm sorry for poor Larisa Dmitriyevna. I'm sorry for her.

VOZHEVATOV. Why are you so sorry for her?

KNUROV. Don't you see? Here's a woman made for luxury. A precious jewel demands a costly setting.

VOZHEVATOV. And a good jeweler.

KNUROV. That's the whole truth. A jeweler and not just an ordinary workman; he has to be an artist. If she's surrounded by poverty and married to a fool besides, she'll either perish or become common.

VOZHEVATOV. But I think she'll throw him over pretty soon. She's like a dead woman now, but when she recovers and takes a closer look at her husband, sees what he's like... *(Quietly.)* There they are now, speak of the devil...

Karandyshov, Madame Ogudalov, and Larisa enter. Vozhevatov stands up and bows. Knurov takes out a newspaper. Larisa sits down on a bench by the railing and looks through binoculars at the Volga.

MME OGUDALOV *(walking over to the table).* Greetings, gentlemen!

Karandyshov follows her over. Vozhevatov gives his hand to both of them. Knurov silently and not rising from his place gives his hand to Mme. Ogudalov, nods slightly to Karandyshov, and buries himself in his newspaper.

VOZHEVATOV. Kharita Ignatyenva, please sit down. *(He moves a chair forward.)*

Mme. Ogudalov sits down.

Wouldn't you like some tea?

Karandyshov sits down some distance away.

MME OGUDALOV. All right, I'll take a cup.

VOZHEVATOV. Ivan, bring a cup and add some boiling water.

Ivan takes the teapot and goes off.

KARANDYSHOV. What a crazy idea to drink tea at this time of day? It amazes me.

VOZHEVATOV. It's a question of thirst, Yuly Kapitonych, but just what I should drink I don't know. Give me your advice, I'd appreciate it.

KARANDYSHOV *(looks at his watch).* At the present moment it's noon, so you could have a small glass of vodka, a chop, and then a small glass of good wine. That's how I always lunch.

VOZHEVATOV *(to Mme. Ogudalov).* Now that's what I call living, Kharita Ignatyenva, it makes a man jealous. *(To Karandyshov.)* If I could only live one little day in your shoes. A bit of vodka, a bit of wine! But we can't do that, sir, we might lose our powers of reasoning. You can do what you want, you're not running through your capital because you don't have any, but we poor devils were born into the world with a lot of big deals to attend to, so we're not allowed to lose our reason.

Ivan brings the teapot and a cup.

Kharita Ignatyenva, please! *(He pours out a cup and hands it to her.)* I drink my tea cold so people won't say I use hot drinks.

MME OGUDALOV. The tea's cold all right. Only, Vasya, you poured mine too strong.

VOZHEVATOV. That doesn't matter, ma'am. Drink it, for my sake! It won't do you any harm in the open air.

KARANDYSHOV *(to Ivan)*. Come to my house tonight to serve dinner.

IVAN. Yes, sir, Yuly Kapitonych.

KARANDYSHOV. And listen, my friend, dress up for it.

IVAN. Of course, a frock coat. As if we didn't understand that, sir.

KARANDYSHOV. Vasily Danilych, tell you what! You come and have dinner with me tonight!

VOZHEVATOV. Thank you so much. And are you going to order me to come in a frock coat too?

KARANDYSHOV. As you wish, don't stand on ceremony. Still, there'll be ladies.

VOZHEVATOV *(bowing)*. Yes, sir. I hope I won't disgrace myself.

KARANDYSHOV *(walks over to Knurov.)* Moky Parmenych, wouldn't you like to come and have dinner with me tonight?

KNUROV *(looks at him in astonishment)*. With you?

MME OGUDALOV. Moky Parmenych, it's the same as with us; this is a dinner for Larisa.

KNUROV. I see, so it's you who's inviting me? Fine, I'll come.

KARANDYSHOV. I'll look forward to seeing you, then.

KNUROV. I already said I'd come. *(He reads his newspaper.)*

MME OGUDALOV. Yuly Kapitonych is my future son-in-law; I'm letting him marry Larisa.

KNUROV *(continuing to read)*. That's your affair.

KARANDYSHOV. Yes, sir, Moky Parmenych, I took the risk. In general I've always been above prejudices.

Knurov hides behind the newspaper.

VOZHEVATOV *(to Mme. Ogudalov)*. Moky Parmenych is stern.

KARANDYSHOV *(moving from Knurov to Vozhevatov)*. I wish that Larisa Dmitri-yevna be surrounded only by choice people.

VOZHEVATOV. Which means I'm one of the elect? Thank you, that's something I wasn't expecting. *(To Gavrilo.)* Gavrilo, how much do I owe you for the tea?

GAVRILO. You had two orders?

VOZHEVATOV. Yes, two orders.

GAVRILO. Then you should know yourself, Vasily Danilych, it's not the first time... Thirteen rubles, sir.

VOZHEVATOV. I just thought it might have gotten cheaper.

GAVRILO. How could it have gotten cheaper! With the rate of exchange and the customs tax, really!

VOZHEVATOV. But I'm not arguing with you, why talk about it! Take your money and forget it! *(He gives him the money.)*

KARANDYSHOV. But why is it so expensive? I don't understand.

GAVRILO. It's expensive for some but not for others. You don't drink that kind of tea.

MME OGUDALOV *(to Karandyshov).* Stop it, don't meddle in other people's affairs.

IVAN. Vasily Danilych, the *Swallow* is coming in.

VOZHEVATOV. Moky Parmenych, the *Swallow* is coming in, wouldn't you like to take a look? We won't go down, we can look from the hill.

KNUROV. Let's go. I'm curious. *(He gets up.)*

MME OGUDALOV. Vasya, I'm going home in your carriage.

VOZHEVATOV. Take it, only send it back soon. *(He goes over to Larisa and speaks quietly with her.)*

MME OGUDALOV *(goes over to Knurov).* Moky Parmenych, we've embarked on a wedding, you just can't believe how many troubles there are.

KNUROV. Yes.

MME OGUDALOV. And suddenly there are unexpected expenses… And tomorrow's Larisa's birthday, I'd like to give her a present.

KNUROV. Good, I'll drop in on you.

Mme. Ogudalov goes off.

LARISA *(to Vozhevatov).* Good-bye, Vasya!

Vozhevatov and Knurov leave. Larisa approaches Karandyshov.

LARISA. Just now I was looking across the Volga. How nice it is on the other side! Let's go to the country as soon as we can!

KARANDYSHOV. You were looking across the Volga? And what was Vozhevatov talking with you about?

LARISA. Nothing really, just little things. I want so much to go to the other side of the Volga, into the woods… *(Thoughtfully.)* Let's go, let's leave here!

KARANDYSHOV. But it's so strange! What could he have to talk with you about?

LARISA. Well, whatever he talked about, what business is it of yours?

KARANDYSHOV. You call him Vasya. Why so familiar with a young man?

LARISA. We've known each other since childhood. When we were little we played together. So I've gotten used to calling him that.

KARANDYSHOV. You'll have to throw off your old habits. There's no reason to be friends with a shallow and stupid boy. It's not possible to tolerate the sort of life you've had so far.

LARISA *(offended)*. There hasn't been anything bad in our life.

KARANDYSHOV. It's been a gypsy camp, miss, that's what it's been. *(Larisa wipes away some tears.)* But why are you so offended!

LARISA. So maybe it has been a gypsy camp, but at least it's been fun. Will you be able to give me something better than this camp?

KARANDYSHOV. Of course.

LARISA. Why do you keep on reproaching me with it? Do you really think I've liked our kind of life? Mama told me how she wanted things, and so, whether I wanted to or not, I had to lead that kind of life. Throwing this gypsy life at me all the time is either stupid or heartless. If I weren't looking for quiet and solitude, I wouldn't be wanting to run away from people, and would I really be marrying you? So try to understand that and don't go assigning my choice to your virtues, I don't see them yet. I still only want to fall in love with you; I'm drawn to the quiet family life, it looks like some kind of heaven. You can see I'm standing at the crossroads, so give me support, I need encouragement and sympathy. Deal with me tenderly, with affection. Seize these moments, don't let them pass.

KARANDYSHOV. Larisa Dmitriyevna, I didn't mean to offend you at all, somehow the words just came to my tongue...

LARISA. What is that "somehow"? You mean you weren't thinking, that you didn't understand your words might be offensive?

KARANDYSHOV. Exactly, I did it without any intent.

LARISA. That makes it even worse. You should think about what you say. Chatter away with others if you like, but with me speak more carefully. Can't you see my position is very serious! I feel every word I say and hear. I've become very sensitive and impressionable.

KARANDYSHOV. In that case please forgive me.

LARISA. All right, only in the future be more careful. *(Thoughtfully.)* Gypsy camp... Yes, that's true... but in that camp have been some good and noble people.

KARANDYSHOV. What noble people? You don't perhaps mean Sergey Sergeyich Paratov?

LARISA. No, please, don't speak of him.

KARANDYSHOV. And why not?

LARISA. You don't know him, and even if you did know him, well... forgive me, but it's not for you to pass judgment on him.

KARANDYSHOV. People are judged by their actions. Do you think he acted well with you?

LARISA. That's my affair. If I'm afraid to, if I don't dare to pass judgment on him, them I'm not going to let you do it.

KARANDYSHOV. Larisa Dmitriyevna, tell me something. Only please, speak frankly.

LARISA. What is it?

KARANDYSHOV. How am I any worse than Paratov?

LARISA. Oh no, don't ask that!

KARANDYSHOV. But why not?

LARISA. Better not, better not! How can there be any comparison!

KARANDYSHOV. That's what I'd like to hear from you.

LARISA. Don't ask, there's no need!

KARANDYSHOV. But why not?

LARISA. Because the comparison will not be to your advantage. By yourself you have value, you're a good and honest man. But in comparison with Sergey Sergeyich you lose everything.

KARANDYSHOV. But those are just words, we need proof. Give him and me a real analysis.

LARISA. Do you know the man you're comparing yourself with! How can you be so blind! Sergey Sergeyich... is the ideal man. Do you understand what ideal is? Maybe I'm wrong, I'm still young and don't know people, but it will be impossible to change this opinion in me, it will die with me.

KARANDYSHOV. I just can't understand what's so special about him, I don't see anything. There's a certain boldness, an impudence... But anybody can have that if he wants.

LARISA. And do you know what boldness is?

KARANDYSHOV. Whatever it is, what's so wonderful about it? All it takes is putting on airs.

LARISA. To show what it is I'll tell you something that happened. There was an officer from the Caucasus passing through here, an acquaintance of Sergey Sergeyich, and he was a wonderful shot. They were both at our place, and Sergey Sergeyich says to him, "I hear you're a wonderful shot." "Yes, not bad," says the officer. Sergey Sergeyich gives him a pistol, puts a glass on his own head, and he goes off to another room, about twelve steps away. "Shoot," he says.

KARANDYSHOV. And he shot?

LARISA. He shot, and, of course, he knocked off the glass, only he turned a little pale. Sergey Sergeyich says, "You shoot beautifully, but you turned pale, and you were shooting at a man, and a man not close to you. Look, I'm going to shoot at a young woman who's dearer to me than anything in the world, and I won't turn pale." He gives me a coin to hold, and, with indifference and a smile, he shoots from the same distance and hits it.

KARANDYSHOV. And you obeyed him?

LARISA. How could I do anything else?

KARANDYSHOV. You really had so much confidence in him?

LARISA. How can you ask! How could I not have confidence in him?

KARANDYSHOV. He has no heart, that's why he's so bold.

LARISA. No, he has a heart too. I saw myself how he helped the poor, how he gave away all the money he had on him.

KARANDYSHOV. So, let's grant that Paratov has some virtues, at least in your eyes, but what about this petty merchant, this Vasya of yours?

LARISA. You're not being jealous, are you? No, you stop all this nonsense. It's degrading, and I won't tolerate it, I'm telling you in advance. Don't worry, I'm not in love with anybody, and I won't fall in love with anybody.

KARANDYSHOV. But what if Paratov should show up?

LARISA. Of course, if Paratov should show up and were free, then it would take only one look from him... But you can set your mind at ease, he hasn't showed up, and even if he should show up now, it's already too late... We'll probably never see each other again.

A cannon shot on the Volga.

What's that?

KARANDYSHOV. Some high and mighty merchant is coming in, so they're firing a salute in his honor.

LARISA. Oh, how it frightened me!

KARANDYSHOV. Why, why should it?

LARISA. My nerves are upset. Just now I was looking down from this bench, and I began to get dizzy. Could one hurt oneself here very much?

KARANDYSHOV. Hurt oneself! Here it's sure death, it's paved with stone below. And it's so high here you'd die before you hit the bottom.

LARISA. Let's go home, it's time.

KARANDYSHOV. I have to go too, I have that dinner, you know.

LARISA *(going to the railing)*. Wait awhile. *(She looks below.)* Oh, oh, hold on to me!

KARANDYSHOV *(takes Larisa by the arm)*. Come on, you're just being childish!

They leave. Gavrilo and Ivan enter from the coffee house.

IVAN. The cannon! The gentleman's come, the gentleman's come, Sergey Sergey-ich.

GAVRILO. I told you it was him. I know—you can tell a falcon by its flight.

IVAN. The carriage is coming uphill empty. That means the gentlemen are coming on foot. There they are! *(He runs off into the coffee house.)*

GAVRILO. Welcome to them. I wish I could figure out what to treat them with.

Paratov enters. He is wearing a single-breasted, close-fitting, black frock coat, varnished high boots, a white service cap; across his shoulder is a traveling bag. With him are Robinson (wearing a cloak, the right flap of which is thrown over his left shoulder, and a tall soft hat perched on one side of his head), Knurov, and Vozhevatov. Ivan runs out of the coffee house with a hand broom to brush off Paratov.

PARATOV *(to Ivan)*. What are you doing! I've just come from the water, there's no dust on the Volga.

IVAN. All the same, sir, it's impossible not to… custom requires it. It's been a whole year since we saw you… we want to welcome you, sir.

PARATOV. All right, fine, thank you. Here. *(He gives him a ruble note.)*

IVAN. Thank you very much, sir. *(He goes off.)*

PARATOV. So, Vasily Danilych, you were expecting men to come on the *Flier?*

VOZHEVATOV. I didn't know you'd be coming on your *Swallow.* I thought you'd be coming with the barges.

PARATOV. No, I sold my barges. I thought I'd get here early this morning. I wanted to pass the *Flier,* but the engineer's a coward. I keep shouting to the stokers, "Stoke away!"—but he takes the wood from them. He climbs out of the hold and says, "If you throw down just one more log, I'll throw myself overboard." He was afraid the boiler wouldn't stand it. He scratched out some figures for me on paper, calculated the pressure. He's a foreigner, a Dutchman, a timid soul; they have arithmetic instead of a soul. But gentlemen, I forgot to introduce you to my friend. Moky Parmenych, Vasily Danilych, I present you—Robinson.

Robinson bows solemnly and shakes hands with Knurov and Vozhevatov.

VOZHEVATOV. And what's his first name and patronymic?

PARATOV. He's just Robinson, that's all, no first name or patronymic.

ROBINSON *(to Paratov)*. Serge!

PARATOV. What is it?

ROBINSON. It's noon, my friend, I'm suffering.

PARATOV. You just wait, we'll be going to an inn.

ROBINSON *(pointing to the coffee house)*. Voilà!

PARATOV. All right, go ahead, have it your own way!

Robinson goes to the coffee house.

Gavrilo, don't serve that gentleman more than one small glass; he has a restless disposition.

ROBINSON *(shrugging his shoulders)*. Serge! *(He enters the coffee house, Gavrilo after him.)*

PARATOV. That, gentlemen, is an actor from the provinces, Arkady Shchastlivtsev by name.

VOZHEVATOV. Then why is he called Robinson?

PARATOV. I'll tell you. He was traveling on some steamboat or other, I don't know which one, with a friend of his, a merchant's son named Neputóvy, both drunk, of course, drunk as could be. They did whatever came into their head, and the passengers put up with it all. At last, to top off all their insane antics, they thought up a dramatic performance. They took off their clothes, cut open a pillow, covered themselves with down and began to play savages. At that point the captain, on the insistence of the passengers, put them ashore on a desert island. We go sailing by that island, I look, and somebody calls out, lifting his arms. Immediately I shout, "Stop," get into a boat myself, and I find the actor Shchastlivtsev. I take him onto our boat and dress him from head to foot in my own clothes since I have extra. Gentlemen, I have a weakness for actors... That's why he's Robinson.

VOZHEVATOV. And Neputovy stayed on the island?

PARATOV. But what good was he to me? Let him get the fresh air. You can judge for yourselves, gentlemen. You know, when you're traveling it can get awfully boring, you're glad for any companion.

KNUROV. Quite right, of course.

VOZHEVATOV. That was lucky, a real stroke of luck! Like finding gold!

KNUROV. Just one drawback, he's given to drunkenness.

PARATOV. No, gentlemen, he can't get drunk with me, I'm strict about that. He has no money, and he can't get anything without my permission. And if he asks me for something, then I make him learn some French conversations from a phrase book I was lucky enough to have. He learns a page first or I won't give him anything. So he sits down and studies, how hard he tries!

VOZHEVATOV. How lucky you are, Sergey Sergeyich! I wouldn't spare anything to have a man like that, but there aren't any around. Is he a good actor?

PARATOV. Well no, hardly! He went through all the roles and was a prompter, but now he plays in operettas. It doesn't matter, he'll pass well enough, he's amusing.

VOZHEVATOV. You mean he's fun?

PARATOV. He's entertaining.

VOZHEVATOV. And can you play jokes on him?

PARATOV. Sure, he's not touchy. Look, to satisfy you I can let you have him for two or three days.

VOZHEVATOV. Thank you very much. If I like him, he won't lose by it.

KNUROV. How is it, Sergey Sergeyich, that you don't feel sorry about selling the *Swallow*?

PARATOV. I don't know what it means to "feel sorry": For me, Moky Parmenych, nothing is sacred. If it's to my advantage, I'll sell anything, no matter what. But now, gentlemen, I have other business and other considerations. I'm going to marry a very rich young woman, I'll be getting gold mines for a dowry.

VOZHEVATOV. A good dowry.

PARATOV. It won't come cheap. I have to say good-bye to my freedom and my life of fun. That's why we should try hard to have a high old time these last days.

VOZHEVATOV. We'll try hard, Sergey Sergeyich, we'll try hard.

PARATOV. My fiancées's father is an important official. He's a strict old man, and he can't stand hearing about gypsies, carousals, and the like. He doesn't even like it if somebody smokes a lot. What you're supposed to do is put on your frockcoat and parlez français! That's why I'm practicing now with Robinson. Only he, maybe for show, I don't know, calls me "la Serge," not simply "Serge." He's terribly funny!

Robinson appears on the steps of the coffee house, chewing something. Gavrilo is behind him.

PARATOV *(to Robinson)*. Que faites-vous là? Venez!

ROBINSON *(with a distinguished air)*. Comment?

PARATOV. What charm! What a tone, gentlemen! *(To Robinson.)* You give up that filthy habit of abandoning respectable society for the tavern.

VOZHEVATOV. Yes, they have a way of doing that.

ROBINSON. La Serge, you've managed to... There was no need to do that.

PARATOV. Yes, forgive me, I gave away your pseudonym.

VOZHEVATOV. We won't give you away, Robinson, you'll pass among us as an Englishman, old man.

ROBINSON. Why this sudden familiarity? You and I haven't drunk any fraternal pledge.

VOZHEVATOV. It doesn't matter... Why stand on ceremony!

ROBINSON. But I don't tolerate familiarity, and I won't permit just anybody...

VOZHEVATOV. But I'm not just anybody.

ROBINSON. Then who are you?

VOZHEVATOV. A merchant.

ROBINSON. A rich one?

VOZHEVATOV. A rich one.

ROBINSON. And generous?

VOZHEVATOV. And generous.

ROBINSON. Now that's something to my taste. *(He extends his hand to Vozhevatov.)* Very pleased to meet you. Now I can permit you to deal with me without formalities.

VOZHEVATOV. That means we're friends, two bodies, one soul.

ROBINSON. And one pocket. What's your first name and patronymic? I mean, your first name, the patronymic's not necessary.

VOZHEVATOV. Vasily Danilych.

ROBINSON. Tell you what, Vasya, in honor of our first acquaintance you pay for me.

VOZHEVATOV. Gavrilo, write it down to my account. Sergey Sergeyich, we're getting up a picnic for tonight on the other side of the Volga. In one boat there'll be gypsies, and we'll be in the other. When we get there we'll sit down on a rug and heat up some hot punch.

GAVRILO. And I, Sergey Sergeyich, have two pineapples that have been waiting for you a long time. They should be broken into to celebrate your arrival.

PARATOV (to Gavrilo). Fine, cut them up! (To Vozhevatov.) Gentlemen, I'm at your disposal, do what you want with me.

GAVRILO. And I, Vasily Danilych, will make all the necessary arrangements. I have a silver saucepan for such occasions, and I'll let my help go off with you.

VOZHEVATOV. All right, very good. Have everything ready by six. If you should get in something extra, it won't be held against you, but you'll have to answer for any lack.

GAVRILO. We understand, sir.

VOZHEVATOV. And when we come back we'll light up colored lanterns on the boats.

ROBINSON. I haven't known him long, and already I've grown fond of him, gentlemen. There's a miracle for you!

PARATOV. The main thing is, there should be a good time. I'm saying goodbye to my bachelor life, so I want something to remember it by. And this evening, gentlemen, I invite you to have dinner with me.

VOZHEVATOV. What a pity! I'm afraid that's impossible, Sergey Sergeyich.

KNUROV. We've been invited elsewhere.

PARATOV. Decline, gentlemen.

VOZHEVATOV. We can't decline. Larisa Dmitriyevna is getting married, so we're having dinner at her fiancé's.

PARATOV. Larisa is getting married! (He becomes pensive.) So then... God be with her! This is even better... I'm a bit guilty towards her, or rather, I'm so guilty I shouldn't show my face to them. But now she's getting married it means the old scores are settled, and I can show up and kiss her little hands, and aunty's too. I call Kharita Ignatyevna aunty for short. You know, I almost married Larisa; that would have given people something to laugh at! Yes, I almost made a fool of myself. So she's getting married... That's very nice on her part; all the same I do feel a bit relieved... and may God grant her health and every blessing! I'll drop in on them, I'll drop in. It'll be interesting, very interesting to have a look at her.

VOZHEVATOV. They'll probably invite you.

PARATOV. Of course, how could they do without me!

KNUROV. I'm very glad. Now at least I'll have somebody at dinner to exchange a word with.

VOZHEVATOV. When we're there we'll talk over how we can pass time to have more fun. Maybe we can think up something else.

PARATOV. Yes, gentlemen, life is short, that's what the philosophers tell us, so we've got to know how to take advantage of it... N'est-ce pas, Robinson?

ROBINSON. Oui, la Serge.

VOZHEVATOV. We'll try hard, you won't be bored, we'll stand on that. We'll take a third boat, and we'll put the regimental band on it.

PARATOV. Good day, gentlemen! I'm going to the inn. Robinson, forward... march!

ROBINSON *(lifting his hat)*.

Long live merriment!
Long live delight![3]

ACT TWO

A room in the home of Mme. Ogudalov. Two doors: an entrance door in the background, the other to the left of the actors. On the right is a window. The furniture is presentable. A piano with a guitar lying on it. Mme. Ogudalov is alone. She is walking toward the door at the left with a small box in her hands.

MME OGUDALOV. Larisa, Larisa! *(Larisa's voice off stage: "I'm getting dressed, Mama.")* Just see what a gift Vasya's brought you! *(Larisa off stage: "I'll look later.")* What things! They must be worth five hundred rubles. He told me, "Put them in her room tomorrow morning and don't say who they're from." But he knows, the scamp, that I won't be able to control myself, that I'll tell. I asked him to stay awhile, but he wouldn't stay. He's going around with some foreigner, he's showing him the town. But Vasya's such a joker you can't tell whether he's thought up something or whether it's the real thing. "What I've got to do," he says, "is show this foreigner all the tavern institutions worthy of note." He wanted to drag that foreigner along to visit us. *(Looking out the window.)* There comes Moky Parmenych! Don't come out, it's better for me to talk with him alone. *(Knurov enters.)*

KNUROV *(in the doorway)*. You're alone?

MME OGUDALOV. Alone, Moky Parmenych.

KNUROV *(enters)*. Very good.

MME OGUDALOV. To what can I ascribe this good fortune! I'm grateful, Moky Parmenych, so very grateful that you've honored us with your visit. I'm so glad I've even lost my bearings. Really... I don't know where to have you sit.

KNUROV. It doesn't matter. I'll sit some place. *(He sits down.)*

MME OGUDALOV. You must excuse Larisa, she's changing. But I suppose I could hurry her up.

KNUROV. No, why bother!

MME OGUDALOV. What made you think of visiting us?

KNUROV. I walk about a lot before dinner, so I just dropped in.

MME OGUDALOV. You can rest assured, Moky Parmenych, that we consider your visit a special stroke of good fortune. I just can't compare it with anything.

KNUROV. So you're marrying off Larisa Dmitriyevna?

MME OGUDALOV. Yes, she's getting married, Moky Parmenych.

KNUROV. There was a groom who'd take her without money?

MME OGUDALOV. Without money, Moky Parmenych. Where do you think we could get any money?

KNUROV. Well then, does he have great means, that groom of yours?

MME OGUDALOV. What means! He has very little!

KNUROV. I see… And how do you feel, do you think you're doing the right thing to marry off Larisa Dmitriyevna to a poor man?

MME OGUDALOV. I don't know, Moky Parmenych. I didn't have anything to do with it, it was her choice.

KNUROV. Well, and this young man, what about him? Do you think he's doing the right thing?

MME OGUDALOV. Why not? I find it praiseworthy on his part.

KNUROV. There's nothing praiseworthy about it; on the contrary it's blameworthy. To be sure, from his point of view he's not being stupid. What is he, who knows him, who's paid any attention to him! But now the whole town'll start talking about him, he's climbing into the best society, he allows himself to invite me to dinner, for example… But here's the stupid part. He didn't think or didn't want to think about how and on what means he's going to live with such a wife. That's something you and I ought to talk about.

MME OGUDALOV. Be so kind, Moky Parmenych!

KNUROV. What opinion do you have of your daughter? What's she like?

MME OGUDALOV. I really don't know what to say. About all I can do is listen to you.

KNUROV. You know as well as I there's none of that commonness in Larisa Dmitriyevna, none of that everyday stuff. Well, you know what I mean, none of the petty triviality you need for a family living in poverty.

MME OGUDALOV. There's none of that, none.

KNUROV. You could call her an ethereal creature.

MME OGUDALOV. An ethereal creature, Moky Parmenych.

KNUROV. She was created for splendor.

MME OGUDALOV. For splendor, Moky Parmenych.

KNUROV. And can your Karandyshov give her that splendor?

MME OGUDALOV. No, how could he!

KNUROV. She won't be able to endure life when it's poor and common. And what will be left for her then? She'll fade away, and then, the way these things go, she'll end up with consumption.

MME OGUDALOV. Oh, how can you say things like that! God forbid!

KNUROV. It would be a good thing if she'd decide very quickly to leave her husband and come back to you.

MME OGUDALOV. But that would be just more misery, Moky Parmenych, what would my daughter and I have to live on!

KNUROV. Well, that's a misery that could be remedied. The heartfelt concern of a strong and rich man...

MME OGUDALOV. How nice if such a concern should turn up.

KNUROV. You should try to gain it. In cases like this it is quite necessary to have a good friend, one who's solid and steady.

MME OGUDALOV. It is quite necessary.

KNUROV. Now you might tell me that she's not even married yet, that the time is still far off when she could leave her husband. Yes, it could well be far off, but then again it could be very close. So it's better to let you know now, so you won't make some kind of mistake, that I won't begrudge a thing for Larisa Dmitriyevna. Why are you smiling?

MME OGUDALOV. It makes me very happy, Moky Parmenych, that you're so well disposed to us.

KNUROV. Do you think, perhaps, that my suggestions are not disinterested?

MME OGUDALOV. Oh, Moky Parmenych!

KNUROV. Take offense if you want, throw me out.

MME OGUDALOV (embarrassed). Oh, Moky Parmenych!

KNUROV. Go find those people who'll promise you tens of thousands for nothing in return, then you can scold me. Only don't bother to look, you won't find them. But I got carried away, that wasn't what I came to talk about. What's that box you have there?

MME OGUDALOV. I wanted to give it to my daughter for a present, Moky Parmenych.

KNUROV (looking over the things in the box). I see...

MME OGUDALOV. But it's all expensive, more than I can afford.

KNUROV (gives back the box). Well, those are just trifles, there are more important things to think about. You have to provide a good wardrobe for Larisa Dmitriyevna, what I mean is, not just good but very good. A wedding dress and everything else that's required.

MME OGUDALOV. Yes, yes, Moky Parmenych.

KNUROV. It would be a great shame for her to be dressed just any old way. So you go ahead and order everything in the best store, and don't count the cost or worry over the kopecks. Just send the bills to me, I'll pay.

MME OGUDALOV. Really, I can't find the words to thank you.

KNUROV. To tell the truth, that was why I came. *(He gets up.)*

MME OGUDALOV. All the same, I'd still like to give my daughter a surprise tomorrow. A mother's heart, you know...

KNUROV *(takes the box)*. Well now, what do we have here? How much does it cost?

MME OGUDALOV. You set a price on it, Moky Parmenych!

KNUROV. Why price it, why bother! Let's say it costs three hundred rubles. *(He takes money from his wallet and gives it to Mme. Ogudalov.)* Good-bye. I'm going to walk a bit more, I expect to have a good dinner tonight. We'll see each other at dinner. *(He goes to the door.)*

MME OGUDALOV. I'm very grateful, very grateful to you for everything, Moky Parmenych, everything! *(Knurov goes off. Larisa enters with a basket in her hand.)*

LARISA *(places the basket on the table and examines the things in the box)*. Are these what Vasya gave me? Not bad. How nice of him!

MME OGUDALOV. "Not bad." They're very expensive. Aren't you glad to get them?

LARISA. I don't feel especially glad about it.

MME OGUDALOV. You thank Vasya, just whisper in his ear, "Thank you." And Knurov too.

LARISA. Why Knurov?

MME OGUDALOV. It's something necessary, I know why.

LARISA. Oh, Mama, you always have your secrets and tricks.

MME OGUDALOV. Tricks! You can't live in this world without tricks.

LARISA *(takes the guitar, sits next to the window, and starts to sing)*.

> Mother mine, so dear to me, sun so warm and mild,
> Mother mine, caress your own tiny baby child.[4]

Yuly Kapitonych wants to enter the election for Justice of Peace.

MME OGUDALOV. That's very nice. For what district?

LARISA. For Zabolotye.

MME OGUDALOV. Aie, isn't that off in the sticks somewhere? Where did he get the idea of going so far?

LARISA. There aren't so many candidates there; he'd probably get elected.

MME OGUDALOV. Well, all right, even there people can live.

LARISA. I don't mind going even to the sticks, just so long as I can get away from here first.

MME OGUDALOV. It could be a good thing living in the sticks for a while. Your Karandyshov will look good there, he might be the first man in the district, and little by little you'll get used to him.

LARISA. But he's a good man here too. I don't see anything bad in him.

MME OGUDALOV. Oh come now! As if there aren't others just as good as him!

LARISA. Of course, some are even better. I know that myself, very well.

MME OGUDALOV. They're better all right, only they're not for the likes of us.

LARISA. Right now even this one's good enough for me. But why talk about it, it's all decided.

MME OGUDALOV. I'm just glad you like him, thank God for that! I'm not going to judge him before you, but we don't have to pretend to each other, you're not blind.

LARISA. I've become blind, I've lost all my feelings, and I'm glad of it. For a long time now everything around me's been like a dream. No, I simply must leave here, I must tear myself away. I'll keep after Yuly Kapitonych. Soon summer will be over, and I want to walk through the woods, to pick berries and mushrooms...

MME OGUDALOV. So that's why you've gotten yourself a basket! Now I understand. Get yourself a straw hat with a wide brim, and then you'll be a shepherd girl.

LARISA. I'll get a hat too. *(She sings.)*

O tempt me not if there's no need...[5]

It's calm and quiet there.

MME OGUDALOV. But when September comes it won't be so quiet; the wind will blow at your window.

LARISA. So what?

MME OGUDALOV. The wolves will howl in different keys.

LARISA. Still, it will be better than here. At least my soul will have some rest.

MME OGUDALOV. Do you think I'm trying to talk you out of it? Go there, please do, and let your soul have its rest. But you must realize, Zabolotye is no Italy. I have to tell you that so you won't be disillusioned. You'd blame me for not warning you.

LARISA. Thanks. But even if it will be wild there, and far away, and cold, for me, after the kind of life I've had here, every quiet nook will seem like heaven. Why Yuly Kapitonych is putting it off is something I can't understand.

MME OGUDALOV. But why should he want to rush off to the country! He wants to do some showing off. And no wonder. He was nothing, and now he's become somebody.

LARISA *(sings)*.

O tempt me not if there's no need...

How irritating, I just can't get the right key... *(She looks out the window.)* Ilya, Ilya! Come in for a minute! I'll take some songs with me to the country to play and sing when I'm bored.

Ilya enters.

ILYA. Happy birthday! May God grant you health and happiness! *(He puts his peak cap on the chair by the door.)*

LARISA. Ilya, give me the right key for "O tempt me not if there's no need." I'm always off key. *(She gives him the guitar.)*

ILYA. Right away, miss. *(He takes the guitar and tunes up.)* That's a pretty song. It's good for three voices, you need a tenor for the second part... It's awful pretty. But you know, an awful thing happened with us, an awful thing!

MME OGUDALOV. What awful thing?

ILYA. Our Anton, he sings tenor.

MME OGUDALOV. I know, I know.

ILYA. He's our only tenor, all the rest sing bass. What basses they are, what basses! But Anton's our only tenor.

MME OGUDALOV. So what about it?

ILYA. He's not fit for the chorus, no good at all.

MME OGUDALOV. He's not well?

ILYA. His health is all right, nothing wrong there.

MME OGUDALOV. Then what's the matter with him?

ILYA. He's bent over on one side, at an angle. He walks like that, bent over at a right angle, and he'll be like that for another week, it's awful! Every man is worth a lot in a chorus, but what can you do without a tenor! He went to the doctor, and the doctor says, "After a week or two it'll go away, you'll be straight again." But we need him now.

LARISA. But I want you to sing!

ILYA. Right away, miss. The guitar's out of tune. It's awful, just awful! In a chorus you've got to stand up straight, and there he is bent over.

MME OGUDALOV. How did he get that way?

ILYA. From stupidity.

MME OGUDALOV. What kind of stupidity?

ILYA. That kind of stupidity our people have. I said, "Watch out, Anton, be careful now!" But he didn't understand.

MME OGUDALOV. And we don't understand either.

ILYA. Well, I hate to tell you, but he went on a spree, and what a spree, what a spree! I said, "Anton, watch out, careful now!" But he didn't understand. Oh it's awful, awful! Right now a man's worth a hundred rubles, that's the business at hand, the kind of gentleman we're expecting, and there's Anton bent over crooked. He was a real straight-up gypsy, but now he's twisted! *(He starts to sing in a bass voice)* "O tempt me not..."

Voice through the window: "Ilya, Ilya, come here! Come quick!"

Why? What do you want?

Voice from the street: "Come, the gentleman is here!"

You're joking!

Voice from the street: "He's really come!"

I don't have any more time, miss, the gentleman's come. *(He puts down the guitar and takes his peak cap.)*
MME OGUDALOV. What gentleman?
ILYA. The one we've been waiting for a whole year, that one! *(He goes off.)*
MME OGUDALOV. Who do you suppose could have come? He must be rich and probably a bachelor, Larisa, since the gypsies are so glad to see him. You can see he spends time with the gypsies. Oh Larisa, have we missed out on a suitor? Why did we have to hurry so?
LARISA. Oh Mama, haven't I suffered enough? No, I've been humiliated enough.
MME OGUDALOV. You used that horrible word "humiliated"! Did you mean to frighten me, perhaps? We're poor folk, and that means being humiliated all our life. So it's better to be humiliated when you're young if you can later live like a human being.
LARISA. No, I can't, it's more than I can bear.
MME OGUDALOV. But you can't get anything easily, and you'd stay nobody all your life.
LARISA. To pretend again, lie again!
MME OGUDALOV. So pretend then, and lie too! Happiness won't come running after you if you run away from it. *(Karandyshov enters.)* Yuly Kapitonych, our Larisa's all set to go to the country, here she's gotten herself a basket for mushrooms.
LARISA. Yes, please, for my sake, let's go right away!
KARANDYSHOV. I don't understand you. Why are you in such a hurry to get there?
LARISA. I want so much to get away from here.
KARANDYSHOV *(in an outburst)*. Who is it you want to get away from? Who's persecuting you? Or could you be ashamed of me?
LARISA *(coldly)*. No, I'm not ashamed of you, I don't know how it's going to be in the future, but so far you haven't given me any cause for that.
KARANDYSHOV. Then why run away, why hide from people? Give me some time to get settled, to pull myself together, to come to my senses. I'm glad, I'm happy. So give me a chance to feel the pleasure of my position.
MME OGUDALOV. To show off.

KARANDYSHOV. Yes, to show off, I won't hide it. My self-respect has suffered many, many wounds, and my pride has been offended more than once. Now I rightly want to be proud and strut some.

LARISA. Then when are you thinking of going to the country?

KARANDYSHOV. After the wedding, whenever you want, even the very next day. Only we absolutely must get married here, so nobody can say we're hiding out because I'm not a good match for you but just the straw a drowning man grabs for.

LARISA. But you know, Yuly Kapitonych, that last part's almost the way it is, it's true.

KARANDYSHOV *(angrily)*. Then keep that truth to yourself! *(In tears.)* Have a little pity on me! At least let the others think you love, that you made a free choice.

LARISA. But why do that?

KARANDYSHOV. What do you mean, "why"? Don't you make any allowance for self-respect in a man?

LARISA. Self-respect! All you think about is yourself! Everybody loves himself! When is anybody ever going to love me? You're going to lead me to ruin.

MME OGUDALOV. That's enough, Larisa, what's gotten into you?

LARISA. Mama, I'm afraid, I'm afraid of something. Now listen. If the wedding's going to be here, then please, as few people as possible, as quiet and simple as possible.

MME OGUDALOV. No, don't you get any crazy ideas! A wedding's a wedding, and I'm an Ogudalov and won't allow any skimping. You'll shine as nobody here has ever shone.

KARANDYSHOV. And I won't begrudge a thing.

LARISA. All right, I'll be quiet. I can see that for you I'm a doll. You'll play with me, break me and throw me away.

KARANDYSHOV. That dinner tonight is going to cost me plenty.

MME OGUDALOV. And I consider that dinner of yours absolutely unnecessary, an unjustified expense.

KARANDYSHOV. But even if it should cost me twice as much, or three times as much, I wouldn't begrudge the money.

MME OGUDALOV. It's something nobody needs.

KARANDYSHOV. I need it.

LARISA. But what for, Yuly Kapitonych?

KARANDYSHOV. Larisa Dmitriyevna, for three years I've been suffering humiliation, for three years I've had to put up with mockery from your friends right to my face. I've got to have my turn to laugh at them.

MME OGUDALOV. What will you think up next! Do you want to get up some quarrel, is that it? In that case Larisa and I won't go.

LARISA. Oh, please, don't offend anybody!

KARANDYSHOV. Don't offend! Though they can offend me? But don't worry, there won't be any quarrel, it'll all be very peaceful. I'll propose a toast to you and thank you publicly for the happiness you are giving me by your choice, for the fact that you haven't treated me the way the others have, that you have valued me and trusted in the sincerity of my feelings. That's all, that's my whole revenge!

MME OGUDALOV. And all that's completely unnecessary.

KARANDYSHOV. No, those great dandies harassed me with their bragging. But they didn't accumulate their wealth on their own, so why should they brag about it? They throw away fifteen rubles on one order of tea!

MME OGUDALOV. Now you're taking it out on poor Vasya.

KARANDYSHOV. Not just Vasya, they're all good at that. Just see what's going on in town, the joy on people's faces. The cab drivers are all in a gay mood, they drive around the streets shouting to each other, "The gentleman's come, the gentleman's come." The waiters in the inns are beaming too, they run out to the street and shout from inn to inn, "The gentleman's come, the gentleman's come." The gypsies have gone crazy, they're suddenly all making a big fuss and waving their hands. At the hotel it's like a congress, a big crowd of people. A little while ago four gypsies, all decked out, drove up in a carriage to congratulate him on his arrival. What a scene! But what I've heard is that that gentleman has run through all his money and sold his last boat. So who's come then? A man who's spent all his money having a good time, a degenerate, and the whole town's glad to see him. Fine morals!

MME OGUDALOV. But who is it that's come?

KARANDYSHOV. Your Sergey Sergeyich Paratov.

Larisa stands up in fright.

MME OGUDALOV. So that's who it is!

LARISA. Let's go to the country, let's go right now!

KARANDYSHOV. Now is just the time we shouldn't go.

MME OGUDALOV. What's the matter, Larisa, why hide from him! He's not a highway robber!

LARISA. Why don't you listen to me! You're destroying me, pushing me into an abyss.

MME OGUDALOV. You're insane.

KARANDYSHOV. What are you afraid of?

LARISA. I'm not afraid for myself.

KARANDYSHOV. For whom then?

LARISA. For you.

KARANDYSHOV. Oh, don't be afraid for me! I won't let myself be put upon. Just let him try picking a quarrel with me, then he'll see.

MME OGUDALOV. No, don't talk like that! God help us! This isn't Vasya. You be careful with him if you value your happiness.

KARANDYSHOV (by the window). There, if you care to look, he's come to visit you. Four pacers abreast and a gypsy on the box with the coachman. He's really showing off. Of course, it doesn't do anybody any harm to let him have his fun, but in reality it's disgusting and stupid.

LARISA (to Karandyshov). Let's go, let's go to my room. Mama, you receive him here. Please, talk him out of any visits!

Larisa and Karandyshov go out. Paratov enters.

PARATOV (during this entire scene with Mme. Ogudalov he adopts a half-joking, half-serious tone). Aunty, your dear hand!

MME OGUDALOV (holding out her hand). Oh, Sergey Sergeyich! Oh, my dear boy!

PARATOV. You desire to embrace me? Permitted! (They embrace and kiss.)

MME OGUDALOV. What wind brought you here? Passing through, perhaps?

PARATOV. I came here on purpose, and my first visit is to you, Aunty.

MME OGUDALOV. Thank you. How are you, how are things going with you?

PARATOV. It would be a sin to complain, Aunty. I'm enjoying life though my business affairs aren't too good.

MME OGUDALOV (after looking at Paratov awhile). Sergey Sergeyich, tell me, dear boy, why did you disappear so suddenly that time?

PARATOV. I received an unpleasant telegram, Aunty.

MME OGUDALOV. What kind of telegram?

PARATOV. While I was away my managers reduced my household to a shell. Because of their operations my ships were about to be auctioned off along with all my property and belongings. So I flew off to save my possessions.

MME OGUDALOV. So you saved everything and arranged everything.

PARATOV. Not really. I arranged things but not completely; there was quite a loss. But I haven't lost heart, Aunty, and I haven't lost my fun-loving disposition.

MME OGUDALOV. I can see you haven't lost it.

PARATOV. We lose in one thing and gain in something else, Aunty; that's how it is with men like us.

MME OGUDALOV. What do you want to gain in? Have you started some new business operations?

PARATOV. It's not for lightheaded gentlemen like us to go starting new business operations! That's how people get into debtors' prison, Aunty, I want to sell my precious freedom.

MME OGUDALOV. I understand. You want to marry for money. How high do you value your precious freedom?

PARATOV. At half a million.

MME OGUDALOV. That's a lot of money.

PARATOV. I can't do it any cheaper, Aunty. If you don't figure it out right, you're in trouble, you know that yourself.

MME OGUDALOV. That's my kind of man!

PARATOV. Right.

MME OGUDALOV. What a falcon! It's a joy to look at you.

PARATOV. It's very flattering to hear that from you. Please allow me to kiss your dear hand. *(He kisses her hand.)*

MME OGUDALOV. But what about the buyers? That is, you have some buyers, don't you?

PARATOV. If one looks for them, they'll be found.

MME OGUDALOV. Pardon me for an indiscreet question!

PARATOV. If it's very indiscreet, then don't ask me. I'm bashful.

MME OGUDALOV. Enough of your jokes! Is there a fiancée or not? If there is, then who is she?

PARATOV. Even if you kill me, I won't say.

MME OGUDALOV. All right, as you wish.

PARATOV. I should like to pay my respects to Larisa Dmitriyevna. May I see her?

MME OGUDALOV. Why not, I'll have her come out right away. *(She takes up the case with its things.)* You know, Sergey Sergeyich, tomorrow is Larisa's birth-day, and I'd like to give her these things for a present, but I don't have enough to buy them.

PARATOV. Aunty, Aunty! You've probably already taken something from three men! I remember those tactics of yours.

MME OGUDALOV *(takes Paratov by the ear).* You joker you!

PARATOV. Tomorrow I'll bring a gift myself, better than that.

MME OGUDALOV. I'll get Larisa for you. *(She goes off.)*

Larisa enters.

PARATOV. You weren't expecting me?

LARISA. No, I wasn't expecting you now. I waited for you a long time, but I stopped waiting a long time ago.

PARATOV. Why did you stop waiting?

LARISA. I had no hopes of your coming. You disappeared so unexpectedly, and not a single letter...

PARATOV. I didn't write because I couldn't write you anything pleasant.

LARISA. That's what I thought.

PARATOV. And you're getting married?

LARISA. Yes, I'm getting married.

PARATOV. And may I ask, did you wait long for me?

LARISA. Why do you want to know that?

PARATOV. It's not to satisfy my curiosity, Larisa Dmitriyevna. I'm interested in the purely theoretical aspect. I'd like to know how soon a woman forgets the man she loves passionately: the day after the parting, a week after, a month after... Did Hamlet have the right to say to his mother "ere those shoes were old," et cetera.

LARISA. I won't answer your question, Sergey Sergeyich. You can think what you want about me.

PARATOV. I shall always think of you with respect, but women in general, after your behavior, lose a lot in my eyes.

LARISA. What behavior of mine? You don't know of anything.

PARATOV. Those "mild, tender looks," the sweet lovers' whisper, every word separated by a deep sigh, those vows... And a month later all that is repeated to somebody else, like a lesson learned by heart. O women!

LARISA. What about "women"?

PARATOV. Frailty is your name!

LARISA. Oh, what right do you have to insult me like that? Do you really know that I fell in love with somebody after you? Are you so sure of that?

PARATOV. I'm not sure, but I'm assuming it.

LARISA. To make such a cruel reproach you should know, not assume.

PARATOV. But you're getting married, aren't you?

LARISA. But what made me do it?... If it's impossible to live at home; if, when it's frightfully and deadly boring, I'm forced to be pleasant and smile; if they push suitors on me that I can't look at without disgust; if there are disgraceful scenes in the house; if I have to run away from the house and even from town?

PARATOV. Larisa, so you? ...

LARISA. So I what? Well, what are you trying to say?

PARATOV. Forgive me! I'm guilty towards you. So you haven't forgotten me, you still... love me?

Larisa is silent.

Well, tell me, speak frankly!

LARISA. Yes, of course. There's no need to ask.

PARATOV *(kisses Larisa's hand tenderly)*. Thank you, thank you.

LARISA. That's all you needed; you're a conceited man.

PARATOV. To give you up is something I can do, I have to do that because of circumstances. But giving up your love would be painful.

LARISA. Really?

PARATOV. If you had preferred somebody else to me, you would have insulted me deeply, and I wouldn't have found it easy to forgive you that.

LARISA. And now?

PARATOV. Now for the rest of my life I shall preserve a most pleasant memory of you, and we shall part the best of friends.

LARISA. In other words, let a woman cry and suffer, just so long as she loves you?

PARATOV. It can't be helped, Larisa Dmitriyevna! In love there's no equality, that wasn't started by me. In love it is sometimes necessary to cry.

LARISA. And it's the woman who has to cry?

PARATOV. Of course, that's not for the man.

LARISA. And why not?

PARATOV. It's very simple. Because, if a man cries, people will call him an old woman, and for a man that nickname is the worst thing invented by the human mind.

LARISA. If love were equal on both sides, then there wouldn't be any tears at all. Does that ever happen?

PARATOV. It happens now and then. Only it turns out to be some sort of fancy cake, some kind of sponge cake.

LARISA. Sergey Sergeyich, I told you something I shouldn't have. I hope you won't take advantage of my openness.

PARATOV. Really, what do you take me for! If a woman is free, then that's a horse of another color… I, Larisa Dmitriyevna, am a man with principles; for me marriage is a sacred thing. I can't stand that freethinking. Let me ask you something. Your future mate, of course, possesses many virtues?

LARISA. No, only one.

PARATOV. That's not much.

LARISA. And yet it's precious.

PARATOV. And what is it exactly?

LARISA. He loves me.

PARATOV. That's truly precious. It's very good for around the house.

Mme. Ogudalov and Karandyshov enter.

MME OGUDALOV. Permit me to introduce you, gentlemen! *(To Paratov.)* Yuly Kapitonych Karandyshov. *(To Karandyshov.)* Sergey Sergeyich Paratov.

PARATOV *(giving Karandyshov his hand)*. We're already acquainted. *(Bowing.)* You see a man with a large mustache and few talents. I beg you to be kind and gracious. I'm an old friend of Kharita Ignatyevna and Larisa Dmitriyevna.

KARANDYSHOV *(with restraint)*. I'm very pleased to meet you.

MME OGUDALOV. Sergey Sergeyich is like a member of the family.

KARANDYSHOV. It's a great pleasure.

PARATOV *(to Karandyshov)*. You're not jealous?

KARANDYSHOV. I hope Larisa Dmitriyevna won't give me any cause to be jealous.

PARATOV. But you know, jealous people are jealous without cause.

LARISA. I guarantee that Yuly Kapitonych will not be jealous on my account.

KARANDYSHOV. Yes, of course, but if...

PARATOV. Oh yes, yes. It would probably be something very frightening.

MME OGUDALOV. Gentlemen, why did you get started on this! Aren't there other things to talk about besides jealousy!

LARISA. Sergey Sergeyich, we're going to the country soon.

PARATOV. From the beautiful local sites?[6]

KARANDYSHOV. And what do you find so beautiful here?

PARATOV. That's an individual matter. Tastes differ.

MME OGUDALOV. True, true, Some like the city, and some like the country.

PARATOV. Aunty, everyone to his taste. One man likes watermelon, another pork gristle.

MME OGUDALOV. Oh you joker! Where did you learn so many proverbs?

PARATOV. I spent some time with the barge haulers, Aunty. That's how one can learn Russian.

KARANDYSHOV. Learn Russian from the barge haulers?

PARATOV. And why not learn it from them?

KARANDYSHOV. Because we consider them...

PARATOV. Who's "we"?

KARANDYSHOV *(becoming heated)*. "We" are the educated people, not the barge haulers.

PARATOV. Now, sir, just what do you consider the barge haulers to be like? I'm a ship owner, and I'm taking their part, for I'm such a barge hauler myself.

KARANDYSHOV. We consider them to be a model of coarseness and ignorance.

PARATOV. So, what else, Mister Karandyshov!

KARANDYSHOV. That's all, there's nothing more.

PARATOV. No, that's not all, you left out the main thing. You have to apologize.

KARANDYSHOV. Me, apologize!

PARATOV. Yes, that can't be helped, it's necessary.

KARANDYSHOV. But why should I? That's my conviction.

PARATOV. Now, now, now, now! You can't worm out of it.

MME OGUDALOV. Gentlemen, gentlemen, what are you doing!

PARATOV. Don't worry, I won't challenge him to a duel over this. Your fiancé will stay healthy, I'm just going to give him a lesson. I have a rule: not to forgive anybody anything; otherwise, they'll forget about fear and go too far.

LARISA *(to Karandyshov)*. What are you doing? Apologize right now, I order you.

PARATOV *(to Mme. Ogudalov)*. It looks as though the time has come to see what I'm like. If I want to teach somebody a lesson, then I lock myself up at home for a week to think up a punishment.

KARANDYSHOV *(to Paratov)*. I don't understand.

PARATOV. In that case you should learn to understand and then engage in conversation!

MME OGUDALOV. Sergey Sergeyich, I'm throwing myself on my knees before you; for my sake forgive him!

PARATOV *(to Karandyshov)*. Thank Kharita Ignatyevna. I forgive you. Only, my dear boy, you should learn to distinguish among people! "I'll whistle not where'er I stray, and those I meet won't get away."[7]

Karandyshov wants to answer.

MME OGUDALOV. Don't answer, don't answer! Or I'll quarrel with you. Larisa, have champagne served, and pour each of them a glass. Let them drink to peace. *(Larisa goes off.)* And now, gentlemen, don't quarrel any more. I'm a woman with a peaceful disposition, I like to have everything friendly and agreeable.

PARATOV. I too have a peaceful disposition, I wouldn't hurt a chicken. I'm never the first to start anything, I can assure you of that.

MME OGUDALOV. Yuly Kapitonych, you're still a young man, you should be more modest, it's not good to get worked up. Now be nice enough to invite Sergey Sergeyich to dinner, you simply must! We find his company very pleasant.

KARANDYSHOV. I wanted to do that myself. Sergey Sergeyich, would you like to have dinner at my place tonight?

PARATOV *(coldly)*. With pleasure.

Larisa enters. She is followed by a manservant carrying a bottle of champagne on a tray.

LARISA *(pours)*. Gentleman, please.

Paratov and Karandyshov take glasses.

I beg you to be friends.

PARATOV. For me your request is a command.

MME OGUDALOV *(to Karandyshov)*. You follow Sergey Sergeyich's example.

KARANDYSHOV. There's no need to talk about me. For me every word of Larisa Dmitriyevna is law.

Vozhevatov enters.

VOZHEVATOV. Where there's champagne there we are. What intuition! Kharita Ignatyevna, Larisa Dmitriyevna, permit a blond man to enter the room!

MME OGUDALOV. What blond man?

VOZHEVATOV. You'll see right now. Enter, blond man!

Robinson enters.

I have the honor to present my new friend, Lord Robinson.

VOZHEVATOV *(to Robinson)*. Kiss their hand.

Robinson kisses the hands of Mme. Ogudalov and Larisa.

Now, my lord, come here.

MME OGUDALOV. Why is it you order your friend about so?

VOZHEVATOV. He's hardly been in the society of ladies at all, so he's shy. Most of the time he's been traveling, by water and by land, and not too long ago he almost became a complete savage on an uninhabited island. *(To Karandyshov.)* Let me introduce you. Lord Robinson, Yuly Kapitonych Karandyshov.

KARANDYSHOV *(giving Robinson his hand)*. Has it been a long time since you left England?

ROBINSON. Yes.*

VOZHEVATOV *(to Paratov)*. I taught him three words of English, and, I'll have to confess, I don't know much more myself. *(To Robinson.)* Why are you looking at the champagne? Kharita Ignatyevna, may we?

MME OGUDALOV. Please do.

VOZHEVATOV. The English, you know, drink champagne all day long, from morning on.

MME OGUDALOV. Do you really drink all day long?

ROBINSON. Yes.*

VOZHEVATOV. They have three meals, and then they have dinner from six o'clock to twelve.

MME OGUDALOV. Can that be possible?

ROBINSON. Yes.*

VOZHEVATOV *(to Robinson)*. All right, you pour.

ROBINSON *(pouring the glasses)*. If you please.*

They drink.

PARATOV *(to Karandyshov)*. Invite him to dinner too. He and I go everywhere together, I can't manage without him.

KARANDYSHOV. What shall I call him?

PARATOV. But who ever calls them by name! You say, "Lord, my lord…"

KARANDYSHOV. But is he really a lord?

PARATOV. Of course he's not a lord, but they like to be called that. Or you could simply say "Sir Robinson."

KARANDYSHOV *(to Robinson)*. Sir Robinson, would you do me the honor of dining at my place tonight?

ROBINSON. I thank you.*

KARANDYSHOV *(to Mme. Ogudalov)*. Kharita Ignatyevna, I'm going home, I have some arrangements to make. *(Bowing to all.)* I await you, gentlemen. I have the honor to present my salutations! *(He goes off.)*

PARATOV *(takes his hat)*. And it's time for us to go too; we have to rest up from the trip.

VOZHEVATOV. To get ready for the dinner.

MME OGUDALOV. Wait a little, gentleman, not all at once.

Mme. Ogudalov and Larisa follow Karandyshov into the anteroom.

VOZHEVATOV. Did you like her fiancé?

PARATOV. What's there to like! Who could like him! What's more, he talks like a web-footed goose.

VOZHEVATOV. Did something happen?

PARATOV. We had a few words. He was in a big hurry to show that he's somebody, he got the idea of trying to show off. But you just wait, my little friend, I'm going to have fun with you, my little friend. *(Striking his forehead.)* Oh, I just had a brilliant thought! Now then, Robinson, I have a hard job for you, so you try hard…

VOZHEVATOV. What is it?

PARATOV. It's this …*(Listening.)* They're coming. I'll tell you later, gentlemen.

---

*In the original Ostrovsky has Robinson speak the asterisked expressions of this scene in English but with a Russian accent. "Thank" is pronounced like "senk." "If" rhymes with "beef," "please" with "fleece."

Mme. Ogudalov and Larisa enter.

I have the honor to present my salutations.
VOZHEVATOV Good-bye.

They bow.

ACT THREE

Karandyshov's study. A room furnished pretentiously but without taste. On one wall, over a divan, is hung a tapestry on which a gun is suspended. Three doors, one in the middle, two on the sides. Yefrosinya Potapovna is on stage. Ivan is coming in through the door on the left.

IVAN. Some lemons, please!

YEFROSINYA POTAPOVNA. What kind of lemons, viper?

IVAN. Messina lemons, ma'am.

YEFROSINYA POTAPOVNA. Why do you have to have them?

IVAN. After dinner some of the gentlemen are drinking coffee but others tea, so they need lemon for their tea.

YEFROSINYA POTAPOVNA. You people have plumb worn me out tonight. Give them cranberry water, it's all the same. Take my decanter over there, but be careful with it, it's old; as it is, the stopper hardly sticks, it's held in with sealing wax. Come on, I'll do the serving myself. *(She goes off through the middle door, Ivan after her.)*

Mme. Ogudalov and Larisa enter from the left.

LARISA. Oh Mama, I didn't know what to do with myself.

MME OGUDALOV. It's just what I expected of him.

LARISA. What a dinner, what a dinner! And as if that wasn't enough, he had to invite Moky Parmenych! What is he trying to do?

MME OGUDALOV. Yes, he gave them a treat, you'll have to say that.

LARISA. Oh, how awful it was! There's nothing worse than the embarrassment you have to feel for somebody else. We're not guilty of anything ourselves, but it's all so embarrassing you just want to run off somewhere. But he doesn't seem to notice a thing. He's even in high spirits.

MME OGUDALOV. But on what basis could he notice anything? He doesn't know anything, he's never seen how decent people eat. He still thinks he's astounded everybody with his splendor, and so he's feeling good. But haven't you really noticed? They're getting him drunk on purpose.

LARISA. Oh, oh! Stop him, stop him!

MME OGUDALOV. How are you going to stop him! He's not a child any more, it's time for him to live without a nursemaid.

LARISA. But he isn't stupid, how is it he doesn't see it!

MME OGUDALOV. He's not stupid, but he's vain. They're playing a trick on him; they praise his wines, and that makes him glad. They themselves only pretend to be drinking, but they keep adding to his glass.

LARISA. Oh! I'm so afraid, I'm afraid of the whole business. Why are they doing it?

MME OGUDALOV. They just want to have a little fun.

LARISA. But don't they realize it's torture for me?

MME OGUDALOV. But there's no need for you to torture yourself. Look, Larisa, you haven't seen anything yet, and already you're in torture. What will it be like later?

LARISA. What's done is done, and one can only regret it, there's no way to make amends.

Yefrosinya Potapovna enters.

YEFROSINYA POTAPOVNA. You've finished eating already? Would you like some tea?

MME OGUDALOV. No, we can dispense with that.

YEFROSINYA POTAPOVNA. And what are those men doing?

MME OGUDALOV. They're sitting there, talking.

YEFROSINYA POTAPOVNA. Well, they've eaten, and they ought to get up. What else are they waiting for? This dinner's already worn me out; what trouble, what expense! Cooks are highway robbers, this one comes into the kitchen like some conqueror, you don't even dare say a word to him!

MME OGUDALOV. But what's there to talk about with him? If he's a good cook, then you don't have to teach him anything.

YEFROSINYA POTAPOVNA. I'm not talking about teaching him, but he uses up such an awful lot of stuff. If it were our own things, from the house or the estate, I wouldn't say a word, but they're bought things, and expensive, so I feel bad about them. Imagine, he insists on having sugar, and vanilla, and fish glue, but that vanilla costs dear and the fish glue even dearer. If he'd only put in just a bit of flavoring, but he piles it on for no reason at all; your heart goes dead just looking at him.

MME OGUDALOV. Yes, of course, for people who are used to being economical...

YEFROSINYA POTAPOVNA. Being economical has nothing to do with it when a man's gone out of his head. Now you take the fish, that sterlet. Doesn't it taste the same whether the fish is large or small? But the difference in price, how great that is! About five rubles would have been plenty for everything, but he went and paid half a ruble for each fish.

MME OGUDALOV. With all he spent on the dinner there could have been a good time on the Volga. It wouldn't hurt him to grow up.

YEFROSINYA POTAPOVNA. Well, you know, a ruble here and a ruble there, a man can pay that if he has a lot of money. When it's a head official or some bishop, that sort of thing's all right, but who else can afford it! He was going to buy some expensive wine, at a ruble and more, but the merchant turned out to be an honest man. Take it, he says, at sixty kopecks a bottle, and I'll stick on any labels you want! And what wine he gave us! You've got to give him credit. I tried a small glass. It's flavored with cloves, and it's flavored with roses, and something else besides. How could it be cheap with so many expensive flavors in it! So it costs a lot of money, sixty kopecks a bottle; it's really worth serving. But we don't have the money to pay dear prices, we live on a salary. A neighbor of ours now got married, and for his dowry they brought him lots of downy things, some feather beds and pillows, all good. And besides all that there were furs: fox, marten, sable! When all that comes into a household a man can afford to spend something. But then an official next to us got married, and for all of his dowry they brought him a lot of old pianos. A man won't get rich that way. In any case, we don't have any reason to put on a show.

LARISA (to Mme. Ogudalov). I ought to run away from here and just follow my nose.

MME OGUDALOV. I'm afraid that's impossible.

YEFROSINYA POTAPOVNA. If you don't feel well, then feel free to go to my room; when the men come and smoke here, you can't even breathe. But what am I doing standing here! I've got to run and check the silver and lock it up. People nowadays don't have any conscience.

Mme. Ogudalov and Larisa go off through the door on the right. Yefrosinya Potapovna goes off through the center door. From the door on the left enter Paratov, Knurov, and Vozhevatov.

KNUROV. Gentlemen, I'm going to the club to eat. I didn't eat a thing.

PARATOV. Wait, Moky Parmenych.

KNUROV. This is the first time something like this has happened to me. He invites well-known people to dinner, but there's nothing to eat... He's a stupid man, gentlemen.

PARATOV. We won't argue that. You have to do him justice, he's really stupid.

KNUROV. And he got tipsy himself before the others could.

VOZHEVATOV. We did pretty well getting him ready for it.

PARATOV. Yes, I put my plan into operation. A little while ago I had the inspiration of getting him good and drunk to see what would come of it.

KNUROV. So that was planned by you?

PARATOV. We agreed on it in advance. It's in cases like these, gentlemen, that your Robinsons are so valuable.

VOZHEVATOV. He's not a man, he's gold.

PARATOV. To get the host drunk you should drink along with him yourself, but you can hardly swallow that mixture he calls wine. But Robinson, his very being is sustained by imitation wines, all that's nothing to him. He drinks it and says it's good; he tries this one and some other, compares them, smacks his lips with the air of a connoisseur. But he won't drink without his host, and that's where our host got caught. When a man's not used to drinking, it doesn't take much to get him high in a hurry.

KNUROV. That's funny, only I'm terribly hungry, gentlemen.

PARATOV. You'll still manage to get something. Be patient awhile longer, we'll ask Larisa Dmitriyevna to sing something.

KNUROV. That's another matter. But where is Robinson?

VOZHEVATOV. They're still drinking there.

Robinson enters.

ROBINSON *(falling onto the divan)*. Oh Lord, help! Well, Serge, you'll have to answer to God for me.

PARATOV. What's the matter, are you drunk?

ROBINSON. Drunk! Have I ever really complained about that? If I could get drunk, that would be lovely, I couldn't want anything better. I came here with that good intention, and it's with that good intention I live in this world. It's the goal of my life.

PARATOV. Then what's the matter with you?

ROBINSON. I've been poisoned, I'm going to shout for help right now.

PARATOV. Which wine did you drink most of?

ROBINSON. Who knows? Am I some kind of chemist? Even a druggist couldn't figure it out.

PARATOV. But what was on the bottle, what did the label say?

ROBINSON. The bottle said "Burgundy," but inside was some kind of weak brandy. I won't get off easy from that concoction, I can feel it already.

VOZHEVATOV. That sort of thing happens sometimes. When they make the wine they put in too much of something, out of proportion. It's easy to make a mistake, a man isn't a machine. Perhaps they put in too many poisonous mushrooms?

ROBINSON. It's not a laughing matter! A man is perishing, and you're glad.

VOZHEVATOV. That's enough! You deserve to die, Robinson.

ROBINSON. Now that's really nonsense, I don't agree to die... Oh, I wonder how this wine will cripple me.

VOZHEVATOV. One eye is sure to pop out, just wait.

Off stage is heard the voice of Karandyshov: "Hey, give us some Burgundy!"

ROBINSON. There it is, you can hear it, that Burgundy again! Save me, I'm perishing! Serge, have a little pity on me. After all, I'm in the flower of life, gentlemen, I show great promise. Why must art be deprived...

PARATOV. Don't cry now, I'll cure you. I know how to help you; it'll all go away like magic.

Karandyshov enters with a box of cigars.

ROBINSON *(looking at the tapestry).* What's that you have there?

KARANDYSHOV. Cigars.

ROBINSON. No, what's that hung there? Stage properties?

KARANDYSHOV. What do you mean, stage properties? Those are Turkish guns.

PARATOV. So now we know who's to blame that the Austrians can't beat the Turks.

KARANDYSHOV. What? What kind of joke is that! Really, what nonsense! How am I to blame?

PARATOV. You took all their worthless good-for-nothing guns from them, and, out of grief, they supplied themselves with good English weapons.

VOZHEVATOV. Yes, yes, that's who's to blame! Now we know. You know, the Austrians won't thank you for that.

KARANDYSHOV. But what's wrong with them? This pistol, for instance. *(He takes a pistol from the wall.)*

PARATOV *(takes the pistol from him).* This pistol?

KARANDYSHOV. Be careful! It's loaded.

PARATOV. Don't worry. Loaded or not, the danger from it's just the same, it won't fire anyway. You can shoot at me from five paces, you have my permission.

KARANDYSHOV. No, sir, even this pistol can be used.

PARATOV. Yes, to drive nails in the wall. *(He throws the pistol onto the table.)*

VOZHEVATOV. No, don't say that! As the proverb says, "If you want, you can even shoot out of a stick."

KARANDYSHOV *(to Paratov).* Would you like some cigars?

PARATOV. They're expensive, right? About seven rubles a hundred, I imagine.

KARANDYSHOV. Yes, sir, about that. A top brand, a very top brand.

PARATOV. I know this brand, Regalia cabbage leaf dos amigos. I keep it for my friends, I don't smoke it myself.

KARANDYSHOV *(to Knurov).* Wouldn't you like some?

KNUROV. I don't want your cigars, I smoke my own.

KARANDYSHOV. They're good cigars, sir, very good.

KNUROV. So they're good cigars, then smoke them yourself.

KARANDYSHOV *(to Vozhevatov)*. Wouldn't you like some?

VOZHEVATOV. For me they're expensive, I might get spoiled. It's not for the likes of us to nibble at the ashberry; the ashberry's a tender berry.

KARANDYSHOV. And you, Sir Robinson, do you smoke?

ROBINSON. Me? What a question! Give me five or so! *(He picks out five cigars, takes a piece of paper out of his pocket, and carefully wraps them up.)*

KARANDYSHOV. But why don't you smoke now?

ROBINSON. No, how could I! Cigars like these have to be smoked outdoors, in a good spot.

KARANDYSHOV. But why?

ROBINSON. Because if you smoke them in a decent home, then they'll probably give you a beating, which is something I can't stand.

VOZHEVATOV. You don't like it when they beat you?

ROBINSON. No, ever since childhood I've had an aversion to it.

KARANDYSHOV. What a character he is! Really, gentleman, what a character! You can see right off he's an Englishman. *(Loudly.)* But where are the ladies? *(Still more loudly.)* Where are the ladies?

Mme. Ogudalov enters.

MME OGUDALOV. The ladies are here, don't worry. *(Quietly to Karandyshov.)* What are you doing? Just look at yourself!

KARANDYSHOV. Me? Really now, I know myself. Just look, they're all drunk, but I'm just a bit high. I'm happy tonight, I'm triumphant.

MME OGUDALOV. Be triumphant, only not so loudly! *(She goes up to Paratov.)* Sergey Sergeyich, stop making fun of Yuly Kapitonych. It hurts us to see it; you're offending me and Larisa.

PARATOV. Oh Aunty, how could I dare do that!

MME OGUDALOV. Haven't you really forgotten your recent quarrel? You ought to be ashamed!

PARATOV. How can you say that! I don't hold grudges, Aunty. Very well then, to please you I'll end all this here and now. Yuly Kapitonych!

KARANDYSHOV. What would you like?

PARATOV. How would you like to join with me in a toast to eternal friendship?

MME OGUDALOV. Now that's something nice. Thank you!

KARANDYSHOV. To eternal friendship, you say? Please, with pleasure.

PARATOV *(to Mme. Ogudalov)*. Ask Larisa Dmitriyevna to come here. Why is she hiding from us!

MME OGUDALOV. All right, I'll bring her. *(She goes off.)*

KARANDYSHOV. So what shall we drink? Burgundy?

PARATOV. No, spare me from Burgundy! I'm a simple man.

KARANDYSHOV. What then?

PARATOV. You know what? Just for kicks let's you and me drink some dear old cognac now. You have cognac?

KARANDYSHOV. Of course! I have everything. Hey, Ivan, bring some cognac!

PARATOV. Why bring it here, we'll drink it there. Only tell them to serve it in regular glasses, I've no use for small wine glasses.

ROBINSON. Why didn't you say before that you had cognac? How much valuable time's been wasted!

VOZHEVATOV. Now he's come to life!

ROBINSON. I know how to get along with that drink, I've adapted myself to it.

Paratov and Karandyshov go off through the door on the left.

(Robinson looks through the same door.) Karandyshov is a goner. I started him, and Serge'll finish him off. Now they're pouring, they're striking up a pose, it's a living tableau. Just see what a smile Serge has! Just like Bertram. *(He sings from Meyerbeer's opera* Robert le Diable*)* "You are my savior."... "I am your savior!"... "And protector."... "And protector." There, he swallowed it. They're kissing. *(He sings.)* "How happy I!"... "O victim mine!" Oh no, Ivan's taking away the cognac, he's taking it away! *(Loudly.)* What are you doing, what are you doing, leave it! I've been waiting a long time for that. *(He runs off.)*

Ilya enters through the center door.

VOZHEVATOV. What is it, Ilya?

ILYA. We're all ready, all gathered together waiting on the boulevard. When do you want to go?

VOZHEVATOV. Right away. We'll all go together, just wait a little.

ILYA. Fine. Whatever you say. *(Paratov enters.)*

PARATOV. Ah, Ilya, are you all ready?

ILYA. We're ready, Sergey Sergeyich.

PARATOV. Do you have your guitar with you?

ILYA. I didn't bring it, Sergey Sergeyich.

PARATOV. We need a guitar, do you hear?

ILYA. I'll run after one right away, Sergey Sergeyich! *(He goes off.)*

PARATOV. I want to ask Larisa Dmitriyevna to sing something for us, and then we'll sail across the Volga.

KNUROV. Our excursion won't be much fun without Larisa Dmitriyevna. If only... I could pay a lot for such a pleasure.

VOZHEVATOV. If Larisa Dmitriyevna would go along, I'd gladly give each rower a silver ruble.

PARATOV. Just imagine, gentlemen, I'm thinking the very same thing. So we're in complete agreement.

KNUROV. But is there a possibility?

PARATOV. In this world nothing is impossible, so the philosophers say.

KNUROV. But Robinson, gentlemen, is superfluous. You've had your fun with him, so let it go at that. He'll get so drunk he'll be a brute, what good is that! This excursion's a serious affair, he's no companion for us. *(Pointing to the door.)* There he is, glued to the cognac.

VOZHEVATOV. So we won't take him.

PARATOV. One way or another he'll insist on coming with us.

VOZHEVATOV. Wait, gentlemen, I'll get rid of him. *(Through the door.)* Robinson!

Robinson enters.

ROBINSON. What do you want?

VOZHEVATOV *(quietly)*. How would you like to go to Paris?

ROBINSON. Paris? When?

VOZHEVATOV. Tonight.

ROBINSON. But we were getting ready to sail across the Volga.

VOZHEVATOV. As you wish. You sail across the Volga, and I'll go to Paris.

ROBINSON. But I don't even have a passport.

VOZHEVATOV. I'll take care of that.

ROBINSON. I suppose I might.

VOZHEVATOV. Then we'll leave here together. I'll take you home to my place; you'll wait for me there, get a rest, take a nap. I have to go to a couple of places on business.

ROBINSON. But it would be interesting to listen to the gypsies.

VOZHEVATOV. Always the artist! Shame on you! Gypsy songs, they're nothing but ignorance. That sort of thing can't compare with Italian opera or a gay operetta! That's what you should listen to. I suppose you played in an operetta yourself.

ROBINSON. Of course! I played in *The Songbirds*.[8]

VOZHEVATOV. What role?

ROBINSON. The notary.

VOZHEVATOV. Well then, how could such an artist not visit Paris? After Paris what a price you'll bring!

ROBINSON. Your hand!

VOZHEVATOV. You're going?

ROBINSON. I'm going.

VOZHEVATOV *(to Paratov)*. He was singing here from the opera *Robert*. What a voice!

PARATOV. He and I'll be a sensation at the Nizhny Fair.

ROBINSON. You should ask whether I'm going.

PARATOV. Why is that?

ROBINSON. I see enough ignorance without going to some fair.

PARATOV. Aha! Now he's started to talk!

ROBINSON. Nowadays educated people go to Europe, they don't hang out at fairs.

PARATOV. Which governments and cities of Europe do you wish to make happy with your presence?

ROBINSON. Paris, of course. I've been meaning to go there for some time.

VOZHEVATOV. He and I are going tonight.

PARATOV. So! Bon voyage! You really ought to go to Paris. That's all you need. But where's our host?

ROBINSON. He's there. He said he was preparing a surprise for us.

Mme. Ogudalov and Larisa enter from the right. Karandyshov and Ivan enter from the left.

PARATOV *(to Larisa)*. Why did you leave us?

LARISA. I don't feel very well.

PARATOV. Your fiancé and I just now drank to eternal friendship. Now we're friends forever.

LARISA. Thank you. *(She presses Paratov's hand.)*

KARANDYSHOV *(to Paratov)*. Serge!

PARATOV *(to Larisa)*. You see how close we are. *(To Karandyshov.)* What would you like?

KARANDYSHOV. Somebody's asking for you.

PARATOV. Who is it?

IVAN. It's the gypsy Ilya.

PARATOV. Then call him in.

Ivan goes off.

Gentlemen, forgive me for inviting Ilya into your society. He's my best friend. Where I'm accepted my friends have to be accepted. That's a rule of mine.

VOZHEVATOV *(quietly to Larisa)*. I know a new song.

LARISA. Is it good?

VOZHEVATOV. Wonderful! It goes "We'll swing the rope she skips, the maid is wearing shoes."[9]

LARISA. That's funny.

VOZHEVATOV. I'll teach it to you.

Ilya enters with a guitar.

PARATOV *(to Larisa).* Allow me, Larisa Dmitriyevna, to ask you to make us happy! Sing us a romance or some little song. I haven't heard you for a whole year, and I'll probably never hear you again.

KNUROV. Allow me to second the request!

KARANDYSHOV. That's impossible, gentlemen, impossible. Larisa Dmitriyevna won't be singing.

PARATOV. But how can you know she won't. Maybe she will.

LARISA. Excuse me, gentlemen, I'm not in the mood today, and I'm not in good voice.

KNUROV. Anything, whatever you want!

KARANDYSHOV. But if I say she won't be singing, then she won't be singing.

PARATOV. We'll see about that. We'll ask as much as we have to even if we have to go to our knees.

VOZHEVATOV. I'll go down right now, I'm flexible.

KARANDYSHOV. No, no, don't even ask, it's impossible, I forbid it.

MME OGUDALOV. What did you say! You can forbid it when you get the right, but for now you can wait with your forbidding, it's too early.

KARANDYSHOV. No, no! I positively forbid it.

LARISA. You forbid it? Then I'll sing, gentlemen.

Karandyshov, sulking, goes off into a corner and sits down.

PARATOV. Ilya!

ILYA. What shall we sing, miss?

LARISA. "O tempt me not."

ILYA *(tuning up the guitar).* Here's where we need a third voice! Oh, what a shame! What a tenor he was! All from his stupidity. *(They sing in two parts.)*

> O tempt me not if there's no need,
> Restoring tenderness of old.
> A disillusioned lover's freed
> From former charms which once turned cold.

In various ways everyone shows delight. Paratov sits with his hands thrust into his hair. In the second stanza Robinson joins in a bit.

> No more a promise do I trust.
> No more does love hold my belief.
> Protect myself I wish and must
> From former dreams which brought me grief.

ILYA *(to Robinson).* Thank you, sir. You came to our rescue.

KNUROV *(to Larisa).* It's a great delight to see you and even more of a delight to listen to you.

PARATOV *(with a gloomy look).* I feel as if I'm going out of my mind. *(He kisses Larisa's hand.)*

VOZHEVATOV. To listen and then be ready to die! *(To Karandyshov.)* And you wanted to deprive us of the pleasure.

KARANDYSHOV. Gentlemen, I no less than you admire the singing of Larisa Dmitriyevna. Now let's drink champagne to her health.

VOZHEVATOV. It's a pleasure to hear such a clever speech.

KARANDYSHOV *(loudly).* Serve champagne!

MME OGUDALOV *(quietly).* Not so loud! Why are you shouting!

KARANDYSHOV Really now, I'm in my own house. I know what I'm doing. *(Loudly.)* Serve champagne!

Yefrosinya Potapovna enters.

YEFROSINYA POTAPOVNA. What do you want champagne for? First it's one thing, then the other.

KARANDYSHOV. Mind your own business! Do what you're told!

YEFROSINYA POTAPOVNA. Go yourself! I've walked myself out, I don't even think I've eaten a thing since morning. *(She goes off.)*

Karandyshov goes through the door on the left.

MME OGUDALOV. Listen, Yuly Kapitonych!... *(She follows Karandyshov.)*

PARATOV. llya, go! Have the boats ready. We'll be coming right away.

llya leaves through the center door.

VOZHEVATOV *(to Knurov).* Let's leave him alone with Larisa Dmitriyevna. *(To Robinson.)* Robinson, look, Ivan is taking away the cognac.

ROBINSON. I'll kill him. It would be easier for me to part with life itself!

Knurov, Vozhevatov, and Robinson go off on the left.

PARATOV. What a charmer you are! *(He looks passionately at Larisa.)* How I cursed myself when you were singing!

LARISA. For what?

PARATOV. I'm not made of wood, you know. To lose a treasure like you, do you think that's easy?

LARISA. And whose fault is that?

PARATOV. Mine, of course, and I'm much more at fault than you think. I ought to despise myself.

LARISA. For what? Tell me.

PARATOV. Why did I run away from you? What have I exchanged you for?

LARISA. Then why did you do it?

PARATOV. Oh, why! It was cowardice, of course. I had to put my estate in order. But who cares about that, the estate! I lost more than the estate, I lost you. I'm suffering myself, and I made you suffer.

LARISA. Yes, to tell the truth, you poisoned my life for a long time.

PARATOV. But wait, wait before you condemn me! I haven't lowered myself completely yet, I'm not completely hardened. I wasn't born mercenary, some noble feelings still stir in my soul. There are still a few moments like that, yes... still a few moments like that...

LARISA *(quietly)*. Keep on.

PARATOV. I'll throw away all my calculations, and there won't be any force to tear you away from me. It would have to take my life along with it.

LARISA. But what do you want?

PARATOV. To see you, to listen to you... I'm leaving tomorrow.

LARISA (lowering her head). Tomorrow.

PARATOV. To listen to your charming voice, to forget the whole world, and to dream only about a certain bliss.

LARISA *(quietly)*. What bliss?

PARATOV. The bliss of being your slave, being at your feet.

LARISA. But how?

PARATOV. Listen, we're going for a boat trip on the Volga. Come with us!

LARISA. Oh, but what about here? I really don't know... What about things here?

PARATOV. What does that mean, "here"? They'll come here in a minute: Karandyshov's aunt, some ladies in colored silk dresses, and they'll talk about salted mushrooms.

LARISA. When are you going?

PARATOV. Right now.

LARISA. Now?

PARATOV. It's now or never.

LARISA. Let's go.

PARATOV. What, you've decided to cross the Volga?

LARISA. Wherever you want.

PARATOV. With us, now?

LARISA. Whenever you want.

PARATOV. I confess I can't think of anything more noble than that. Charming creature! My commander!

LARISA. It's you who are my commander.

Mme. Ogudalov, Knurov, Vozhevatov, Robinson, Karandyshov, and Ivan enter. Ivan is carrying a tray with glasses of champagne.

PARATOV *(to Knurov and Vozhevatov)*. She's coming.

KARANDYSHOV. Gentlemen, I propose a toast to Larisa Dmitriyevna.

All take glasses.

Gentlemen, just now you admired the talent of Larisa Dmitriyevna. Your praises are nothing new for her. From childhood on she has been surrounded by admirers who have praised her to her face at every good opportunity. Yes, gentlemen, she really has many talents. But it is not for them that I wish to praise her. The main thing, the priceless merit of Larisa Dmitriyevna is this, gentlemen... is this, gentlemen...

VOZHEVATOV. He's mixed up.

PARATOV. He'll snap out of it, he memorized it.

KARANDYSHOV. Is this, gentlemen, that she knows how to evaluate and choose people. Yes, gentlemen, Larisa Dmitriyevna knows that all is not gold that glitters. She knows how to distinguish gold from tinsel. Many glittering young men have surrounded her, but she wasn't carried away by the glitter of tinsel. She did not seek for herself a man of glitter but a man of merit...

PARATOV *(approvingly)*. Bravo, bravo!

KARANDYSHOV. And she chose...

PARATOV. You! Bravo, bravo!

VOZHEVATOV AND ROBINSON. Bravo, bravo!

KARANDYSHOV. Yes, gentlemen, I not only dare, but I have the right to be proud, and I am proud. She understood me, esteemed me, and preferred me to everyone. Forgive me, gentlemen, perhaps this isn't pleasant for everyone to hear, but I consider it my duty to thank Larisa Dmitriyevna publicly for this preference so flattering to me. Gentlemen, I myself drink to and invite you to drink to the health of my fiancée!

PARATOV, VOZHEVATOV AND ROBINSON. Hurrah!

PARATOV *(to Karandyshov)*. Is there any more champagne?

KARANDYSHOV. Of course, how couldn't there be? How can you ask? I'll go get some.

PARATOV. We have to drink another toast.

KARANDYSHOV. Which?

PARATOV. To the health of the happiest of mortals, to Yuly Kapitonych Karandyshov.

KARANDYSHOV. Oh, yes, and you'll make it up? You make it, Serge! And I'll go and see about getting the champagne. *(He goes off.)*

KNUROV. Well, that's enough of that. Good-bye. I'll get a bite and then go right away to the meeting place. *(He bows to the ladies.)*

VOZHEVATOV *(pointing to the center door)*. Go that way, Moky Parmenych. There's an exit straight to the anteroom, nobody will see you.

Knurov goes off.

PARATOV *(to Vozhevatov)*. We'll go now too. *(To Larisa.)* You should get ready.

Larisa goes off to the right.

VOZHEVATOV. Aren't we going to wait for the toast?

PARATOV. This way it's better.

VOZHEVATOV. How's that?

PARATOV. It'll be funnier.

Larisa enters with hat in hand.

VOZHEVATOV. It will be funnier at that. Robinson! Let's go.

ROBINSON. Where to?

VOZHEVATOV. Home to get ready for Paris.

Robinson and Vozhevatov bow and leave.

PARATOV *(quietly to Larisa)*. Let's go! *(He goes off.)*

LARISA. Good-bye, Mama.

MME OGUDALOV. What are you doing! Where are you going?

LARISA. Either you'll be happy for me, Mama, or you'll be searching for me in the Volga.

MME OGUDALOV. God be with you! What are you doing!

LARISA. It's clear you can't escape your fate! *(She goes off.)*

MME OGUDALOV. So that's what it's finally come to, a general flight! Oh, Larisa!... Should I run after her or not? No, why! Whatever happens, in any case there'll be people around her... But here, even if she gives all that up, it's no great loss.

Karandyshov and Ivan enter with a bottle of champagne.

KARANDYSHOV. Gentlemen, I... *(He looks around the room.)* But where are they? Have they gone? Now that's polite, I must say! Oh well, so much the better! But when did they manage to do it? And maybe you'll go away too? No, you and Larisa Dmitriyevna stay awhile. Were they offended? I understand! Well and good. That leaves our snug family circle...But where is Larisa Dmitriyevna? *(He goes to the door on the right.)* Aunty, is Larisa Dmitriyevna with you?

YEFROSINYA POTAPOVNA *(entering).* Your Larisa Dmitriyevna isn't with me.

KARANDYSHOV. But what's going on, really! Ivan, where did all the gentlemen and Larisa Dmitriyevna disappear to?

IVAN. Larisa Dmitriyevna must have gone off with the gentlemen... Because the gentlemen were getting ready to go across the Volga, they were having some kind of picnic.

KARANDYSHOV. How could they have it across the Volga?

IVAN. They're going on the boats, sir. The utensils and the wine all came from us, sir. We sent them off a little while ago, and the help too, all in proper order, sir.

KARANDYSHOV *(sits down and grabs his head).* Oh, what is this, what is this!

IVAN. And the gypsies, and the band of musicians with them, all in proper order.

KARANDYSHOV *(heatedly).* Kharita Ignatyevna, where is your daughter? Answer me, where is your daughter?

MME OGUDALOV. I brought my daughter here to you, Yuly Kapitonych. You tell me where my daughter is.

KARANDYSHOV. So this was all thought out, all planned. You people were all agreed in advance... *(With tears.)* It's cruel, it's inhumanly cruel!

MME OGUDALOV. It was too soon for you to be triumphant!

KARANDYSHOV. Yes, this is ridiculous... I'm a ridiculous man... I know myself I'm a ridiculous man. But are people punished because they're ridiculous? So I'm ridiculous, all right then, go ahead and laugh at me, right to my face! Come eat with me, drink my wine, make fun of me, and laugh at me, I deserve it. But to break open a man's chest and tear out his heart, to throw it underfoot and then stamp all over it! Oh, oh! How am I going to live! How am I going to live!

YEFROSINYA POTAPOVNA. That's enough now, stop it! It's just not worth making yourself unhappy over it!

KARANDYSHOV. And they're not highway robbers either, they're respectable people... They're all friends of Kharita Ignatyevna.

MME OGUDALOV. I don't know a thing.

KARANDYSHOV. No, you're all one gang, all in cahoots. But you should know, Kharita Ignatyevna, that even the mildest of men can be provoked to fury. Not all criminals are villains, and a peaceful man can make up his mind to a crime when he has no other way out. If all I have left in the world is either to hang myself from shame and despair or to take revenge, then I'll take revenge. For me now there's no fear, no law, no pity; I'm just overwhelmed by ferocious spite and a craving for revenge. I'll get revenge on every one of them, every last one, until they kill me. *(He grabs the pistol from the table and runs out.)*

MME OGUDALOV. What was that he took?

IVAN. A pistol.

MME OGUDALOV. Run, run after him, shout, make them stop him.

ACT FOUR

Setting of the first act. A bright summer night. Robinson (with a billiard cue in his hand) and Ivan are coming out of the coffee house.

IVAN. That billiard cue, please!

ROBINSON. I won't give it up. I want you to play with me! Why won't you play?

IVAN. How can I play with you when you don't pay your money!

ROBINSON. I'll pay you later. My money's with Vasily Danilych, he took it with him. Don't you believe me?

IVAN. How come you didn't go with them on the picnic?

ROBINSON. I fell asleep, and he didn't dare disturb me by waking me up, so he went off alone. Let's play!

IVAN. I can't, sir, the game's not equal. I place money, but you don't. If you win, you take, but if you lose you don't pay up. Place your money, sir.

ROBINSON. What is this, don't I have any credit? That's really something! This is the first time I've seen such a town. Everywhere I've been, all over Russia, I've had all kinds of credit.

IVAN. I can easily believe that, sir. Whatever you want we'll give you. Knowing Sergey Sergeyich and Vasily Danilych, what gentlemen they are, we're obliged to give you credit, sir. But a game requires money, sir.

ROBINSON. Then you should have told me. Take your cue and give me a bottle of... What should it be?

IVAN. That port's not bad, sir.

ROBINSON. You know I don't drink anything cheap.

IVAN. We'll give you the expensive brand, sir.

ROBINSON. And tell them to cook up something for me... you know that... what it is...

IVAN. We could cook some double snipe for you, would you like that?

ROBINSON. Of course, precisely, double snipe.

IVAN. Yes, sir. *(He goes off.)*

ROBINSON. They wanted to play a joke on me; very good, I'll play one on them. Out of grief I'll run up a bill of some twenty rubles, let them pay that off. If they think I need their company, they're mistaken. All I need is their credit, with that I won't miss them even when I'm alone, I can play a solo role and be very happy. To complete my satisfaction I could borrow some money...

Ivan enters with a bottle.

IVAN *(puts down the bottle)*. The double snipe has been ordered, sir.

ROBINSON. I'm leasing a theater here.

IVAN. That's a good thing, sir.

ROBINSON. I don't know who to give the concession to. Do you think your boss might take it?

IVAN. How could he fail to take it, sir!

ROBINSON. Only the way I do things, I have to keep everything in good order! And to guarantee that, I require a sizable deposit at the start.

IVAN. No, he's had some experience with that, he won't put down any deposit. Two men have already tricked him that way.

ROBINSON. Two already? I see, if it's already two...

IVAN. Then he won't trust a third.

ROBINSON. What people! I can't get over it. Everywhere somebody's gotten there first. Where you might have gotten something, it's all taken already, there's no virgin territory. Well, never mind, I don't need it. Don't say a word to him, so he won't get the idea I wanted to cheat him. I have my pride.

IVAN. Yes, sir; that's it, of course... You know, you should have seen how mad Mr. Karandyshov got when all his guests suddenly left! He got awfully mad, he even wanted to kill somebody, he left the house with a pistol.

ROBINSON. A pistol? That's not good.

IVAN. He was drunk. I suppose it'll pass off after a while. He went up and down the boulevard a couple of times... there he comes now.

ROBINSON *(becoming frightened)*. You say he had a pistol? He wanted to kill somebody... was it me?

IVAN. I can't tell you. *(He goes off.)*

Karandyshov enters. Robinson tries to hide behind the bottle.

KARANDYSHOV *(approaches Robinson.)*. Where are your comrades, Mr. Robinson?

ROBINSON. What comrades? I don't have any comrades.

KARANDYSHOV. But what about those gentlemen who had dinner with you at my place?

ROBINSON. What kind of comrades are they! They're just passing acquaintances.

KARANDYSHOV. Then you don't know where they are now?

ROBINSON. I couldn't say, I try to steer clear of that bunch. I'm a peaceful man, you know... a family man.

KARANDYSHOV. You're a family man?

ROBINSON. Very much of a family man... For me a quiet family life is the highest good. God deliver us from any discontent or quarrel. What I like is to carry on a conversation, but it must be clever and polite, about art, for example... And with a man of nobility, a man like you, it's even possible to take a little drink. Wouldn't you like one?

KARANDYSHOV. I don't want one.

ROBINSON. As you wish. The main thing is that there shouldn't be any unpleasantness.

KARANDYSHOV. But you really should know where they are.

ROBINSON. They're off carousing somewhere, what else can they do!

KARANDYSHOV. People say they went across the Volga, is that true?

ROBINSON. That's very possible.

KARANDYSHOV. Didn't they invite you along?

ROBINSON. No, I'm a family man.

KARANDYSHOV. When will they be coming back?

ROBINSON. I don't think they know themselves. They'll be back by morning.

KARANDYSHOV. By morning?

ROBINSON. Maybe even earlier.

KARANDYSHOV. In any case I'll have to wait. There's something I've got to have out with some of them.

ROBINSON. If you're going to wait, you could do it at the pier. Why would they come here! From the pier they'll go straight home. What more could they want? They'd have had all they wanted to eat and drink.

KARANDYSHOV. What pier? We have lots of piers.

ROBINSON. Any one you want, only not here. You won't find them by waiting here.

KARANDYSHOV. Well, all right, I'll go to the pier. Good-bye. *(He gives Robinson his hand.)* Wouldn't you like to go with me?

ROBINSON. No, please, I'm a family man.

Karandyshov leaves.

Ivan, Ivan!

Ivan enters.

Set the table for me inside, and bring the wine there.

IVAN. It's stuffy inside, sir. Why do that!

ROBINSON. The night air is bad for me, the doctor forbade it. And if that gentleman asks abut me, tell him I'm not here. *(He goes off into the coffee house.)*

Gavrilo comes out from the coffee house.

GAVRILO. Did you take a look at the Volga? You didn't see our people?

IVAN. They must have arrived.

GAVRILO. Why do you say that?

IVAN. Because down the hill there's some noise, the gypsies have started to make a racket. *(He takes the bottle from the table and goes off into the coffee house.)*

Ilya and a mixed chorus of gypsies enter.

GAVRILO. Did you have a good trip?

ILYA. Very good! I can't tell you how good!

GAVRILO. Did the gentlemen enjoy themselves?

ILYA. They had themselves a spree, they really did, to the limit! They're coming here, and they'll carry on all night, you'll see.

GAVRILO *(rubbing his hands).* Then go ahead, sit down, people! I'll tell them to serve the women tea, and you go to the buffet, and get a bite to eat.

ILYA. Tell them to add some rum to the old women's tea; they love that.

Ilya, Gavrilo, and the gypsies go off into the coffee house. Knurov and Vozhevatov enter.

KNUROV. It looks as though the drama's about to start.

VOZHEVATOV. That's the way it seems.

KNUROV. I saw that Larisa Dmitriyevna had shed some tears.

VOZHEVATOV. Tears come cheap with women.

KNUROV. Say what you will, her position's not one to envy.

VOZHEVATOV. It will work itself out one way or another.

KNUROV. Hardly.

VOZHEVATOV. Karandyshov will get angry a bit, he'll make a fool of himself, as much as he needs, and then he'll be the same as before.

KNUROV. But she won't be the same. After all, to abandon her fiancé almost on the eve of the wedding there has to be some basis. Just think, Sergey Sergeyich came for one day, and for him she abandons her fiancé, the man she's supposed to live with all her life. That means she was putting her hopes on Sergey Sergeyich. What else could he be for her!

VOZHEVATOV. So you think there was some deception, that his words led her on once again?

KNUROV. I'm sure of it. And there must have been some promises, definite and serious. Otherwise how could she trust a man who'd already deceived her once?

VOZHEVATOV. I wouldn't be surprised. Sergey Sergeyich won't stop at anything, he's a reckless man.

KNUROV. But no matter how reckless he is, he's not going to give up a fiancée worth a million for Larisa Dmitriyevna.

VOZHEVATOV. Of course not! What could he gain from that!

KNUROV. So think what it must be like for the poor girl.

VOZHEVATOV. But what can you do! It's not our fault, we're only bystanders.

Robinson appears on the steps of the coffee house.

VOZHEVATOV. Ah, my lord! What did you dream about?

ROBINSON. About rich fools, the same as I see in real life.

VOZHEVATOV. I see. And tell me, my poor sage, how have you been spending your time here?

ROBINSON. Very well. I've been leading a life of pleasure and running up a bill besides, on your account. What could be better than that!

VOZHEVATOV. One has to envy you. And do you intend to delight in such a pleasant life for long?

ROBINSON. You're really quite a character, I can see that. Think now, what would I gain from refusing such delights!

VOZHEVATOV. There's something there I don't remember. I didn't give you carte blanche, did I?

ROBINSON. You promised to take me with you to Paris. Isn't that the same thing?

VOZHEVATOV. No, it's not the same. What I promised I'll carry out. For me a word is law, what I've said is sacred. Ask me, have I ever deceived anybody?

ROBINSON. But while you're getting ready to go to Paris, what am I supposed to live on, air?

VOZHEVATOV. There was no agreement about that. We can go to Paris right now.

ROBINSON. It's too late now; let's go tomorrow, Vasya.

VOZHEVATOV. Tomorrow then, let it be tomorrow. Listen, tell you what, you better go on alone, I'll give you the fare there and back.

ROBINSON. How can I go alone? I won't find my way.

VOZHEVATOV. They'll drive you there.

ROBINSON. Listen, Vasya, I'm not at all fluent in French… I want to learn, but I never have enough time.

VOZHEVATOV. But what do you need French for?

ROBINSON. What do you mean, shouldn't one speak French in Paris?

221

VOZHEVATOV. But that's not at all necessary, nobody there speaks French.

ROBINSON. The capital of France, and they won't be speaking French there! What kind of fool do you take me for?

VOZHEVATOV. What capital! What's the matter with you, are you in your right mind? What Paris are you thinking of? The inn on our public square is called "Paris." That's where I wanted to go with you.

ROBINSON. Bravo, bravo!

VOZHEVATOV. And you thought I meant the real Paris? You should have used your head a little. And you consider yourself a smart man! So why should I take you there, for what purpose? Should I make a cage and put you on exhibit?

ROBINSON. You've been to a good school, Vasya, a good one. You'll turn out to be a real merchant.

VOZHEVATOV. Good enough, I've heard people think well of me.

KNUROV. Vasily Danilych, drop him. I want to talk with you.

VOZHEVATOV *(approaching)*. What would you like?

KNUROV. I've been thinking about Larisa Dmitriyevna. It seems to me she's now in such a predicament that we who are her close friends are not only permitted but even obliged to take part in her fate.

Robinson listens.

VOZHEVATOV. What you're trying to say is that now that a good opportunity presents itself you'd like to take her with you to Paris, is that it?

KNUROV. Yes, I suppose that's what it adds up to, if she's agreeable.

VOZHEVATOV. So what's holding things up? Who's in your way?

KNUROV. You're in my way, and I'm in yours. Maybe you're not afraid of a rival? I'm not very much afraid either, but all the same it's awkward and troublesome. It would be a lot better if the field were clear.

VOZHEVATOV. You can't buy me off, Moky Parmenych.

KNUROV. Why buy anyone off? We can settle it some other way.

VOZHEVATOV. Look, here's the best way. *(He takes a coin out of his pocket and puts it under his hand.)* Heads or tails?

KNUROV *(in reflection)*. If I say heads, I'll lose. *(Decisively.)* I take tails.

VOZHEVATOV *(lifting his hand)*. You win. That means I go to Paris alone. I haven't lost anything, there'll be less expenses.

KNUROV. Just one thing, Vasily Danilych, you've given your word, so keep it. You're a merchant, you must understand what your word means.

VOZHEVATOV. You're insulting me. I know myself what a merchant's word is. I'm dealing with you, you know, not Robinson.

KNUROV. There comes Sergey Sergeyich with Larisa Dmitriyevna. Let's go into the coffee house so we won't disturb them.

Knurov and Vozhevatov go off into the coffee house. Paratov and Larisa enter.

LARISA. Oh, how tired I am. I've lost all my strength, I could hardly get up the hill. *(She sits down at the rear of the stage on a bench near the railing.)*

PARATOV. Ah, Robinson! Tell me, are you going to Paris soon?

ROBINSON. Who with? I'll go with you, la Serge, wherever you want, but I'm not going with any merchant. No, I'm finished with merchants.

PARATOV. Why is that?

ROBINSON. They're ill-bred.

PARATOV. Really? How long ago did you figure that out?

ROBINSON. I've always known it. I've always been for the nobles.

PARATOV. That does you honor, Robinson. But your pride is out-of-date. Adapt yourself to circumstances, my poor friend. The era of enlightened patrons, the era of a Maecenas has passed. Now we see the triumph of the bourgeoisie, now art is worth its weight in gold, and the golden age in the full sense has set in. But don't be too condemning. Now and again they'll give you your fill, if only with shoe polish, and for their own pleasure they'll roll you down a hill in a barrel, onto some Medici.[10] But don't leave me, I'll need you!

ROBINSON. For you I'd go through fire and water. *(He goes off into the coffee house.)*

PARATOV *(to Larisa)*. Let me thank you for the pleasure, no, that's not saying enough, for the happiness you've given us.

LARISA. No, no, Sergey Sergeyich, don't use empty words with me. Just tell me, what am I, your wife or not?

PARATOV. First of all, Larisa Dmitriyevna, you need to go home. We'll still have time to discuss it in detail tomorrow.

LARISA. I'm not going home.

PARATOV. But you can't stay here. To take a trip with you on the Volga before nightfall, that's permissible. But having a good time all night at a tavern, in the center of town, and with people who have a reputation for bad conduct! You'll be giving people food for gossip.

LARISA. What do I care about gossip! With you I can be anywhere. It was you who took me away, so it's you who should take me home.

PARATOV. You can go with my horses, isn't that just the same?

LARISA. No, it isn't the same. You took me away from my fiancé, Mama saw us leave, she won't be upset, no matter how late we return… She's calm, she's sure of you, she'll simply be waiting for us, waiting… to give us her blessing. I must either go home with you or not at all.

PARATOV. What does that mean, that "not at all"? Where are you going to go?

LARISA. For unhappy people there's a lot of space in God's world. There's the park, there's the Volga. Here you can hang yourself on any branch, and on the Volga you can pick any spot you want. It's easy to drown yourself anywhere if you have the desire and enough strength.

PARATOV. How exalted! You can live, and you must. Who will deny you love or respect! And there's your fiancé, he'll be overjoyed if you show him favor again.

LARISA. How can you say that! If I don't love my husband, then at least I should respect him, and how can I respect a man who calmly puts up with mockery and all kinds of humiliation! That affair is finished, for me he doesn't exist. I have only one fiancé, and that's you.

PARATOV. Forgive me, don't take offense, but you hardly have the right to be so demanding of me.

LARISA. What did you say! Have you really forgotten? Then I'll go over it all from the beginning. I suffered for a year, for a year I couldn't forget you, life became empty for me. I finally decided to marry Karandyshov, almost the first man I came on. I thought family responsibilities would fill up my life and reconcile me to it. Then you showed up and said, "Give all that up, I'm yours." Doesn't that give me the right? I thought your word was sincere, that I had earned it through suffering.

PARATOV. All that's very fine, and we'll talk it all over tomorrow.

LARISA. No, tonight, right now.

PARATOV. You insist?

LARISA. I insist.

Knurov and Vozhevatov can be seen in the doorway of the coffee house.

PARATOV. As you wish. Listen, Larisa Dmitriyevna, can you admit the possibility of a momentary passion?

LARISA. I can. I myself am capable of being carried away.

PARATOV. No, I didn't express myself properly. Can you admit the possibility that a man chained hand and foot by unbreakable chains could be so carried away that he would forget everything in the world, that he would even forget the reality oppressing him, even forget his chains?

LARISA. Well, so what! It's a good thing he does forget them.

PARATOV. A state of mind like that is a very good thing, I won't argue with you, but it's not long-lasting. The intoxication of ardent passion soon wears off, leaving the chains and common sense, which says that it's impossible to break those chains, that they're unbreakable.

LARISA *(pensively)*. Unbreakable chains! *(Quickly.)* Are you married?

PARATOV. No.

LARISA. But all other chains are no hindrance! We'll carry them together, I'll share this burden with you, I'll take the greater share of the weight myself.

PARATOV. I'm engaged.

LARISA. Oh!

PARATOV *(showing the engagement ring).* You see the golden chains by which I'm chained for the rest of my life.

LARISA. But why didn't you tell me? It's shameless, shameless! *(She sits down on a chair.)*

PARATOV. But was I really in a condition to remember anything! I saw you, and nothing more existed for me.

LARISA. Look at me!

Paratov looks at her.

"Your eyes shine bright like heaven's light…"[11] Ha, ha, ha! *(She laughs hysterically.)* Get away from me! I've had enough! I'll do my own thinking about myself. *(She rests her head on her hand.)*

Knurov, Vozhevatov, and Robinson come out onto the steps of the coffee house.

PARATOV *(going toward the coffee house).* Robinson, go look for my carriage. It's there by the boulevard. You'll take Larisa Dmitriyevna home.

ROBINSON. La Serge! He's here, he's going about with a pistol.

PARATOV. Who's "he"?

ROBINSON. Karandyshov.

PARATOV. What does that have to do with me?

ROBINSON. He'll kill me.

PARATOV. A matter of importance! Do what you're told! Without arguments! I don't like that, Robinson.

ROBINSON. I'm telling you, as soon as he sees me with her, he'll kill me.

PARATOV. Whether he'll kill you or not is still a question, but if you don't do right away what I've told you, then I'll kill you for sure. *(He goes off into the coffee house.)*

ROBINSON *(threatening with his fist).* Oh you barbarians, you highway robbers! What company I've fallen in with! *(He goes off.)*

Vozhevatov goes up to Larisa.

LARISA *(looking at Vozhevatov).* Vasya, I'm lost!

VOZHEVATOV. Larisa Dmitriyevna, my dear! What can you do! It can't be helped.

LARISA. Vasya, you and I have known each other since childhood, we're almost relatives. What am I to do? Teach me.

VOZHEVATOV. Larisa Dmitriyevna, I respect you, and I'd be glad… there's nothing I can do. Believe me.

LARISA. But I'm not asking you for anything, I'm only asking you to show me a little pity. Well, perhaps cry a bit with me.

VOZHEVATOV. I can't, there's nothing I can do.

LARISA. Do you have chains too?

VOZHEVATOV. I'm in irons, Larisa Dmitriyevna.

LARISA. What kind of irons?

VOZHEVATOV. A merchant's word of honor. *(He goes off into the coffee house.)*

KNUROV *(approaches Larisa).* Larisa Dmitriyevna, listen to me and don't take offense. I have no intention of offending you. I only wish you the good and happiness you so fully deserve. Wouldn't you like to go with me to Paris, to the exposition?

Larisa shakes her head no.

And have full security for the rest of your life?

Larisa remains silent.

Don't be afraid of shame, there won't be any condemnations. There are boundaries which condemnation does not cross. I can offer you such tremendous wealth that even the meanest critics of other people's morals will have to keep still and open their mouths in astonishment.

Larisa turns her head to the other side.

I wouldn't hesitate a moment to offer you my hand, but I'm married.

Larisa remains silent.

You're upset, I don't have the right to hurry your answer. Think about it. If you feel you can give my offer a favorable reply, let me know, and from that very moment I'll be your most devoted servant, and I'll carry out absolutely exactly all your wishes and whims no matter how strange or expensive. For me the impossible would be too little. *(He bows respectfully and goes off into the coffee house. Larisa is left alone.)*

LARISA. A little while ago I looked down over the railing, my head was spinning, and I almost fell. And if one falls down there, they say it's... certain death. *(She thinks.)* It would be a good thing to throw myself down! No, why throw myself down!... If I stand by the railing and look down, I'd get dizzy and fall... Yes, that would be better... unconscious, no pain... I wouldn't feel a thing! *(She goes to the railing, and looks down, She bends over, grabs firmly onto the railing, and then jumps back in horror.)* Oh, oh, how horrible! *(She almost falls and grabs onto the arbor.)* How my head is spinning! I'm falling, I'm falling, oh! *(She sits down at a table by the arbor.)* Oh, no... *(In tears.)* To part with life isn't nearly so simple as I thought. I just don't have the strength! How unlucky I am! But some people find it easy. It must be absolutely impossible for those people to go on living, nothing attracts them, nothing is dear to them, there's nothing they can't part with. And me!... There's nothing really dear to me either, and it's impossible for me to live, there's no reason for me to live! Then why can't I make up my mind? What's holding me back from this precipice? What's in the way? *(She becomes pensive.)* Oh no, no... It's not Knurov... luxury, glitter... no, no... I'm far from earthly things... *(Shuddering.)* Depravity... oh no... It's just that I don't have any will power. It's a pitiful weakness to want to live, somehow or other... when it's impossible to live and one shouldn't. How pitiful I am, how unlucky. If only somebody would kill me now... How nice it would be to die... while I still don't have anything to reproach myself for. Or to die from illness... And I think I will be ill. How awful I feel!... To be ill for a long time, to find peace, to reconcile myself with everything, to say good-bye to everybody and to die... Oh, how awful I feel, how my head is turning. *(She supports her head with her hand and sits oblivious to everything.)*

Robinson and Karandyshov enter.

KARANDYSHOV. You say you were told to take her home?

ROBINSON. Yes, sir, I was told to do that.

KARANDYSHOV. And you say they treated her badly?

ROBINSON. How could it be worse, how more humiliating!

KARANDYSHOV. She herself is at fault, and what she did deserves a punishment. I told her what kind of people they are. She could have noticed it herself, she had the time to see the difference between me and them. Yes, she's at fault, but I'm the only one who has the right to judge her, not speaking of humiliating her. It's my own business whether to forgive her or not, but I'm obliged to be her defender. She doesn't have any brothers or close friends, I'm all she has. I alone must stand up for her and punish those who wronged her. Where is she?

ROBINSON. She was here. There she is!

KARANDYSHOV. When she and I have things out there mustn't be any outsiders around, you'll be in the way. Leave us.

ROBINSON. With the greatest pleasure. I'll say that I handed Larisa Dmitriyevna over to you. My best wishes. *(He goes off into the coffee house.)*

Karandyshov goes up to the table and sits down opposite Larisa.

LARISA *(raising her head)*. How disgusting you are to me, if you only knew! What are you doing here?

KARANDYSHOV. Where am I supposed to be?

LARISA. I don't know. Anywhere you want, so long as it's not where I am.

KARANDYSHOV. You're wrong, I must always be with you, to protect you. And I'm here now, to avenge the wrong you've suffered.

LARISA. The most painful wrong I could suffer is your protection. Nobody wronged me.

KARANDYSHOV. You're too hard on me. Knurov and Vozhevatov cast lots to see who'd get you, they tossed a coin. Isn't that wronging you? Fine friends you have! What respect for you! They don't look on you as a woman, as a person. A person has some control over his fate, but they look on you as a thing. Well, if you're a thing, that's another matter. Naturally a thing belongs to the man who's won it, and a thing can't be wronged.

LARISA *(deeply hurt)*. A thing… yes, a thing! They're right, I am a thing, and not a person. I've just become convinced of it, I experienced it… I'm a thing! *(With heat.)* At last the word for me's been found, and you found it. Now go! Please leave me alone!

KARANDYSHOV. Leave you? How can I leave you, who to?

LARISA. Every thing has to have its owner. I'll go to my owner.

KARANDYSHOV *(with heat)*. I'll take you, I'm your owner. *(He seizes her by the hand.)*

LARISA *(pushing him away)*. Oh no! Every thing has its price… Ha, ha, ha… I'm too expensive, too expensive for you.

KARANDYSHOV. What did you say! How could I ever expect to hear such shameless words from you?

LARISA *(in tears)*. If one has to be a thing, there's one consolation, to be expensive, very expensive. Do me one last favor, go send Knurov to me.

KARANDYSHOV. What's wrong with you, what's gotten into you? You're out of your mind!

LARISA. All right, then I'll go myself.

KARANDYSHOV. Larisa Dmitriyevna! Stop! I forgive you, I forgive you everything.

LARISA *(with a bitter smile)*. You forgive me? Thank you. Only I don't forgive myself for taking it into my head to tie up my fate with such a nonentity as you.

KARANDYSHOV. Let's go away, let's go away from this town right away, I agree to everything.

LARISA. It's too late. I asked you to take me right off from the gypsy camp, but you couldn't manage that. It's clear enough I have to live and die in a gypsy camp.

KARANDYSHOV. I beg you, make me happy.

LARISA. It's too late. Gold has already flashed before my eyes. Diamonds have sparkled.

KARANDYSHOV. I'm ready for any sacrifice. I'll endure any humiliation for you.

LARISA *(with disgust)*. Go away. You're petty, you're too insignificant for me.

KARANDYSHOV. But tell me, how can I deserve your love? *(He falls on his knees.)* I love you, I love you.

LARISA. That's not true. I was looking for love and didn't find it. People looked on me and still look on me as a toy. Nobody ever tried to look into my soul. I didn't get any sympathy from anybody, I didn't hear a warm or kind word. And when you live like that, life is cold. It's not my fault. I was looking for love and didn't find it... it doesn't exist in the world... there's no point in looking for it. I didn't find love, so I'll look for gold. Go away, I can't be yours.

KARANDYSHOV *(getting up).* Oh, don't punish yourself for the past! *(He places his hand behind the breast of his suit coat.)* You must be mine.

LARISA. If I'm going to be anybody's I won't be yours.

KARANDYSHOV *(vehemently).* Not mine?

LARISA. Never!

KARANDYSHOV. Then nobody'll get you! *(He shoots her with his pistol.)*

LARISA *(grabbing her breast).* Oh! Thank you! *(She sinks onto a chair.)*

KARANDYSHOV. What have I done, what have I done... oh, I'm mad! *(He drops the pistol.)*

LARISA *(tenderly).* My dear, what a nice thing you did for me! Put the pistol here on the table. I did it myself... myself. Oh, what a nice thing...*(She lifts the pistol and puts it on the table.)*

Paratov, Knurov, Vozhevatov, Robinson, and Ivan come out of the coffee house.

ALL. What happened, what happened?

LARISA. I did it myself... Nobody's guilty, nobody... I did it myself... *(Off stage the gypsies begin a song.)*

PARATOV. Tell them to be quiet! Tell them to be quiet!

LARISA *(with a gradually weakening voice).* No, no, what for!... Let them be merry, anyone who can... I don't want to be in anyone's way! Live, everybody live! You have to live, and I have to... die... I have no complaints against anybody, no resentment against anybody... you're all good people... I love you all... all of you. *(She sends a kiss.)*

Loud chorus of the gypsies.

CURTAIN

NOTES

1. Name of a town of the Volga which existed in the seventeenth century.

2. Altered quotation from the fable "The Fox and the Grapes" *(Lisitsa i vinograd)* by I. Krylov based on Aesop's fable with the same title.

3. From "The Tomb of Askold" *(Askol'dova mogila),* opera by A.N. Verstovsky, libretto by M.N. Zagoskin.

4. From a romance by A.L. Gurilev, words by Nirkomsky.

5. "O tempt me not if there's no need…" *(Ne iskushai menia bez nuzhdy…)* Romance by M.I. Glinka, words by E.A. Baratynsky.

6. From "I Retire to the Desert" *(Ia v pustyniu udaliaius'),* song by M.V. Zubova (d. 1799).

7. "I'll whistle not where'er I stray, and those I meet won't get away" *(Ia edu-edu, ne svishchu, a naedu-ne spushchu).* From Pushkin's narrative poem *Ruslan i Liudmila.*

8. Operetta *(La Périchole)* by Jacques Offenbach (1819-80).

9. "We'll swing the rope she skips, the maid is wearing shoes *(Verev'iushki verev'iu, na baryshne bashmachki).* Russian folksong.

10. The reference is to Lorenzo de' Medici (1449-92), Florentine ruler and patron.

11. "Your eyes shine bright like heaven's light…" *(V glazakh, kak na nebe svetlo…).* From M. Lermontov's poem "To a Portrait" *(K portretu).*

AFTERWORD

Without a Dowry (Bespridannitsa) was conceived in November, 1874 and finished some four years later on October 17, 1878. Though Ostrovsky wrote other plays during that time, it was *Without a Dowry* which he valued most, spending an unusually long time as well as meticulous care on it. It was passed almost immediately by the censor for performance, later published in the No. 1, 1879 issue of *Fatherland Notes (Otechestvennye zapiski)*. The Moscow premiere occurred on November 10, 1878, then in St. Petersburg on November 22, 1878. Though some of Ostrovsky's contemporaries volunteered that they considered the play Ostrovsky's best, it was not really successful on the stage until 1896 when the great actress Vera Komissarzhevskaya played Larisa.

The play is remarkably unified, each scene directly or indirectly bearing on the fate of Larisa, whom all the male principals want to have at their disposal and whom her mother wants to dispose of. Seemingly free to make choices denied most of Ostrovsky's earlier heroines, in actuality she is not, since she has no realizable options that would be both attractive and honorable. Like it or not, she has to perform in her mother's entertainment center while being on display as a marketable commodity for potentially interested men.

Larisa has grown up in the artistic milieu of the gypsies where she, obviously talented to begin with, has received an excellent musical training. Her performance is appreciated by even the most mercenary-minded in the play. What Karandyshov disparagingly calls the "gypsy camp" is Larisa's spiritual ally, and she, herself of gypsy lineage through her mother, is attracted to the fun-loving gypsies. On the other hand, in contrast to her amoral mother, Larisa has moral principles, and she longs for an honorable life elsewhere.[1]

It has been generalized that when Ostrovsky's heroines are in love, that love becomes their whole world. This is certainly true for Larisa, who, once in love with Paratov, is ready at any given moment to trust, idealize, and forgive him. For Paratov love is like a good meal—to be enjoyed for the moment—but for Larisa it's a full and lasting commitment of her very life which she makes without looking back or, for that matter, ahead.

Larisa is disgusted by her mother's way of surviving through ingratiation and even trickery, but at this point her only honorable escape seems to be marriage, for which her prospects are limited. All she has to offer is herself, no dowry. After Larisa has given up hope that Paratov, following his first desertion, might return to her, Larisa settles for the faithful but dull and mediocre Karandyshov. She fantasizes that since she respects Karandyshov, even though she doesn't love him (though one can easily wonder if this respect isn't based on her strong need to believe in it), that they will be able to have a decent family life elsewhere, away from the insincere hurly-burly bazaar of her home, where she already senses, without being able to articulate it, that she is treated as a thing.

Like Larisa, Karandyshov is a pathetic victim of people and circumstances but at the same time a victim of his limitations, for which he tries to compensate by being spitefully envious of those with higher status. He even goes so far as to use his pending marriage with Larisa to get in some revenge, boasting that she has chosen him over the others. Compared to the other male principals he is a "good man" morally (as none of them are), but only in the sense of not doing conventionally bad things rather than in doing anything positively good. He can always be counted on to be honest, which is hardly a sure-fire asset in his case.

All the same, as most seem to agree, Karandyshov, along with his perverse possessiveness, does love Larisa for herself and has endured a good deal of abuse while waiting for her to come his way. He is sensitive enough to see through the other male principals, and it is he who finds the right word for Larisa: "thing." True, he's nasty to Larisa, but she has also been nasty to him and hasn't made it easy for him to show her the affection and support she now feels the need of. Proud and envious, much in the manner of Dostoevsky's underground man, Karandyshov oscillates between inevitable submission to humiliation and precipitous thrusts in society which make him look ridiculous, something Larisa finds impossible to forgive.

The little satire of the play is directed mostly against Knurov. In his setting Knurov is a giant whose every act is justified since money's might makes right. However, Ostrovsky exposes him for what he is—a cynical, callous, self-righteous, pompously arrogant snob, whose cleverness backed by wealth helps him to maintain his prestige and bring him the pleasures he desires. When he makes his proposition to Larisa that she become his kept woman, he feels he has to mention the prejudice some might have about it, but he reassures her that there's nothing at all to worry her pretty head inasmuch as the all-powerful whitewashing capacity of his money will make everything fine.

In Act Two Knurov demonstrates a skill which shows that while he is not interested in others for their own sake, he knows how to deal with them for his own ends. He bargains with Mme. Ogudalov for her sympathetic alliance, giving her three hundred rubles, a thinly disguised retainer fee for her potential lobbying services on his behalf relative to Larisa. He assumes (and maybe even finds it congenial) that Larisa will marry Karandyshov, but he has no trouble making the quick-minded Mme. Ogudalov realize that when the marriage inevitably goes downhill, then he, Knurov, will be ready, able, and only too willing to rescue poor Larisa from the tedium of everyday family humdrum.

Paratov has his demonic side, reminding some of Pechorin, the hero of Lermontov's *Hero of Our Times,* and he's close enough to the truth when he claims that for him nothing is sacred. When he causes Larisa grief, it bothers him a little, but not overly; after all, it's a woman's lot to weep! He cares for Larisa somewhat, almost certainly more than he has ever cared for another woman, but not to the point of losing anything by it. If it becomes necessary to sell his assets to pay for the pleasures of life he's become accustomed to, then he'll do it, even to the point of selling his matehood. But if Paratov were only a black villain as just described, we would be puzzled by Larisa's attraction to him. So Ostrovsky makes Paratov charismatic. Paratov is charming, a bit sophisticated, self-assured, intelligent, imaginative, playful in speech, and appreciative of beauty, qualities contributing to Larisa's enchantment. It's easy enough to see how Larisa would prefer the dashing Paratov over the petty and lackluster Karandyshov.

Robinson as an outsider who knows the score, so to speak, from the ground up sees Knurov, Vozhevatov, and Paratov for what they are and says so but guardedly, for Robinson's main interest is self-interest. While we won't admire Robinson for his pliability, we can sympathize with him since he, paralleling Larisa, is treated as a thing.

The off-stage chorus of the gypsies at the end may be considered symbolically as a hymn in Larisa's honor. Paratov wants the gypsies silenced, but Larisa says no, let them have their fun, that she doesn't want to get in anyone's way, that she loves everybody. Some may find this a bit histrionic, but it's all consistent with her past life when all she asked for was true love and during which she hurt nobody except Karandyshov (that at least partly forgivable in the circumstances).

The play rushes with an intense pace, taking place within a represented time span of little more than twelve hours. The psychological compression is heightened by each succeeding act's being shorter than the preceding one.

Some, including me, consider *Without a Dowry* to be Ostrovsky's finest play. The Russian critic Yefim Kholodov has this to say:

> But neither before nor after *Without a Dowry* did Ostrovsky rise to such dramatic heights, attain such artistic force, reach such psychological subtlety in the portrayal of characters. It may now be considered generally accepted that "opus 40" is the best play of the best Russian playwright of the past century.

NOTE

1. VI. Filippov discussed Larisa's mixed background as the daughter of a Russian nobleman (apparently long dead) and a gypsy mother, Mme. Ogudalov. He noted that Kharita was a name often given to gypsy women, and also that Ignat, from which the patronymic for Mme. Ogudalov would be derived, was often used as a nickname for gypsy men.

Filippov assumed that, as was not uncommon at the time, Larisa's father married Mme. Ogudalov after ransoming her from a gypsy camp. At one point Vozhevatov makes a point of telling Knurov that Mme. Ogudalov is not Russian, and Filippov claimed that she uses a number of non-Russian phrases.

Fillipov conjectured that what he considered to be contradictory traits in Larisa could be attributed to her mixed parentage. Larisa clearly has much of the gypsy in her, but in her moral values is hardly her mother's daughter. Filippov's remarks accompanied an anthology of Ostrovsky's plays (A. N. Ostrovskii, *Izbrannye proizvedeniia,* Moscow, 1965, 404).

TALENTS AND ADMIRERS

A Comedy in Four Acts

(1882)

CAST OF CHARACTERS*

ALEXÁNDRA NIKOLÁVNA NYÉGIN (SÁSHA). An actress in a provincial theater. Young and unmarried.

DÓMNA PANTELYÉVNA NYEGIN (MME. NYEGIN). Alexandra's mother, a widow and very simple woman over forty. Her husband was a musician in a provincial orchestra.

PRINCE IRÁKLY STRATÓNYCH DULYÉBOV. An imposing gentleman in the old style. Elderly.

GRIGÓRY ANTÓNYCH BÁKIN. A provincial official in a important position. About thirty.

IVÁN SEMYÓNYCH VELIKÁTOV. A very rich landowner, owner of well-run estates and factories. A retired cavalry officer with a practical mind. His behavior is modest and well-controlled. He has constant dealings with merchants, and he clearly tries to imitate their tone and manners. Middle-aged.

PETER YEGÓRYCH MELÚZOV (PÉTYA). A young man who has finished the university and is awaiting a teaching position.

NÍNA VASÍLYEVNA SMÉLSKY. An actress. Older than Alexandra.

MARTÝN PROKÓFYICH NARÓKOV. Assistant to the stage director and also property man. An old man, who is dressed very well, though cheaply. His manners are refined.

GAVRÍLO PETRÓVICH MIGÁEV (GAVRYÚSHKA). Theater manager.

YERÁST GROMÍLOV (*also called* TRAGEDIAN). Tragedian.

VÁSYA. A young merchant of pleasant appearance and proper manners.

MATRYÓNA. Cook in the Nyegin household.

CHIEF TRAIN CONDUCTOR.

TRAIN CONDUCTOR.

RAILROAD STATION CLERK.

VARIOUS PASSENGERS and RAILROAD STATION WORKERS.

A VARIED PUBLIC, mostly of the merchant class (in Act Two).

---

*Meanings which would probably or possibly be suggested to Ostrovsky's contemporaries: Nyegin—comfort, bliss, tenderness; Dulyebov—blockhead, simpleton; Bakin—eloquent; Velikatov—majestic, eminent; Meluzov—groats, chaff; Smelsky—bold; Narokov—reproach; Gromilov—devastate, loot, fulminate (against).

ACT ONE

The action takes place in a provincial town [Bryakhimov]. The actress Nyegin's apartment. On the left of the actors is a window. In the corner in the background is a door to the anteroom. On the right is a partition with a door into another room. There is a table with some books and notebooks on it by the window. The furniture is cheap.

MME NYEGIN *(alone, talking through the window)*. Come back in three or four days. After the benefit performance they're giving for us we'll pay you everything. Eh? What? Oh, he's deaf! He doesn't hear me. I say we're getting a benefit performance, so after that we'll pay you everything. Well, he's gone. *(She sits down.)* All those debts, all those debts! A ruble here, a couple there... And what they'll take in at the box office is anybody's guess. In the winter there was a benefit for us, and after expenses there were only forty-two and a half rubles. And there was that half-crazy merchant who brought some turquoise earrings... a lot of good they were! What a thing to do! But now that the fair is here we ought to be getting some two hundred rubles from it. But even if we should get three hundred it's not likely we'll keep it long; it'll go through our fingers like water. My Sasha just doesn't have any luck! She behaves the way she ought to, but the public isn't well disposed to her, she doesn't get any gifts worth speaking of, nothing like the ones the others get, those who... if... Take the prince now... What would it cost him! Or Ivan Semyonych Velikatov... they say his sugar factories are worth millions... What would it cost him to send a couple pounds of that sugar? It would last us a long time... Those people sit buried up to their ears in money and don't think of helping a poor girl out. I'm not talking about the merchants, what could anyone get out of them! They don't even go to the theater, they'd have to go plumb crazy first, get blown there by the wind... disgraceful things is all you can expect from them...

Narokov enters.

Oh, Prokofyich, hello.

NAROKOV *(gloomily)*. Hello, Prokofyevna.

MME NYEGIN. My patronymic isn't Prokofyevna but Pantelyevna, what's the matter with you!

NAROKOV. And I'm not just Prokofyich but Martyn Prokofyich.

MME NYEGIN. Oh, excuse me, Mister Actor Man!

NAROKOV. If you want to be familiar when you speak with me, then call me simply Martyn. At least that would be more suitable. But "Prokofyich"! That's vulgar, madam, very vulgar!

MME NYEGIN. You and I, my dear sir, are small fry. Why spout all that fine talk?

NAROKOV. Small fry? I'm not small fry, pardon me!

MME NYEGIN. Then I suppose you're somebody big?

NAROKOV. Big.

MME NYEGIN. So from now on we'll know. And exactly why have you, such a big man, come to see us little people?

NAROKOV. Must we continue in this tone, Domna Pantelyevna? Why are you so grumpy?

MME NYEGIN. So I'm grumpy, why hide it! I like to do my work, and bothering to talk with you is something I don't care for.

NAROKOV. But where did your grumpiness come from? From nature or upbringing?

MME NYEGIN. Oh Lord, what from, what did it come from?... But what else could you expect? I lived my whole life in poverty, among lowdown people. Cursing in the house every day and never a chance to rest or catch your breath. I was never in any boarding school, wasn't brought up with any fine ladies. All that happened to people like us was that time passed, and everybody cursed everybody else. You know, it's the rich people who've thought up all those delicate things.

NAROKOV. It all makes sense. I understand now.

MME NYEGIN. So I don't say tender things to everybody, with every person, if I may say so... I might've said something to you, but I didn't mean to offend. Do you speak respectfully to everybody?

NAROKOV. I'm familiar when I speak with the common folk...

MME NYEGIN. "The common folk"! You don't say! And what sort of a fine gentleman are you!

NAROKOV. I'm from the gentleman class, a genuine gentleman... Well, all right, let's you and I speak together on familiar terms, that's nothing special.

MME NYEGIN. Nothing special at all, but a very common thing. And in what way are you of the gentleman class?

NAROKOV. I can tell you that I'm like King Lear, every inch a gentleman. I'm an educated man, I studied in an educational institution, I was rich.

MME NYEGIN. *You?*

NAROKOV. Yes, me!

MME NYEGIN. Is that really true?

NAROKOV. Do you want me to take an oath on it?

MME NYEGIN. No, what for? There's no need for an oath, I believe you. But then how come you work as a prompeter?

NAROKOV. I'm not a prompeter nor even a prompter, Madam, I'm assistant to the stage director. This theater was once mine.

MME NYEGIN *(with astonishment)*. Yours? You don't say!

NAROKOV. I maintained it for five years, and Gavryushka was my clerk. He copied out the roles.

MME NYEGIN *(with great astonishment)*. Gavrila Petrovich, the theater manager here?

NAROKOV. The very same.

MME NYEGIN. You poor man! So that's how it is. It seems God didn't give you any happiness in this theater play business.

NAROKOV. Happiness! I didn't know what to do with my happiness, I had so much of it!

MME NYEGIN. Then why have you come down so? Did you take to drink? What did you do with your money?

NAROKOV. I never drank. I spent all my money for my happiness.

MME NYEGIN. And what was your happiness?

NAROKOV. It was a happiness that I made into a love affair. *(Pensively.)* I love the theater, I love art, I love actors, can you understand that? So I sold my estate, got a lot of money, and became a theater manager. Eh, wasn't that happiness? I rented the theater here and did everything over, the sets and the costumes. I got together a good troupe and began to live in seventh heaven... I didn't care whether we had a good take at the box office, and I paid everybody a good salary and on time. And so I passed five happy years, till I saw that my money was running out. At the end of the season I paid off all the actors, gave them a farewell dinner, gave each one an expensive gift to remember me by...

MME NYEGIN. And what happened then?

NAROKOV. And then Gavryushka rented my theater, and I started working for him. He pays me a small salary and a little for my keep. That's the whole story, my dear.

MME NYEGIN. And that's all you live on?

NAROKOV. Well, no, I can always earn my bread. I give lessons, I write items for newspapers, I do translations. But I work for Gavryushka because I don't want to leave the theater, I love art so much. So here I am, an educated man, with fine taste, living among coarse people who offend my artistic feeling every step of the way. *(Going to the table.)* What kind of books are these?

MME NYEGIN. Sasha is studying, she has a teacher come.

NAROKOV. A teacher? What sort of teacher?

MME NYEGIN. He's a student. Peter Yegorych. Do you know him by any chance?

NAROKOV. I know him. A dagger in his chest right up to the hilt![1]

MME NYEGIN. So cruel?

NAROKOV. Without pity.

MME NYEGIN. You better wait before sticking him, he's Sasha's fiancé.

NAROKOV *(with fright)*. Fiancé?

MME NYEGIN. It will work out, of course, as God wills, but anyway we call him a fiancé. She met him somewhere, and he started visiting us. So what could you call him? Well, we call him a fiancé, otherwise what would the neighbors say! I'll marry her off to him as soon as he gets a good position. It isn't easy to find eligible bachelors. A merchant with a lot of money would be nice, but a good one wouldn't take her, and some of them are awfully disgusting, no great joy from them. So why shouldn't she marry him then, he's a peaceful lad, Sasha loves him.

NAROKOV. Loves? She loves him?

MME NYEGIN. And why shouldn't she love him? As a matter of fact, why should a young woman wear herself out in the theater? There's just no way to get a good foothold in life there!

NAROKOV. And *you* can say that?

MME NYEGIN. I can say that, and I've been saying it a long time. You can't get anything good from the theater.

NAROKOV. But your daughter has talent, she was born for the stage.

MME NYEGIN. For the stage, for the stage, you hit the nail right on the head! When she was little you couldn't drag her out of the theater; she'd stand behind the wings, all aflutter. My husband, her father, was a musician, he played the flute. So whenever he'd go to the theater, she'd go after him, staying in the wings, not even breathing.

NAROKOV. So there you are. The only place for her is on the stage.

MME NYEGIN. A beautiful place that is!

NAROKOV. But she has a passion for the theater, you must understand, a passion! You said that yourself.

MME NYEGIN. And what if she does have a passion for it, what's the good of that? That's nothing to brag about. That kind of passion is for you homeless and dissipated people.

NAROKOV. Oh ignorance! A dagger in the chest right up to the hilt!

MME NYEGIN. You and your daggers! There's mighty little good on that stage of yours, and I'm keeping my daughter on the road that ends up in marriage. Men keep coming at her from all sides, trying to get on her good side and whispering all kinds of stupid things in her ear... That Prince Dulyebov's been coming a lot. In his old age he's taken it into his head to go courting... Is that good? What do you say to that?

NAROKOV. Prince Dulyebov! A dagger in his chest right up to the hilt!

MME NYEGIN. You've gone and stuck an awful lot of people.

NAROKOV. A lot.

MME NYEGIN. And they're still alive?

NAROKOV. Why not? Of course they're alive, and all in good health, may they live to a ripe old age. Here, give this to her. *(He gives her a notebook.)*

MME NYEGIN. What is it?

NAROKOV. It's a role. I copied it out for her myself.

MME NYEGIN. What's the great occasion? On thin paper and tied up with a rose-colored ribbon!

NAROKOV. Well, all you have to do is give it to her! Why all this talk!

MME NYEGIN. But what use is this tenderness when we're so hard up? You spent your last twenty kopecks on that ribbon, didn't you?

NAROKOV. Suppose I did, so what? She has such nice hands, and her soul is even better, so I couldn't give her a messy notebook.

MME NYEGIN. But what for? What's it all for?

NAROKOV. Why be so surprised? The whole thing's very simple and natural. That's how it should be because I'm in love with her.

MME NYEGIN. Oh good heavens! It gets worse every minute! You know, you're an old man, you're nothing but an old clown. What kind of love could you want?

NAROKOV. But isn't she beautiful? Tell me, isn't she beautiful?

MME NYEGIN. So she's beautiful, what's it to you?

NAROKOV. And who doesn't love what's beautiful? You too love what's beautiful. Do you think that because a man is in love, there has to be a big racket... that he must get all excited? My soul is full of fine perfumes. But how could you understand that!

MME NYEGIN. You know, when I look at you I can see you're some kind of freak!

NAROKOV. Thank God you've realized. I know myself that I'm a freak. Were you trying to call me names?

MME NYEGIN *(by the window)*. Could that be the Prince who drove up? That's who it is.

NAROKOV. Well, in that case I'll leave now, through the kitchen. Adieu, madame.

MME NYEGIN. Adieu, moosir!

Narokov goes out behind the partition. Dulyebov and Bakin enter.

MME NYEGIN. She's not home, Your Excellency, please excuse us. She went shopping.

DULYEBOV. That's all right, it doesn't matter. I'll wait.

MME NYEGIN. As you wish, Your Excellency.

DULYEBOV. You just go about your business, don't go to any trouble, please. I'll wait.

Mme. Nyegin goes off.

BAKIN. Sir, we've both come at the same time.

DULYEBOV. What difference does that make? There's room here for both of us.

BAKIN. No, one of us is extra, and the extra one is me. That's just my luck. I dropped in on Smelsky too, and Velikatov was sitting there. He didn't say a word.

DULYEBOV. But you should have started a conversation. You know how to talk, so the chances are on your side.

BAKIN. It doesn't always work out that way. Velikatov is more convincing when he's quiet than I am when I talk.

DULYEBOV. Why is that?

BAKIN. Because he's rich. You know how the proverb goes, "Never rival men of wealth; don't fight strong men, guard your health." So I give way. Velikatov is rich, and you are strong with your sweet talk.

DULYEBOV. And how do you intend to win?

BAKIN. With boldness, Prince. Boldness, they say, is what takes cities.

DULYEBOV. It's probably easier to take cities… Still, that's your affair. If you're not afraid of losing, then why not try boldness?

BAKIN. I'd rather suffer defeat than go in for compliments.

DULYEBOV. Every one to his liking.

BAKIN. To go courting, pay compliments, resurrect the days of chivalry, that's just too much honor for our ladies!

DULYEVOV. Every one to his viewpoint.

BAKIN. It seems to me it's enough just to come right out with it: "Here I am, just as you see me. I offer you such and such. Would you care to love me?"

DULYEBOV. Yes, but you know that would be offensive for a woman.

BAKIN. Well, that's their business, whether to take offense or not. At least I'm not deceiving them. After all, with all the things I'm busy with, I can't take up love seriously. So why should I pretend to be in love, to delude somebody with hopes that might not be realized! Isn't it a lot better to have a clear understanding?

DULYEBOV. Every one to his own style. Tell me, please, what kind of man is Velikatov?

BAKIN. I know as much about him as you do. He's very rich. He has a splendid estate in the next province, a sugar beet factory, a stud farm, and a distillery too, I think. He comes here to the fair, but whether it's to buy or sell horses I don't know. I don't know how he talks with the horse dealers either, but with us he's quiet most of the time.

DULYEBOV. Does he have tact?

BAKIN. Very much so. Instead of arguing, he agrees with everybody, and you can never tell whether he's serious or pulling your leg.

DULYEBOV. But he's very courteous.

BAKIN. Terribly. In the theater he knows absolutely everybody by name: the cashier, the prompter, even the property man, and he shakes hands with all of them. And he's charmed the old women completely. He knows everything and puts himself into everything that interests them. In other words, he treats all the old women like a most respectful and obliging son.

DULYEBOV. But he doesn't seem to show any preference for the young ladies; he shies away from them.

BAKIN. In that regard you can set your mind at rest, Prince, he's not a dangerous rival for you. For some reason he's shy with young ladies, and he never speaks first to them. When they address him, all he says is, "What would you like? What do you want?"

DULYEBOV. But perhaps this coldness is calculated. Couldn't be he trying to get them interested in him?

BAKIN. But what can he count on? He's leaving tomorrow or the day after.

DULYEBOV. Is that so?... Really?

BAKIN. It's a sure thing. He told me so himself. He has everything ready for departure.

DULYEBOV. That's too bad! He's a very pleasant man, so steady, so calm.

BAKIN. It seems to me his calmness comes from his limitations. A man just doesn't keep his intelligence to himself, he shows it in some way, but he keeps quiet, which means he's not bright. Still, he's not stupid either, because he figures it's better to stay quiet than to say stupid things. He has just enough intelligence and ability to behave properly and not squander what papa left him.

DULYEBOV. That fact is, papa left him a ruined estate, and he built it back up again.

BAKIN. All right, so give him credit for some practical sense and thrift.

DULYEBOV. Add a little more, and he'll turn out to be a very clever and practical man.

BAKIN. For some reason I don't care to believe that. But it doesn't really matter to me whether he's smart or stupid. What bothers me is that he's so rich.

DULYEBOV. He is?

BAKIN. Yes. I can't get it out of my head that it would be a lot better if I were rich and he were poor.

DULYEBOV. Yes, that would be better for you, but why for him?

BAKIN. Oh the hell with him, what's he to me! I'm talking about myself. But it's time to go to work. I yield you the field uncontested. Good-bye, Prince.

DULYEBOV *(giving his hand)*. Good-bye, Grigory Antonych.

Bakin leaves. Mme. Nyegin enters.

MME NYEGIN. He left? He didn't wait?

DULYEBOV. What do you pay for this apartment?

MME NYEGIN. Twelve rubles, Your Excellency.

DULYEBOV *(pointing to the corner)*. Am I right in saying that it must be damp there?

MME NYEGIN. You get the kind of apartment you pay for.

DULYEBOV. You'll have to change it. *(Opening the door to the right.)* And what's there?

MME NYEGIN. That's Sasha's bedroom. And on the right is my room, and there's the kitchen.

DULYEBOV *(to himself)*. It's pitiful. Yes… of course, this is impossible.

MME NYEGIN. It's in keeping with our means, Your Excellency.

DULYEBOV. Please, don't talk about what you don't understand. A good actress can't live like this. It can't be done, I tell you, it's impossible. It's not proper.

MME NYEGIN. But where can we get the revenue?

DULYEBOV. What kind of word is that, "revenue"?

MME NYEGIN. From what income, Your Excellency?

DULYEBOV. But why should we be concerned about your income?

MME NYEGIN. But where are we going to get it, Your Excellency?

DULYEBOV. You and your "Where are we going to get it"! Who cares! It's nobody's business, get it where you want. Only it's impossible to live like this, it's… well, it's just not proper, that's all there is to it.

MME NYEGIN. Now if we had a salary…

DULYEBOV. Well, whether it's a salary or something else, that's your business.

MME NYEGIN. What we get from the benefit performances for her is very small.

DULYEBOV. And whose fault is that? To get a lot from benefit performances you have to know the right people, how to choose them, how to manage things… I can give you the names of about ten people you have to get on your side, then you'd have wonderful benefit performances, even with prizes and gifts. It's simple enough, something everybody's known for a long time. You have to entertain the right people… And how can you do that here! What's here? Who's going to come here?

MME NYEGIN. But you know, the audience seems to like her, but when it comes to a benefit performance, then… you just can't attract them at all.

DULYEBOV. What audience are you talking about? The students, the shopkeepers, the petty officials! They're very happy to clap their hands off, they'll call back the actress Nyegin ten times, but for all that, they're no-good trash, they won't pay a kopeck extra at a benefit performance.

MME NYEGIN. That's the gospel truth, Your Excellency. Of course, if we had some acquaintances, it would be quite a different matter.

DULYEBOV. No question. You can't blame the public, the public is never at fault. The same for public opinion, it's ridiculous to complain against that. You must know how to earn the love of the public. What's necessary is for your daughter to be surrounded all the time by rich young men, or, more properly speaking, her main friends should be us, the solid people. We're all busy the whole day long, some of us with family and household business, some of us with public affairs, so we only have a few hours free in the evening. So where can we find a suitable place, if not with a young actress, where we can relax, so to speak, from our burdens? For one man it's getting away from his domestic problems, for another from the problems connected with his area of responsibility.

MME NYEGIN. That's too hard for me to understand, Your Excellency. You better say those words to my Sasha.

DULYEBOV. Yes, I'll tell her, I'll most certainly tell her. That's what I came here for.

MME NYEGIN. There, I think she's coming now.

DULYEBOV. Only don't you get in our way.

MME NYEGIN. Really now, do you think I'm my own child's enemy? *(Alexandra enters.)* What took you so long? The Prince has been waiting a long time for you. *(She takes her daughter's hat, umbrella, and cloak. She goes off.)*

DULYEBOV *(approaches and kisses Alexandra's hand)*. Ah, my joy, at last you've come.

ALEXANDRA. Excuse me, Prince. I'm having so much trouble with my benefit performance. It's agony... *(She becomes pensive.)*

DULYEBOV *(sitting down)*. Tell me, please, my dear friend...

ALEXANDRA *(coming out of her pensiveness)*. What would you like to know?

DULYEBOV. What was that play you last played in?

ALEXANDRA. "Uriel Acosta."[2]

DULYEBOV. Yes, yes... You played wonderfully, wonderfully. How much feeling, how much nobility! I'm not joking when I say that.

ALEXANDRA. Thank you, Prince.

DULYEBOV. They write such strange plays now; you can't understand a thing.

ALEXANDRA. But that play was written long ago.

DULYEBOV. Long ago? Was it by Karatygin[3] or Grigoryev?[4]

ALEXANDRA. Neither. It was by Gutzkow.

DULYEBOV. Ah! Gutzkow... I know, I know. He also wrote a comedy, a wonderful comedy, "A Russian Remembers a Good Deed."

ALEXANDRA. That one's by Polevoy,[5] Prince.

DULYEBOV. Oh yes... I got them mixed up... Polevoy... Nicholas Polevoy. He came from the lower middle class... He taught himself French, wrote learned books, took it all from the French... Only then he had an argument with somebody... with some learned men or some professors. Now how could he do a thing like that! How was it possible, how was it proper! So, they told him not to write any learned books, and they ordered him to write some vaudeville pieces. Later on he himself was grateful for that, he made more money that way. "I wouldn't have thought of it," he said. Why are you so sad?

ALEXANDRA. I have many cares, Prince.

DULYEBOV. My beauty, you should be jollier, it's still too early for you to be thinking about things. Find some distraction, amuse yourself with something. Just now I was talking with your mother...

ALEXANDRA. What about, Prince?

DULYEBOV. Why naturally about you, my treasure, what else? You have a bad apartment here... It's impossible for an actress, a beautiful young woman, to live in such a hut. It's not proper.

ALEXANDRA *(a bit offended)*. A bad apartment? Well, what of it? I know myself there are better apartments... I should think, Prince, you'd be a little sorry for me and not remind me of my poverty. Even without you I feel it every hour, every moment.

DULYEBOV. But don't you think I'm sorry for you? I'm very sorry for you, my beauty.

ALEXANDRA. Then keep your sympathy to yourself, Your Excellency! Your sympathy doesn't do me any good, and it's unpleasant to hear it. You find my apartment bad, but I find it acceptable, and I don't need a better one. If you don't like my apartment, if it's unpleasant for you to be in such an apartment, then nobody's keeping you.

DULYEBOV. Now don't get excited, don't get excited, my joy! You haven't heard me to the end, and you're being angry with a man who's devoted to you heart and soul... That's just not right...

ALEXANDRA. Please go ahead and speak, I'm listening.

DULYEBOV. I'm a man of tact, I never humiliate anybody, I'm known for my tact. I never would have dared to criticize your apartment if I didn't have in view...

ALEXANDRA. What, Prince?

DULYEBOV. To offer you another, one much better.

ALEXANDRA. At the same rent?

DULYEBOV. Well, what do we care about the rent?

ALEXANDRA. There's something here I don't understand, Prince.

DULYEBOV. You see, my delight, it's like this. I'm a very kind and tender man, everybody knows it... In spite of my years I've kept onto all my freshness of feeling... I can still fall in love, like a young man...

ALEXANDRA. I'm very glad for you. But what does that have to do with my apartment?

DULYEBOV. It's very simple. Don't you really see? I love you... I want to cherish you, to spoil you... that would be a delight for me... that's my necessity. I have a lot of tenderness in my soul, I need to shower affection on somebody, I can't manage without it. So, come to me, my little bird!

ALEXANDRA *(gets up)*. You're out of your mind!

DULYEBOV. That's rude, my friend, it's rude!

ALEXANDRA. Where did you ever get an idea like that? Really! I gave you no cause at all... How could you dare say such things?

DULYEBOV. Take it easy now, take it easy, my little friend!

ALEXANDRA. But what is this! To come into somebody else's home and just like that, for no good reason, to start a stupid and offensive conversation.

DULYEBOV. Now take it easy, take it easy, please! You are still very young to talk like that.

ALEXANDRA. I like that! "You are still young"! That means you can offend young people as much as you want and they have to keep quiet.

DULYEBOV. But where's there any offense here? Where's the offense? It's a most ordinary sort of business. You don't know life or proper society, and yet you dare to pass judgment on a respected man! In actuality it is you who are offending me!

ALEXANDRA *(in tears)*. Oh, my God! No, this is more than I can bear...

DULYEBOV. For everything there's a proper form, young lady! You just don't have good breeding. If you didn't like my offer, then you should have thanked me all the same and told me your unwillingness politely, or somehow made a joke of it.

ALEXANDRA. Oh, leave me alone, please! I don't need your moral admonitions. I know myself what I should do. I know what's good and bad. Oh, my God!... I just don't want to listen to you.

DULYEBOV. But why shout?

ALEXANDRA. And why shouldn't I shout? I'm in my own home, who's there to be afraid of?

DULYEBOV. Very well! Only remember this, my joy. I don't forget an insult.

ALEXANDRA. All right, all right, I'll remember it.

DULYEBOV. I'm sorry, but I thought you were a well-brought-up young woman. There was no way to expect that because of some little trifle or other you would burst into tears and show a lot of emotion, just like some kitchen woman.

ALEXANDRA. All right, fine, I'm a kitchen woman, only I want to be a woman of honor.

Mme. Nyegin appears in the doorway.

DULYEBOV. Congratulations! Only honor itself isn't enough. You have to be more intelligent, and more prudent, so you won't cry afterwards. Don't send me any of those tickets at sponsors' prices. I won't be going to your benefit performance, I don't have the time. And if I do decide to go, then I'll send to the box office for a regular-priced ticket. *(He leaves.)*

Mme. Nyegin enters.

MME NYEGIN. What is it? What's going on here? Has the Prince left? He wasn't angry, was he?

ALEXANDRA. Let him be angry!

MME NYEGIN. What are you saying! Come to your senses! Before a benefit performance? Are you in your right mind?

ALEXANDRA. But it's just impossible! The things he says! If you could have heard!

MME NYEGIN. But what's that to you! Let him talk. Words won't kill you.

ALEXANDRA. But you don't know what he said. It's really none of your business.

MME NYEGIN. I know, I know it all very well, what men say.

ALEXANDRA. And we can listen to that and stay calm?

MME NYEGIN. But what's the harm! Let him talk away as much as he wants. Let him spout all his nonsense. You just laugh to yourself!

ALEXANDRA. Oh, don't give me lessons! Leave me alone, please! I know how to behave.

MME NYEGIN. I can see what you know. Right before a benefit performance you quarrel with a man like that!

ALEXANDRA. Mama, can't you see I'm upset? I'm trembling all over, and you keep after me.

MME NYEGIN. No, now you just wait! Listen to sense from your mother! How can you quarrel before a benefit performance when you need certain people?... Couldn't you have waited a bit? Afterwards you can quarrel as much as you want, I won't say a word. Because I realize you can't let them get away with everything, you've got to hold them back. But now they'll call you a scarecrow!

ALEXANDRA. Mama, that's enough...

MME NYEGIN. No, it's not! Before that benefit performance you should have been polite...

ALEXANDRA. But I didn't quarrel with him. I just felt offended and told him to leave me alone.

MME NYEGIN. And that's where you were stupid, yes, stupid! You should have tried to be as polite as you could, say to him, "Your Excellency, we are always very much pleased with you and always very grateful to you. Only we don't find pleasure in listening to those vile things. We are completely opposed to what you understand of us." That's what you should have said! Because that way it's honorable, it's noble, it's polite.

ALEXANDRA. What's done is done. There's no point in talking about it now!

MME NYEGIN. Maybe I'm not educated, but I know how to talk with people. And you have a teacher teaching you...

ALEXANDRA. Why bring that up about a teacher? ... You just don't understand any of this business so you have no reason to interfere.

MME NYEGIN. But what is there to understand? He's a student like any other. What's so important about him, tell me that! He's nothing high and mighty! We've seen plenty from his class in life. Nothing but talk... They're the poorest of the poor. They can only show off, but they don't have a decent frock coat to their name.

ALEXANDRA. What has he done to you? ... Why talk like that? Why are you tormenting me?

MME NYEGIN. Just look now, what an important man we have here! Don't dare say a word about him! No, my dear, nobody's going to stop me; if I want, I'll curse a man out, right to his face. I'll pick out the most insulting words I can think of and let him have it... I want you to know what it means to quarrel with a mother, what it means to talk with a mother.

ALEXANDRA. Go away!

MME NYEGIN. And now it's "Go away!" You can go away yourself if I'm crowding you.

ALEXANDRA. I think somebody's just driven up... Go, Mama! Who wants to listen to the kind of stupid talk we've been having!

MME NYEGIN. Just for that I'm not going to leave... Look at her, she insults her mother in the worst way and then acts high and mighty... Stupid talk. I'm no more stupid than you or that student of yours, with all that shaggy hair.

ALEXANDRA *(looking out the window)*. It's Velikatov! This is the first time he's visited us... and the way things are here...

MME NYEGIN. Don't worry your precious head, miss, Mamselle Nyegin, famous actress, some of us aren't any worse in dealing with people than you are... let me remind you.

ALEXANDRA. Nina Smelsky is with him.

MME NYEGIN. Yes, I'll have you know there are people who know how to...

ALEXANDRA. What horses, what horses!

MME NYEGIN. Nina Smelsky can go riding, but we go on foot.

Nina Smelsky and Velikatov enter.

MME NYEGIN. Come in, please come in, Nina Vasilyevna!

NINA. Hello, Domna Pantelyevna! I've brought you a guest, Ivan Semyonych Velikatov. *(Velikatov bows.)*

MME NYEGIN. I'm so pleased to meet you. I've known you for a long time, and I've seen you often at the theater, but I've never had a chance to meet you.

NINA. Hello, Sasha! I was getting ready to visit you, and I'd already put on my hat when Ivan Semyonych dropped in. So he's tagged along. You don't mind, do you?... She's our hermit, you know.

ALEXANDRA *(gives Velikatov her hand)*. Really, how can you say that! I'm very glad to meet you. You should have thought of coming much sooner, Ivan Semyonych.

VELIKATOV. I didn't dare, Alexandra Nikolavna. I'm a shy man.

NINA. Yes, shy, that's him exactly!

ALEXANDRA. Proud would be better.

MME NYEGIN. That's where you're wrong. Ivan Semyonych is pleasant with everybody, I've seen that myself. He's not proud at all.

VELIKATOV. Not at all, Domna Pantelyevna.

MME NYEGIN. I like to tell the truth.

VELIKATOV. So do I, Domna Pantelyevna.

ALEXANDRA. Sit down, Ivan Semyonych.

VELIKATOV. Don't go to any trouble, please! You two probably have something to do, don't pay any attention to us. I'll have a little chat with Domna Pantelyevna. *(He sits down by the table.)*

Alexandra and Nina speak in a whisper.

ALEXANDRA. That's how it was, Nina…

NINA. Really?

ALEXANDRA. Yes. I don't know what to do.

NINA. You don't know what to do? You should… *(She speaks in a whisper.)*

MME NYEGIN. What are you doing whispering over there? Do you call that polite?

VELIKATOV. Don't bother them. Everyone has their own affairs.

MME NYEGIN. What affairs! It's all nonsense. You see, I know what they're talking about. About clothes. That's what their affairs are!

VELIKATOV. For you and me clothes may be nonsense, but for them it's something important.

MME NYEGIN. She doesn't have a dress for her benefit performance nor the money for it.

VELIKATOV. There, you see! And you say it's nonsense. *(Looking out the window.)* Are those your hens?

MME NYEGIN. Which ones?

VELIKATOV. Those Cochins there.

MME NYEGIN. No, how could we ever breed Cochins! We did have four hens and a rooster—an eagle he was, not a rooster—but they were all stolen.

VELIKATOV. And do you like hens, Domna Pantelyevna?

MME NYEGIN. I'm crazy about them, sir. I love all kinds of birds.

Meluzov enters.

ALEXANDRA *(to Velikatov)*. Allow me to introduce you. Peter Yegorych Meluzov. Ivan Semyonych Velikatov.

NINA. You know what, Ivan Semyonych? Peter Yegorych is a student, he's Sasha's fiancé.

VELIKATOV *(giving his hand)*. I'm very pleased to meet you.

MELUZOV. But why should you be pleased? That's just an empty expression. We were introduced, now we're acquainted, that's all.

VELIKATOV *(politely)*. That's quite true. Very many empty words get spoken, I agree with you there. But what I said, pardon me, was not an empty expression. I am pleased that actresses are marrying the right and proper people.

MELUZOV. Well, if that's the way it is... thank you! *(He approaches and shakes Velikatov's hand warmly.)*

ALEXANDRA. Come, Nina, I'll show you my dress! Take a look and see if anything can be made of it. *(To Velikatov.)* Excuse us for leaving you. But I know you won't be bored; you'll be talking with an educated man, not the same as with us. Mama, come with us, open up the dresser.

Alexandra, Nina and Mme. Nyegin go off.

VELIKATOV *(noticing the books on the table)*. Books and notebooks.

MELUZOV. Yes, we're learning little by little.

VELIKATOV. There's some progress?

MELUZOV. Some, relatively speaking.

VELIKATOV. Even that's sufficient. Alexandra Nikolavna has little time. Almost every day a new play, and she has to prepare her role, to think about her costume. I don't know how you feel about it, but it seems to me that it's rather difficult to learn roles and grammar at the same time.

MELUZOV. Yes, it doesn't make for much comfort.

VELIKATOV. At least there's the urge, the desire. That in itself is a great thing. Honor and glory to you.

MELUZOV. But what's the glory for, may I ask?

VELIKATOV. For your noble intentions. Who would ever take it into his head to teach grammar to an actress!

MELUZOV. You're not making fun of me, are you?

VELIKATOV. No, not at all, I never permit myself that, I'm very fond of young people.

MELUZOV. Really?

VELIKATOV. I love to listen to them... it renews the spirit. Such high and noble plans... I'm even envious.

MELUZOV. But what's there to be envious about? Who's stopping you from having your own high and noble plans?

VELIKATOV. No, how could people like us have them, really! The prose of life has overwhelmed us. I'd be happy to be in such a heaven, but my sins won't let me.

MELUZOV. What kind of sins?

VELIKATOV. Serious ones. Practical considerations, material calculations, those are the sins of people like me. I'm constantly moving in the sphere of the possible and the attainable. In that realm a man's soul becomes petty, and high and noble plans don't enter his head.

MELUZOV. And what do you call noble plans?

VELIKATOV. Plans that have very noble intentions and very little chance of success.

Alexandra, Nina, and Mme. Nyegin enter.

NINA *(to Alexandra)*. All that, my dear, won't be any use.

ALEXANDRA. I see that too. Making a new dress will be very expensive.

NINA. But what can be done! It's just impossible!... Let's go, Ivan Semyonych.

VELIKATOV. At your service. *(He gives his hand to Alexandra.)* I have the honor to present my regards!

ALEXANDRA. What horses you have! I'd love to ride with them sometime.

VELIKATOV. Whenever you want, just say the word. *(He gives his hand to Meluzov, then to Mme. Nyegin.)* Domna Pantelyevna, my respects! You know, you resemble my dear aunt!

MME NYEGIN. Really?

VELIKATOV. It's quite amazing... such a resemblance... I almost called you "Aunty."

MME NYEGIN. Then call me that, what's in the way!

NINA. All right, then, let's go. Good-bye, Sasha. Good-bye. *(She bows to all.)*

VELIKATOV *(to Mme. Nyegin)*. Good-bye, Aunty.

Nina and Velikatov leave. Mme. Nyegin sees them to the door.

MME NYEGIN. Oh, what a mischievous boy he is! *(To Alexandra.)* And you say he's proud! He's not proud at all. He's just very well mannered. *(She goes off.)*

ALEXANDRA *(at the window)*. How they drove off! What style! She's lucky, that Nina! One has to envy her.

Meluzov embraces her.

Oh, you and your bear hugs!... I don't like them at all. No, Petya, stop bothering me.

MELUZOV. Sasha, you haven't shown me any tenderness at all. A fine engaged couple we make!

ALEXANDRA. Later, Petya, later. Let me calm down a bit. I can't think about that now.

MELUZOV. If you can't think about that then let's get down to our studies.

ALEXANDRA. Studies! I can't get the benefit performance out of my mind. I don't have a dress, that's what's so awful.

MELUZOV. Let's not talk about the dress, that's not my field, I'm no good as a teacher in that line.

ALEXANDRA. What I need now is not teaching but money.

MELUZOV. I'm weak in that line too. As soon as I get a position I'll buckle down to work, and then we'll live in comfort. But now, Sasha, it's time for our confession!

ALEXANDRA. Oh, that's always so hard for me!

MELUZOV. Do you feel ashamed with me?

ALEXANDRA. No, but somehow it's painful... unpleasant.

MELUZOV. You have to master that unpleasant feeling in yourself. After all, it was you who asked me to teach you how to live. So, how can I teach you if I don't give you lessons? Simply tell me what you've felt, said and done, and then I'll tell you how you ought to feel, talk and act. That way you'll improve gradually, and in time you'll be...

ALEXANDRA. What'll I be, my dear?

MELUZOV. You'll be an absolutely good woman, the kind that's needed, the kind that's required nowadays by your fellow man.

ALEXANDRA. Yes, I feel grateful to you. I've already become so much better, I can feel it myself... And I owe it all to you, my darling... All right, let's start.

MELUZOV *(sits down by the table)*. Sit next to me.

ALEXANDRA *(sits down next to him. Meluzov puts an arm around her)*. Listen. This morning Prince Dulyebov dropped in on me. He said my apartment's no good, that's it's not proper to live like this. Well, that offended me, and I told him that if he didn't like my apartment nobody was forcing him to stay here.

MELUZOV. Good for you, Sasha! Go on.

ALEXANDRA. Then he proposed that I move into another apartment, a good one.

MELUZOV. Why does he want that?

ALEXANDRA. Because he has a lot of tenderness in his soul and nobody to shower his affection on.

MELUZOV *(laughs loudly)*. Now there's a syllogism for you! Since I don't have anybody to shower my affection on but need to shower my affection, then this apartment is no good, and you have to move to a new apartment. *(He laughs loudly.)* Good work, Prince, we're much obliged!

ALEXANDRA. You can laugh all you want, but I was crying.

MELUZOV. Which is how it should be. I should laugh, and you should cry.

ALEXANDRA. But why?

MELUZOV. Just think. If such conversations should make you laugh and me cry, would that be good?

ALEXANDRA *(thinking)*. Yes, that would be very bad. Oh, what a brain you have! *(She strokes his head.)* Tell me, Petya, why is it you're so smart?

MELUZOV. Whether I'm smart or not is an open question, but there's no doubt I'm smarter than a lot of you. And that's because I think more than I talk, but you people talk more than you think.

ALEXANDRA. Well, now I'll tell you something very secret… Only please, don't you get mad at me. This is a vice we women have. Today I was envious.

MELUZOV. Who can you be envious of, my dear? What for?

ALEXANDRA. But don't get mad! I'm envious of Nina… because she has so much fun, she goes riding with such horses. That's bad, I know it's bad.

MELUZOV. Envy and jealously are dangerous feelings. Men know that all too well and take advantage of your weakness. Because of envy and jealousy a woman can do bad things.

ALEXANDRA. I know, I know, I've known cases. It just came into my head for a moment, then I got the better of it.

MELUZOV. We need just one thing, Sasha. You and I want to live a life of honest work, so why should we think about horses!

ALEXANDRA. Yes, of course! And a life of work has its own pleasures. That's so, isn't it, Petya?

MELUZOV. Exactly!

ALEXANDRA. You have dinner with us. And after dinner I'll read a role to you. That way we can have the whole day together. We'll be getting used to a quiet family life.

MELUZOV. What could be better!

ALEXANDRA *(listening)*. What's that? Somebody drove up.

Nina enters carrying two packages.

NINA. Here, Sasha, this is for you! *(She gives her one of the packages.)* Ivan Semyonych bought these pieces of material for a dress for each of us. That one's for you, and this one's for me.

They unwrap the packages and look at the two pieces of material.

MELUZOV. But what right does he have to give presents to Alexandra Nikolavna?

NINA. Oh please, lay off your sermons! Your philosophy's out of place here. It's not a gift at all. He's giving it to her in return for a ticket to her benefit performance.

MELUZOV. And what's he giving you yours for?

NINA. What business is that of yours! It's because he loves me.

ALEXANDRA. It's exactly what I need, Nina. Oh, how nice!

NINA. You know, I picked it out, I know what you need. Well, let's go Sasha, let's go quickly.

ALEXANDRA. Where?

NINA. For a ride. I have Ivan Semyonych's horses. And after that we'll have dinner at the railroad station restaurant. He's invited the whole company, he wants to say good-bye to everybody. He's leaving soon.

254

ALEXANDRA *(pensively)*. I really don't know what to say.

NINA. But what's gotten into you! What's there to think about! How can you say "no"? You really ought to thank him.

MELUZOV. I'm curious. What are you going to do in this case?

ALEXANDRA. Do you know what, Peter Yegorych? I think I must go. Otherwise it would be impolite. I could get all of the public against me. The Prince is already mad at me, and Velikatov could take offense too.

MELUZOV. And just when are we going to get used to the quiet family life?

NINA. That'll come after the benefit performance, Peter Yegorych. This is hardly the time to think about family life. That's even funny. There'll still be time for family life to bore you, but now we have to take advantage of an opportunity.

ALEXANDRA *(decisively)*. No, Peter Yegorych, I'm going. It would really be bad to refuse.

MELUZOV. Do what you want. It's your affair.

ALEXANDRA. It's not a question of what I want. Maybe I don't want it, but it's necessary that I go. It's really necessary, and there's nothing to discuss.

MELUZOV. Then go!

NINA. Come on, get ready.

ALEXANDRA. Right away. *(She goes off behind the partition with her package.)*

NINA. You haven't taken it into your head to get jealous, have you? Then don't worry about it, for he's leaving the day after tomorrow. And anyway, I'm not going to give him up to Sasha.

MELUZOV. "I'm not going to give him up." You'll have to excuse me, but I don't understand such relations between men and women.

NINA. And how could you understand! You don't really know life at all. But you just live with us awhile, and you'll learn to understand everything.

Alexandra enters dressed up.

Well, let's go! Good-bye. *(She leaves.)*

ALEXANDRA. Petya, you come here tonight. We'll study, and I'll be smart. I'll always obey you in everything, but this time forgive me. Well, good-bye, my dear! *(She kisses him and rushes out.)*

MELUZOV *(pulls his hat down low on his forehead)*. Hmm! *(Thinking.)* Time to walk home! What else is there to do!

ACT TWO

A town garden. To the right of the actors is the rear corner of a wooden theater with a stage-entrance door. Closer to the front of the stage is a garden bench. On the left, in the foreground and under trees, are a bench and a table. In the background under trees are small tables and garden furniture. The tragedian is sitting at a table, head lowered on hands. Narokov comes out of the theater.

TRAGEDIAN. Martyn, is it the intermission?

NAROKOV. The intermission. Are you on another binge?[6]

TRAGEDIAN. Where's my Vasya? Where's my Vasya?

NAROKOV. How should I know?

TRAGEDIAN. Martyn, come here!

NAROKOV *(approaching)*. Well, here I am. What is it?

TRAGEDIAN. Have you any money?

NAROKOV. Not even a kreutzer.

TRAGEDIAN. Martyn... for a friend! That's a sublime word!

NAROKOV. I don't even have a sou. You can turn my pockets inside out.

TRAGEDIAN. That's disgusting.

NAROKOV. It's even worse.

TRAGEDIAN *(shaking his head)*. O people, people!...[7]

Silence.

Martyn!

NAROKOV. What now?

TRAGEDIAN. Go borrow some money.

NAROKOV. Who from? You and I don't have a lot of credit.

TRAGEDIAN. O people, people!

NAROKOV. Yes, it really is a case of "O people, people!"

TRAGEDIAN. And you, Martyn, is something bothering you?

NAROKOV. There's some kind of vile devilish plot going on.

TRAGEDIAN *(threateningly)*. A plot? Where? Against who?

NAROKOV. Against Alexandra Nikolavna.

TRAGEDIAN *(still more threateningly)*. Who's the man? Where is he? Tell him from me that he's going to have to deal with me, with Yerast Gromilov!

NAROKOV. You won't do a thing. Be quiet, don't irritate me! As it is I'm all upset, and you make a lot of noise but no sense. All the trouble you give me! You people all have a lot you don't need, but there's a lot you don't have enough of. It wears me out just looking at you. The comics have too much of the comic, and you have too much of the tragic. And you don't have enough grace... grace, or a sense of measure. And it's a sense of measure that makes for art... You're not actors, you're only buffoons!

TRAGEDIAN. No, Martyn, I'm noble... Oh, how noble I am! The one thing that hurts, brother Martyn, is that I'm noble only when I'm drunk... *(He lowers his head and sobs in a tragic manner.)*

NAROKOV. So, you see what a buffoon you are, you're a buffoon!

TRAGEDIAN. Martyn! People say you're crazy. Tell me, is that true or not?

NAROKOV. That's true, I'll go along with that, but only on one condition. If all of you here are smart, then I'm crazy, then I won't argue.

TRAGEDIAN. Do you know, Martyn, what you and I are like?

NAROKOV. What?

TRAGEDIAN. Do you know *King Lear?*

NAROKOV. I know it.

TRAGEDIAN. Then you remember, there in the forest and out into the storm... I'm Lear, and you're my fool.

NAROKOV. No, don't delude yourself. There are no Lears among us, and as to which of us is the fool, I'll let you figure it out for yourself.

Alexandra comes out of the theater.

ALEXANDRA. What's going on, Martyn Prokofyich? What are they doing to me?

NAROKOV *(grasping his head)*. I don't know, I don't know. Don't ask me.

ALEXANDRA. It hurts me so much I could cry.

NAROKOV. Oh, don't cry. Those people aren't worth your tears. You're a white dove in a flock of black crows, and they're pecking away at you. Your whiteness is what offends them, your purity.

ALEXANDRA *(in tears)*. Listen, Martyn Prokofyich, you know it was in your very presence, you remember, he promised to let me play before my benefit performance. But I've been waiting, I haven't played for a whole week, and today's the last day before the benefit. So what does the nasty man do! He assigns the role of Frou-frou[8] to Nina!

NAROKOV. A dagger in the chest right up to the hilt!

ALEXANDRA. They set up ovations for her on the eve of my benefit, they bring her bouquets, and the public has forgotten me completely. What kind of a take can I get at the box office!

TRAGEDIAN. Ophelia, get thee to a nunnery!

ALEXANDRA. I tried to talk to him, but he just makes a joke of it and laughs in my face.

NAROKOV. He's as hard as an oak tree.

TRAGEDIAN. Ophelia, get thee to a nunnery!

ALEXANDRA. Martyn Prokofyich, you're the only one who loves me.

NAROKOV. Oh yes, more than life, more than the world.

ALEXANDRA. I understand you and love you myself.

NAROKOV. You understand, you love? Well, then I'm happy, yes... yes... *(He laughs quietly.)* Happy as a child.

ALEXANDRA. Martyn Prokofyich, do me a favor, go look for Peter Yegorych. Tell him to come to me at the theater.

NAROKOV. I'm so happy it'll be a pleasure to get your lover.

ALEXANDRA. He's a fiancé, Martyn Prokofyich, not a lover.

NAROKOV. It's all the same, the same thing, my white dove! Fiancé, husband, but if you love him, then he's your lover. But I'm not jealous of him, I'm happy myself.

ALEXANDRA. And drop by at the box office. Find out if they're taking in anything for my benefit. I'll wait for you in my dressing room. We'll have some tea.

Narokov leaves.

TRAGEDIAN. If you'll have it with rum, then I'll come too.

ALEXANDRA. No, it won't have any rum. *(She goes off into the theater.)*

TRAGEDIAN. Where's my Vasya? Where's my Vasya? *(He goes off into the depths of the garden.)*

Prince Dulyebov and Migaev enter.

DULYEBOV. I'm telling you, Alexandra Nyegin doesn't suit us. It's your obligation to please the noble public, the good society, not the gallery. And besides, she's not to our taste. She's too simple. She has no manners, no tone.

MIGAEV. She doesn't have a good wardrobe, but she has a lot of talent, sir.

DULYEBOV. Talent, you say! A lot you understand, my dear fellow!

MIGAEV. That is so, Your Excellency, there's a great deal I don't understand. But you know, we judge... excuse me, Your Excellency, by what we can pocket, and she brings in a lot at the box office. Which means she has talent.

DULYEBOV. Why yes, of course. You people are materialists.

MIGAEV. You're absolutely correct, Your Excellency, when you choose to call us materialists.

DULYEBOV. What you don't understand is that... delicate... how should I put it?... That style.

MIGAEV. We do understand it, Your Excellency. But let me tell you that last year I sent away for a celebrity with style so she could play high society roles.

DULYEBOV. And what happened?

MIGAEV. We suffered a loss, Your Excellency. There wasn't any beauty, no joy either.

DULYEBOV. No beauty? Now how can you say such a thing, that there wasn't any beauty?

MIGAEV. My mistake, Your Excellency. There was some beauty when she'd get dressed for her part and the whole company would crowd around her dressing room, some at the door, some at the cracks. You see, our dressing rooms are transparent—the way they're built you can see through them.

DULYEBOV *(laughs loudly)*. Ha, ha, ha! So you see! There was joy after all.

MIGAEV. Yes, sir, there was joy... for Your Excellency. But for me it was grief.

DULYEBOV. Ha, ha, ha! How you play with words.

MIGAEV. We can't get along without that, a little bit of everything, or we're lost. That's what our calling is like, Your Excellency.

DULYEBOV. You should write vaudeville sketches, old man. Excuse my familiarity; it's from good will.

MIGAEV. And why do we knock ourselves out if not for that good will? Just make us happy, Your Excellency... if you want to be familiar or not, it really doesn't matter.

DULYEBOV. No, don't say that! I'm polite, and I'm always respectful. So tell me, why not write vaudeville sketches?

MIGAEV. I tried, Your Excellency.

DULYEBOV. And what happened?

MIGAEV. The Theater Commission wouldn't accept them.

DULYEBOV. That's strange. Why not?

MIGAEV. I don't know, Your Excellency.

DULYEBOV. Next time you write something, tell me. Right away I could... in the Commission I have... well, why go into it now? Only tell me.

MIGAEV. Yes, Your Excellency.

DULYEBOV. And I'll take care of it right away... In the Commission I have... well, why talk about it, only tell me... And instead of that Alexandra Nyegin I'll send for a real actress for you. A pretty one *(He spreads his hands.),* with my compliments! You'll lick your fingers.

MIGAEV. Licking fingers I can put up with, but have you ever had to wipe away tears with your fist, Your Excellency?

DULYEBOV. Ha, ha, ha! You really play with words! No, you really should write vaudeville sketches, I urge you to. But that actress, I'm telling you, she's a delight.

MIGAEV. What about the cost, Your Excellency?

DULYEBOV. Well, the cost, of course, is rather high.

MIGAEV. And from what sources are we to pay it, Your Excellency? Where do you think we can get it from? Every year our costs go up and the box office take goes down. We pay out salaries recklessly, like millionaires. Could we go halves, Your Excellency?

DULYEBOV. "Go halves"! What do you mean, "go halves"?

MIGAEV. Fifty-fifty. You pay half her salary, and I'll pay half.

DULYEBOV. Ha, ha, ha! Well, all right... So, what about this Alexandra Nyegin? What kind of a leading actress is she? She's dull, old man. She doesn't bring any life to our society, she leaves us dejected.

MIGAEV. What can you do! If Your Excellency wishes, I won't renew her contract.

DULYEBOV. Don't renew it, don't.

MIGAEV. Her contract is expiring.

DULYEBOV. Good, fine. All our public will be grateful to you.

MIGAEV. You mean your public, Your Excellency, just the first row of seats.

DULYEBOV. But we're the ones who set the tone.

MIGAEV. Let's hope we haven't made a mistake.

DULYEBOV. Oh no, don't worry your head about that! The public's grown cold to her. Just watch, her benefit performance will take in hardly anything at the box office. Want to bet on it?

MIGAEV. I won't argue with you.

DULYEBOV. It's out of the question to argue with me. I know the public better than you, and I understand this business. And I'll send off for an actress who'll put some life into everybody here. Then we'll be singing with the larks.

MIGAEV. Singing with the larks? If only we don't howl with the wolves, Your Excellency.

DULYEBOV. Ha, ha, ha! You really play with words, you really do. Oh, excuse me for getting so carried away in a friendly conversation, but in general I'm tactful... I'm tactful even with servants... *(He takes out a cigar case.)* Would you care for a cigar?

MIGAEV. Please. *(He takes a cigar.)* Are they expensive, Your Excellency?

DULYEBOV. I don't smoke cheap ones.

MIGAEV. I have something that's troubling me, Your Excellency.

DULYEBOV. What's that?

MIGAEV. Our tragedian is on a binge. There he is now, in the garden.

DULYEBOV. Are his papers in order?

MIGAEV. Are their papers ever in order, Your Excellency?

DULYEBOV. Then you could scare him. Say you'll have the police send him back to his place of registration.

MIGAEV. No, trying to scare people like him doesn't work; I always come out the loser.

DULYEBOV. How's that?

MIGAEV. Tragedians are full of spirit, Your Excellency. He says to me, "Even if you send me all the way to Kamchatka, you're still a scoundrel!" And he puts so much expression into that word "scoundrel" that I can't say anything, I just want to get away.

DULYEBOV. Yes, in that case it's better to be friendly.

MIGAEV. Friendly is right. People are astonished, Your Excellency, that lion tamers can go into a lion cage, but that doesn't impress us. I'd much rather go in to the lions than to a tragedian when he's in a bad mood or drunk.

DULYEBOV. Ha, ha, ha! They've really struck fear into you. I'm going to look for some of my friends. *(He goes off behind the theater.)*

The tragedian enters.

MIGAEV *(offering him a cigar)*. Would you care for a cigar?

TRAGEDIAN. One of those two-kopeck cigars? One could hardly expect a good one from you.

MIGAEV. No, it's a good one, one of the Prince's.

TRAGEDIAN. Then why aren't you smoking it yourself?

MIGAEV. My own are better. *(He takes out a silver cigar case.)*

TRAGEDIAN. You have a cigar case like that, but you say you have no money.

MIGAEV. Yes, I'm a queer one, I should have pawned it long ago, but I can't. It's a gift, a remembrance, I guard it like the apple of my eye. You can see the inscription: "To Gavriil Petrovich Migaev from the public."

TRAGEDIAN. You gypsy you!

MIGAEV. Talk with yourself if you don't understand sense. There's the audience, the act must be over. *(He goes off.)*

TRAGEDIAN *(shouts after him)*. You gypsy you! *(He sits down at a table.)* O people, people! *(He lowers his head onto his hands.)*

Dulyebov, Velikatov, Bakin and Vasya enter.

BAKIN. It's great, that's how to teach those people a lesson, in the future they'll act smarter. I inquired at the box office; they've taken in fourteen rubles.

VASYA. Not much, sir. But they'll sell more tickets tomorrow morning and evening; they'll take in something.

BAKIN. A hundred rubles. No more.

VASYA. Even that is money, sir.

BAKIN. Not a whole lot. And she surely must have some debts, for clothes here and there. Actresses can't live without that. *(To Vasya.)* Doesn't she owe you anything?

VASYA. We don't give credit, sir.

BAKIN. You're covering up for her. I like that, it's nice when public opinion is so friendly. *(To Velikatov.)* How do you feel about that?

VELIKATOV. I agree with you completely.

BAKIN. In the person of the Prince our society has been insulted by her, so society is paying her back with its indifference, letting her realize it has forgotten her existence. When she won't have anything to eat, she'll learn proper manners.

VASYA. But how did Miss Nyegin insult His Excellency?

BAKIN. You know Prince Irakly Stratonych, don't you?

VASYA. How could I help knowing him, sir? Who in our region doesn't know His Excellency?

DULYEBOV. Yes, we've known each other a long time, I knew his father too…

BAKIN *(to Vasya)*. Then you know what kind of a man he is, don't you? A man respected in the highest degree, our most learned critic. The soul of our society, a man with great taste, one who knows how to live well. He loves art and understands its fine points. A patron of all artists, actors and especially actresses…

DULYEBOV. Isn't that enough?

BAKIN. To each according to his merits. Not only that, this is a man who's generous, hospitable, an excellent family man. Take note of that, gentlemen! For that's something rare in our day. In a word, a man respected in all respects. Isn't that so?

VASYA. Exactly, sir.

BAKIN *(to Velikatov)*. There can't be two opinions about it?

VELIKATOV. I agree with you completely.

BAKIN. And this man, gentlemen, a man respected in all respects and an excellent family man, wanted to make a young woman, Miss Nyegin, happy by bestowing his favor on her. I ask you, what's bad about that? He says to her very politely, "How would you like being kept by me, my dear?" But she took it into her head to take offense and start crying.

DULYEBOV. No, really now, Grigory Antonych, do me a favor, give it a rest!

BAKIN. But why, Prince?

DULYEBOV. When you start praising somebody, the man respected in all respects ends up completely disrespected.

BAKIN. As you wish. I don't know… I always speak the truth. Allow me, Prince, to continue a bit more. So, please note, Miss Nyegin took offense. There wasn't any reason for her to take offense, or even think of it, because in essence there's nothing offensive there. It turns out there's an outside influence.

DULYEBOV. Yes, I heard.

BAKIN. That young lady has a student teaching her, and that explains the matter quite simply.

DULYEBOV. They've even infiltrated the theater.

BAKIN. If they knew what was good for them, they'd stick to cutting up their dogs and frogs, but they've taken it into their head to educate actresses. And in actresses learning is a dangerous thing. We have to take immediate steps against it.

DULYEBOV. Absolutely.

BAKIN. And suppose they really would educate them. What would the Prince and I do with ourselves then?

DULYEBOV. All right now, that's enough! Please!

BAKIN. As you wish, I've finished. *(To Velikatov.)* Am I correct in thinking you wanted to leave today?

VELIKATOV. One can't always plan things for certain. I really did want to leave today, but now I see the possibility of an operation I wasn't counting on.

BAKIN. You're tempted by the chance of gaining something?

VELIKATOV. It's a business with a risk. I could gain something, but I could very easily lose too.

BAKIN. It would be nice if we could eat together tonight.

VELIKATOV. That's all right by me.

BAKIN. And how about you, Prince?

DULYEBOV. Yes, fine, let's do it.

BAKIN. We'll meet here after the performance and go somewhere. What's going on there now? The divertissement?

VASYA. Some storyteller's doing his thing.

DULYEBOV. Good, let's go in for a laugh or two.

BAKIN. If he pleases you, Prince, add something for him.

Bakin, Dulyebov, and Velikatov leave.

TRAGEDIAN. Where's my Vasya?

VASYA *(approaching)*. Here's your Vasya. What do you want?

TRAGEDIAN. Where did you disappear to, brother?

VASYA. What do you want from me?! Speak fast!

TRAGEDIAN. What do I want?! I want respect. Do you mean to tell me you don't know your obligation?

VASYA. Well, you just be patient, and I'll learn to respect you. Since you've waited so long for it you can wait a while longer. I'm going in to hear the storyteller, all my friends are there. So be nice about it and don't hold me up.

TRAGEDIAN. Go on! I'm noble.

Vasya leaves. Alexandra, Nina, and Meluzov come out of the theater. Meluzov is carrying a plaid for the shoulders and Alexandra's short cloak.

NINA. Yes, Sasha, your position is very unpleasant, I understand that. But none of it's my fault, Sasha. I'm in a lot of trouble too.

ALEXANDRA. That can't be, what trouble are you in! I can't believe it. It's all so easy for you, things are going your way.

263

NINA. I'll tell you…*(She leads Alexandra aside.)* The Prince is showing me a lot of attention.

ALEXANDRA. So what! That's your affair.

NINA. I know it's my affair. But I don't want to let go of Velikatov.

ALEXANDRA *(with some agitation).* You mean Velikatov is showing you attention too?

NINA. He's strange. He comes to see me every day, he carries out my every wish, but he doesn't say anything… He must be shy, there are types like that. I just don't know how to act. If I'm cold to the Prince, I'll gain a enemy. But Velikatov's leaving tomorrow, and I could lose him. If I'm nice to the Prince, I'll be ungrateful to Velikatov, and anyway, I like Velikatov a lot more.

ALEXANDRA. Of course! Naturally… who wouldn't like him!

NINA. You feel that way? And what I learned about him! He's a millionaire, he just puts on being a simple man. I just don't know what to do. Believe me, Sasha, it's made a wreck of me.

ALEXANDRA. But I don't understand any of this. Go ask Peter Yegorych.

NINA. How can you say that! What does he understand? He'd grind out that philosophy of his, a lot I need that. And you, Sasha, dear, you're wasting your time listening to him! Don't listen to him, don't listen, for your own good. He just gets you mixed up. That philosophy is good enough in books, but just let him try living it in our situation! Is there really anything worse than the situation we women are in! You're on your way home, let's go together.

ALEXANDRA. I'd like to speak with Gavrilo Patrovich. I'm waiting for him.

NINA. Then I'll wait too.

They approach Meluzov, who is looking at the tragedian.

TRAGEDIAN *(raises his head and speaks to Meluzov).* Who are you? What are you doing here?

ALEXANDRA. He came with me.

TRAGEDIAN. Alexandra Nikolavna!… Sasha! Ophelia! What is he doing here?

ALEXANDRA. He's my fiancé, my teacher.

TRAGEDIAN. Teacher! What does he teach you?

ALEXANDRA. All that's good.

TRAGEDIAN *(to Meluzov).* Well now, come here!

Meluzov approaches.

Give me your hand!

Meluzov gives him his hand.

I'm a teacher too, yes, a teacher. Why are you looking at me like that? I'm teaching a rich merchant.

MELUZOV. May I ask something?

TRAGEDIAN. Ask away!

MELUZOV. Exactly what are you teaching him?

TRAGEDIAN. Nobility.

MELUZOV. That's a serious subject.

TRAGEDIAN. I think it is. Yes, sir... I think it is. Not like that geography of yours. So, you and I are teachers. Wonderful. Such an occasion calls for a drink at the buffet. On you, of course.

MELUZOV. I'm sorry. In that field I'm not your colleague. I don't drink.

TRAGEDIAN. Sasha, Sasha! Alexandra! Who are you bringing to us artists, to the temple of the muses!

MELUZOV. But we can go! You drink wine, and I'll have a glass of water.

TRAGEDIAN. Go to hell! Take him away! *(He lowers his head.)* Where's my Vasya?

Dulyebov, Velikatov, and Vasya enter. Behind Vasya comes a waiter from the buffet with a bottle of port and some wineglasses. Some of the audience also enter and remain in the background. Dulyebov sits down on a bench on the right side, Nina sitting down next to him. Not far from them Meluzov and Alexandra sit down. Velikatov and Bakin approach them from the left side. The tragedian, sitting in his former position, is approached by Vasya and the waiter; the latter places the bottle and wineglasses on the table before going off to the side. Some of the audience stand while some sit down at the small tables in the background.

VASYA *(to the tragedian, while pouring a glass of wine)*. Please, I humbly beg you.

TRAGEDIAN. Don't beg, I don't need that to drink. Why all those words. "Please, I humbly beg you"! Just say, "Drink!" You see how simple it is, just one word but what a deep thought.

Migaev walks out from the theater.

ALEXANDRA. Gavrilo Patrovich, come over here, please.

MIGAEV *(approaching Alexandra)*. What do you want?

ALEXANDRA. You kept avoiding me in the theater. Now I want to have a talk with you here, in the presence of others.

MELUZOV. Yes, it would be interesting to hear the motives for your actions.

MIGAEV. What actions, sir?

MELUZOV. You scheduled the benefit performance for Alexandra Nikolavna at the very end of the fair.

MIGAEV. That's the very best time, sir. According to the contract I'm obliged to give Miss Nyegin a benefit performance during the fair, but it doesn't say whether it's to be at the beginning or the end. That's up to me, sir.

MELUZOV. You're within the law, I understand that. But besides the law there also exist moral obligations for men.

MIGAEV. What is this, sir, why all this talk?

MELUZOV. Listen. You put off the benefit performance till the last day. You gave out the playbills late. And you didn't let Alexandra Nikolavna perform before her benefit. Those are your actions.

MIGAEV. Quite right, sir.

MELUZOV. But Alexandra Nikolavna didn't deserve that because she always brought you a full take at the box office, which can't be said for others. So try to justify your behavior.

TRAGEDIAN. You gypsy you!

MIGAEV. To the best of my knowledge you don't work in our theater, and I don't give an account of my business to outsiders, sir.

DULYEBOV. Of course not. What kind of inquest is this! He's the boss in his theater, so he can act in his own best interests.

MELUZOV. Nevertheless such actions are called improper, and the gentleman who permits himself such a course of action does not have the right to consider himself a man of honor. Concerning which I have the honor to declare to you in public. Upon which we consider ourselves satisfied.

MIGAEV. As you wish, as you wish, sir, that doesn't matter to me. Public tastes differ, you can't please everybody. You may not like my actions, but the Prince approves of them.

MELUZOV. What do I care about the Prince! The moral laws are alike for all.

Migaev approaches the Prince.

BAKIN. Why waste rhetoric preaching honor to Migaev?! How naive can you get? For a long time now he's considered honor a prejudice, and for him there's no difference between an honorable or dishonorable act, not until he's been given a thrashing. But when he gets boxed on the ear two or three times, that'll start him thinking: I must've done something pretty bad if they're beating me like this.

TRAGEDIAN. And they'll be beating him, you'll see, I predicted it long ago.

MIGAEV *(approaching Alexandra)*. So, Miss Nyegin, is it your pleasure to be dissatisfied with me?

ALEXANDRA. Of course. How can you still ask?

MIGAEV. In that case what compels you to work with me? Our contract is coming to an end.

ALEXANDRA. Yes, but you yourself asked me to renew it.

MIGAEV. I'm sorry, miss, but I've changed my mind. By public demand I have to invite another actress to take your place.

Alexandra stands in amazement.

TRAGEDIAN. Ophelia, get thee to a nunnery!

ALEXANDRA. You should have warned me earlier. I had offers from other managers, and I turned them all down. I believed your word.

MIGAEV. And you're wrong to believe words. We can't answer for our every word. We depend on the public, and we have to fulfill its desires.

ALEXANDRA. Now I just don't know where to turn. You've put me in such a position…

MIGAEV. I'm sorry, miss. With another actress I wouldn't have done it, but you have so much talent you won't be hurt at all. They'll be glad to take you on anywhere.

ALEXANDRA *(in tears)*. Now you're making fun of me… But it's a good thing you told me before my benefit… Tomorrow I'll say good-bye to my public… which loves me so… It should be printed up, that I'm playing for the last time.

VASYA. We'll spread the word even without the playbills.

ALEXANDRA *(to Velikatov)*. Ivan Semyonych, you're not leaving before tomorrow, are you?

VELIKATOV. No, I won't be leaving yet, miss.

ALEXANDRA. So you'll be in the theater?

VELIKATOV. Without fail.

BAKIN. Only don't you take credit for it. He's not staying over for your benefit performance. He has some unfinished business, some operation in mind.

VELIKATOV. That's true. The operation's no secret, gentlemen, I won't keep it from you. I want to buy up Alexandra Nikolavna's benefit. I might even make something on it.

ALEXANDRA. What? You want to buy up my benefit? You're not joking? Is this some new hurt, am I being made fun of again?

VELIKATOV. I'm not joking at all. How much is your benefit worth to you, what would you like to receive for it?

ALEXANDRA. It isn't worth anything to me, it has no value. God grant there's no loss.

VASYA. You're wrong to be so upset, miss. Your benefit is certainly worth buying.

VELIKATOV. How much could the beneficiary receive if the theater is full and the prices are high? Did anyone ever take in very much at his benefit?

TRAGEDIAN *(striking the table with his fist)*. I did.

VASYA. At the beginning of the fair he and I took in three hundred and fifty rubles.

VELIKATOV. Would you be willing to take three hundred and fifty rubles?

ALEXANDRA. I can't, that's a lot, it's a gift… I don't want to take gifts. It's not in keeping with my principles.

VELIKATOV. What a pleasure hearing such words from a young actress! One can see right away you have a good teacher, a man with honorable and noble convictions.

VASYA. But that's not a high price at all, Alexandra Nikolavna, really! For if Ivan Semyonych is latching onto this business, that means you'll have the whole fair with you tomorrow. I'll raise the price fifty rubles. Would you take four hundred rubles?

VELIKATOV. No, excuse me, but I won't back out. I offer Alexandra Nikolavna five hundred rubles.

VASYA. Count me out, I won't go higher. That's a real price.

ALEXANDRA. But what are you doing, gentlemen? You know that after expenses I get half the profit.

VASYA. People like us won't lose a thing, miss, we're businessmen. By eleven tomorrow there won't be a single ticket left. *(To Velikatov.)* Please, give me a share! Let me have two boxes and a dozen orchestra seats.

VELIKATOV. Get them at the box office, and tell the ticket seller to send me right away the money for what he's sold, also to send me all remaining tickets except those in the high balcony. I'll wait here.

VASYA. Fine, I'll tell him, sir. Let me pay you for the two boxes and the dozen orchestra seats. *(He gives the money.)*

VELIKATOV *(taking the money)*. There's a hundred rubles here.

VASYA. Exactly, sir. You know, we have four of our merchants here, so maybe there'll be some takers among them. I'll run along now. *(He goes off through the rear of the stage.)*

VELIKATOV. I still haven't received your consent, Alexandra Nikolavna.

ALEXANDRA *(to Meluzov)*. What should I do, Peter Yegorych? I don't know. Whatever you say I'll do.

MELUZOV. I don't know either. I don't have any competence in such matters. For now it looks as though everything's legitimate. Agree.

ALEXANDRA *(to Velikatov)*. I agree. Thank you.

VELIKATOV. There's nothing to thank me for, I'll be making money. I ought to thank you.

MIGAEV *(to Dulyebov)*. And you, Your Excellency, wanted to make a bet.

DULYEBOV. Well, no one could have expected this. It's a completely special case.

BAKIN *(to Velikatov)*. Set aside a ticket for me! This will be an interesting performance.

Vasya returns.

VASYA. The ticket seller's going to bring the tickets and the money right away, he's just counting the receipts. I took ten more orchestra seats at five rubles each. Here's your money. *(He gives Velikatov fifty rubles.)*

VELIKATOV. Isn't that a high price?

VASYA. It's not high at all. Just now I sold four tickets at five rubles each. Tomorrow my first-row tickets will go for ten rubles, and even at ten rubles they'll be a gift.

DULYEBOV. A man would have to be an absolute fool to pay ten rubles for an orchestra seat in a provincial theater.

VASYA. But they're in the first row, Your Excellency. The box office has only one seat left there.

DULYEBOV. In that case, Ivan Semyonych, set that one aside for me.

VELIKATOV. At ten rubles, Prince?

DULYEBOV. It can't be helped since everyone's gone out of his mind.

VASYA. So, Gavrilo Petrovich, you can close up shop! As soon as Alexandra Nikolavna leaves, you won't be in business any more! That'll be the end! You won't be able to lure them into the theater for love or money, so now you know what to expect!

ALEXANDRA. Give me my coat, Peter Yegorych. Good-bye, gentlemen. Thank you! You gave me such comfort, when I was on the point of crying. Really, gentlemen, it was such a blow to me, such a blow...

Meluzov gives her her coat, and she puts it on.

TRAGEDIAN. Vasya, ask for champagne!

VASYA. Is that really necessary?

TRAGEDIAN. You're something, brother, how can you ask such a thing? You've acted nobly, so we have to congratulate you.

VASYA. You should have said so in the first place. Waiter, a bottle of champagne!

ALEXANDRA. Good-bye, gentlemen.

VELIKATOV. Allow me to offer you my carriage.

NINA. You're offering her your carriage, and I suppose you're offering yourself to accompany her?

VELIKATOV. No, why that! Alexandra Nikolavna will ride with her fiancé. *(To Meluzov.)* The coachman will drive you home too, and then you can send him back.

MELUZOV. Excuse me, but I consider your concern for me unnecessary. *(He wraps himself up in his plaid, Velikatov helping him.)* You're troubling yourself to no good purpose, I'm used to managing without other people's help. That's my principle.

VELIKATOV. But that's hard to maintain. People can't get along without mutual aid.

ALEXANDRA *(to Velikatov)*. You're such a noble person, and so tactful... I'm so grateful to you, I can't express it... I'll give you a kiss tomorrow.

VELIKATOV. That will make me very happy.

NINA. Tomorrow? That's a long time to wait. *(To Dulyebov.)* Prince, I'll give you a kiss today, right now.

DULYEBOV. At your service, my beauty. I'm at your disposal!

Nina kisses Dulyebov.

ALEXANDRA. So, good-bye, gentlemen, good-bye! *(She sends a kiss with her hand.)*

TRAGEDIAN. Ophelia! O nymph! Remember me in thy orisons.

ACT THREE

Scenery of Act One. Evening. Two candles on the table.

MATRYONA *(at the door).* Who is it? *(Voice of Mme. Nyegin off stage: "It's me, Matryona!")* I'll open up right away. *(Mme. Nyegin enters.)* Has the the-AYter crowd left yet?

MME NYEGIN. Not yet, not completely. It'll take about a half hour more. I came home early on purpose, to get the tea ready. I don't want Sasha to wait when she comes. Do you have the samovar ready?

MATRYONA. I lit it. Any time now it'll start making its noises.

MME NYEGIN. When it starts making noises, cover it up.

MATRYONA. Why cover it up! That samovar of ours may start making noises, but it's not about to boil soon. First it's got to sing, sing all kinds of tunes, huff and puff away. But all that's little use, and if you try blowing up the fire, it gets worse, like it's making fun of you. I've used lots of bad words with it.

MME NYEGIN. I got tired out in that theater, it was so hot and stuffy. I was really glad when I could rush out of there.

MATRYONA. That's how it is, sitting inside four walls in the summer. A big crowd was there?

MME NYEGIN. The theater was absolutely full, jam packed.

MATRYONA. You don't say! And they kept beating their hands together?

MME NYEGIN. The whole works. You go take a look at the samovar and set it up in her room. But wait, somebody's come. It's too soon for Sasha.

Matryona opens the door, and Velikatov enters. Matryona goes off.

VELIKATOV. Hello, Domna Pantelyevna.

MME NYEGIN. Hello, Ivan Semyonych. What brings you here?

VELIKATOV. I have some business, Domna Pantelyevna.

MME NYEGIN. Then it should wait till tomorrow. It's late now, it's out of place, we don't have men here at this hour.

VELIKATOV. Don't worry, Domna Pantelyevna, I won't be waiting for Alexandra Nikolavna. And nobody's going to say anything bad about you and me.

MME NYEGIN. Oh you joker you!

VELIKATOV. So, Aunty, you don't have anything to be afraid of.

MME NYEGIN. But what kind of an aunty am I to you?

VELIKATOV. Do you mean I'm not good enough to be your nephew?

MME NYEGIN. It's not that, who could be better! Such a fine fellow, our handsome lad!

VELIKATOV. I've brought you the money from the benefit performance, Domna Pantelyevna.

MME NYEGIN. Thank you, thank you very much! I just can't tell you how much we need it. The first thing, Ivan Semyonych, is the debts. How can one live without them? Is that possible?

VELIKATOV. It's not possible.

MME NYEGIN. We're all people.

VELIKATOV. All human beings, Domna Pantelyevna.

MME NYEGIN. And those debts we have, even if they're small, still, if a person has a conscience, then it's a worry.

VELIKATOV. A worry, Domna Pantelyevna, a worry. *(Giving a package with money.)* Here, give this to Alexandra Nikolavna.

MME NYEGIN. We're grateful, very grateful to you, Ivan Semyonych! Wouldn't you like some tea?

VELIKATOV. Thank you very much, but I can't. Spare me from tea, Domna Pantelyevna. For some reason nothing agrees with me now, especially tea. It's as though I have some kind of melancholy, Domna Pantelyevna, as if I'm all upset.

MME NYEGIN. It's what's called the pachondria.

VELIKATOV. Yes, Domna Pantelyevna, the pachondria.

MME NYEGIN. A lot of money and nothing to do. That's when it latches onto people.

VELIKATOV. You hit it right on the head. That's exactly what it comes from.

MME NYEGIN. If it wasn't for that, you wouldn't have any reason for melancholy.

VELIKATOV. You're quite right, no reason. But I am suffering from melancholy, Domna Pantelyevna, and I've been rushing about at the fair from tavern to tavern. Could you believe it, this is the second week running that I've been drunk twice a day... What I think, Domna Pantelyevna, is this: either it's from evil spirits or it's God's will.

MME NYEGIN. It's from loneliness.

VELIKATOV. Loneliness, Domna Pantelyevna. Your words are pure gold, no more to be said, it's loneliness.

MME NYEGIN. So choose yourself a life companion.

VELIKATOV. And where would you advise me to find one?

MME NYEGIN. Get married, get yourself a nice young lady. Anyone would marry you, even one from the very best of families.

VELIKATOV. But I'm afraid, Aunty.

MME NYEGIN. Come now, what's there to be afraid of, what's so frightening about it?

VELIKATOV. Life will be sadder.

MME NYEGIN. Oh no, that's where you're wrong. How could that happen! There's a world of difference between a married man and a bachelor.

VELIKATOV. They like to play the piano a lot, and I can't stand that.

MME NYEGIN. All the same it's music. But what pleasure does a bachelor have? Aside from a drink with his friends he doesn't have any joy in life.

VELIKATOV. But the household, Domna Pantelyevna? What would you say about that?

MME NYEGIN. Well, of course, if a man maintains a household...

VELIKATOV. That's a sin I have. In the country I have a nice little home with about forty rooms, quite a lot of horses, a little garden laid out for almost two thirds of a mile, with arbors, with ponds...

MME NYEGIN. What you're saying is that everything is the way it should be with a good landowner. Isn't that it?

VELIKATOV. Everything's in good order, Domna Pantelyevna. If you get bored indoors, you can go out on the porch, and the turkey cocks are going through the yard, all of them white.

MME NYEGIN. White! You don't say!

VELIKATOV. So you shout out to them, "Hello there, boys!" And they answer back, "We wish you health, honorable sir."

MME NYEGIN. They're trained?

VELIKATOV. Trained. So you can amuse yourself with them. Peacocks sit on the roofs and fences, and their tails play in the sun.

MME NYEGIN. Peacocks too? Good heavens!

VELIKATOV. You go out in the park for a walk, and you see swans swimming in the lake. They're always in pairs, always in pairs, Domna Pantelyevna.

MME NYEGIN. And you really have swans? That's heaven itself! If only I could set my eyes on it.

VELIKATOV *(looking at his watch)*. We've had such a nice pleasant talk, Aunty, I hate to leave. I'd like to talk some more, but there's not time. Excuse me, I have some business.

MME NYEGIN. I'd like to talk some more too, it's so pleasant with you... A nice well-mannered man like you I've never seen in all my life...

VELIKATOV. I made some money from the benefit, Domna Pantelyevna, so let me offer you a little gift. *(He goes off to the entry and brings back a package wrapped in paper, which he gives to Mme. Nyegin.)*

MME NYEGIN. What is it?

VELIKATOV. It's a kerchief.

MME NYEGIN *(unwrapping the paper)*. You call this a kerchief? Say rather it's a whole shawl, such as I've never sewn my whole life. How much did it cost?

VELIKATOV. I don't know, I got it for nothing from a friendly merchant.

MME NYEGIN. But what's it for, sir? Really, I don't know what to do... I'll just give you a kiss, allow me that, dear friend... my heart can't hold out.

VELIKATOV. Do me the favor, as much as you want.

Mme. Nyegin kisses him.

Good-bye. Give my respects to Alexandra Nikolavna. We might not be seeing each other. *(He leaves.)*

Mme. Nyegin sees him to the entry and returns.

MME NYEGIN. Where did such people come from! Good heavens! *(She puts on the shawl.)* I won't even take it off now. *(She looks in the mirror.)* I'm a lady, a real lady! What a man! But what good are those others we have? I'd rather not lay eyes on them. Still, there are worthwhile people in the world. *(She listens.)* Who could that be?

Narokov enters with wreaths and bouquets.

NAROKOV. Here, take them! Those are your daughter's laurels! You can be proud!

MME NYEGIN. Whoever saw the like! Why bring us these wreaths? What good are they!

NAROKOV. Ignorance! These wreaths signify enthusiasm, they signify the recognition of talent in return for the happiness it provides. Laurels are a diploma representing honor and respect.

MME NYEGIN. How much money thrown away on this brushwood! The money would have been better, with that we could have found a place, but this pile of junk... what can we do with it? Just throw it in the stove.

NAROKOV. You'd only run through the money, but this will always stay with you as a memento.

MME NYEGIN. Yes, of course, we've got to save every bit of trash! I'll throw it out the window this very night. You look at this! *(She shows him the shawl and turns around before him.)* Now that's what I call a gift! It's nice, charming, delicate.

NAROKOV. Well, to each his own, I won't be jealous of you; it's your daughter I'm jealous of. I'll just take a few little leaves for a memento. *(He tears off a few little leaves.)*

MME NYEGIN. You can take them all if you want, I won't cry.

NAROKOV *(takes a sheet of paper out of his pocket)*. Give this to Alexandra Nikolavna.

MME NYEGIN. Now what? A note from somebody? I'm so fed up with these stupid things.

NAROKOV. It's from me... a poem... I was born in Arcadia too.[9]

MME NYEGIN. Where, Prokofyich, where did you say?

NAROKOV. It's far from here. You've never been there and never will be. *(He shows his poem to Mme. Nyegin.)* You see there, that little border; it has forget-me-nots, pansies, cornflowers, and ears of corn. And look there, a bee sitting, and a butterfly flying... I was a whole week drawing it.

MME NYEGIN. Then you should give it to her yourself.

NAROKOV. It's embarrassing. Look here. *(He points to his head.)* I'm bald, what little hair I have is gray! But my feelings are young, fresh, full of youth, and I'm embarrassed. Here, you give it to her. Only don't you throw it away! You're really a coarse woman, you have no feeling. You coarse people like to throw things away, to trample on everything tender, everything refined.

MME NYEGIN. Oh you! You're so sensitive. But everyone can't be like that. Just set it on the table, she'll see it when she comes.

NAROKOV *(puts the paper on the table).* Yes, that's true, I'm a sensitive man. Good-bye. *(He leaves.)*

MME NYEGIN. That man is crazy! But he's all right, he has a good heart, I'm not afraid of him. Others do things a lot worse, smash crockery and run around biting people. But this one's peaceful. Somebody's there, it must be Sasha. *(She goes to the door.)*

Alexandra enters carrying a bouquet and a box. She puts them on the table.

ALEXANDRA. Oh, how tired I am! *(She sits down at the table.)*

MME NYEGIN. Should I have the coachman go?

ALEXANDRA. No, why do that! I'll just rest a bit, and then we'll take a ride, for the fresh air. It's still not too late. After all, he's been hired for the whole evening.

MME NYEGIN. In that case let him wait, you don't want to pay out that money for nothing!

ALEXANDRA. What's that shawl you're wearing?

MME NYEGIN. Velikatov gave it to me. He says he made money on the benefit. What do you thing, is it pretty?

ALEXANDRA. It's a wonderful shawl, and expensive.

MME NYEGIN. He says he got it for nothing.

ALEXANDRA. And you believe him! He's always saying things like that. So he was here?

MME NYEGIN. Yes, he dropped by and brought the money.

ALEXANDRA. Why didn't he try to see me?

MME NYEGIN. I don't know. He was in a hurry to go somewhere, maybe he's leaving.

ALEXANDRA. That's possible. How strange he is, you can't understand him at all. *(Pensively.)* I think a man like him, if he wanted, could sweep a woman right off her feet.

MME NYEGIN. No question about it! And you couldn't blame the woman either, how could you blame her! After all, the heart's not a stone, and fine fellows like him are few and far between, I don't suppose you'd meet another man like him your whole life. Not like those meek ones who don't do anything worth thinking of. He was telling me about his estate in the country. What a wonderful household he has there!

ALEXANDRA. That's not surprising, he's very rich.

MME NYEGIN. Don't you want some tea?

ALEXANDRA. No, wait awhile. *(Looking at the table.)* What's that?

MME NYEGIN. It's what Prokofyich brought you as a remembrance.

ALEXANDRA *(looking over the paper)*. Oh, how nice! What a kind, nice old man he is!

MME NYEGIN. Yes, he's a kind, good man. It's just that he had a bankrupture, and that made him crazy. Well, how are we going to figure out that money?

ALEXANDRA. What's there to figure out! First of all we have to pay the debts, and we'll live on what's left over.

MME NYEGIN. And there'll be only a little left, nothing to get rich on.

ALEXANDRA. Yes, it's going to be harder now, without any salary. And where can I go, whom do I know? And I need clothes again.

MME NYEGIN. About two hundred, maybe two hundred and fifty, there won't be any more than that left, no matter how we twist it. That's what we have to live on all summer. Allow a kopeck and a half a day, and a day's still a day. In the fall they'll call us to Moscow, they say actresses are needed there.

ALEXANDRA. I could give up the stage and get married, but Peter Yegorych hasn't found a position yet. If I could only do some kind of work.

MME NYEGIN. What, give up the stage! You've just got in one day what you wouldn't earn in three years at some other work.

ALEXANDRA. We get a lot, but we have to spend a lot.

MME NYEGIN. Any way you look at it, Sasha, this life of ours isn't too sweet. I'll have to tell you, I'm sick of our being so poor.

ALEXANDRA. Sick of it... yes... sick of it... I've thought and thought till I've simply given up thinking. Well, let's sleep on it, we'll talk it over tomorrow.

MME NYEGIN. All right, but now let's have some tea. *(She listens.)* Who could that be this time?

Bakin enters.

275

BAKIN. I've come for a drink of tea, Alexandra Nikolavna!

ALEXANDRA. Oh, excuse me, I can't receive you. I'm very tired, I must rest. I want to be alone, to calm down.

BAKIN. But a half hour, what's a half hour!

ALEXANDRA. I really can't, I'm so worn out.

BAKIN. Very well, then I'll drop back in ten or fifteen minutes. That'll give you time to rest up.

ALEXANDRA. No, no, do me a favor! Come tomorrow, whenever you want, only not tonight.

BAKIN. Alexandra Nikolavna, for some reason or other I don't like changing my intentions. I always want to carry out what I've thought of, and, with my persistence, I succeed.

ALEXANDRA. I'm very glad you succeed, but you must excuse me, I'm going to leave you, I'm very tired.

BAKIN. All right, you can leave, but I'm going to stay on in this room. I'll sit right through the night in this chair.

ALEXANDRA. Now stop joking! This has gone far enough.

BAKIN. You don't believe me? Then I'll prove to you I'm a resolute man.

MME NYEGIN. And I, dear sir, am a resolute woman who's about to shout for help.

BAKIN (to Alexandra). Listen, are you afraid somebody will find me here with you?

ALEXANDRA. I'm not afraid of anybody or anything.

BAKIN. All your admirers are eating supper now at the railroad station. The Prince, Velikatov, and Nina Smelsky are with them. And they're staying there till morning.

ALEXANDRA. That's no concern of mine!

BAKIN. And your fiancé is probably asleep. But then I don't even believe you love him.

ALEXANDRA. Oh my God, this is unbearable! I don't care what you believe.

BAKIN. You only keep him near you as protection against other men's attentions, but when you find a man you like you'll throw him over. It's always that way.

ALEXANDRA. All right, I heard you.

BAKIN. You're being terribly fastidious. What are you waiting for? What blessing? You see before you a man who is educated, secure… If I don't come courting, if I don't say sweet nothings, if I don't make a declaration of love, it's because those aren't my principles. We're not children, so why pretend! Let's talk like grown-up people.

ALEXANDRA. Good-bye. (She goes off.)

MME NYEGIN. Well, sir, you've had your little talk. It's time now to give people some peace! But if you want to talk, do it with me; I have a ready tongue.

BAKIN *(loudly)*. All the same I'll drop in again. *(He goes off.)*

MME NYEGIN. I'll lock up the entrance. I won't let a soul in now, not even if he's dying there. *(She goes off.)*

A sharp exchange of words is heard off stage. Alexandra enters.

ALEXANDRA What's going on there?

Mme. Nyegin, Vasya, and the tragedian enter. Vasya has a bottle of champagne.

MME NYEGIN. They're depraved, they're really depraved! They forced their way in, they won't listen to reason at all.

VASYA. But you can't act like that, Domna Pantelyevna. We simply must drink to the health of Alexandra Nikolavna, that's something we can't do without. What is all this! We've come here with honorable and noble intentions, with all due respect! There's nothing disgraceful at all, really now!

TRAGEDIAN. Of course not! Since I'm here.

ALEXANDRA. But you're troubling yourselves for nothing. I won't drink anything.

VASYA. If that's the way you want, miss. There'll be all the more left for us, we'll drink by ourselves. *(He shouts in the direction of the partition.)* You there, my dear smart girl, bring us some glasses!

MME NYEGIN. Give me that, I'll open it. *(She takes the bottle and goes off.)*

TRAGEDIAN. You say you won't drink anything, but I'd like to see you not drink with me here!

VASYA. You shouldn't force her, sir.

TRAGEDIAN. I won't force her, I'll ask her.

Mme Nyegin returns. She places the bottle and glasses on the table.

VASYA *(pours)*. We'll start with you, elders first, ma'am.

MME NYEGIN. I don't know whether to drink or not. I'm afraid of getting tipsy.

VASYA. What is all this! What's there to be afraid of? It's getting on in the night, so even if you do get tipsy, it's no great catastrophe. He and I aren't afraid of that.

MME NYEGIN *(takes the glass)*. Well, Sasha, congratulations! *(She drinks.)*

VASYA *(carries a glass to Alexandra)*. Now let me ask you.

ALEXANDRA. I already told you I won't drink anything.

VASYA. You can't do that to us, miss. We've come with nothing but good will. Just half!

TRAGEDIAN *(falling to his knees)*. Sasha, Alexandra! Look who's asking you! Look who's at your feet! It's Gromilov, Yerast Gromilov himself!

ALEXANDRA. Well, all right, I'll drink a little bit. Only I won't drink more than that for anything. *(She drinks.)*

VASYA *(helping the tragedian to his feet).* As much as you want, miss. *(He takes her glass.)* We'll drink what's left and find out your thoughts. *(He pours glasses.)* Now we'll drink, sir. *(He gives a glass to the tragedian.)*

TRAGEDIAN. Congratulate her for the two of us. My eloquence isn't in good shape tonight.

VASYA. It is my honor, miss, to congratulate you on your success. A hundred years of life and a million rubles! *(He clinks glasses with the tragedian, and they drink.)*

TRAGEDIAN *(giving his glass).* Pour some more. *(Vasya pours; the tragedian drinks.)* Is that all?

VASYA *(showing the bottle).* That's all.

TRAGEDIAN. I see. Let's go.

VASYA *(to Alexandra).* Farewell! Please give me your hand, miss. And excuse our ignorance, miss. Our thanks to this house, now we'll go to another.

They leave.

MME NYEGIN. What muddleheads! Going through town like a whirlwind. Now I'll lock up, they were just too much for us. *(She goes off and soon returns.)* Well, now we can drink our tea!

ALEXANDRA. I'll be glad to have some.

MME NYEGIN *(at the partition).* Matryona, pour each of us a cup of tea. *(To Alexandra.)* Hand me over that gift there.

ALEXANDRA *(giving a small box).* But you've already seen what's there, some earrings and a brooch.

MME NYEGIN. I just want to put them away. You know they're worth a lot. *(She puts the small box into her pocket.)* What's good about things like these, what's so pleasant about them, is that in time of need they can be pawned straight off. Not like all that brushwood.

Matryona brings two cups of tea and goes off.

ALEXANDRA *(sipping the tea).* You should see the bouquet Velikatov brought me. Look!

MME NYEGIN. Well, what about the bouquet! A bouquet's a bouquet. Money thrown away for nothing, that's what I think. *(She drinks her tea.)*

ALEXANDRA. No, look! The flowers are all expensive. Where do you suppose he got them?

MME NYEGIN *(looking over the bouquet).* Yes, it is pretty, you have to say that. *(She finds a note.)* But what's this?

ALEXANDRA *(reads the note to herself).* Oh, oh!

MME NYEGIN. What is it?

ALEXANDRA *(grabbing onto her head).* Oh no, wait! I have another note. And I forgot it. *(She takes a note out of her pocket.)* It's from Peter Yegorych, he gave it to me at the stage door. *(She reads it to herself.)*

MME NYEGIN. Read it out loud! What kind of secrets does anybody keep from a mother!

ALEXANDRA *(reads).* "Yes, dear Sasha, art is not nonsense, I am beginning to understand that. Tonight I found so much warmth and sincerity in your acting that I simply must tell you I was amazed. I am very happy for you. These are rare and precious qualities of the soul. After the performance some people will probably visit you at home. In the presence of your guests I always feel something unpleasant, either embarrassment or vexation, I feel awkward. They all look at me in a hostile or mocking way, which you yourself know I don't deserve. Because of these considerations I won't drop in on you after the theater, but if you should find two or three free minutes, then run out into the garden, I'll be waiting for you there. Of course, I could drop in on you tomorrow morning, but, excuse me, my heart is filled to the brim, to the point of overflowing…" *(She wipes away tears.)*

MME NYEGIN. Well, read the other one.

ALEXANDRA. No, Mama, I don't want to, it's embarrassing!

MME NYEGIN. Embarrassing! You get a lot of letters that are embarrassing, and you read those to me.

ALEXANDRA. All right, Mama, prepare yourself. *(She reads.)* "I fell in love with you at first sight. To see and hear you is an inexpressible delight for me. Forgive me for making my declaration in a letter, but because of inborn timidity I would never dare to transmit my feelings to you aloud. My happiness now depends on you. And my happiness, what I dream about, my adorable Alexandra Nikolavna, is this. At my country home, in my splendid castle, in my palace, there is a young lady of the house to whom all, starting with me, bow, whom all obey like slaves. Thus the summer passes. In the fall my charming lady and I go to one of our southern towns. She goes onto the stage of a theater which is completely dependent on me; she goes on in full glory, and I rejoice and take pride in her successes. Beyond that I do not dream, we shall live and see. Don't be angry with me for my dreams, for everyone can dream. I shall read my sentence tomorrow in your eyes, they'll tell me if you accept me. If you don't accept me, I will go away with a broken heart but without complaint, punished by your scorn for my boldness. Your Velikatov." *(In tears.)* Mama, what is this? What is this disgusting man writing here? Who gave him permission?

MME NYEGIN. What permission?

ALEXANDRA. That… to fall in love with me.

MME NYEGIN. Oh you silly girl, does a man have to ask permission for that!

ALEXANDRA I could kill him.

Silence.

MME NYEGIN *(pensively)*. Swans... He says swans swim on the lake.

ALEXANDRA. Oh, what do I care about that!

Silence.

MME NYEGIN. Sasha, my own little Sasha, you know you and I have never had a serious talk about some things, and now's the time. You live in poverty, and here's a chance for wealth! But good heavens, could this be some kind of calamity?! A temptation?! Is it the devil, Lord forgive us, who's turned up here? At the very time... when we've started thinking about our need. That's just like the devil. But how much kindness is in this man, how much of every virtue! So, my flighty girl, let's you and I have a serious talk about this business.

ALEXANDRA. "Serious," you say, a serious talk about such business. But what do you take me for! Is this a "business"? It's shameful, that's all! You remember what he said, it was he who said it, my dear boy, my Petya! How can I do any thinking about this, what's there to think about, what's there to discuss! And if you can't stand the uncertainty, then take tea leaves or something and tell from them what I'm going to do! Yes, I'll be in your hands. And that's the end of it. *(She takes Meluzov's note.)*

MME NYEGIN. But what's gotten into you! How could I!... It's your affair. Lord help me! May God and all good people...

ALEXANDRA *(reads from Meluzov's note)*. "But if you should find two or three free minutes, then run out into the garden, I'll be waiting for you there." Oh, my poor, poor boy! How little I've loved him! While I feel now that I love him with all my soul. *(She takes Narokov's letter.)* Oh, and this one too! I'll have to save this all my life! Nobody will ever love me like that. Give me my shawl. I'm going.

MME NYEGIN. Where are you going, where? What's gotten into you?

ALEXANDRA. Oh, stop it, it's none of your business!

MME NYEGIN. How is it none of my business! You're my daughter.

ALEXANDRA. All right, I'm your daughter, you can do what you want with me. But my soul's my own. I'm going to Petya. He really loves me, he feels for me, he's taught me what's good and right.

MME NYEGIN. But what about that other business? Just say something.

ALEXANDRA. Oh, that business, that! All right, tomorrow, tomorrow, let's leave it for tomorrow. But right now don't you get in my way. Now I'm good and honorable, such as I've never been before, and such as I might not be tomorrow. I feel very good in my soul now, very honorable, and you shouldn't get in the way.

MME NYEGIN. All right, all right, do what you want, do what you want.

ALEXANDRA *(covering herself with the shawl)*. I don't know, I might come back right away, I might stay till morning... But don't you say a word to me, no look...

MME NYEGIN. Why say that, don't you think I'm your mother, don't you think I'm a woman! Don't I understand I shouldn't get in your way, do you think I don't have a soul?

ALEXANDRA. I'm going then.

MME NYEGIN. Wait, wrap yourself up good and warm, don't catch cold. Anyway, you really have a heart of gold. I won't lock up, I'll drink tea and wait up for you awhile.

Alexandra leaves. Mme. Nyegin goes off behind the partition. The stage is empty awhile, and then Bakin enters.

BAKIN. There's nobody here, the door's not locked, and somebody sneaked out, it had to be her. But where was she going, who to? If it's to her fiancé's place, there's no point, he can come here. She's probably gone into the garden for a breath of fresh air. I'll wait for her here. She won't drive me away, she'll surely let me stay at least a half hour. I made a bet with Velikatov that I'd drink tea with her and stay till morning. And I don't feel like losing it. I wanted to let him know whether she received me or not. Ah, here's what I'll do, I'll send the coachman to say I've stayed here. If she drives me out, then I'll walk around somewhere till it's dawn. *(He opens the window.)*

At this moment Meluzov and Alexandra enter. She goes behind the partition.

Ivan, drive to the railroad station and tell them I've stayed here.

MELUZOV. No, you won't be staying here. Tell the coachman to wait, for you're leaving here right now. What do you think you're doing! All right, then I'll tell him. *(Through the window.)* Ivan, stay! Your gentleman is coming out right away.

BAKIN. What right do you have to give orders in somebody else's apartment? I don't know you and don't want to know you.

MELUZOV. No, really, why do you want to lie like that? And you're lying with a bad intent. Do you want to give a girl a bad reputation?

BAKIN. "A bad reputation"? Does a visit after the theater give somebody a bad reputation? Well now, what do you know about it?

MELUZOV. But why were you going to send the coachman to say you were staying here?

BAKIN. You sit up there in the balcony, so how can you understand what goes on between actors and that part of the audience that sits in the front rows of the orchestra!

MELUZOV. Here's something I understand: that you, with your front seat in the orchestra, are going to leave here while I, with my seat in the balcony, am going to stay here.

BAKIN. You're going to stay here?

MELUZOV. Yes, I'm going to stay.

BAKIN. How nice! At least I've made a discovery I can share with...

MELUZOV. With anyone you want.

BAKIN. Still, haven't you been bragging a bit too much, in all your excitement?

MELUZOV. No, you can count on it, I'm going to stay.

Alexandra enters, dressed in an overcoat.

ALEXANDRA *(places her hand on Meluzov's shoulder)*. Yes, he's going to stay.

MELUZOV. So now your doubts are over, which means you have just one thing left to do...

ALEXANDRA. To leave.

MELUZOV. And the sooner the better.

BAKIN. The better! I know myself what's better for me.

MELUZOV. No, you don't know, you didn't let me finish. The sooner you leave the better for you, because then you can leave through the door, but if you take a long time to get ready, you'll fly off into space through the window.

ALEXANDRA *(embracing Meluzov)*. Oh, darling.

BAKIN. Young man, you're going to remember this! *(He leaves.)*

ALEXANDRA. Oh, dear Petya, my darling, let's go driving now, all night long. The horses are here.

MELUZOV. Where to, Sasha?

ALEXANDRA. Anywhere you want, anywhere at all. Everything, everything will be as you want it till morning. Mama, good-bye, lock the door. We're going driving.

Meluzov and Alexandra leave.

ACT FOUR

Railroad station's waiting room for first-class passengers. On the right of the actors is a doorway in the form of an arch; it leads into another waiting room. Directly facing is a glass door, behind which can be seen a platform and cars. In the middle, stretching along the room, is a long table, on which are eating utensils, bottles, a candelabra, and a vase with flowers. The tragedian is sitting at the table. From the platform are heard voices: "The station is Bryakhimov. There will be a stop of twenty minutes. A buffet is provided. Bryakhimov! There will be a stop of twenty minutes."

TRAGEDIAN. Where's my Vasya? Waiter! *(He bangs on the table.)*

The waiter enters.

WAITER. What would you like?

TRAGEDIAN. Where's my Vasya?

WAITER. Really now, how many times have you asked that already! How are we supposed to know?

TRAGEDIAN. Then in that case, my friend, you can go away.

The waiter leaves.

Where's my Vasya?

Vasya enters.

VASYA. Here's your Vasya. What do you want?

TRAGEDIAN. Look, friend, where did you disappear to?

VASYA. What will you ask next! If I disappeared, there was a reason. Tell me what you want!

TRAGEDIAN. Inform me, friend, what is there that you and I haven't drunk today?

VASYA. What? I think we've drunk everything except vitriol. And I'll tell you something else! That should be enough for a while!

TRAGEDIAN. But do you love me or not?

VASYA. So now you've found another topic for conversation.

TRAGEDIAN. What is it you love me for?

VASYA. For the fact that our house is a mess and that you have talent. So, that conversation's ended. But listen! Why wine and more wine all the time? Let's give that a little rest.

TRAGEDIAN. All right, let it rest.

VASYA. I'm sending my assistant to Kharkov, so I've got to make things good and clear to him. Let's go into the third-class waiting room. We can stretch our legs there and relax a bit.

TRAGEDIAN. All right, let's go. *(He gets up.)*

They go toward the doorway. They are met by Narokov and Meluzov, who are coming from the other waiting room.

NAROKOV *(stopping Vasya).* Wait, wait! Here, take my watch. *(He takes out his pocket watch and gives it to Vasya.)*

VASYA. But why are you giving me your watch, Martyn Prokofyich?

NAROKOV. Give me ten rubles for it, give them to me, please.

VASYA. But you're crazy, I don't need your watch.

NAROKOV. Do me a favor, do me a favor! It's an emergency.

VASYA. But if it's an emergency, I'll trust you for it.

NAROKOV. There's no need for that, no need. Take the watch, I'll buy it back. It's expensive, I'll buy it back soon.

VASYA. But what do you need the money for? Tell me, take me into your confidence.

NAROKOV. Oh, why do you go on tormenting me like this? Tell me, will you give me the money or not?

VASYA. I'm just curious to know, my friend, what kind of business you have here, what kind of commerce.

NAROKOV. Excuse me for troubling you. I shouldn't have.

VASYA. Well, all right, all right. *(He puts the watch into his pocket and takes money out of his wallet.)* There you are. I won't take any interest, don't worry.

NAROKOV *(takes the money and shakes Vasya's hand)*. Thank you, thank you, you've saved my life.

Vasya and the tragedian go off into the other waiting room.

MELUZOV. They're not here. You must have been mistaken.

NAROKOV. No, I know it, and my heart tells me she's going away. You can see I still haven't recovered.

MELUZOV. But it's just not likely. Why should she hide it from me, why deceive me! This morning I received a note from her, and here's what she wrote: *(He takes a note from his pocket and reads.)* "Petya, don't visit us today. Stay home and wait for me. I'll drop in on you myself in the evening."

NAROKOV. Yes, it's incomprehensible, but she's leaving, that's certain. I tried to drop in on them, but they wouldn't let me in. Domna Pantelyevna came out and shouted at me, "We can't be bothered with you, not with you, we're leaving by train right away." I saw the suitcases, the handbags, the bundles... and I went running to you.

MELUZOV. Let's go take a look in the other waiting room; we'll wait for them at the entrance.

NAROKOV. I've lost my memory. What is it, morning or evening? I don't know a thing. When does the train leave?

MELUZOV. Seven p.m., in about twenty minutes.

NAROKOV. Oh, then they'll still come. Let's go.

They go off into the other waiting room. Through the glass door enter Alexandra carrying a traveling bag, Mme. Nyegin, Nina Smelsky, Dulyebov, Bakin, and Matryona carrying pillows and packages. Alexandra and Nina come forward. Dulyebov and Bakin sit down at the table. Matryona places the packages and pillows on the divan near the door. Mme. Nyegin sorts out the packages and conceals something in them.

NINA. How soon you got ready, Sasha, and not a word to anyone.

ALEXANDRA. When could I tell anyone! I got the telegram today and began getting ready right away.

NINA. If the Prince and I hadn't dropped in at the station, then you'd have left without saying good-bye.

ALEXANDRA. I didn't have any time, I haven't said good-bye to anyone. I got ready all of a sudden. I planned to write you from Moscow.

NINA. Then you're going to Moscow?

ALEXANDRA. Yes.

NINA. On what conditions?

ALEXANDRA. They're offering very good ones, but I still haven't made up my mind. I'll write you from there.

DULYEBOV (to Bakin). I thought Velikatov would have to leave today, so I came to catch him. I said to myself, I'll drink a bottle of champagne with him to punish him for going off on the sly.

BAKIN. Me too and for the same reason.

DULYEBOV. But the train's already in, and he's still not here, so he must have stayed in town.

BAKIN. You know, these gentlemen millionaires love to show up at the very last moment.

NINA (to Alexandra). But what about Peter Yegorych?

ALEXANDRA. Oh, don't talk about him, please!

NINA. You told him?

ALEXANDRA. No, he doesn't know. I'm afraid he'll come here. If only we could leave soon.

BAKIN. There's Ivan Semyonych!

Velikatov and the head conductor enter from the other waiting room. They stop by the doorway.

HEAD CONDUCTOR (to Velikatov). The station master has given the order to add a special parlor car.

VELIKATOV. Yes, I was the one who asked him. *(He nods to Dulyebov and Bakin.)*

BAKIN. Are you traveling?

VELIKATOV. No, I'm seeing off Alexandra Nikolavna and Domna Pantelyevna. *(To the head conductor.)* When everything's ready, then arrange for these things to be transferred. And take pains to make sure that everything is good and comfortable.

HEAD CONDUCTOR. Don't worry.

MME NYEGIN. Ivan Semyonych, did you get the tickets?

VELIKATOV. I got them, Domna Pantelyevna, and I registered all your luggage.

MME NYEGIN. Then give me the tickets. They won't let us on without tickets.

VELIKATOV. I'll give them to you later, when you sit down in the car.

MME NYEGIN. If only we're not late, Ivan Semyonych. They might leave without us, my heart's all jumpy.

HEAD CONDUCTOR. Don't worry. I'll come for you and seat you myself, without me the train won't move. And I'll have them come for your things right away.

MME NYEGIN. Get somebody reliable to keep everything safe.

VELIKATOV. See to it.

HEAD CONDUCTOR (touching his cap). I'll give the orders right now. (He goes off.)

VELIKATOV. Gentlemen, to see them off we have to drink off a bottle, I've already ordered it to be served. Alexandra Nikolavna, Nina Vasilyevna, please join us.

MME NYEGIN. Yes, and before we leave everybody has to sit for a moment. Matryona, you sit too.

They all sit down at the table on the side facing the arch. The waiter enters with a bottle of champagne, puts it on the table, and walks off. Velikatov pours the champagne into the champagne glasses.

VELIKATOV (raising his glass). A happy journey, Alexandra Nikolavna! Domna Pantelyevna!

Dulyebov and Bakin stand up and bow.

MME NYEGIN. Happiness to you who stay, gentlemen!

NINA (kissing Alexandra). I wish you happiness, Sasha! Write me, please!

A conductor enters.

CONDUCTOR. Which things would you like taken?

MME NYEGIN. Over there, sir! Matryona, show him. And go after him, keep a good eye on things.

The conductor picks up the articles.

Conductor!

CONDUCTOR. Yes?

MME NYEGIN. You be careful with those pillows, don't drag them on the floor.

ALEXANDRA. Mama!

MME NYEGIN. What do you mean, "Mama"! It's a lot better when you tell them. (To the conductor.) Don't touch that bag there, the one on the end! I say not to touch it, it has some rolls. You'd probably spill them out.

Dulyebov and Bakin laugh.

ALEXANDRA. Mama!

MME NYEGIN. What! Try counting on them!

ALEXANDRA. Take all of it, take it all!

A bell rings on the platform.

MME NYEGIN *(gets up quickly from her chair).* Aie! They're going.

VELIKATOV. Don't worry, Domna Pantelyevna. They won't go without you.

CONDUCTOR. That ring was for the third-class passengers, there's still plenty of time. *(He goes off, Matryona after him.)*

MME NYEGIN. They frightened me to death. They wear a person all out with those damn bells.

Narokov enters from the other room, followed by a waiter with a bottle and then Meluzov. Narokov sits down at the end of the table, near the arch. The waiter sets the bottle in front of him. Meluzov stops by the doorway.

ALEXANDRA *(goes up to Meluzov).* Not a word, for God's sake, not a word! If you really love me, be quiet. I'll tell you everything later. *(She goes off and sits down at her place.)*

NAROKOV *(to the waiter).* You had your doubts looking at me, didn't you, whether I'd pay you? All right! You're a good waiter! Here's a reward for your virtue! *(He gives him ten rubles.)* That's for the champagne, keep the change.

WAITER. Thank you, thank you very much, sir! *(He goes off.)*

Meluzov sits down next to Narokov, who, pouring glasses for himself and Meluzov, stands up.

BAKIN. A speech, a speech, gentlemen! Let's listen.

NAROKOV. Alexandra Nikolavna! The first glass is to your talent! I take pride in being the first to notice it. But then who here beside me could notice and appreciate talent! Can they really understand art here? Do they really want art here? Is it really possible here that… oh damn it!

BAKIN. You've gotten mixed up, Martyn Prokofyich.

NAROKOV *(angrily).* No, I haven't gotten mixed up. In the shy steps of an actress making her debut, in the first, still naive babbling I foresaw the future celebrity. You have talent. Cherish it, develop it! Talent is the best wealth, the best happiness of man! To your talent! *(He drinks.)*

ALEXANDRA. Thank you, Martyn Prokofyich!

BAKIN. Bravo!

DULYEBOV. But he speaks quite well.

NAROKOV *(to Meluzov).* Pour some for me and yourself.

Meluzov pours. Narokov raises his glass.

The second glass is to your beauty!

ALEXANDRA *(gets up).* Oh, why say that! What for!

NAROKOV. You don't acknowledge your beauty? No, you're a woman of beauty. For me where talent is, that's where beauty is! All my life I've bowed to beauty, I'll bow to it till the grave… To your beauty! *(He drinks and puts down the glass.)* Now allow me on parting to kiss your hand. *(He falls to his knees before Alexandra and kisses her hand.)*

ALEXANDRA *(in tears).* Stand up, Martyn Prokofyich, stand up.

VELIKATOV. That's enough, Martyn Prokofyich! You're upsetting Alexandra Nikolavna!

NAROKOV. Yes, it's enough! *(He stands up, takes several steps toward the glass door, and stops.)*

In the doorway of the other waiting room appear the head conductor, station attendants, and several passengers.

> Not tears, dismay,
> Not dreams of weight,
> But roses gay
> Will be your fate.
> Those roses fair
> Has God esteemed;
> In vain has ne'er
> The poet dreamed.
> When joys enthrall
> In happy reign,
> You must recall
> The poet's pain.

He goes off toward the doorway.

> No mercy had
> From will divine,
> The wretch but glad
> In joys of thine.*

He walks toward the doorway.

---

* Genuine verses by an unknown actor of the forties. *(Ostrovsky's note.)*[10]

VELIKATOV AND ALEXANDRA. Martyn Prokofyich, Martyn Prokofyich!

NAROKOV. No, enough, enough. I can't stay any longer. *(He leaves.)*

ALEXANDRA *(with a sign she calls over the head conductor).* Say that it's time to leave. Please.

HEAD CONDUCTOR *(looking at his watch).* It's still a bit early. But if that's what you'd like. Ladies and gentlemen, won't you please take your seats in the train?

MME NYEGIN. Oh, let me go ahead, gentlemen! Let me go or I won't make it in time.

HEAD CONDUCTOR. To the right, please, the last car!

Mme. Nyegin exits, followed by the head conductor, Alexandra, Nina, Velikatov, Dulyebov and Bakin. Alexandra soon returns.

ALEXANDRA. So, Petya, good-bye! My fate's been decided.

MELUZOV. What? What's that? What did you say?

ALEXANDRA. I'm not yours, my dear! It was impossible, Petya.

MELUZOV. Whose are you then?

ALEXANDRA. Well, why should you know! The result's the same for you. It had to be this way, Petya. I thought for a long time, Mama and I both thought… You're a good person, very good! Everything you said was true, all true, but it was impossible… how much I cried, how much I curse myself…It's something you can't understand. You see, that's the way it is, it's always been that way…All of a sudden I was alone… isn't it even ridiculous?

MELUZOV. Ridiculous? Even ridiculous?

ALEXANDRA. Yes. What you said is true, it's all true, people ought to live like that, they really should… But if I have talent… if I have fame ahead of me? What should I do, give that up, should I? And later regret it, grieve over it the rest of my life?… If I was born an actress?

MELUZOV. How can you say that, how can you, Sasha! Are talent and depravity *ity* really inseparable?

ALEXANDRA. No, it's not depravity! How can you! *(She cries.)* You don't understand a thing… and you don't want to understand me. After all, I'm an actress. But you expect me to be some kind of a heroine. Can every woman be a heroine? I'm an actress… If I had married you, I'd soon have left you and gone off to the stage, even for a small salary, just to be on the stage. Do you think I can live without the theater?

MELUZOV. That's news to me, Sasha.

ALEXANDRA. News! The reason it's news is that you haven't gotten to know my soul. You thought I could be a heroine, but I can't… and I don't even want to. Why should I be a reproach to others? It's as if I'd be saying, that's what you women are like, but look at me, an honorable woman!… And that other woman might not be guilty at all. There can be all kinds of circumstances. You can figure them out yourself: one's family... or some kind of deception... So am I going to reproach others? God forbid!

MELUZOV. Sasha, Sasha, is an honorable life really a reproach to others? An honorable life is a good example for imitation.

ALEXANDRA. That must mean that I'm stupid, that I don't understand anything... But that's how Mama and I decided it... we cried, but we decided it... Yet you want me to be a heroine. No, where could I get the strength for the struggle?... What kind of strength do I have! But all you said was true. I'll never forget you.

MELUZOV. You won't forget me? Thanks for that!

ALEXANDRA. They were the best days of my life, I won't have any more like them. Good-bye, darling!

MELUZOV. Good-bye, Sasha!

ALEXANDRA. When I was getting ready I cried the whole time over you. Here! *(She takes some hair wrapped in paper out of her traveling bag.)* I cut off half a braid for you. Take it as a memento!

MELUZOV *(puts it into his pocket).* Thank you, Sasha.

ALEXANDRA. If you want, I'll cut off some more, right now. *(She takes scissors from her bag.)* There, cut some off yourself.

MELUZOV. No, no.

Velikatov opens the door.

VELIKATOV. Alexandra Nikolavna, please come! They're about to ring the last bell.

ALEXANDRA. Right away, right away! Go on! *(Velikatov goes off.)* Good-bye then. Only don't be mad at me! Don't scold me! Instead forgive me! Or it'll be painful for me, I won't have any joy at all. Forgive me! I'll beg you on my knees.

MELUZOV. Don't, don't. Live as you please, as best you can. All I want is that you be happy. Just manage to be happy, Sasha! You forget about me and my words, but somehow or other, in your own way, manage to find yourself happiness. That's all there is to it, and the question of life is decided for you.

ALEXANDRA. Then you're not mad at me? That's nice... how nice that is! Only listen, Petya. If you're ever in need, write me.

MELUZOV. What a thing to say, Sasha!

ALEXANDRA. No, please, don't refuse. I'll be like a sister to you... like a sister, Petya. So give me that satisfaction... Like a sister! How can I ever repay you for all your goodness!...

The head conductor enters.

HEAD CONDUCTOR. I've come for you. Please take your seat. The train's leaving right away!

ALEXANDRA *(throws her arms around Meluzov's neck).* Good-bye, Petya! Good-bye, my dear, my darling! *(She tears herself from his embrace and rushes to the door.)* Write me, Petya, write. *(She leaves, the head conductor after her.)*

Meluzov looks at the open door. The bell rings. The conductor's whistle is heard, then the whistling sound of the engine, and the train starts. From the other waiting room enter the tragedian and Vasya.

TRAGEDIAN. What did you say? She's left?

VASYA. Yes, brother, our Alexandra Nikolavna's left us. Good-bye! Just like that and she's gone.

TRAGEDIAN. Well, so be it. You and I'll cry together into one urn, and now that she's gone we'll wish her a happy journey.

Nina, Dulyebov, and Bakin enter.

BAKIN *(laughs heartily).* I've never seen anything like it! I shout to him, "Get off, or they'll take you along!" And he says, "Let them take me along, it won't hurt my feelings. Good-bye, gentlemen!" I've never seen anything like it! Does that mean he took them off to his estate?

NINA. It was obvious, I guessed it right off. Do you think Alexandra could travel in a parlor car? On what money? She and her mama would travel in a third-class car, squeezed up in a corner.

BAKIN. But why did he tell a lie, saying he's seeing them off?

NINA. To avoid talk. If he said he'd be going with them, right off people would make fun of them. There'd be jokes, and you'd be the first to start. Whether that embarrasses him or he simply doesn't like such talk I don't know. But he was smart to act as he did.

DULYEBOV. I told you he was a smart man.

BAKIN. And there we were wishing Miss Nyegin a happy journey! So what could be happier? Well, if I had known all that, my cordial traveling wish for Velikatov would have been for him to break his neck. And you know, that sort of thing happens, Prince; a switchman drinks himself dead drunk... A train comes from the other direction, and suddenly bang!

Meluzov rushes toward the door.

What are you doing, where are you going? To save him? You won't be in time. But don't worry. People like Velikatov don't perish, they pass unharmed through fire and water.

Meluzov stops.

Let's have a little talk, young man. Or are you perhaps in a hurry to shoot yourself? In that case I won't get in your way, shoot yourself, shoot yourself. After all, students shoot themselves at every setback.

MELUZOV. No, I'm not going to shoot myself.

BAKIN. You don't have the wherewithal to buy a pistol? Then I'll buy you one at my expense.

MELUZOV. Buy one for yourself.

BAKIN. So what are you going to do now? What will you take up, teaching again?

MELUZOV. Yes. What more is there to do? That's our occupation, our obligation.

BAKIN. Another actress?

MELUZOV. Possibly another actress.

BAKIN. And you'll fall in love again, spin your dreams again, think of yourself as a fiancé?

MELUZOV. Go on, make fun of me, I won't get mad, I deserve it. I'll disarm you, I'll make fun of myself along with you. After all, it's ridiculous, really ridiculous. Here we have a poor man who's been taught to work for his living, so let him work. But he took it into his head to fall in love! No, that's a luxury not meant for people like us.

NINA. Oh, how nice he is! *(She sends him a kiss with her hand.)*

MELUZOV. We poor devils, we workers, have our own joys that you know nothing about, they're inaccessible to you. Friendly conversations over a glass of tea, about books over a bottle of beer, books you don't read, about the progress of science, which is something you don't know anything about, about the successes of civilization, which is something you're not interested in. What more could we want! But I encroached, so to speak, on the domain of others, going into the region where time is passed without sorrow or care, into the sphere of beautiful and jolly women, into the sphere of champagne, of bouquets, of expensive gifts. Well now, isn't that ridiculous? Of course, it's ridiculous.

NINA. Oh, how nice he is!

BAKIN. I can see you're not touchy about it. And I thought you might be challenging me to a duel.

MELUZOV. A duel? What for? You and I have a duel as it is, a constant duel, an unending duel. I enlighten, and you deprave.

TRAGEDIAN. That's noble! *(To Vasya.)* Ask for champagne!

MELUZOV. So let's fight. You do your business, and I'll do mine. And we'll see who gets tired first. You'll give up first, There's nothing very attractive in being lightheaded. You'll reach a good age, and your conscience will prick you. Of course, there are some people with such happy natures that to deep old age they preserve the capacity to fly with astonishing lightness from flower to flower, but they're the exception. As for me, I'll do my business to the end. But if I do stop teaching, if I do stop believing in the possibility of improving people, or if I do cowardly bury myself in idleness and give up on everything, then at that time you can buy me a pistol, and I'll say thank you. *(He pulls his hat down on his head and wraps himself up in his plaid.)*

VASYA. A bottle of champagne!

TRAGEDIAN. Make it six.

CURTAIN

NOTES

1. Paraphrase of a line from Schiller's play *The Robbers*.

2. The tragedy *Uriel Acosta* (1847; Russian translation 1872) is considered the best work of the German playwright Karl Gutzkow (1811-78). As many of the audience in Ostrovsky's time would have realized, Dulyebov's remarks at this point in the play expose his muddleheaded ignorance of theatrical culture.

3. P.A. Karatýgin (1805-79), Russian actor and dramatist.

4. P.I. Grigóryev (1806-71), Russian actor and dramatist.

5. N.A. Polevóy (1796-1846), Russian writer, dramatist, and journalist.

6. In the sense of "binge" Narokov actually quotes the first four words of the Russian folksong "Beyond the Urals, beyond the river the Cossacks carouse" *(Za Uralom, za rekoi kazaki guliaiut)*.

7. From Schiller's *The Robbers*.

8. Heroine of Frou-frou, a French play (1869) by Henri Meilhac (1831-97) and Ludovic Halévy (1834-1908).

9. "I was born in Arcadia too." Opening lines of Schiller's poem "Resignation."

10. The "unknown actor" and author of the verses was actually D.A. Gorev. Although Ostrovsky was generally good-natured, one may suspect that here he was getting back a bit at Gorev, who had insisted that he was a co-author of Ostrovsky's first significant play *It's All in the Family*.

AFTERWORD

Ostrovsky conceived *Talents and Admirers* in the summer of 1881, started to write it at the end of October, and finished it on December 6, 1881. It was published in the No. 1, 1882 issue of *Fatherland Notes (Otechestvennye zapiski)*.

The premiere in Moscow on December 20, 1881, boasting an outstanding cast, enjoyed great success. Especially noteworthy was the performance of Márya Nikoláyevna Yermólov, who played Alexandra Nyegin as a basically innocent young actress sacrificing her love for art, while A. P. Lénsky played a Velikatov whose every move was calculated and certain. Both interpretations have been influential. The St. Petersburg premiere on January 14, 1882, was also successful, though less so than that in Moscow. However, the play did not become popular until the Soviet period.

To properly interpret this play I consider it essential that we try to avoid simplification, to be leery of hastily making black and white judgments, especially about Alexandra and Velikatov. *Talents and Admirers* is a complex play which sends out inconsistent signals, and it behooves us to try to determine as well as we can the ultimate truth known only for sure by its creator. One critic by implication aptly characterizes the play as a labyrinth.

Let's start with Alexandra, whom I'll discuss at relative length. Keep in mind that Ostrovsky is not just interested in portraying Alexandra's character but also in emphasizing her situation: her sudden predicament effectively forces her to make a crucial decision without delay.

Alexandra is obviously devoted to the theater and a talented actress. However, in this provincial city's theater acting talent is not enough to guarantee security for an actress. Her fate may depend on powerful male sponsors, such as Dulyebov, who are admirers of actresses with appropriate extracurricular talents. Early on, as we see, Alexandra indignantly rejects Dulyebov's proposition, and we can only accept her indignation as genuine. And yet, while it is true that Alexandra is relatively naive, I would like to suggest that, sexually speaking, she is hardly the innocent child she seems to be in this scene, that she is not nearly so surprised as she seems but is acting a bit in order to make things more difficult for Dulyebov. It is also possible that in general she puts on a puritanical pose as a protective tactic, but at base she is certainly not puritanical—her night fling with Meluzov is probably acceptable as sufficient proof of that. It is of some significance for what comes later that her highly pragmatic mother, whose views on sexual matters are of concern to Alexandra, is not overly disturbed by Dulyebov's proposition, indeed more by Alexandra's blunt response to it.

At this point one might assume that Alexandra should not have any man problem since she is engaged to Meluzov, but while there's never any doubt about Meluzov's love for Alexandra, it gradually becomes clear that Alexandra doesn't love Meluzov other than platonically. This becomes obvious when at one point she rejects Meluzov's embrace (significantly, when she's watching Velikatov drive off with Nina), provoking him to complain that she never shows him any affection. We need no more to rule out the interpretation that Alexandra sacrifices love for art or career.

But does Alexandra perhaps love Velikatov? It seems impossible to answer that with a yes or no, but it's clear that from the very beginning she is impressed by him and finds him attractive. At his first visit with astounding forwardness she makes a thinly disguised request that he take her driving sometime with his wonderful horses. She herself may well not be conscious of how attracted to Velikatov she is, but we can see it now and later. Especially pertinent is her reaction when Velikatov buys out her benefit performance; she not only understandably expresses her gratitude to Velikatov but goes on to promise him a kiss on the morrow. But why not today? Maybe because the kind of kiss she has in mind is one better not witnessed? Nina sees what's up and gives Dulyebov a kiss on the spot!

In view of the above why does Alexandra tell her mother that Velikatov is a "disgusting man" for having written his letter to her?

My guess is that she doesn't find him disgusting at all but is putting out a safe feeler to learn the reaction of her mother, who probably was reared in a morally conservative milieu. After Mme. Nyegin finds Velikatov acceptable and the proposed enterprise quite feasible, Alexandra feels free to make her sudden decision to accept Velikatov's offer, though the audience, which has been in suspense during the intermission between Acts III and IV, could only realize this in retrospect. Her choice is the play's climax, the fourth act the denouement.

Into the final meeting of Alexandra and Meluzov Ostrovsky sneaks a surprise. For Alexandra tells Meluzov that were she to give up the stage, she would lose her chance for fame! That in itself is enough to show that, devoted to theatrical art as she surely is, it's not all she lives for.

Finally something should be said of Alexandra's decision to go with Velikatov. Obviously it gives her a guaranteed chance to act as well as security to her and her mother (whom Alexandra would never think of abandoning in any way), and we know that Velikatov attracts her. But is her step "immoral," as Meluzov judges? She refuses to accept Meluzov's verdict though I suspect she might have some misgivings if only because Meluzov, whom she so much respects, is so sure about it. While Alexandra is not one to philosophize about morality or, for that matter, anything, the play suggests to me that she has her own responsible moral code and that her realization, probably influenced by her attraction for Velikatov, that she does not really love Meluzov makes her understand that it would be marrying Meluzov without love which would be immoral.

A key question for the interpretation of Velikatov is whether he is a thoroughgoing hypocrite, as some have maintained, or not. I'll discuss the hypocrisy claim later, but for the immediate discussion I am assuming that Velikatov is by turns sincere and insincere.

Enigmatic though he be, mostly because he is so reticent about himself and his views, there is still quite a bit we can say about Velikatov, especially if we're willing to venture some conjectures.

Velikatov did not inherit his wealth but, having rebuilt his father's ruined estate, went on to accumulate others and to become a millionaire from his ownership of factories, especially a sugar-beet factory. However, Velikatov can hardly be summed up as just another moneymaker. Ostrovsky has informed us in the list of characters that Velikatov is a retired cavalry officer, which suggests the possibility that he loves horses and that he maintains his stud farm as a hobby. We also learn near the end that he has his own theater, which certainly suggests the possibility that he has cultural sympathies. Moreover, unlike some people of wealth, he seems able and willing to talk democratically with people regardless of their station. So we have enough to posit Velikatov as a man of parts, an unusual individual not readily pigeonholed. Ostrovsky tells us that Velikatov tries to imitate the tone and manners of the merchants he deals with, but that does not mean that he imitates their business methods.

Given Velikatov's shyness, when he falls in love with Alexandra at first sight, he has a tactical problem. My guess is that he decides to use the readily accessible Nina to get closer to Alexandra while feeling his way. If this suspicion be on the mark, I would consider his so using Nina his one clearly unforgivable sin in the play. In any case it seems reasonable to suppose that Velikatov's first visit with Nina to Alexandra's apartment was his idea and not that of Nina, whose remarks to Meluzov at one point show that she considered Alexandra a potential rival for Velikatov's favor. In this scene Alexandra gives Velikatov encouragement with the result that he immediately has Nina bring Alexandra the dress material she needs. Moreover, being the brilliant opportunist he is, he has Nina invite Alexandra on his behalf to a farewell party he's giving the troupe. The decision to give such a party was probably made on the spot on the basis of his reception by Alexandra.

If at this point we can agree that Alexandra and Velikatov have been playing a game with each other involving either love or flirting, a game with each taking initiatives, then we can summarily dismiss the interpretation of Velikatov as predator and Alexandra as victim.

If Velikatov loves Alexandra, then why, since he's free, does he not propose marriage? We can only speculate. His conversation with Mme. Nyegin at one point suggests the possibility that as a bachelor of rather long standing he may be afraid of marriage. Perhaps he prefers to learn more about Alexandra at close quarters before making a binding commitment.

Finally, there's the charge that Velikatov is basely insincere, which is expressed most succinctly by the critic A. I. Revyakin when he writes that "Velikatov from beginning to end is insincere, false."[1] But how can we be so sure of that? Beginning to end? Every act and thought? Isn't that a parti pris? To be sure, using the term rather loosely, Velikatov is often enough insincere in the sense of being manipulative (he butters Mme. Nyegin up shamelessly) and, more to the point, of being habitually agreeable, and of lying more than once.

However, on this last point let me hasten to emphasize that his lies are the kind of white or perhaps even grayish lies which probably most of us have engaged in at one time or another (in the specific cases they don't bother Alexandra or Nina), and none seem to do any great harm. I think it may be apropos to note that because a man lies sometimes doesn't mean he lies all the time.

The negative social types in the play are Dulyebov, Bakin, and Migaev. Dulyebov is a snobbish old noble whose self-importance overwhelms what intelligence he has. For him the theater is a convenience store stocked with actresses who will be only too honored to perform offstage to his satisfaction. He's spent much time in the theater, but, despite his pretension of being a connoisseur, he clearly has no genuine esthetic appreciation of it.

Bakin is bright and discerning but also a self-centered, coarse, and brazen cynic. He goes straight for whatever he wants regardless of others' feelings, and his vaunted persistence makes him confident that he'll get Alexandra into his stable, preferably quickly and without unnecessary fuss. Of course Bakin's insolent aggressiveness is the worst approach to use with Alexandra, if for no other reason than it enhances Velikatov's considerable tact.

Migaev, reportedly representative of many provincial theater directors of the time, has risen from a low position in the theater to become director, but he has no understanding of theatrical art—his only concern is the take at the box office. He has no concept of honor or dishonor, but disgusting though we must find him, on reflection we might be willing to judge him less harshly than Dulyebov and Bakin since his evildoing is close to being unthinkingly animalistic.

Narokov is the play's defeated artistic conscience. A most likeable but pathetic old man, he has sacrificed his possessions for the theater he's always loved. He idolizes Alexandra as an artistic ally with considerable justification, but Narokov is the only one whose entire life finds meaning solely in art, especially theatrical. He stands in sharp contrast to Dulyebov and Bakin, who tolerate him as a harmless eccentric but don't take him seriously. They are not about to waste much of their valuable time with a man who can say that his "soul is full of fine perfumes."

Last, but certainly not least, there's Meluzov, the play's defeated moral conscience. As some have noted, he bears a resemblance to Bazarov, the gruffly independent medical-studies graduate in Ivan Turgenev's novel *Fathers and Sons,* who deems art useless. Meluzov shows no appreciation of art until near the end of the play when his views start to change under the influence of Alexandra's benefit performance, suggesting the possibility that he had not seen her act before.

Meluzov is certainly quixotic, perhaps at his most honorably ridiculous when he tells Migaev roundly off for his maltreatment of Alexandra, and then is satisfied with himself for having done his duty (though it's clear he hasn't helped Alexandra's cause at all). However, overly idealistic though we might consider Meluzov to be, we are sure that he has the stuff to endure privations and troubles while fulfilling his mission as teacher. Ostrovsky bestows a deserved honor on Meluzov when he has him basically end the play with a stout rejoinder to his spiritual enemy Bakin: "A duel? What for? You and I have a duel as it is, a constant duel, an unending duel. I enlighten, and you deprave… So let's fight. You do your business, and I'll do mine. And we'll see who gets tired first… As for me, I'll do my business to the end."

NOTE

1. *Istoriia russkoi literatury XIX veka,* v. 2, 336. Moscow, 1963.

OSTROVSKY'S PLAYS IN RUSSIAN

Translations of the titles are sometimes borrowed, in whole or in part, sometimes wholly my own. The first date is that of initial publication. The second is the date of the initial stage production as it has usually been given in Soviet sources. However, in some cases, some earlier performaces of a rather unsubstantial nature were given; for the details see the end commentaries in A. N. Ostrovskii: *Polnoe sobranie sochinenii,* Moscow, 1973-1980.

1. *Kartina semeinogo schast'ia* (Picture of Family Happiness). 1847, 1857.
2. *Svoi liudi-sochtemsia* (It's All in the Family). 1850, 1861. Originally entitled *Bankrot* (The Bankrupt).
3. *Utro molodogo cheloveka* (A Young Man's Morning). 1850, 1853.
4. *Neozhidannyi sluchai* (Unexpected Incident). 1851, 1902.
5. *Bednaia nevesta* (The Poor Bride). 1852, 1853.
6. *Ne v svoi sani ne sadis'* (Don't Sit in Another's Sleigh). 1853, 1853.
7. *Bednost' ne porok* (Poverty's No Vice.) 1854, 1854.
8. *Ne tak zhivi, kak khochetsia* (Don't Live as You Please). 1855, 1854.
9. *V chuzhom piru pokhmel'e* (Trouble Caused by Another). 1856, 1856.
10. *Dokhodnoe mesto* (A Profitable Position). 1857,1863.
11. *Prazdnichnyi son—do obeda* (A Holiday Dream Before Dinner). 1857, 1857.
12. *Ne soshlis' kharakterami* (Incompatibility of Character). 1858, 1858.
13. *Vospitannitsa* (The Ward). 1859, 1863.
14. *Groza* (The Thunderstorm). 1860, 1859.
15. *Staryi drug luchshe novykh dvukh* (An Old Friend Is Better than Two New Ones). 1860, 1860.
16. *Svoi sobaki gryzutsia, chuzhaia ne pristavai* (We Won't Brook Interference). 1861, 1861.
17. *Za chem poidesh', to i naidesh'* (You'll Find What You Go After). 1861, 1863. Also called *Zhenit'ba Bal'zaminova* (Balzaminov's Wedding).
18. *Koz'ma Zakhar'ich Minin-Sukhoruk* (Kozma Zakharyich Minin-Sukhoruk). The first version was initially published in 1862 but never performed. The second version was first published in 1904 and first performed in 1866.
19. *Grekh da beda na kogo ne zhivet* (Sin and Sorrow Are Common to All). 1863, 1863.
20. *Tiazhelye dni* (Difficult Days). 1863, 1863.
21. *Shutniki* (Jesters). 1864, 1864.
22. *Voevoda* (Voivode). First version: 1865, 1865. Second version: 1890, 1886. Also called *Son na Volge* (Dream on the Volga).
23. *Na boikom meste* (At the Jolly Spot). 1865, 1865.
24. *Puchina* (The Abyss). 1866, 1866.
25. *Dmitrii Samozvanets i Vasilii Shuiskii* (The False Dmitry and Vasily Shuisky). 1867, 1867.

26. *Tushino* (Tushino). 1867, 1867.

27. *Vasilisa Melent'eva* (Vasilisa Melentyeva). 1868, 1868. In collaboration with S. A. Gedeonov.

28. *Na vsiakogo mudretsa dovol'no prostoty* (To Every Sage His Share of Folly). 1868, 1868.

29. *Goriachee serdtse* (An Ardent Heart). 1869, 1869.

30. *Beshenye den'gi* (Easy Come, Easy Go). 1870, 1870.

31. *Les* (The Forest). 1871, 1871.

32. *Ne vse kotu maslianitsa* (Feasting Can't Last Forever). 1871, 1871.

33. *Ne bylo ni grosha, da vdrug altyn* (Not Even a Copper, Then Lo a Goldpiece). 1872, 1872.

34. *Komik XVII stoletiia* (Comic of the 17th Century). 1873, 1872.

35. *Snegurochka* (The Snowmaiden). 1873, 1873.

36. *Pozdniaia liubov'* (Late Love). 1874, 1873.

37. *Trudovoi khleb* (Hard-earned Bread). 1874, 1874.

38. *Volki i ovtsy* (Wolves and Sheep). 1875, 1875.

39. *Bogatye nevesty* (Rich Brides). 1876, 1875.

40. *Pravda khorosho, a schast'e luchshe* (Truth Is Fine, but Good Luck's Better). 1877, 1876.

41. *Schastlivyi den'* (Happy Day). 1877, 1877. In collaboration with N. Solovyov.

42. *Posledniaia zhertva* (A Last Sacrifice). 1878, 1877.

43. *Zhenit'ba Belugina* (Belugin's Wedding). 1878, 1877. In collaboration with N. Solvyov.

44. *Bespridannitsa* (Without a Dowry). 1879, 1878.

45. *Dikarka* (Wild Woman). 1880, 1879. In collaboration with N. Solovyov.

46. *Serdtse ne kamen'* (The Heart Is not a Stone). 1880, 1879.

47. *Nevol'nitsy* (Bondwomen). 1881, 1880.

48. *Svetit da ne greet* (It Gives Light but not Warmth). 1881, 1880. In collaboration with N. Solovyov.

49. *Blazh'* (Whim). 1881, 1880. In collaboration with P. Nevezhin.

50. *Talanty i poklonniki* (Talents and Admirers). 1882, 1881.

51. *Staroe po-novomu* (The Old in a New-fashioned Way). 1882, 1882. In collaboration with P. Nevezhin.

52. *Krasavets-muzhchina* (Handsome Man). 1883, 1882.

53. *Bez viny vinovatye* (Without Guilt Guilty). 1884, 1884.

54. *Ne ot mira sego* (Not of This World). 1885, 1885.

OSTROVSKY'S PLAYS IN ENGLISH TRANSLATION

Artistes and Admirers (Talanty i poklonniki). Tr. by Elisabeth Hanson. Manchester U. Press; Barnes and Noble, New York; 1970.

At the Jolly Spot. Tr. by Jane Paxton Campbell and George R. Noyes. *Poet Lore,* no. 1, 1925.

Bondwomen. Tr. by Schöne Charlotte Kurlandzik and George R. Noyes. *Poet Lore,* no. 4, 1925.

A Cat Has Not Always Carnival (Ne vse kotu maslianitsa). Tr. by J. P. Campbell and G. R. Noyes. Poet Lore, no. 3, 1929.

The Diary of a Scoundrel (Na vsiakogo mudretsa dovol'no prostoty). Adapted by Rodney Ackland. Marston, London, 1948. Included in vol. 2 of The Modern *Theatre* (Eric Bentley, ed.). Doubleday, Garden City, 1955. Also published as *Too Clever by Half* by Applause Theatre Bk. Pubs., 1988.

A Domestic Picture (Kartina semeinogo schast'ia). Tr. by E. L. Voynich in *The Humour of Russia.* Walter Scott, London; Scribner, New York, 1909.

Easy Money (Beshenye den'gi), and two other plays: *Even a Wise Man Stumbles (Na vsiakogo mudretsa dovol'no prostoty),* and *Wolves and Sheep.* Tr. by David Magarshack. Allen & Unwin, London, 1944. Reprinted by Greenwood Press, Inc.; Westport, Conn. *Easy Money* is included in *From the Modern Repertoire,* Series II (Eric Bentley, ed.), Indiana U. Press.

Enough Stupidity in Every Wise Man (Na vsiakogo mudretsa dovol'no prostoty). Tr. by Polya Kasherman. In *The Moscow Art Theatre Series of Russian Plays.* Second series, New York, 1923.

Fairy Gold (Beshenye den'gi). Tr. by Camille Chapin Daniles and G. R. Noyes. *Poet Lore,* no. 1, 1929.

Five Plays. Tr. by Eugene K. Bristow. Pegasus, New York, 1969. Contents: *It's a Family Affair—We'll Settle It Ourselves, The Poor Bride, The Storm, The Scoundrel (Na nsiakogo mudretsa dovol'no prostoty), The Forest.*

The Forest. Tr. by Clara Vostrovsky Winlow and G. R. Noyes. S. French, New York, 1926.

The Forest. Tr. by Serge Bertennson. Reproduction of typewritten copy in New York Public Library.

Incompatibility of Temper. Tr. by E. L. Voynich. In The Humour of Russia (see above under A Domestic Picture).

The King of Comedy Is Speaking to You. Vol. One. Tr. by J. McPetrie. Contents: *A Sprightly Spot, Late Love.* Stockwell, London, 1938. Copies in the British Museum, Library of Congress, and Grosvenor Library at Buffalo.

Larisa (Bespridannitsa) Tr. by Michael Green and Jerome Katsell, *The Unknown Russian Theater,* Ardis, Ann Arbor, 1991.

A Last Sacrifice. Tr. by Eugenia Korvin-Kroukovsky and G. R. Noyes. *Poet Lore,* no. 3, 1928.

Plays. Edited by G. R. Noyes. Contents: *A Protégée of the Mistress (Vospitannitsa), Poverty Is No Crime, Sin and Sorrow Are Common to All, It's a Family Affair-We'll Settle It Ourselves.* Charles Scribner's Sons, New York, 1917. Reprinted by AMS Press, Inc., New York, London.

Plays. Tr. by Margaret Wettlin. Contents: *Poverty Is No Crime, The Storm, Even the Wise Can Err (Na vsiakogo mudretsa dovol'no prostoty), More Sinned Against than Sinning (Bez viny vinovatye).* Progress Publishers, Moscow, 1974.

The Poor Bride. Tr. by John Laurence Seymour and G. R. Noyes. In *Masterpieces of the Russian Drama,* vol. one (G. R. Noyes, ed.). Dover, New York, 1960 (originally D. Appleton, New York, 1933).

The Storm. Tr. by Constance Garnett. Duckworth, London, 1899.

The Storm. Tr. by George F. Holland and Malcolm Morley. Allen & Unwin, London, 1930.

The Storm. Tr. by F. D. Reeve. In *An Anthology of Russian Plays,* vol. one. Vintage, New York, 1961.

The Storm. Tr. by David Magarshack. In *The Storm and Other Russian Plays.* Hill and Wang, New York, 1960. Also Ardis, Ann Arbor, 1988.

Thunder. Tr. by Joshua Cooper. In *Four Russian Plays.* Penguin Books, Baltimore, 1972.

The Thunderstorm. Tr. by Florence Whyte and G.R. Noyes. S. French, New York, 1927. Included in *World Drama,* vol. two (Barrett H. Clark, ed.) Dover, New York, 1933.

The Thunderstorm. Tr. by Andrew MacAndrew. In *19th Century Russian Drama.* Bantam, New York, 1963. Also in *A Treasury of the Theatre,* vol. one, ed. by John Gassner.

Too Clever by Half. See *The Diary of a Scoundrel.*

We Won't Brook Interference. Tr. by J. L. Seymour and G. R. Noyes. Banner Play Bureau, San Francisco and Cincinnati, 1938.

Wolves and Sheep. Tr. by Inez Sachs Colby and G. R. Noyes. *Poet Lore,* no. 2, 1926.

You Can't Live Just as You Please. Tr. by Philip Winningstad, G. R. Noyes, and John Heard, *Poet Lore,* no. 3, 1943.

OSTROVSKY CRITICISM IN ENGLISH

I am indebted to Herbert R. Smith for some items below.

Bristow, Eugene. See the preface, introduction, and notes in his translation of Ostrovsky: *Five Plays.*

Beasley, Ina. "The Dramatic Art of Ostrovsky." *The Slavonic Review,* vol. 6 (1927-28), 603-17.

Cizevskij, Dmitrij. Wide-ranging and perceptive discussion in Volume Two of his *History of Nineteenth-Century Russian Literature* (translated from the German). Vanderbilt U. Press, Nashville, 1974.

Cox, Lucy. "Form and Meaning in the Plays of Alexander N. Ostrovsky." Diss. U. of Pa., 1975.

Dana, H. W. L. Discussion in *A History of Modern Drama,* edited by Barrett H. Clark and George Freedley. Appleton, New York and London, 1947.

Esam, Irene. "An Analysis of Ostrovsky's *Ne ot mira sego* and the Play's Significance in Relation to the Author's Other Works." *New Zealand Slavonic Journal (NZSJ),* Summer, 1969, 68-91.

— "Folkloric Elements as Communication Devices in Ostrovsky's Plays." *NZSJ,* Summer, 1968, 67–88.

— "A Study of the Imagery Associated with Beliefs, Legends and Customs" in *Bednost' ne porok. NZSJ,* Winter, 102-22.

— "The Style of *Svoi liudi-sochtemsia." NZSJ,* Summer, 1972, 79-105.

— Grylack, Bevin Ratner. "The Function of Proverbs in the Dramatic Works of Ostrovsky." Diss. New York U., 1975.

Henley, Norman. See the brief end materials in English in his editing of Ostrovsky's *Groza* (The Thunderstorm), a text intended for Russian-reading students. Bradda, Letchworth, 1963.

— "Ostrovskij's Play-Actors, Puppets, and Rebels." Article in *The Slavic and East European Journal (SEEJ),* no. 3, 1970, 317-25.

— Review of Ostrovsky's *Artistes and Admirers., SEEJ,* no.3, 1971, 382-85.

Hoover, Marjorie L. *Alexander Ostrovsky.* Twayne, Boston, 1981. Only full-length study of Ostrovsky's life and works in English and within the limits of the Twayne format a useful work. Reviewed by Andrew R. Durkin *(Russian Review,* 41(4), 525-26), Felicia Hardison Londré *(Theatre Journal,* 34 (4), 561), Cynthia Marsh *(Modern Language Review,* vol. 77, 763-64), and Peter Petro *(Canadian- American Slavic Studies,* 16 (4), 525-26).

Kaspin, Albert. "Character and Conflict in Ostrovskij's *Talents and Admirers," SEEJ,* no. 1, 1964, 26-36.

— "Dostoevsky's Masloboyev and Ostrovsky's Dosuzhev: A Parallel." *The Slavonic and East European Review,* vol. 39, 222-26.

— "Ostrovsky and the *Raznochinets* in his Plays." Ph.D. dissertation, U. of Cal., 1957. A valuable study not so specialized as the title might suggest.

— "A Re-examination of Ostrovsky's Character Lyubim Tortsov." *Studies in Russian and Polish Literature in Honor of Waclaw Lednicki.* 's-Gravenhage (The Hague), 1962, 185-91.

— "A Superfluous Man and an Underground Man in Ostrovskij's *The Poor Bride." SEEJ,* no. 4, 1962, 312–21.

Kersten, Peter Andrew. "The Russian Theater in the Plays of A.N. Ostrovskij." Informative M.A. thesis, U. of Wisconsin, 1962.

Magarshack, David. "Alexander Ostrovsky, the Founder of the Russian Theatrical Tradition." Introduction to the Ardis edition of *The Storm,* 5–13.

Mirsky, D. S. Discussion in his A *History of Russian Literature.* Alfred A. Knopf, New York, 1949. Also published by Vintage Books.

Patrick, George Z. "A. N. Ostrovski: Slavophile or Westerner." In *Slavic Studies,* ed. by Alexander Kaun and Ernest Simmons, Cornell U. Press, Ithaca, 1943.

Peace, R.A. "A. N. Ostrovsky's *The Thunderstorm:* the dramatization of conceptual ambivalence." *Modern Language Review,* v. 84, 99-110. Valuable discussion with emphasis on double meanings of *volia* (freedom versus will, the latter equated with outer constraint) and *serdtse,* literally "heart"(tender emotions versus anger).

Ralston, William. Discussion in *The Edinburgh Review,* July, 1968.

Slonim, Marc. Nonduplicating discussions in his *The Epic of Russian Literature* (Oxford Pr., New York, 1950) and *Russian Theater from the Empire to the Soviets* (Collier, New York, 1962). Slonim is good on Ostrovsky.

Valency, Maurice. Discussion in his *The Breaking String.* Oxford U. Press, London, and New York, 1966.

Varneke, B.V. Chapter in his *History of the Russian Theatre* (translated from the Russian). Macmillan, New York, 1951.

Wettlin, Margaret. "Alexander Ostrovsky and the Russian Theatre Before Stanislavsky." Introduction to her translations of four Ostrovsky plays (See earlier section under "Plays"). 7-79.

Whittaker, Robert. "The Ostrovskii–Grigor'ev Circle Alias the 'Young Editors' of the *Moskvitianin.*" *Canadian-American Slavic Studies,* v. 24, no. 4 (1990), 385- 412. Illuminating discussion touching on Ostrovsky's professional life in the early 1850's.

Wiener, Leo. Discussion in his *The Contemporary Drama of Russia.* Little, Brown & Co., Boston, 1924. Reprinted by AMS Reprints, New York and London.

Zohrab, Irene (a.k.a. Irene Esam. See above). "Problems of Style in the Plays of A.N. Ostrovsky." *Melbourne Slavonic Studies,* no. 12, 1977.